MRS CARRUTHERS IS BLACK

John Carruthers

The Book Guild Ltd
Sussex, England

First published in Great Britain in 2005 by
The Book Guild Ltd
25 High Street
Lewes, East Sussex
BN7 2LU

Copyright © John Carruthers 2005

The right of John Carruthers to be identified as the author of this work has been asserted by him in accordance with the Copyright, Designs and Patents Act 1988.

All rights reserved. No part of this publication may be reproduced, transmitted, or stored in a retrieval system, in any form or by any means, without permission in writing from the publisher, nor be otherwise circulated in any form of binding or cover other than that in which it is published and without a similar condition being imposed on the subsequent purchaser.

Although this book features some real people, this is a work of fiction.

Typesetting in Baskerville by
Keyboard Services, Luton, Bedfordshire

Printed in Great Britain by
Antony Rowe Ltd, Chippenham, Wiltshire

A catalogue record for this book is available from
The British Library

ISBN 1 85776 926 0

Contents

1	The African Learning Curve	1
2	The Lady in Black	24
3	The Search	30
4	Uganda Affairs	49
5	Whirlwind Romance	65
6	Willi Becomes Mrs	71
7	Frivolities	82
8	Events at the Club	92
9	The Coup and the Parrot	105
10	Changed Days	126
11	Mother Meets Daughter	131
12	The Aftermaths	145
13	The Army	160
14	Visits, to and from	171
15	Fleeing Uganda	188
16	The End of an Era	198
17	White Mischief	204

18	Going West	220
19	Meetings and Visits	240
20	Comedy and Tragedy	260
21	Life in Nigeria	278
22	Wind-down	284
23	Working in England	300
24	Homecoming	312
25	New Experiences	321
26	The Past Catches Up	337
27	Back from Exile	351

Chapter 1

The African Learning Curve

Carruthers, perspiring heavily, struggled up the patchy green slope. It had been a long haul and he had walked miles and miles. Vultures circled overhead and the hot African sun beat down on him cruelly. His bearer followed him. 'God, it's hot,' Carruthers said to himself as he pushed his way through the thorn bushes that ringed the green oasis in front of him. There was sand to the left of him and sand to the right of him. He was sure he saw a snake slithering away. He paused and moved his hat to the back of his head.

He had suspected what he was going to find and cursed when his suspicions were confirmed. Bedded deeply in the sand was his nearly new Dunlop 65, only half of it visible. He swore as his first attempt to hit the golf ball out of the bunker simply drove it deeper in. He shook his head in disgust. Eventually after three more shots he got it on the green and holed out. But there was no satisfaction there. Just frustration.

He was glad there was only one more hole to play. It was so tedious playing badly by oneself. His elderly partner had dropped out after the ninth hole, pleading exhaustion. Carruthers knew he would find him at the bar leering at the club waitresses. With the present state of his golf Carruthers wished he had done the same. A slight hangover also didn't help.

The plus side was that he was getting some exercise in very pleasant but hot surroundings. Also he didn't have to carry his own golf clubs, as he would in the UK. Caddies were inexpensive and widely available. They also at times gave impromptu golf lessons on the way round. And, God, didn't he need them!

On the other hand, the caddies sometimes could be bloody rude. His erstwhile partner's caddie had remarked that while he could see he was enjoying his golf, he wouldn't at that age, in his opinion, get any better. Bloody cheek! No wonder his partner had stomped off.

Carruthers reflected on the past few months of his life as he loped downhill to the 18th and final tee. Everything seemed to be happening so fast. He had arrived ten months and one week ago, on 2nd January 1962 to be exact, in the then colonial Kenya. At 24, he was bright-eyed and bushy-tailed and all ready for an exciting future. He had come to Nairobi to work in an insurance broker's office, part of a large UK group. He had been offered a job in London but felt if he was going to be away from home he might as well be far away.

He had thought long and hard about the move to London. It was an opportunity not offered to many in the Edinburgh Head Office and he was well thought of by his bosses. However, he felt he would not exist in bedsitter land and had decided that the lure of the African unknown would take precedence over London, which he considered a place where one had to have friends and money to succeed. He had neither but he was determined to make money and return to London and make his mark. Perhaps he could even end up as Chairman of the company, he thought. Who knows?

Fleeing from a broken love affair in Edinburgh, he was still a bachelor and eager to make a successful romantic conquest. Perhaps a well-heeled settler's daughter who would make a fine Chairman's wife some time in the future.

He was thinking in terms of a white conquest rather than a black one. In fact his aunt in Edinburgh, a stern-faced woman, had warned him prior to his departure to be careful of the black women, a remark which had quite shocked his mother, who hadn't even given it a thought. Carruthers had wondered then what on earth she meant.

The previous afternoon he had overindulged at the Long Bar at Nairobi's New Stanley Hotel, and later at the Harlequin Rugby Club, both of which had become his favourite haunts and given him a taste for the locally made Pilsner. Dinner and drinks in the evening at the Lobster Pot with its sawdust-covered floor in the basement bar had not helped. In the company of young fellow expatriates and local white Kenyans he had been able to let his hair down, as he did most weekends in a society which, on the eve of Independence, was still largely white-dominated and thus privileged in many walks of life.

In fact, come to think of it, he was astonished that he, a new arrival, would be able to vote in Kenya's Independence elections, which would shortly take place. He had been deeply impressed last week, as he had listened to two senior African politicians in Jomo Kenyatta's political party, Kanu. They had managed at least partly to allay the fears of many in the all-white business audience at Nairobi's City Hall regarding their future under a black-controlled government. Many whites, however, were pessimistic and feared having to give up their privileged positions.

Carruthers was ambivalent. While he could sympathise with his white acquaintances who had grown up in a privileged society, he could not agree that such a system should continue. The black Kenyans had campaigned vigorously and often violently for the right to govern themselves. The largest tribe, the Kikuyu, had formed a secret society, the Mau Mau, to fight the colonialists and many of that tribe, including the future President, Jomo Kenyatta, had been imprisoned. Bowing to such pressure, the British colonial government eventually had to agree to give up control after nearly 60 years, but many, many miles of prime farmland would remain in colonial settlers' hands.

When Kenya's elections were held, Carruthers duly cast his vote for a candidate of Kenyatta's Kanu party, which formed the first independent government, and he remembered a long night of celebration when results began to trickle through. Kenyatta commanded the respect of many when he then refused to carry out a witch-hunt of his former white antagonists.

Carruthers lodged with an elderly white couple who had immigrated to Kenya from South Africa many years ago. They lived in a bungalow in a Nairobi suburb mainly populated by white families – Indians and Africans had their own separate areas of residence in various suburbs around Nairobi. The wife was a feisty old bird and her husband a cynic. They certainly hadn't looked forward to Independence. It was a somewhat strained relationship for Carruthers, especially when his hosts had their long-established white friends around for dinner and discussed the future. They couldn't understand why Great Britain should give Kenya independence and felt they had been betrayed. Carruthers' attempt to provide an alternative friendly argument was met with outright hostility. They talked about tearing up their British passports and complaining to the Queen. Carruthers often felt quite uncomfortable as his views, the views of a 'new boy', were treated with contempt. He cautioned himself to keep his mouth shut as far as possible and give guarded respect to his elders.

During one after-dinner discussion Carruthers' remark, 'Aren't we all socialists in Africa?' was met with fury and, as he later realised, he had been a bit naive to say this. However, in his opinion independence and socialism in Africa went together as far as the locals, black and white, were concerned. One of the male dinner guests, a burly white newspaper editor, was so angry at Carruthers' remark that his pent-up energy broke the fragile chair on which he was sitting. No one laughed. Carruthers had made his excuses and gone to bed quickly. He couldn't understand the continued anger at the inevitable political situation, and surely a newspaperman should break news rather than chairs. The editor had left soon after Independence, not being able to stomach the change.

On another occasion, when his cynical landlord came across Carruthers playing with the three-year-old son of one of the house servants on the red polished verandah steps, he had shouted angrily at the young boy in Swahili to go to the quarters where he belonged. The *mtoto* had run away terrified, while Carruthers felt like a scolded schoolboy.

After a few months Carruthers had decided to move out and seek a place of his own. He had to make a new life for himself in new surroundings; he belonged in the future not the past. Such a move was also prompted by a letter from his Edinburgh ex-girlfriend, who announced that in a couple of months she was flying out to Nairobi at her own expense to attempt a reconciliation. Parting had obviously made her heart grow fonder. Carruthers was in two minds about this. He was still sowing – or rather hoping to sow – his wild oats in a new and exciting environment and relished his freedom. However, he was still very fond of his ex-girlfriend and regularly exchanged letters with her. In fact his landlord had drooled over a photograph of her in a swimsuit. That had taken his mind off the political situation for a short while! The white girls of his own age group whom he had met in Nairobi and who had been brought up in Kenya seemed to be jealously guarded by their parents and their white Kenyan boyfriends respectively.

They were probably correct. Tensions were high and people were nervous. He had been shocked, for instance, to see one of his white male acquaintances physically attacking a black waiter at the Thorntree Café in the New Stanley Hotel during a dispute over a bill. Both ended up rolling on the floor, punching and kicking each other, and had to be pulled apart and forced to apologise to each other. Years earlier, the waiter would have been sacked immediately. It was a changing and difficult time.

At times Carruthers felt himself being sucked into a colonial mentality. On one occasion he felt outrage when a white police officer accused him of jumping a red light at a set of traffic lights. Surely his job was to protect whites not harass them! It was a frustrating time for many, and Carruthers felt ashamed at such thoughts. He patted his caddie on the back and asked him to clean his golf ball before teeing off.

Generally, however, life was very pleasant for Carruthers when he ignored the tense political situation. Apart from the scenic attractions of Kenya, the attractive city of Nairobi, with its bougainvillea-lined streets and highways, boasted hotels and restaurants of international standards. The climate was perfect, although around June and July it was common for log fires to be lit in houses as the weather turned cloudy and cold; but it wasn't like the constant cold of the European winter.

Nairobi also boasted some excellent Indian restaurants where Carruthers was introduced to curries for the first time. To remind himself of these wonderful meals, he once punched a couple of holes in a chapatti from a restaurant and filed it on his return to the office after lunch. The look on his colleague's face when he came across it was a sight to behold.

On the outskirts of the city, Nairobi Racecourse could take its place amongst the best of British racecourses. The monthly race meeting was one of the social events not be missed. On one occasion Carruthers backed five winners in a row through the Tote, the first time that had ever happened to him. Unfortunately, the winnings were shared with another four punters but nevertheless he won a tidy sum. He and a colleague had spent a night out on the town to celebrate, including visits to various nightclubs. If only he had staked more money, he kept thinking. Luckily, his good fortune did not encourage him to gamble on a regular basis because he was sure it would not happen again.

A favourite place Carruthers used to visit was the National Museum in Nairobi, an old colonial stone building surrounded by beautiful gardens with an adjoining snake park. The museum was where the famous Kenyan anthropologist Dr Louis Leakey was based when not on location at anthropological sites in Kenya or on his overseas lecture tours in the US. It was the Leakey family who had proved through the discovery of ancient human fossils that Africa, more especially Eastern Africa, was the cradle of the human race – and indeed anyone living in Africa for some time would not fail to feel that and would always want to return to this cradle as if drawn by an unseen hand.

Another fine building in Nairobi was the Macmillan Library, which Carruthers joined. Both his father and mother were librarians in Edinburgh, and from an early age he was used to having many books to read. He felt at home in libraries; certainly more at home than on the golf course, he thought as he took a few practice swings.

Kenya was, of course, famous for its wildlife and game parks, which covered large tracts of land. One such park was on the edge of Nairobi and Carruthers spent many happy hours there viewing lions, giraffe, zebras etc. An early morning visit just as dawn was breaking was exciting stuff. Next to the game park was a drive-in cinema and the international airport, both of which provided a strange contrast.

The scenery of Kenya was magnificent, and standing at the top of the road going from Nairobi down into the Great Rift Valley was like standing on the edge of the world – that is, if the world has an edge. Carruthers made many trips along this road, every time experiencing the excitement of the unknown. Italian prisoners had constructed part of it during the Second World War and built a small church at the side of the road to worship in. The road eventually reached Uganda, a country he had not yet visited. He had heard the women there were beautiful. What an intriguing thought, the mystery of the unknown – just like the final hole in front of him.

Another trip he relished was driving down the murram road through the bush to Mombasa on the Kenyan coast, where excellent hotels and sandy beaches abounded. Elephants could often be seen at the side of the road, their dust-covered hides blending in with their dusty brown surroundings, mainly baobab trees, rough scrub and thorn trees.

Carruthers' early visits to the East African coast remained vividly in his mind, from the old musty-smelling hotel bedroom in Tanga, a small town on the Tanganyika coast, with a mosquito net and a slowly whirling fan on the ceiling which had little effect on the oppressive humidity, to the luxury air-conditioned bedroom of the Mombasa city hotel where ships of all sizes entering the harbour from the Indian Ocean slipped past the bedroom window.

He remembered his first visit to Tanganyika, when he had driven to the towns of Moshi and Arusha. Passports weren't necessary and one simply drove across the border where a sign said you were entering Tanganyika. The roads were mainly murram, which produced clouds of swirling red dust. Sometimes there were two strips of tarmac the width of car wheels. These were perfectly adequate when no other traffic was on the road but when an approaching vehicle appeared, one wheel would remain on the tarmac while the other would be on the murram; the approaching vehicle would adopt a similar position; quite a clever conception and a lot cheaper than fully tarmacking a long road.

One of the most beautiful sights on this trip was the snow-capped Mount Kilimanjaro suddenly appearing way above him as if by magic. He was too busy looking at giraffes by the roadside as he drove along to appreciate the fact that the famous mountain was in fact always in front of and above him. It really was astonishing. One of his colleagues had once rounded a bend on the same road and hit a giraffe that fell seated onto the bonnet of his car and then got up and trundled away. He had some trouble explaining this to his insurance company when claiming for a dented bonnet!

Carruthers' return to Nairobi on that first trip had been delayed because the Greek manager at the sisal factory denied having received any correspondence from Carruthers' company for the past six months. This was the reason for his visit – to get replies. (Sisal, used in making ropes, was an important export for Tanganyika and was mainly grown by Greek farmers.) Carruthers refused to move from the manager's office, so the manager eventually pulled open a drawer in his desk and, expressing astonishment, pulled out six months' correspondence. He promised to work on this immediately, and Carruthers as a result was forced to spend another night in the comfortable hotel at Arusha.

On the return journey to Nairobi Carruthers made a terrible mistake. Looking at the map, he saw there was a murram road, which was half the distance of the longer tarmac road to the Kenyan border, and he decided to take it. At first it seemed a good choice as he bowled along at a good speed on the well-kept road, dust clouds billowing behind him; later, however, the road became very stony and hilly, with lots of bends. At one stage he had to reverse up a steep stony road, as the forward gears of his car couldn't make it. Then a fearsome-looking Masaii warrior with a sharp-looking long spear barred his way and demanded a lift. Half a mile further on, another two warriors had to be given a lift. Carruthers felt quite nervous with three fearsome-looking Masaii in his car, spears standing between their legs. Eventually they asked to be let out at a junction in the road, much to his relief.

On the dashboard of the car a blinking red light had come on. It was the oil warning light. Luckily, about a mile further on a petrol station appeared and Carruthers was able to fill up with oil. In what seemed a very short time but was probably about half an hour, the red light was on again. Carruthers swore to himself. He was in the middle of nowhere on a road which seemed to have been deserted by all other cars. There was no point in stopping where he was so, heart in mouth, he drove on and eventually reached another petrol station. He found that in his journey up the stony hill he had torn a small hole in the sump and the oil was leaking out. The bush petrol stations had no proper mechanical facilities but they did try and block the tear. As an added precaution he bought six one-pint tins of oil. He eventually reached Nairobi hours later than he would have had he taken the longer tarmac road, stopping at frequent intervals to pour oil into the engine. This seemed to work because there was no lasting damage to the engine, but it was a frustrating experience and a lesson in map-reading in Africa for a motorist. Keep to the main recommended routes whenever possible unless you are in a Land Rover or other high-clearance four-wheel-drive vehicle.

When Carruthers had first arrived in Nairobi he wasn't in a position to drive very far outside the city, due to a cost-cutting exercise which he was convinced would save him a fortune: he bought a Vespa scooter instead of a car. After being knocked down by an Asian lady driving a large Mercedes who denied all liability, and then being thrown onto the tarmac one night after hitting a pothole after a long session at the rugby club, he had to invest in the safety of a car. He fingered the scar on his forehead as he ruefully thought about these incidents.

His first car was an Austin Mini, not much bigger than his scooter, some wags said. Anyway, at least it had four wheels and enabled him to get about much more easily. It was also easier to persuade a girl to get into a car than on the back of the scooter.

All sorts of cars were available in Nairobi, new and second-hand. Despite the fact that Kenya was a British colony, the most popular cars were French Peugeots specially built for the African terrain. However, the

British were superior with their heavy vehicles – Leyland lorries and Land Rovers.

Carruthers smiled to himself when he remembered that soon after his arrival he decided, as he didn't have a car, that he would visit Mombasa travelling by bus from Nairobi. It was ridiculously cheap, which appealed to him after his Scottish upbringing. All his friends told him he was mad and as it turned out they were correct, although it had been an interesting experience. He was the only European on the bus and the African lady sitting next to him clutched a hen, which kept taking an unwelcome interest in him. It was hot and dusty and bloody uncomfortable. The bus stopped halfway to Mombasa for the passengers to have refreshments, first in front of a superior-looking hotel suitable for the European. The rest of the passengers would be taken to a cheaper hotel nearby. Carruthers declined to get off at the first stop to show his solidarity with his fellow passengers, also not wanting to draw too much attention to himself. They all bought some hard-boiled eggs and lemonade. Some young white Kenyans he met in Mombasa during his long weekend gave him a lift back to Nairobi in their car, which was more speedy and comfortable, although he ended up paying for most of the petrol. He had a feeling he had been conned.

There was a good overnight passenger train service from Nairobi to Mombasa, which Carruthers sometimes used. It passed through the game park outside Nairobi and first-class passengers could enjoy a very palatable dinner on the train. Some even dressed for dinner. The railway line went all the way from Mombasa through Nairobi to Kampala in Uganda and when first built was known as the Uganda railway. That was when the then British Colonial Secretary Winston Churchill, after a visit to the country, had urged the British Government to open up Uganda – the Pearl of Africa, as he called it, and a name which was still used 70 years later.

It was because of the railway that the Nairobi staging post grew as a city, and its construction was the reason for the presence of a large number of Indians brought in by the British from the sub-continent. They would remain in East Africa as traders and artisans and wield an important influence in the economy of the three East African countries.

Carruthers usually stayed at a beach hotel, the Jadini, on the coast south of the coral island of Mombasa. A ten-minute ferry ride took him and his car off the island to the road south, where if you kept going you would reach Tanganyika. The hotel was composed of a series of cottages on the edge of a white sandy beach lined by palm trees. The coral reef kept the sharks away from the beach area so snorkelling was a popular activity, watching the many varieties of brightly coloured fish swimming and darting about. Air-conditioning was not a feature of coast hotels; however, one soon got used to the humidity of the coast, especially when cooled by the frequent breezes off the Indian Ocean.

On one of his stays at the hotel he was told that the European couple occupying one of the cottages came regularly every year at the same time. He evidently was a priest and she a female companion helping him to break his vows of celibacy. Being a Scottish Presbyterian, that appealed to Carruthers' jaundiced sense of humour.

One could get bored, however, lying on the beach every day, so Carruthers occasionally drove into Mombasa to see the sights. One he would always remember was walking into a day and night bar on Kilindini Road around 11 in the morning. There must have been at least 50 black girls there, all sitting quietly around tables and not a single drink between them. As he entered the bar they all applauded. Carruthers, taken aback, bowed with a sheepish grin on his face and went to join the only customer sitting at the bar, an older white man. He was told that the girls were all prostitutes; they had their own union and were sitting waiting for their president to arrive for a meeting. He was amused to learn that his bar companion was the local magistrate. He was not there officially, he said, but many of the girls had been up before him over the years. Carruthers wondered how many times the magistrate had been up before the girls but didn't ask. The two of them had a beer or two together, and Carruthers met some of the girls again that evening as he did a tour of the nightclubs.

Mombasa was a great place to wander about. Stalls full of carvings and other ornaments abounded on the palm-tree-lined streets. Ivory and African jewellery was particularly attractive and reasonably priced. In the old port with its narrow winding streets, dhows could be seen which traded up and down the coast of Eastern Africa and as far as Arabia.

As a port Mombasa was very busy both with freighters and passenger liners. (The Kenya navy was also berthed there and the British and US navies often made visits. No wonder the girls needed their own union!)

Another added attraction to the coast was deep-sea fishing and Carruthers usually went out fishing on his visits there. The largest fish he ever caught was a hammerhead shark, but the regular fishers often caught marlins, sail fish and the like. Carruthers found the experience exhilarating, and luckily he never got seasick.

While Carruthers relished visiting Mombasa for a holiday, he didn't feel he would like to work there because of its constant humidity. Most expatriates wore shorts and knee length stockings because of the heat. The Nairobi climate was much healthier and dress was more formal. Mosquitoes were present at the coast and malaria was a very real threat. As a protection, Paludrine tablets taken daily were a must at the coast but not necessarily Nairobi.

Having decided to move out of his Nairobi 'digs' – a decision which was noticeably welcomed by his hosts – before the arrival of his ex-girlfriend, Carruthers busied himself with searching for a suitable place to house the two of them, and found a small two-bedroomed bungalow near the golf course. If things worked out between them they could get married quickly enough, but he was doubtful about the whole situation. He still relished his freedom.

In that respect the sightseeing he was doing in the bars and nightclubs was, he thought, as exciting as the sightseeing in the game parks. However, there wasn't much to surpass the excitement of being escorted through the African bush by an armed white hunter to reach places such as the famous Treetops Hotel built in trees overlooking a water hole in the middle of a game park. He had stayed there with friends and spent much of the night huddled in a blanket looking down at various wild animals using the water hole and licking salt only yards from where he sat.

His girlfriend hadn't arrived in time to accompany him to Treetops on that trip, or indeed to see Cliff Richard and the Shadows performing live in an open-air concert in Nairobi. That had been a new experience for the Kenya Police, who expected trouble from pop stars, and a squad of the riot police had been on hand. However, everyone had been on their best behaviour and the evening was a great success.

All these past events went through his mind as he patiently waited to tee off on the final hole of his so far disastrous golf round. Two ladies in front of him were in the middle of the fairway and if he hit a good drive it could easily reach them, he thought optimistically. He had to be patient and wait.

His life in Kenya up until now had been brimming with excitement. It hadn't been all pleasure though and there had been a few instances where he had only managed to get himself out of trouble with a certain amount of difficulty and embarrassment. But it had been all of his own making, he had to admit.

Once, a white Kenyan BOAC stewardess had nearly raped him. What should have been a pleasurable nightcap and chat had turned into a battle of the sexes as he fought her off. With the imminent arrival of his ex-girlfriend he hadn't wanted any complications, but he had not told the stewardess. That was his mistake. Her father had introduced them at the golf club and that particular evening she had been his partner at a formal ball to celebrate something or other. Perhaps if she had been black, Carruthers mused, he might have given in.

He had been known to visit the red light district of Nairobi on occasions. In fact he had been chased by a British military police patrol in a jeep one night. On seeing a young white face driving through the streets of that particular district, they had assumed he was one of their boys. When they eventually caught up with him after a prolonged chase through the outskirts of Nairobi, he had a job explaining to them that he was in fact a civilian and could go where the hell he wanted. In their frustration Carruthers thought they were going to beat him up.

Another dangerous situation had only just been avoided because, luckily, he had a membership card of the ruling Kenya political party, which he had joined soon after arriving in the country. He had been in the company of a black girl in a bar on the outskirts of

Nairobi and on leaving had been surrounded by a group of political youth wingers who had objected to his being with one of their kind. They had started shouting and pushing him around. There was no way of escape but on hastily producing his party membership card and waving it about, a very nervous Carruthers had then been welcomed as a hero! There weren't many white card-carrying members, especially of his age. That had cost him quite a few beers subsequently and the excited youth wingers had soon calmed down, much to Carruthers' relief.

To add insult to injury he had, later that night, been followed home from the same bar by a white police officer from the Special Branch well known for hanging around such bars and spying on fellow expatriates. He had managed, driving his souped-up Austin Mini to outwit his pursuer by turning off his car lights at various turnings and keeping his foot off the brake pedal so that no tell-tale red light would indicate his presence. The perils of doing that were rudely brought home to him when he very nearly went into the back of an unlit lorry parked at the side of the road. He was glad to fall into the bed of his temporary new abode, having lost the police officer in the chase. He might have been raped! The man was single!

On another occasion, walking through a dark alleyway on his way from a nightclub to collect his car in the centre of Nairobi, he had an uneasy feeling he was being followed. Glancing back, he saw a tall black African man silhouetted against lights from the main street bending down to pick up a large stone and running towards him. Carruthers took off at a speed which would have made his great grandfather, a noted Scottish professional runner, very proud, and managed to reach one of the main streets, where he saw a couple of guards were standing outside a bank. He hovered around near them and watched the end of the alley. His pursuer stopped at the edge of the alley, noticed the presence of the guards and decided to retreat. Carruthers, heart beating violently, was then able to reach his car and get back to the safety of his home, cursing his own recklessness.

Reckless or not, he had a deep desire to get to know and mix with Africans. He couldn't take a blinkered approach and only socialise with white friends. Being young, he found he was accepted by African society more readily than older white men, whose main object of socialising with Africans was seen as an excuse to meet African women solely for sex.

That was enough reminiscing, he thought. The fairway ahead was clear. He viciously hit his next and final tee shot, sending it disappointedly just past the ladies' tee. Serves you right, he muttered to himself. Bloody women, it's all their fault. Why did they have these ladies' tees that just put you off your game, particularly if there was a good-looking woman hanging around the tee. He had never had it on the golf course, he thought. More enjoyable than what he was presently engaged in, no doubt.

Hurrying down the fairway of the 18th hole, the ground hard beneath him, Carruthers could see the 19th hole, the clubhouse housing the bar, where iced beer awaited. The two ladies in front of him were already on the green. He was hot, sweaty and lustful. Hopefully waitress No. 4, the beautiful and black Bernadette, would be on duty clad in the hip-gripping black mini skirt and white blouse that he knew concealed at least a 34B bra, of which he had occasionally seen flashes, white flashes, certainly covering dark erect nipples. He licked his dry lips and completely mishit his approach shot to the green.

What a state to be in, he thought. No wonder his game was going to the dogs. His mind was always somewhere else. He just could not concentrate on his golf and he wondered if he should give it up for a time. That very afternoon had been three hours of frustration, hitting a wee white ball round what could best be described as an arboretum of torture.

More humiliation waited on the green and he eventually sank his final putt for a painful nine strokes. Ignoring his smirking caddie, he strode purposefully towards the bar and joined his erstwhile golfing partner, who was now drunkenly revived. All the woes of his golf round were forgotten when Bernadette approached and smilingly took his order. As she walked seductively away he sighed and imaginatively ran his right hand up and over her glistening black thighs. His left-hand unfastened, so he imagined, the white bra. Perhaps it was all worth it after all, he mused.

He was finding it very difficult, or perhaps too easy, to settle down in a society where the local females were all so enticing. His ex-girlfriend from Edinburgh was due to arrive in ten days. She also played golf and he would have to be very careful to hide the lust in his eyes when Bernadette brought drinks to their table at the golf club. Women noticed these things rather quickly.

As Carruthers (now on his third lager) mused about the future, he began to hatch a plan on how to satisfy his lustful desires and yet keep the women in his life satisfied and separated.

The bar area was now getting quite noisy and Bernadette, although being kept very busy, noticed again, as she had on many similar occasions, the glances of Carruthers and his fellow drinkers. Carruthers, she thought, was quite handsome and although she had only once before slept with a white man, she knew she could probably give him something to think about, given the chance. Bernadette's old man had died a couple of years ago from alcoholic poisoning and left her with two young kids, so she had to satisfy her sexual and monetary needs somehow – and who better than a newly arrived white man instead of some of these pot-bellied MPs who frequented the club and thought they were God's gift to women? Their wives certainly didn't think so but they were mostly fat bags anyway, she noted.

Finishing his sixth lager, mumbling farewell to some of his cronies, Carruthers looked meaningfully at Bernadette and staggered off, vowing in his mind to slip her a written note of his desire on his next visit to the club. He hoped that in the not too distant future he would also be able to slip her something else.

Carruthers' plan was as follows: On his next visit to the golf club, shortly before the arrival of his girlfriend, he slipped two notes to Bernadette. The first note quite crudely told Bernadette that he wanted her and he knew she already knew that, so why hang about? However, he had to be careful and so had she, especially as a certain Minister in the Government was abusing her regularly, although with her consent. He didn't need any trouble from politicians, especially on the eve of Independence. The first note told Bernadette to destroy it once read, while the second one, couched in more formal tones, and which she could keep for posterity or rather for evidence, inquired if she could find someone to work in the Carruthers' household as a maid – and in fact, if she was so minded, she could take on the job herself at a substantial increase in her present salary. To Carruthers' delight she accepted.

* * *

The arrival of his ex-girlfriend did nothing to stifle Carruthers' lust. She certainly didn't wear a white bra, preferring black, and in fact in that department was more man than woman. She could, however, hit a long four iron and soon became a respected member of the ladies' golf section.

Members sadly lamented Bernadette's departure from the golf club and Carruthers thought it wise not to mention to fellow golfers where she had relocated. It was also subsequently noticed that Carruthers did not hang around the bar area as much as he used to and was even known to rush off early and send his driver back later to collect his girlfriend from the club. But she relished all the gossip from the lady members, and that is, of course, how she came to learn more of former waitress No. 4.

One of the lady members who was more interested in the female sex than the male, mentioned to her golfing cronies that she really missed Bernadette and wondered where she had gone to. She would have loved to undo her bra again. His ex-girlfriend thereupon innocently said that although it could be a coincidence there was a Bernadette working in her household who talked a lot about members of the golf club. Could it be her, she asked?

And there the dye was cast. Poor Bernadette, the lover of Carruthers, encountered the lustful desires of the female golfer, who now insisted on regularly visiting the Carruthers' home to be nearer her quarry. This, of course, suited Carruthers, who was now able to cover his tracks by insisting that his almost constant presence at home was as a result of trying to protect Bernadette from female predators. Naively, his ex-girlfriend praised Carruthers' heroism and loyalty

As a result Carruthers' work (and golf) suffered. His

sexual prowess, however, improved and Bernadette derived a certain amount of pleasure in coaching him on the various positions to give maximum sexual pleasure.

It was the leather whips which eventually led to the break-up of the liaison between Carruthers, his ex and Bernadette. In an effort to increase their sexual pleasure Bernadette, hoping to revive the abuse she used to suffer and enjoy from the Minister boyfriend of days gone by, brought into her love nest, the one-room servant's quarters, a couple of whips. The only whipping Carruthers knew about was whipped cream and he was devastated by the new experience, which he found rather painful.

One evening, on returning home early from the golf club, his ex heard moans of pain emanating from the servant's quarters and on investigation found Carruthers being given a whipping by Bernadette. Thoroughly shocked and wishing to protect him, she grabbed the whip and began beating Bernadette, who responded, to her surprise, with moans of pleasure. One thing led to another. The whip cracked and cracked, and the shamed Carruthers fled painfully naked and alone to the main house, the two women having decided to spend the night together in the servants' quarters comforting each other.

Carruthers' humiliation was complete. He had lost his girlfriend and perhaps his future wife, he was sure he was going to lose his job and he couldn't even get that bloody white ball out of a bunker properly.

If he wanted to remain in Kenya and retain his job, he knew he would be expected to conform or he could be shipped back home by his employer. Conforming meant marrying his white girlfriend and settling down. In a way, that could fit in with his plans to make a name for himself as well as some money. However, so far he hadn't managed to do either and he should really get down to it and make a start on realising his ambition to become someone. He knew in his heart that he wouldn't be able to settle down. He was young and there were too many other temptations. He also felt that because of racial divides he would have to pitch his tent in one of two camps, African or European. He wasn't mature enough yet to live with a foot in each camp. Yet he didn't feel he wanted to return to UK, where life was not nearly so exciting.

It was time to move on, Carruthers decided. He applied for and to his delight got a job with a sister company in neighbouring Uganda, and his company agreed to transfer him. He had made a brief visit there on business a few months before and had been enchanted by Kampala, which was more of an African city than Nairobi and completely multi-racial. He had felt very much at home there.

Carruthers packed his golf clubs into his Austin Mini, gave Bernadette one for the road and thoroughly whipped his ex, who wept profusely with pleasure. It was December 1963. He suggested she return to UK forthwith as their reunion had not worked out as envisaged, and on no account was she to follow him to Uganda. Carruthers had no idea at the time that by going to Uganda he would be moving from the frying pan into the fire.

Chapter 2

The Lady in Black

Over the border in neighbouring Uganda a very attractive young black lady was locking the doors of her shop on the main street of the capital, Kampala. It was Saturday afternoon and she was going to meet some of her girlfriends for a stroll along the long and busy main street.

Her name was Wilfrieda and her shop, a joint venture with her parents, stocked upmarket lingerie. Her clientele were mostly well-off ladies of all races and sometimes the odd man.

Business was good and the income generated enabled Wilfrieda, her parents and various brothers and sisters to maintain a comfortable lifestyle. They all lived in a large red tiled bungalow just outside the city centre.

Her father, recently retired, was an ex-Minister in the Kabaka's Government. The Kingdom of Buganda, in which Kampala was situated, was ruled by the Kabaka, or King, and his government. Wilfrieda was related to the Kabaka on both her mother and father's side.

There were several kingdoms in Uganda whose traditional rulers could date their ancestry back many centuries. While the country as a whole was governed by a popularly elected central government, the kingdoms' Ministers and Members of Parliament were appointed by their respective kings. It was a system which up until then had worked well. Soon, however, jealousies between the central government and the kingdoms would erupt into violence.

Unlike its neighbour Kenya, Uganda had never been a colony. A colony is defined as a body of people who settle in a country distant from their homeland but are still under its control. Thus the white settlers in Kenya who had been there since the early twentieth century controlled the economy of Kenya and its African inhabitants under the rule of their homeland, Great Britain.

Uganda was never colonised as such. There was no colonial government-sponsored settlement, yet surprisingly the railway built by the British from Mombasa to Nairobi and then to Kampala was built especially to 'open up Uganda'. Instead, Uganda became a protectorate, a territory largely controlled by a stronger state, namely Great Britain.

The first white inhabitants of Kenya were in the main settlers from Great Britain who came to farm; in Uganda they were Scottish Presbyterian and Church of England missionaries followed by the Catholic Mill Hill Fathers from England.

The British Government considered Kenya ripe for settlement by its citizens because in their eyes there was no system of local government in existence. There were only warring tribes whom the British wished to tame, exploit and subdue.

Conversely in Uganda, particularly Buganda where the Kabaka reigned, a system of local government already existed through the long-established kingdoms. This was nearer to the hearts of the British politicians, most of them strong royalists. The British therefore did not seek to colonise but certainly wished to control, and this they did by appointing a Governor of the whole country and sending out teams of civil servants. They also wished to keep out the influence of the Germans, French, Belgians and the Sudanese Arabs.

After 50-odd years of British control, Uganda regained its independence in 1962, a year before Kenya. By then Wilfrieda's father had retired from the Kabaka's Government but as a respected elder continued to play an important role in society.

Fixing her wide-brimmed hat firmly on her head, Wilfrieda headed to the Greek-owned teashop on Kampala Road where she would meet her girlfriends. Her short skirt showed off her shapely legs, which drew admiring glances as she sauntered along the road. She had no shortage of admirers but was cautious with her liaisons and indeed was a bit conservative due to her strict Catholic upbringing. The fact that her father was a Papal Knight and her mother had been brought up in the royal court influenced her outlook on life. She could retreat, and often did, into her prayer book. One of her sisters was a nun.

She had only had one brief serious love affair, which had caused her much anguish when she discovered that her lover was married. Girls in Uganda matured much quicker than males of the same age and unfortunately for well-intentioned girls like her, married men had a field day.

Reaching the teashop, she joined up with four of her girlfriends and they proceeded along Kampala Road, window-shopping and greeting friends. There were no high-rise buildings in Kampala and a walk along Kampala Road was really a pleasant stroll.

Wilfrieda sometimes wished she didn't have such a nice figure as it often drew unwanted attention from men old enough to be her father. Some were even white. She resisted all such approaches with good grace but it was a bit of a bore. She really needed someone to take her seriously, but where was he? He certainly wasn't on Kampala Road that Saturday and after a couple of hours Wilfrieda and one of her friends went to 5 o'clock mass at Christ the King Church just off Kampala Road and then headed home.

There her father had a visitor, an old friend of his who was a Member of Parliament. She greeted them both in the traditional way by kneeling in front of them and inquiring after their health, then went out of the sitting room, leaving the door slightly ajar so she could hear what they were talking about.

She was horrified to hear her father suggesting to his guest that she would make a good wife to one of his sons. That would happen over her dead body, she said to herself. Her father's friend said it was early days yet as he wanted his sons to finish university first. Such arranged marriages were not uncommon and at least she had breathing space.

The two men's conversation turned to politics. There were tensions in the three main political parties, brought about by tribalism, religion, power and greed. The face of politics was changing as old allegiances became open to bribery and unfulfilled promises. There was fear that the army was going to be used as a political tool and that the kingdoms could lose much of their influence and autonomy.

Wilfrieda had heard much of this before but this time there seemed to be an added urgency to the discussion. The two men agreed that they must voice their fears to their King, the Kabaka, and indeed they decided to do so the very next day. However, it turned out that as it was a Sunday, the Kabaka had proceeded to his country palace and gone on a hunting trip, so their approach was thwarted.

The English-educated former Grenadier Guards officer the Kabaka of Buganda met the two men at the Palace on the following Tuesday. Once again Wilfrieda was able to eavesdrop on the conversation when the two men returned and she served them drinks. They were furious. The Kabaka had pooh-poohed their concerns and sent them away with a flea in their ear. He had even told them that the Prime Minister wanted to appoint him President of the country and he had accepted. Traditionally Kabakas did not get involved in central government politics, and the two men were convinced that their King was being manipulated by a more experienced and wily politician who had his own political agenda. His name was Milton Obote.

Wilfrieda went to talk to her mother, who told her she wasn't surprised at what was happening. She had been privy to many intrigues in the past when she was growing up in the royal court. Men, especially kings, were all too likely to listen to advice from their inner circle and ignore the counsel of others, especially if they were of another religion. It would all end in tears, she said. One of the King's inner circle was not even of the same tribe.

They decided, with the agreement of her father, that Wilfrieda should keep her stock at the shop to a minimum. If there were going to be riots or whatever, all shops on the main road would be easy targets. They should also review the lease on the shop and consider not renewing it when it expired if events warranted it.

All this made Wilfrieda quite sad. On the face of it Kampala seemed quiet and people were moving about enjoying themselves. Bars, restaurants and nightclubs were doing a roaring business. Why was it that men always wanted to fight each other, she wondered? They gave little respect to women but it was often the women who had most to contribute. Yet these same men had been brought up by women who knew their secrets, their desires and weaknesses. The fools.

That evening she had samosas and Pepsi-Cola at the Greek shop with a boyfriend and afterwards they went to see a film. She was determined not to let herself get too miserable. However, she was determined also that if Mr Right came along she would grab him quickly and not let him get away.

It didn't cross her mind that Mr Right could also be white! She didn't really know many white people, apart from the ladies who came into her shop. Most of them were a bit stand-offish and annoyingly pretended to know everything. She got on better with the Asian ladies, who liked a good laugh.

Another week was nearly gone and she thought of her weekend ahead. She decided that on the Sunday she would go and visit two of her sisters who were at a boarding school some 20 miles outside Kampala. They would be so pleased to see her.

She had a couple of dresses being made for her by a Goan seamstress and she planned to go directly there after closing the shop on Saturday. Her friends would as usual be expecting her to join them in their promenade along Kampala Road. This time they had arranged to pop into a well-known basement bar where there was a jukebox. They were going to play Jim Reeves, Elvis Presley and Beatles records and drink Babycham.

She was very much looking forward to that, and if her dresses were ready she would wear one of them. It might bring her luck in her search for some man to be in her life. She would, as it turned out, not be disappointed!

Chapter 3

The Search

Carruthers, with a new job in a new country and a bit of experience under his belt, albeit probably the wrong experience, felt he could take life a bit more slowly and perhaps settle down again – if he had, for that matter, ever settled down. All his past activities in his first overseas posting seemed related to pleasure rather than to work. He would have to buckle down and start making a real career for himself and not spend so much time on the pleasures of life, he decided. Once he was a chairman he could indulge himself again. That's what chairmen did, wasn't it?

    The journey from Nairobi to Kampala by road took Carruthers about eight hours. Much of the road was tarmac but there was a lengthy stretch of murram on the Kenya side leading up to the Uganda border. The change in the scenery entering Uganda was quite dramatic. From the dusty brown of the Kenya countryside one entered a green almost botanical garden through which the straight tarmac road went all the way to Kampala. At Jinja, the source of the Nile, 50 miles east of Kampala, one crossed the huge Owen Falls Dam, which provided electricity for the whole of Uganda and some for Kenya. The waters of Lake Victoria, the second largest inland lake in the world, went through the dam and became the Nile River, which would flow through

Uganda, Sudan and Egypt eventually to reach the Mediterranean Sea three months later.

Carruthers found, on reaching Kampala and his new job, that he had to share a guesthouse attached to the company managing director's residence with another young expatriate. The residence was situated on a hill overlooking the city of Kampala, which was built on seven hills, three of them housing in turn a mosque, a Catholic cathedral and a Protestant cathedral. On top of another hill stood the Palace of the Kabaka, the King of Buganda. Notably, Kampala had no racial divides concerning housing, as in Nairobi; Africans, Asians and Europeans dwelt happily side-by-side.

The day after Carruthers' arrival a party had been organised by various expatriates to celebrate Kenya's Independence on 12th December 1963. This was to take place at his managing director's residence. As a resident in the guesthouse, Carruthers was automatically invited, but his name was not on the invitation list, which as it turned out was a blessing in disguise.

The invitations appeared racist in their wording, saying that so and so was invited 'to celebrate the giving up of the white man's burden in Kenya'. A Union Jack fluttered at the top of a white flagpole in the garden, with a spotlight on it.

The party became known as The Tank Hill Party because the MD's residence was on top of a hill which was also occupied by a large water tank. The dress was to be fancy dress and many dressed up as Africans, colonial administrators etc. Carruthers put on a white dinner jacket, short trousers and long stockings, and carried a flywhisk. The great majority of the guests were white.

At midnight the British National Anthem was played and the Union Jack lowered. Drinking and merry-making carried on until the early hours. Someone lost his wife; she turned up mid-way through the next morning and refused to say where she had been.

At that particular time in Uganda's history the country was independent under a civilian government whose Prime Minister was one Milton Obote. He was having a major political problem over the price of coffee, Uganda's major export and earner of foreign currency, which was controlled by a government-owned marketing board, and he desperately needed some excuse to divert attention away from the problem of falling exports and thus income.

A white racist party held at a house flying the Union Jack in an independent African country was a golden opportunity too good to miss for such an astute and ruthless politician.

In the following days, newspapers, radio and TV most of them state-controlled, gave details, some true, some false, of what had gone on at the party. Obote said it was an insult to the country and he wasn't going to have white colonialists degrading Africans. Around 20 expatriates were deported from Uganda and Carruthers' managing director felt obliged to leave too, although he had only lent his house as he was away from Kampala at the time. Carruthers survived because he hadn't been there officially and having only been in the country literally one day, nobody knew him. He had in fact left the party early, finding it boring.

Special Branch policemen searched his company's offices in the week following and took away all the tapes from the office tape recorders. They suspected some imperialist plot and must have been very bored listening to work tapes about various insurance covers.

As far as the expatriates were concerned, it was a prank which had gone seriously wrong. It was a lesson to others, however, not to take newly independent governments for granted. Somebody should have known better. It was rumoured that it was an expatriate in the Ministry of Information who had leaked details of the party to Government.

Obote was a clever politician and knew how to milk any given opportunity for all it was worth. He would later use to the same effect an incident where a British diplomat in Kampala was kidnapped and kept on an island in Lake Victoria for some days. The kidnapping had been carried out by Indians and it was rumoured that the diplomat had collaborated with his captors to draw attention to the fact that Indian residents in East Africa had not been granted British citizenship. He was eventually found by the Government security agencies, for which Obote took full credit. Instead of being sacked on the spot, the diplomat was merely transferred to another post, which seemed astonishing to Carruthers.

'Don't want to rock the boat, old boy,' a British diplomat told him.

Shortly after the party incident, Carruthers found that he had to seek alternative living accommodation. On the Sunday following the party he had gone with some friends to spend the day at Entebbe, 20 miles from Kampala on the edge of Lake Victoria. On returning late in the afternoon, he noticed as he drove up hill to the house that a fire engine was standing outside and wisps of smoke were rising up from the charred ashes of what had once been his MD's large double-storeyed, red-roofed tiled house.

Youth wingers from the largest political party, which formed the Government, had marched up the hill from Kampala and thrown petrol bombs into the house. The main residence had no tenant at the time, although the guesthouse was of course occupied by Carruthers and his colleague. Luckily the fire had been put out in time and had not reached the guest wing, so he was able to retrieve his property. Thank goodness it had not happened when he was there, he thought, as he could have been attacked or burnt alive. This time Obote didn't use the incident for any diversionary action.

There must have been a jinx on that house because years later the expatriate who bought and rebuilt it was killed by invading troops when trying to flee Kampala during the overthrow of Idi Amin.

That evening Carruthers spent the night in a hotel. After a couple of days the company found accommodation for him and he started settling in to his new residence and job. He made friends with young Ugandans his own age and started hitting the nightspots after office hours. Life was back to normal!

The difference was, however, that he was mixing with Uganda Africans of his own age and class, which he had not found possible in Kenya. At that time Kenya had a lot of catching up to do in that respect.

Carruthers awakened to the sound of water being thrown on his car windows. Bloody hell, where was he? What was that white froth running down the glass? Then it all came back to him. He had left the nightclub about three in the morning and, on reaching his small bungalow, found that he had forgotten his keys. He hadn't had to worry about keys in his previous, burnt-out residence. The houseboy had the spare keys but wouldn't be on duty until 7 a.m., so he had crashed out on the back seat of his car. Now the houseboy was carrying out his daily early morning ritual of washing the car and obviously had not seen the inert body inside. Gingerly easing himself up, Carruthers met the astonished and frightened gaze of his houseboy, who seeing him through the soapsuds thought he was a ghost. He gave a shriek, knocking over his bucket. 'Morning, Festus,' Carruthers mumbled as he opened the door and staggered into the bungalow to have a bath and some tea and toast. Festus backed away rapidly.

Things are getting out of hand, Carruthers mused as he crunched his toast. Every other night in a nightclub was not doing his liver any good. He must settle down and find a steady girlfriend. Single white girls were few and far between and the married ones all looked washed out, and anyway he felt it would be too dangerous to have an affair with a married woman in what was a relatively small expatriate community.

The local girls were gorgeous and his past dalliance with Bernadette from across the border had whetted his appetite. And he still had one of those whips, he thought.

Festus came in, bucket in hand and a disapproving look on his face.

'Have you got any nice sisters, Festus?' Carruthers asked cheekily. Festus' disdainful grunt soon ended that conversation.

Ah well, down to the office, he thought. He was director in charge of sales and marketing for various insurance products in his position as a broker, reporting upwards only to his managing director, another expatriate about ten years older than him. He was sure his MD was having it off with his own secretary, a married expatriate girl who was a bit of all right. Oh God, why did he have to think about sex all the time! It must be the constant hot weather. It was never like this in Edinburgh, where his parents lived. He wouldn't have left if it had been!

By 11 a.m. he had chatted up a few of the secretaries

in the office, mainly pretty Indians, arranged to have lunch with a client at the club and was hoping that his MD would invite him into his office around noon for a drink and a chat.

He swirled round in his chair to glance out of the window and noticed that in the offices above and opposite his, across the car park below, people were clustered round the windows and staring at something. He stood up and looked down but there was nothing there of any interest. The phone rang and he soon forgot about the staring faces.

His hoped-for meeting with his MD didn't unfortunately take place in the manner he had hoped. The case of the staring faces was solved just before noon when the caretaker of the office building, a retired expatriate sergeant major with a large white moustache, marched indignantly into Carruthers' office and demanded that he had a word with his MD on a rather delicate matter, which he reported to Carruthers in hushed tones.

Evidently the MD, in his office next door, had been spotted by staff in the offices opposite feverishly kissing the exposed white breasts of his secretary. A rallying cry had soon emptied all the desks as office workers crowded the windows. They didn't often see white breasts. The caretaker, who happened to be passing the open door of the offices, had wondered what everyone was looking at and soon found out.

'We can't have office workers being distracted by such goings-on,' barked the ex-sergeant major, his moustache quivering, and stalked out, his face bright red.

Carruthers' first inclination was to ignore the situation. It would all be too embarrassing to tell his MD. The staring faces had gone, so presumably the petting had stopped. Lucky blighter. However, it could happen again, he thought, and as he liked his MD, and the MD's wife, incidentally, he felt he must warn him personally that his antics had been observed.

Checking that the secretary was back at her desk, his eyes drawn automatically to her breasts, he strode resolutely into his MD's office and, somewhat hesitant at first, repeated what the caretaker had said.

The MD, like the caretaker, went bright red and said, 'Absolute rubbish, absolute rubbish.'

Carruthers fled, knowing he wasn't going to be offered a drink this time. He winked as he passed the secretary and told her he was on his way to lunch.

My God, I really need that drink, thought Carruthers as he drove to the club, sometimes known as the Top Club as it was also on a hill. Fifteen minutes later he was sipping his first pink gin as he awaited his guest in the men's bar. 'No ladies beyond this point' said the notice on the verandah outside. A bastion of peace and safety, Carruthers thought.

He couldn't very well repeat the story of that morning's incident to his guest as he was a valued client of the company, plus the fact the MD's secretary's husband worked for this client. News like that travelled fast.

The client arrived, was duly signed in the visitors' book and a pink gin was thrust in his hand. This gave Carruthers the opportunity to order another one for himself.

The client was German and Carruthers always felt uneasy in this very British club when some common friends invariably greeted the German with a click of the heels and a Nazi salute and a finger across their upper lips. Anyway, his guest didn't seem to mind too much, he thought, although you never knew with these Germans. He might get his own back one day.

Carruthers was starving, having missed out on dinner the night before. Lots of beer and a couple of samosas was all he had had – and quite a few dances, he remembered. He moved to the club restaurant with his guest. Both started off with rollmops from the hors d'oeuvre trolley followed by roast lamb, then biscuits and cheese, all washed down with a bottle of Chianti. As they ate their rollmops Carruthers idly wondered if his German guest was Jewish. A quick glance in the toilet would solve that one, he thought, but there again such a glance could be misinterpreted. Carruthers had done that not so long ago to the club secretary, who had merely raised his eyebrows and given him a knowing smile. He blushed slightly as he remembered that unfortunate experience and glanced nervously around to see if he was present.

The dining room was open to males and females, and situated at the other end of the verandah from the all-male bar. Being a Friday, it was busy; mainly expatriate businessmen making use of their expense accounts. He spotted the club secretary sitting with his wife and gave them a sheepish grin. 'What a nice young man,' the wife remarked to her husband, who nodded his head sagely and wondered if an approach would be welcomed as he remembered that covert glance in the toilet.

Lunch over, back at his desk Carruthers finished off a couple of reports, had a cup of tea and thought about the coming weekend. He must take up golf again to take his mind off sex, although it didn't seem to help his MD, who was a two-handicap golfer. Maybe he would go to the Saturday night dance at the university – the leading university in East Africa – and check out the local academic talent.

On Friday evenings it was usual for many of the younger expatriates to meet at the Rugby Club for a few beers after the office, and that's where Carruthers now headed.

The Rugby Club was a popular meeting point for young expatriates and the occasional local. The rugby team was of quite a good standard and played in East African competitions. On away games at Jinja Rugby Club, one of the Jinja players they would play against was called Idi Amin. Carruthers himself didn't play any longer, having seriously injured his knees playing rugby in Scotland.

I must have an early night, Carruthers promised himself as he parked his car on his way home from the office in the Rugby Club car park. After quite a few beers and a hot curry in his stomach, which he had shared with some of the lads at an Indian restaurant, he was ready for bed. He slept soundly and dreamt of breasts. White and black. Black and white. He woke up sweating.

Saturday morning was a working day, with office dress being casual. On weekdays ties and long-sleeved shirts were worn. The senior staff usually had a drink with the MD around noon on Saturdays. Later, as Carruthers sat in the MD's office sipping an iced lager, his eyes took in the offices opposite and he imagined how the scene of yesterday must have looked to those cramming the windows. The MD, who smiled grimly at him, must have known what he was thinking. Carruthers smiled back.

Drinks over, Carruthers left the office and dug out the shopping list which Festus had given him and made his purchases in various shops, storing everything in the boot of his car.

Kampala was really an Indian city. Most of the buildings and shops had been built and were owned by Indians. Sunday evenings resembled Bombay, people said, as the Asian community did a walkabout. The colonial government had encouraged the Indians to settle and trade in Uganda after their services were no longer needed on completion of the Uganda Railway. Sometimes this caused friction between the indigenous population and their new competitors but generally the races got on reasonably well together (until Idi Amin and his henchmen, jealous of their wealth and acumen, threw them out in 1972).

One of the Indian shopkeepers complained bitterly to Carruthers during his Saturday shopping that an expatriate businessman and fellow Scot whom Carruthers knew well had not paid his bill for three months, and he was going to complain to the British High Commissioner. Carruthers assured him that that would not do the slightest good and he would be better off threatening to beat the chap up. Alternatively, he could start an affair with his wife, who he knew was also not getting satisfaction, although not in the bills department. In that way, he jokingly told the shopkeeper, the expatriate could pay off his bills through what could be termed sexual credit. Carruthers never did find out if the bills were paid but the shopkeeper's complaining stopped subsequently and he noticed that at certain functions the expatriate's wife sometimes wore a sari, while her husband had developed a slight nervous tic.

That was a particularly good shop because, apart from giving credit, it also stocked good champagne. From time to time Carruthers held brainstorming sessions in the office on a Sunday morning and he would phone the shop to put a bottle on ice, to be collected later to assist in the deliberations. The shop, incidentally, was situated next to a popular bar where Carruthers was to meet the love of his life.

His purchases safely locked in the boot, Carruthers went for a beer at the adjacent bar, the Crested Crane, where he was meeting a well-known local African businessman who had become a close friend. He was newly divorced (his ex-wife had the dubious claim to fame of having two of her extra-marital partners die on the job with her) so they had much in common in their search for women.

It was in that bar, gazing up at the girls walking on the street above him, that he saw the most fantastic sight, which would affect him for the rest of his life.

She was brown and beautiful, with the most fantastic legs, and was wearing a stunning orange hat –a real eye-catcher. Carruthers turned to his friend and muttered, 'Look at that, wow.'

He was told that she was the daughter of some local bigwig. Unfortunately, she moved off along the street with some girlfriends and did not return. Carruthers was assured that she would probably pass again next week at the same spot – where he would undoubtedly be lurking, he promised himself.

By now visibly excited, he accepted his friend's invitation to lunch at his house, together with his friend's current girlfriend. More beer and music followed at the house and also a bit of dancing. It was a very pleasant afternoon just the three of them, and the dancing increased Carruthers' lust so much that when his host disappeared to spend a penny he managed to persuade the girlfriend to go off with him before he returned. As he peed, his erstwhile host heard the crunch of tyres on the gravel of the drive. The remainder of the afternoon was even more enjoyable, although Carruthers wondered, slightly uneasily, what the reaction of his friend would be to having his girlfriend stolen from under his nose – or, to put it more exactly and crudely, from under his member.

Carruthers never did make it to the university dance. He need not have worried about his friend's reaction.

On bumping into him at lunchtime the next day, Sunday, in another bar, minus the girlfriend, he had laughed uproariously and said he was astonished that Carruthers had had the cheek to act so outrageously. In fact he was so amused he insisted that Carruthers accompany him, in a brand-new Mercedes Benz he had just collected, to the City Bar, at the other end of town. Carruthers was placed in the back seat, with his friend pretending to be his driver. On arriving at the bar his friend alighted, opened the back door and saluted as Carruthers sheepishly got out. There was then a lot of laughter as various friends waved and greeted them. Quite a lot of drinking followed, mainly at Carruthers' expense, and the rest of the day was a blur.

(Carruthers' friend would in time become chairman of the company where Carruthers worked. However, by then he was not in good health and losing his memory. Carruthers had agreed with him that because of his health another chairman should replace him and that this would be brought up at the next board meeting. He would always remember his acute embarrassment when his friend came to the item on the agenda 'Resignation of Chairman' and asked, 'What is this?' His memory had failed him at this most crucial moment.

As Carruthers cringed in his chair, the other directors sat impassively. After a whispered explanation to the Chairman, it was agreed to accept his resignation and appoint a new chairman. It was too early in Carruthers' career for him to be appointed chairman but the possibility had crossed his mind. He couldn't leapfrog over his MD at the present. Soon after that, his friend was admitted to hospital for treatment but never really recovered. He would later, during Carruthers' exile, be found dead at the side of the road, probably murdered as he walked home; it was a sad death for someone who had been such a nice man and close friend and who had taken Carruthers under his wing almost immediately he arrived in the country. Carruthers never forgot him.)

Mercedes Benz cars were the ultimate status symbol in Uganda. Carruthers' friend could afford one as he had many business interests. On a previous Sunday morning Carruthers had seen an Asian acquaintance handing over the keys of a new Mercedes to a Government Minister on the main street of Kampala. Thinking about it later, he assumed it must have been a bribe for some favour carried out by the Minister, and the Asian had been shrewd enough to do it in public and perhaps had someone secretly record it on film. (Such transactions would subsequently rebound on the Asian community when Idi Amin expelled them from Uganda.)

At that time corruption in Uganda was not nearly as widespread as it would later become through political instability and the lack of adequate finance to pay proper salaries – people had to exist somehow and live by their wits. But a British civil servant in Uganda had recently been 'caught on the fiddle' and imprisoned. To the amusement of many and to the shock of some, the civil servant had carried out a similar exercise while in the local prison. He was subsequently deported to the UK.

The company which employed Carruthers had some years previously sold a 25 per cent shareholding for a nominal amount to the newly set up Government Trading Corporation. That was not corruption as such but done in order to show solidarity and provide some income to a corporation which had been formed to promote the interests of the African businessman. Although the cost of the shares was minimal, the company's generosity was never returned. Requests for help in securing insurance business for the corporation itself and other Government corporations were always turned down, which did nothing to induce confidence in Government's stated wish to form such partnerships. One had the feeling that whatever Government's announced intentions, the politicians and their lackeys in Government-owned companies had their own agenda – and to hell with anyone else.

Over a period of some months Carruthers' duties had taken him all over Uganda to visit city and town councils. In this way he was able to enjoy the different aspects of Uganda from the lush and populous south to the arid and sparsely populated north. He drove by himself everywhere with his golf clubs in the boot of his car. At times he would be the only person on some upcountry golf course. Being a former colonial protectorate, in Uganda every town boasted a members' club, often adjoining the golf course. One had to buy a book of coupons to be used for bar purchases – yet another colonial legacy. But there was always someone to talk to at these clubs who was eager to get news of what was happening in the big city.

The roads were very well kept; if not well-maintained tarmac then they were well-maintained murram. He had even driven so far north one day that he came across a sign pointing to Juba in southern Sudan. He felt he must have crossed the border involuntarily, and turned back. No one was about and he was all alone. (In later years the place would be bristling both with army and rebels and no one would venture there alone.)

Carruthers was impressed, too, with the well-maintained council offices and chambers throughout the country. Most of the local governments operated successfully and the various council officials were given the respect they deserved. These were the days of a virtually non-corrupt society in local government.

When Carruthers and a fellow director from Nairobi were first trying to secure the council business, it initially involved securing the business of Jinja Town Council at the source of the Nile. Numerous council meetings were attended, culminating in one acrimonious occasion when their proposals were thrown out. After the meeting, Carruthers suggested to his colleague that they should go and drown their sorrows at a local bar, the Black Cat. They sat there downing some beers at the bar, quite despondent. Then, turning round to survey the rest of the bar, Carruthers noticed that a group of drinkers in the corner were some of the councillors from the meeting who had been in the forefront of objecting to their proposals. Trade unionists!

Carruthers suggested to his colleague that they go and join them. His colleague was a bit apprehensive but Carruthers insisted and they marched up to the group and said they had come to buy them drinks. Two hours later they had drunk quite a few beers and gone over their proposals again. Outside the formal council meeting it was much easier to have a heart-to-heart dialogue, and with further explanations the group of councillors eventually agreed with the proposals and promised to pass them at the next council meeting. This they did, and all councils in Uganda followed suit. The Black Cat was again busy the evening after the successful outcome of the meeting. Carruthers was never one to let an opportunity pass!

Accommodation on such business safaris was not a problem. Government-owned hotels had been built in all the major towns to a very high standard and were staffed by well-trained Ugandans. The long-term plan was to privatise these hotels, along with other industries owned by the parastatal Uganda Development Corporation, thus enabling indigenous Ugandans to develop their skills in a wider business environment. (However, it would be another 30 years before a forward-looking government began such privatisation. Previous governments hadn't wanted to sell off profit-making enterprises as it was against their socialist principles. However, like many socialist principles, these didn't help the common man but merely increased Government's hold over the country. Eventually, incompetent managers who were happy to take all the profits out for their own use instead of reinvesting in the enterprises to strengthen and increase their profitability would run down many such Government-owned parastatal companies.)

Certain highly educated and well-placed competent Ugandans were already benefiting from foreign-owned companies that were either doing business in Uganda or setting up businesses, and required local partners who were businessmen rather than politicians. They were appointed to local boards and offered shares and did very well just because they happened to be of the calibre needed and, more importantly, were around at the right time.

(Sadly, most of these people would be targeted by Amin and have to flee the country into exile. Amin was a very jealous man, maliciously so, and not just to Asians but also to his own countrymen. These same Ugandan businessmen would return when stability was resumed, but that would not be for many years. Exile was a painful business, no matter the state of one's finances, and to many their shareholding in their own country as citizens was worth more to them than pieces of paper in the form of share certificates in commercial companies.)

One of Carruthers' clients with local shareholders was the managing director of a brewery. Carruthers liked calling on him in Kampala, and his visits were always arranged around 11 a.m. so that when business was finished it was time to partake of the local brew. Sometimes this spilled over into lunch at the Top Club. The brewery was situated on the edge of the lake where steamers came into Port Bell from Kenya and Tanzania. In the old days flying boats used to land there on their way to Kenya, Rhodesia and South Africa. Next to the brewery was a distillery, another useful client, and an instant tea factory, but that was not on Carruthers' itinerary.

The distillery produced Uganda Waragi, a cheap but good-quality type of gin. This sold in small plastic packs and bottles and was very popular. The raw spirit came from bananas, which grew in great abundance in Uganda. Unfortunately, the taste didn't remain after distillation so a banana-flavoured essence had to be imported from UK to give it an authentic taste. When introducing the product to the Uganda market, various essences with different flavours were tried and free samples given to several clubs and popular bars to gauge the public's reaction, resulting in some dreadful hangovers.

Carruthers had a relatively quiet week, vowing to himself that he should remain reasonably sober for his intended and hoped-for introductory meeting with the beauty he had seen on the Saturday before. He only had one late night.

In the office building during the week he had bumped into the caretaker, who said that the MD now just ignored him as if he didn't exist. That certainly proved the MD's guilt. The caretaker said he couldn't care less as he was leaving the country soon, after completion of his tour of duty, and hoped he wouldn't come across any more indecent exposures. Carruthers found it hard to keep a smile off his face.

(Strangely enough, the MD was later to get his own back on Carruthers in a somewhat similar incident – although it wasn't to take place in the office.)

Saturday came and Carruthers was back in the Crested Crane next to the Asian shop. To his utter delight the same beauty passed by and this time actually descended the stairs with her companions and sat in the bar drinking sodas. They giggled as they noticed Carruthers' constant stare. Plucking up his courage he offered to buy some drinks when the group had finished their sodas and introductions were soon being made. Coins went into the jukebox for Jim Reeves, The Beatles and Elvis. *Heartbreak Hotel* was an apt choice, Carruthers thought.

He learned that the future Mrs Carruthers was called Wilfrieda, her father was a former Minister in the Government and she managed a ladies' clothes shop, which her mother and father owned. Hearing that one of her sisters was a nun, a mother superior, Carruthers mentally vowed he would not repeat his past errant ways if he was going to go anywhere with the delicious Willi. Surely some chairmen had black wives? He must think positively on this arising situation.

Promises were made to meet during the week and Carruthers was invited to visit the ladies' clothes shop. That would be a new experience, he thought.

Chapter 4

Uganda Affairs

Carruthers' Scottish accent had softened since his stay in Uganda, not out of choice but of necessity. The Luganda language had few 'r's' in it, these being replaced by 'l's'. When Carruthers first met Willi, the battery of his Austin Mini had gone flat and he duly gave his diagnosis to Willi as they sat in the stalled car. Willi couldn't immediately comprehend what a battery was, with Carruthers stressing the 'r' in his Scottish accent. Eventually she said in a very posh voice, 'Oh you mean the battery,' with no stress at all on the 'r'. They both fell about laughing at this. Ever since then Carruthers had consciously softened his 'r's'.

He was soon head over heels in love with Willi. Of course he knew that such a good-looking chick must already have other liaisons and that over the future weeks they would come to light – my God, he was already jealous!

Once, they were chased in their car by a spurned university professor who objected to the two of them dancing so closely at a Saturday night dance. They managed to elude him on their way back to Carruthers' bungalow, giggling all the way but nervously looking behind them.

On another occasion he was working, in his position as treasurer, on the books of the Uganda Club in the manager's office when a visiting Tanzanian Cabinet Minister asked to use the telephone. To Carruthers' consternation, on dialling the number he had asked to speak to Wilfrieda and suggested meeting her again. Carruthers seethed and shifted in his chair but kept his peace. Was this his Willi? When confronted, Willi laughed it off and said she had met him before Carruthers came on the scene. He was, however, deeply suspicious over the next few months, especially when Tanzanian delegations made visits. Of course a girl with such beautiful legs must have had many admirers. He knew he should feel proud at her being lusted after by other men, but it wasn't easy.

Twice, local admirers of Willi had attacked him. One had punched him on the chin, knocking him to the floor, and another had torn his shirt in a scuffle. Well, Carruthers thought, that is the price of love and it was worth it.

Wilfrieda was, however, very proper in their relationship. She said she would dump any boyfriends she had, but first she had to tell them. Before she introduced Carruthers to her parents she insisted he meet her sister the nun and another elder sister for their approval. Carruthers passed with flying colours.

It was the bath in the bungalow that led to Carruthers' embarrassing confrontation with his MD. One Saturday afternoon Carruthers and Wilfrieda decided to take a bath together. The laughter, splashing and screams of lust aroused one of the neighbours from her afternoon nap and she was not amused. Being an expatriate spinster, she was also jealous; and as she was the personal secretary to the chairman of an important client, she complained to Carruthers' MD, saying that she didn't consider it becoming behaviour for an employee of a well-known British company – and with a black girl!

It was with a certain amount of satisfaction therefore that the MD brought Carruthers' attention to this episode. Soon after, the lady neighbour married her boss the Chairman, and Carruthers was convinced the incident had revived old memories for her so everything was not in vain. However, after that he preferred showers. It was much easier standing up.

Carruthers was now able to concentrate more on his office work. The Nairobi-based Chairman came on a visit, bringing his golf clubs and camera with him as they were going upcountry. He looked like a tourist, Carruthers thought. They had dinner together, getting to know each other as they had not met. The next morning the golf clubs were put in the boot of the car along with their suitcases, and there was just enough room in the back seat for the office files they were taking with them on safari. Off they sped, Carruthers at the wheel, heading towards the tea estates of Western Uganda. He would obtain some insight into how a chairman behaved, he thought, which would surely stand him in good stead.

Between them, Carruthers and the Chairman had finished off a bottle of Jack Daniel's whiskey the night before. The Tennessee mash kept repeating on them and the car was full of whisky fumes. After dinner, the Chairman had insisted on being taken to a night club, which Carruthers had felt very guilty about and certainly didn't intend to mention to his beautiful Willi.

Carruthers felt the effects of the night before every time the car went over a bump in the road. The Chairman was completely incommunicado, only giving the occasional grunt. However, a cold beer or two at a roadside bar two hours into their journey, which was halfway to their destination, sorted both of them out, although the beers, on top of the previous night's Jack

Daniels appeared to bring the Chairman back to his previous inebriated state. Carruthers realised this when the Chairman started fishing in his briefcase in the car, bringing out some pornographic photographs of white girls in various poses and waving them under Carruthers' nose.

'What d'you think of these?' he slurred.

As he was driving quite fast, Carruthers started to swerve, one eye on the road in front and the other, now bulging, eye on the photographs. Eventually sanity was restored; the Chairman returned the photographs to his briefcase and promptly fell asleep. Carruthers wiped his brow and drove on resolutely, heart pounding.

He remembered the last time he was in a swerving car, which had ended disastrously for the car and nearly for him. He had been driving back to Kampala after visiting a client near the Kenya border and was alone in the car, which belonged to his MD and was only one week old. The road was tarmac; it was afternoon and pouring with rain. Ahead of him a cyclist going in the opposite direction on the other side of the road seemed to lose confidence as he saw the speeding car approaching out of the rain. He started to wobble all over the road and Carruthers was forced to slam on his brakes. Before he could sense what was happening, the car skidded, turning completely round, and slid off the road into the bush. A following taxi just missed him. Luckily he was not wearing his seat belt and also luckily the front seat was a bench-type seat. He was thrown across to the passenger's side, the force of his momentum breaking open the door, and he dropped out to land sitting on the grass. He watched in awe as the car rolled over and over away from him. He couldn't believe he was completely unharmed and didn't even have a bruise.

He brought his attention back to the present.

The first part of the journey had been on tarmac, which soon turned into murram that had been well looked after. It was early in the morning and schoolchildren in their bright pink, blue or green uniforms thronged the sides of the road on their way to school. They were all well-behaved, very smart and a credit to their parents, most of whom would be poor subsistence farmers or traders. There were many schools in Uganda, which was reflected in the fact that the first university in East Africa, Makerere, was situated in Kampala, as was the first medical school. The Uganda Civil Service was renowned for its efficiency and honesty. The investment made therefore by both parents and Government provided an excellent return, as many of the schoolchildren ended up in the Civil Service.

At one stretch in the road Carruthers had difficulty in passing a convoy of army lorries full of armed soldiers. As it was a murram road full of bends and the lorries wouldn't give way, he made a decision to put his foot down and overtake, which he managed to do with his heart in his mouth. Things are hotting up politically, he thought, and wondered where the lorries were headed. Probably the Congo, he surmised.

The soldiers reminded him of his own two years' National Service, mostly spent in Cyprus at the time of Eoka terrorism prior to Independence. On arrival in Nicosia he had a rifle thrust into his hand and with others he was ordered to guard a playground of service personnel's school kids. Further guard duties and patrols, some of them quite frightening, had given him a fatalistic outlook in life. He had even got a medal. He had also visited his first brothel in Nicosia and yet did not make any purchase, the reason being that the two ladies available were in his opinion quite horrible. He had used the money he would have spent on flesh on a flash for his camera, instead of flashing himself. There were flashes and flashes, after all. He remembered he had at the time come in for a certain amount of ridicule from his mates, who had participated.

On another occasion he was the armed escort to an officer going off duty from his base to his house in Nicosia. They had been caught up in a demonstration in the middle of the city, and chanting students waving Greek flags and banging their fists on their car surrounded them. There were hundreds of them. The officer ordered Carruthers to fire a warning shot, which he refused to do, reckoning that such action would infuriate the mob, who would only turn over the car and set it alight or whatever. Eventually the crowd broke away. The officer, who had been more frightened than Carruthers, falteringly thanked him for keeping a cool head when he dropped him off home.

Because there was a state of emergency in Cyprus, all letters sent home had to be censored by officers, which must have been a very boring job – especially when people like Carruthers heaped abuse on certain officers he didn't like. The only other place he had encountered censorship was on a visit to Banda's Malawi, when imported newspapers regularly had headlines, photographs and text blacked out; another very boring job.

He had really experienced fear in Cyprus when on patrol on the outskirts of Nicosia. His patrol and another patrol mistook each other in the dark for terrorists. Luckily, it was sorted out soon after guns had been cocked and firing positions taken. He had felt fear, foolishness and then anger at that moment.

Thinking back, the main reason for censorship in Cyprus at that time was the British Government's decision to attack Egypt in its bid to retake the Suez Canal, which Egypt had possessed. Cyprus was used as a staging post, and before the invasion a build-up of supplies, men and aircraft took place on the island. This was obvious to all military personnel based in Cyprus, and as Anthony Eden, the British Prime Minister, was making his plans without the backing of his allies, the USA, it was imperative that no advance warning of the invasion was leaked. It was, however, a failure – leading to Eden's resignation. Another failure was the attempt by Britain to hold on to Cyprus. It became independent, and Archbishop Makarios returned from exile in the Seychelles – where, coincidentally, a Kabaka of Uganda was also once exiled. Colonised islands had their uses in those days.

The journey continued through the lush countryside. Coffee, tea and sugar could all be seen growing in the fields. Herds of cattle were grazing in the distance. All the ingredients were there for a cuppa, Carruthers thought. The smell of the tea bushes alerted him to the fact that they were nearing their destination. The smell was like that of turnips, which the English insisted on calling swedes for some strange reason.

They arrived at the tea planters' club, situated in the middle of the tea estates, where they were to meet the client at whose house they were staying that night. He was an old friend of the Chairman. Two hours and many beers later, the tea planter had not shown up but had sent a message saying the guests should proceed to his house, where he would catch them up later after dinner. He and his wife had been called away unexpectedly and wouldn't be back until late.

Carruthers and the Chairman sat down to dinner in

the tea planter's house in a dimly lit room, after having showered and downed a couple of aperitifs – two snifters from a then unopened bottle of Glenmorangie found on a table in the lounge.

A servant placed a bowl of chicken curry on the table. The rice, what there was of it, was cold. The chicken seemed to have disappeared. All that could be found were chicken bones in gravy. The servants must have taken the meat. They left the table completely unsatisfied and attacked the bottle of Glenmorangie. They weren't sure where they were to sleep so they had to await the return of their hosts.

The Glenmorangie almost finished, Carruthers and the Chairman fell asleep in their chairs. On the table in front of them lay the pornographic photographs, which Carruthers had been able to study more carefully with both eyes this time. They had shown up a side of the Chairman which he hadn't heard about before. He was sure that wasn't one of the qualifications needed to be a chairman! Well, it takes all types, Carruthers thought.

They awakened slumped in their chairs to the sound of sobbing. Opposite sat their host sipping a glass of whisky, his face impassive. His wife was the one sobbing as she clutched the photographs.

'You beasts, you beasts,' she shouted, throwing down the photographs, and fled the room.

Carruthers and his Chairman stared back blearily. It turned out, as related by their host over a second bottle of Glenmorangie, that one of the girls in the photographs was his wife's daughter from a previous marriage whom she had not seen or heard from for at least ten years. She had recognised her from the large birthmark on her left buttock. Luckily she hadn't recognised the Chairman, whose face was obscured by her daughter's large breasts.

They left early the next morning with massive hangovers. There was no sign of their hostess but their host was up and about to see them off. 'Not very clever, old boy, not very clever,' he said to the Chairman as they drove off.

Carruthers was at a loss what to say. The Chairman grunted, then belched.

Their next port of call was to Kilembe copper mine at the foot of the Mountains of the Moon, which rose above them as they drove. Inside the perimeter of the mining compound it was like a small town and it was run by a Canadian mining company. Most of the technicians were white South Africans smuggled in with the approval of the Uganda Government. In the days of apartheid, South Africans were not welcomed officially, but in this case a blind eye was turned. It was an economic necessity. So much for political rhetoric.

A herd of elephants blocked their way for a while as they passed through the Queen Elizabeth National Park on their way to the mine. They waited at a safe distance while the herd crossed the road 20 yards in front of them. Herds of tan-coloured kobs grazed all along the roadside. It was a magical part of their journey and bought home to Carruthers the natural beauty of the country he was living in, and in comparison the ugliness of some of the nightclubs he had visited and the painted women in them, as so vividly portrayed in the Uganda poet Okot p'Bitek's epic poem, *The Song of Lawino*. Africa indeed was a land of great contrasts.

They checked into the Margharita Hotel perched on top of a small hill at the base of the mountains. The hotel was named after the snow-topped peak of the highest mountain in the Rwenzori range, which could sometimes be glimpsed from the hotel if and when the almost constant cloud cover lifted. It was well worth seeking out.

After checking into the hotel they had lunch. Then Carruthers and the Chairman agreed to meet at 4 p.m. for a round of golf at the nine-hole golf course adjacent to the hotel which the expatriates working at the mine frequented. Afterwards they were due at the managing director's house at the mine for dinner.

Golf, while enjoyable, was frustrating because the course was on the side of a hill. Anyway, the weather was good and the exercise dispelled much of the morning's hangover. Carruthers and the Chairman came off the course both leaning to one side; it was a bit like trying to find one's balance after a rough sea voyage.

Dinner was excellent at the managing director's delightful bungalow perched on the side of a hill. Strategically placed lights showed up a beautifully kept garden with exotic plants peculiar to that area and a stream tumbling down through it. The managing director's wife was justifiably proud of her bungalow and garden and wallowed in the praise showered upon her. Wallowed was the correct word as she was a lady of ample proportions. As she bent over him to pour some coffee, Carruthers couldn't help noticing a frayed white bra. Size 40 at least, he thought. He told his hostess, Flora, about Wilfrieda's parents' shop in Kampala and the exquisite range of underwear available, including bras.

After dinner, brandies were served in the largest brandy glasses that Carruthers had ever seen, along with Dutch cigars. What looked like a splash of brandy in the foot of the glass was in fact equal to a couple of doubles. They were both well oiled as they left for the hotel, and their host had enjoyed leering at the Chairman's photographs after his wife had gone to bed.

Carruthers parked the car at the edge of the hotel car park and they both decided to have a nightcap in the hotel bar. Carruthers assumed his Chairman was behind him as he weaved and waved his way into the bar, greeting the few couples there at that time of night. Plonking himself down on a bar stool, he ordered a couple of large Remy Martins. Of the Chairman there was no sign but Carruthers was past caring. The Chairman appeared half an hour later, completely dishevelled, in his bare feet and holding one shoe. Evidently when he got out of the front passenger seat he had not realised the car was on the edge of a very steep drop to the golf course below. Luckily it was grass rather than rocks which he slid down into, but he had great trouble climbing up the slippery slope, nearly reaching the top a few times, only to slide back down. He had eventually taken his shoes and socks off to get a better grip and managed at last to make it. Carruthers laughed and laughed but it took quite a few more brandies for the Chairman to see the funny side. At first he had accused Carruthers of parking the car there on purpose, and for a moment Carruthers could see another job and his future ambitions slipping away.

At the end of the corridor leading to the hotel bedrooms a blackboard had been strategically placed so that guests could chalk up the time they wanted their early morning tea to be delivered. The next morning many of the guests complained they had their tea delivered at least an hour early. If they had stayed awake a bit longer the night before they would have heard the giggling of Carruthers and his Chairman as they set to with duster and chalk.

They left early the next morning after breakfast, smiling inwardly as they heard some of their fellow guests complaining bitterly to the desk clerk about their early morning wake-up.

Preparing to leave the car park, when Carruthers lifted the gear lever to go into reverse, he found he was holding it aloft, oil dripping down. Great consternation. The Chairman raised his eyebrows. Carruthers found a nut and bolt had dropped out. Luckily he was able to find them and was thus able to fix the gear lever back in a reasonably short time.

He drove at a leisurely pace down into the game park and up through the steep escarpment, clouds of red dust billowing behind on their way back to Kampala. They stopped at the Tropic Inn at Masaka for lunch and were in Kampala by mid-afternoon.

On such visits by road to the mine one would cross the equator twice. The equator was marked by large white-painted concrete circles on each side of the road and were popular spots to stop and take photographs. However, the Chairman was not interested. It was now apparent to Carruthers that he had other uses for his camera.

The Chairman was dining that evening with the MD of the Kampala office and his wife, who would pick him up from his hotel later. He confided in Carruthers that he knew the MD and his wife were having personal problems and he didn't want a long dinner, fearing the MD's wife would bend his ear, so to speak. He therefore planned to tell the MD that he had to meet Carruthers at 10 p.m. as he was going to introduce him to an important Minister in the Government at the Uganda Club.

This meant that Carruthers would not get an early night as planned and not even have time to touch base – or anything else – with his beautiful Willi, who he was sure was eagerly awaiting his return. He did, however, have time to nip into her shop to say he was back. He noticed a new line in bras was on display and wondered if there was a large enough size for the mine managing director's wife. He would make inquiries before his next visit to the mine. Frayed bras needed replacing.

Carruthers knew that he was going to end up in a nightclub, or worse, with the Chairman after a couple of drinks at the political club, where the Chairman would be dropped after dinner. And that in fact is what happened. They had a few drinks at the club and did meet a couple of Ministers, after which the Chairman insisted on seeing a bit of nightlife. They left the club in reasonably good spirits. Set in an acre of ground, the club had an accommodation block to house MPs and visitors which adjoined the bungalow-type buildings housing the bar, restaurant, library etc.

By contrast the Top Life Club was a different kettle of fish and was a local nightclub where good Congolese music was played by a live band. Carruthers was feeling a bit jaded after his long drive and was quite happy when, after a few drinks at the bar, the Chairman suggested it was time to take him back to his hotel. This done, Carruthers suddenly felt such great relief at having the Chairman off his hands he decided to return to the Top Life Club for a final nightcap. He had spotted a few people he knew, mainly girls, but at the time he hadn't wanted to introduce them to the Chairman.

The Chairman must have been very quick off his mark and picked up a fast taxi almost immediately after Carruthers had dropped him off at his hotel. To Carruthers' astonishment, as he ordered himself a beer at one end of the Top Life Club's long bar, there at the other end was the Chairman doing likewise! He couldn't believe his eyes. They nodded at each other. The Chairman was a man of many parts, Carruthers thought as he downed his beer quickly and bolted, not looking back. God knows what the Chairman was up to, but he could guess.

It turned out later, as Carruthers learnt from some of the girls present that night, that the Chairman had in fact gone round asking if they knew Wilfrieda, that white man's girlfriend, and if so, did she have other boyfriends, go around nightclubs etc? Carruthers was furious but he decided to keep quiet because he knew the answers the Chairman got were negative.

Still anxious to have a nightcap, Carruthers stopped at a small pub he knew kept open into the early morning. It was near the office of the Uganda Russian Friendship Society. The pub was deserted, except for another white person propping up the bar. Trying to strike up a conversation with the other occupant, Carruthers asked him where he worked, lived etc. It turned out he was a Russian on a visit to Uganda. Thinking that Carruthers was a security man, he insisted on producing his passport to prove who he was and stressed that he was doing no harm and just having a quiet drink. Carruthers laughed but couldn't convince the man that he was only a fellow tippler. He decided to leave the man to his suspicions and went home. Russia must be a scary place to live, he thought.

The next evening it was the MD's mistress, his white secretary, who came under investigation similar to Willi's from the Chairman – but of a much more serious nature. Telling the MD and Carruthers that he wanted an early night before returning to Nairobi the next day and would look after himself, he had persuaded the MD's secretary, swearing her to secrecy, to meet him for a sundowner at his hotel. Telling her that he wanted to show her some papers relating to her boss which he kept in his briefcase in his bedroom, and having got her through the door, he nearly raped her. It was only with difficulty that she managed to escape him and flee the hotel, as she revealed to her boss the next morning.

The MD was not one to keep quiet on such matters and confronted the Chairman. He mumbled that he knew about the MD's affair and wanted to test her to see if she was the type of girl who would give in to anyone. What an excuse! The MD was not amused.

As events had turned out, visits from the Chairman were difficult to say the least. Unfortunately, his wife rarely accompanied him. She evidently was the only person who could tame him. She was present at one dinner party where the Chairman disappeared under the table and was found, under cover of the long tablecloth, peering up the ladies' skirts and muttering to himself. A swift kick had soon sorted that problem out.

But the Chairman's visit was not yet over. The next morning Carruthers and his Chairman crossed the River Nile at its source at Jinja, the bridge over the dam and its integral power station being their chosen route – and indeed the only route if you were travelling by car. They were on their way to visit the most important Asian businessman in Uganda at his offices and home in the centre of huge sugar estates started up by his father many years before. He also owned various factories, including a brewery, in and around Jinja.

Business over at the sugar factory, they adjourned to his sumptuous house, where they were treated to an excellent lunch and a wide variety of beers, not only of his own brand. Even then, years before Amin came on the scene, the businessman had been shrewd enough to ensure that his family's main wealth was safely outside the country. He loved Uganda and would use most of his energies in developing his business interests in that country, much of it for the benefit of Ugandans, but his own family wealth was out of reach of greedy and jealous hands.

The journey back to Kampala was uneventful and, his business visit to Uganda over, the Chairman left for Nairobi from Entebbe Airport that evening – first calling in at a massage parlour on the way, where he was given a good kneading with extras thrown in. Carruthers waited patiently in the car outside. The things he had to do! After the Chairman's departure, life was going to get back to normal, if that was the correct description. The life of a chairman certainly seemed interesting, Carruthers thought.

Chapter 5

Whirlwind Romance

Wilfrieda's emotions were in turmoil. She seemed to be falling in love with a white man and she wasn't quite sure how to handle the situation.

Apart from being white, he was the ideal catch: young and handsome, with a good job. She herself felt no embarrassment at moving around with a white man, although some of her African male acquaintances were not amused. Some threatened her and she laughed in their faces.

Her family was the main problem, especially her father. Two of her sisters had been introduced to Carruthers and they had been favourably impressed and offered encouragement. The two sisters were highly educated, both university graduates, one a teacher and the other a reverend sister, and she felt strong in her resolve with their support.

Her mother was sympathetic, but her father was hostile and went as far as calling her a prostitute. How could she take up with a white man from a country whose masters had caused such grief to his own King, who had been exiled by the British although allowed to return to his own country? All this had happened only a few years ago. Where was her loyalty, he had wondered? To him this was typical of the British colonial divide and rule policy. He was not amused! He forced her to leave the family house and she had to go and stay with a sister. However, her love for Carruthers and his for her managed to heal in part the pain she had caused to her father and, as a result, herself. Carruthers had assured her that everything would eventually work out, and she believed him.

Willi was aware that her father's anxiety had been increased by the political situation, a feeling that Willi also shared. Her father's loyalties, and her own for that matter, were to her King, the Kabaka, and also to the opposition party in Parliament.

The arrogance of the ruling party and their determination to crush all opposition was very worrying to her and her father. The army were also being drawn into politics and were in effect openly campaigning for the political party in power, the Uganda People's Congress of Milton Obote. Despite his marriage to a lady of Willi's tribe, Obote was hostile to and envious of the wealthy elite, the King's loyal subjects. Willi wondered how she could have married such a man.

Her love for her white man wavered at times because Carruthers was an open supporter of Obote and his Ministers, some of whom he knew well. He was treasurer of their social club and she hated going there to be leered at and lusted after by uncouth politicians. She had in fact decided to keep away from the place.

Carruthers had asked her to marry him and she had accepted, but she worried what would happen to them. Carruthers kept saying everything would be okay; she wasn't so sure. His intention to move eventually to London as Chairman of a company seemed to her a bit farfetched as he didn't seem to know anyone in London. At least he kept her smiling and she considered him a very amusing guy. His antics at her shop, 'modelling' various pieces of underwear, were hilarious.

However, she and her family had decided to give up the shop and someone had expressed interest in buying it. Her father had experienced riots before in Kampala and he could sense all was not well and that it was time to consolidate.

Carruthers had told her that he was due to go back to Scotland shortly to visit his parents. She would not be going with him, he said, because it would be too much of a shock for his parents if he were to arrive with a black girl. Naturally she felt disappointed, but thinking of the problems she had with her own father, she could understand Carruthers' dilemma.

At least Carruthers' absence would give her the opportunity to close down the shop and get rid of the stock. She was going to miss him terribly and she would have to keep a low profile lest some of her ex-boyfriends heard of his absence and started pestering her.

Closing down the shop was easier than she thought. She held a closing-down sale and, apart from a few items, mainly large sizes of underwear, everything was sold quite quickly and she even realised a tidy profit. Even the hard furnishings sold quickly and profitably.

On Saturday morning she locked the now empty shop for the last time and without looking back, although feeling a little sad, made her way along Kampala Road to meet some of her girlfriends.

The next week youth wingers of the ruling political party staged a demonstration in Kampala, for or against what she never discovered, and some white residents were roughed up and threatened. Some families of white residents decided to leave the country and Willi then realised that her family's decision to close the shop had been the right one.

She corresponded regularly with Carruthers in Scotland and eagerly awaited his letters to her. He didn't seem entirely happy and wanted to get back to her as soon as he could. However, he couldn't disappoint his parents and had to serve his time, so to speak.

Willi now threw herself into sorting out a land title for a piece of land in Kampala near to the King's palace and given to her by her mother. Once she had transferred the title into her name, she hoped to erect a small house which she could then rent out.

Carruthers had also talked about building a house where both of them could live. He had secured a plot of land on the outskirts of Kampala overlooking Lake Victoria. However, it was about ten miles from the city centre and Willi felt that was too far. But Carruthers loved the view and was adamant that was where they would live. He had told her that if she didn't want to live there then he would live there by himself! Willi smiled to herself and thought that there wasn't much difference between white and black males when it came to taking decisions on behalf of their female partners. She knew she would move there.

Willi was eagerly looking forward to a holiday Carruthers had promised her on his return. They were going by train to Mombasa on the Kenyan coast. She had never been there so it was going to be a new and exciting experience. He had made all the bookings and bought the train tickets, she boasted to her friends. They couldn't believe how lucky she was. Now they started asking if Willi's boyfriend had expatriate friends who might be interested in them.

As it turned out, some of Carruthers' friends were interested in Willi's friends, but their affairs were short-lived. Most of the expatriate friends were not interested in long-term relationships as they didn't intend to stay too long in Uganda, whereas John had demonstrated his long-term commitment to remain in the country.

Although not living at home, Willi was still able to visit her parents and talk to her mother and father. Her father's mind had been largely taken off his daughter's affiliation with a white man by the increasing political tension. He was a very worried man.

It was obvious that Obote was an extremely shrewd politician. He had persuaded many of the opposition MPs to cross to his own party, including those MPs closely associated with their King, who was now the appointed President of Uganda.

Willi's father and his friends could see the dangers. However, their views were ignored by the King's close confidants, who were mainly Protestants, even although they themselves might have the same misgivings, because such opinions were being expressed by their age-long adversaries the Catholics!

Her father and his friends couldn't do much about the situation except talk. There were few like-minded people in the army. Anyway, they were peaceful people and organising an uprising against a government where the President was their own King was unthinkable. Of course Obote was well aware of that. He was the mastermind behind the whole situation.

Willi heard all these fears from both her mother and father. She wondered if they should actually be considering building a house for themselves when there was obviously such trouble on the horizon. Why couldn't Carruthers ask his company to transfer him back to the UK, she thought?

She wouldn't write to him about the current troubling situation as it would only worry him and she didn't want to spoil his leave, although he was obviously not all that happy anyway.

However, knowing Carruthers and his connections with the ruling party, she was sure he wouldn't share her and her family's fears. She was also fearful that if she said too much to him he might very well, wittingly or unwittingly, blurt out something to his political cronies at his club. She had better keep quiet, she thought.

She read the last letter he had written to her, expressing his undying love for her. He would actually be home next week. Surely her worries would vanish then!

Chapter 6

Willi Becomes Mrs

Such was their passion for each other that Carruthers and his beautiful Willi, as he liked to call her (often causing consternation, puzzlement or amusement to whoever overheard), decided to go on an advance honeymoon to his usual coastal hotel at Mombasa on the Kenya coast. This, however, would have to be after Carruthers' first home leave. He made the necessary arrangements in the name of Mr and Mrs Carruthers for two and half months hence, after he would have returned from UK.

Going back to the UK in winter meant that Carruthers would have to search out what warm clothes he could find. He had only a couple of thick jumpers, having lost the raincoat with which he had originally arrived. His new Ugandan friend who was the clerk to the National Assembly kindly presented him with his own raincoat, which, he said, he had last used on a visit to the UK. He didn't want it back.

The story of Carruthers' lost raincoat was strange. On his first visit to Mombasa, when he went by bus and stayed with friends, he had taken his raincoat, as he had no idea of the climate and whether it might rain. Being overly cautious, he had ignored the advice of friends not to take it. It had hung unused in the wardrobe of the guest room he was sharing with another young man, who was leaving that weekend by sea from Mombasa on his annual leave to the UK. This was the first time Carruthers had met him and he was amiable enough. Carruthers and his hosts all went down to the port to see him off and had drinks in his cabin. When Carruthers noticed a raincoat similar to his own hanging in the cabin closet, he thought nothing of it. That was until he returned to his guest room and saw that his own raincoat no longer hung there. Quietly furious, Carruthers got his acquaintance's UK address and wrote to him. The letter would be waiting for him when his ship docked in three weeks' time. The pilferer did have the courtesy to reply, saying that as Carruthers would have no need for it, he, going to a cold climate, felt it would be of more use to him. He apologised and promised to return it but he never did.

At that time UK leave of three months was the norm after a three-year contract. Carruthers was quite happy where he was and didn't really relish going back to a UK winter, but then he had to see his parents, who were missing him. He felt it would be too much of a shock to his parents if Willi accompanied him, and decided he would have to ease them in gently to the prospect of their having a black daughter-in-law. It wasn't going to be easy.

To break them into the idea, during his home leave he took them to the film *Guess Who's Coming to Dinner* depicting the clashes which a black Sidney Poitier and a white Grace Kelly had with her parents (Spencer Tracy and Katharine Hepburn) over their planned marriage. Unfortunately it had little effect on Carruthers' parents, who sided with the film parents. When Carruthers broached the subject, his father was so shocked he couldn't speak and his mother declared that he would only marry a black girl over her dead body. Regular letters from Willi dropping through the letterbox didn't help matters and were looked upon with great suspicion and anger by his mother.

It was a difficult and uneasy time for Carruthers. He was deeply in love with Willi but he also loved his parents. He longed to be back in East Africa, and in fact he only had a few weeks' leave left in Scotland. To add further unease and misery to his stay, his mother had told him he was expected to be best man at his brother's wedding, which was taking place at the same time as he and Willi were to be in Mombasa. Carruthers, while angry that his brother had never written to him in Kampala about this, still felt it was his duty to take on such a task and pondered about extending his UK leave by a couple of weeks. The more he pondered the more uneasy he became.

He had made all the bookings for their coastal holiday and he had not seen Willi for nearly three months. To write to Willi and cancel their visit to Mombasa could have a devastating effect on their relationship. She had plenty of other admirers who could take advantage of the situation. Torn between love and family loyalties, Carruthers guiltily chose the former. He was now certainly the black sheep of the family, a not inappropriate term in the circumstances, and he prepared for his departure.

His mother was certain he would change his mind but, having inherited an obstinate streak from her, he stuck to his guns. Departure was a sad affair, but once he was on the aircraft Carruthers' spirits, like the aircraft, soared and he had a couple of large scotches to help him on his way. His reunion with Willi at Entebbe Airport was emotional – only marred by a Sikh customs officer confiscating one of his two bottles of duty-free whisky. He would reclaim it later and pay the damned duty.

Willi was amused about his parents going to see *Guess Who's Coming to Dinner*. (Some years later, Carruthers and Willi would together view the same film in a Kampala cinema when Sidney Poitier in person appeared on stage. He was on a cultural visit from the USA, just as Louis Armstrong had been some years earlier. This same cinema was the one that advertised a family film called *Tales of the Vienna Woods*, starring Little Red Riding Hood. Having nothing else to do one evening with Willi away in Nairobi, Carruthers and a colleague had gone to see the film. To their amazement the opening scene showed Little Red Riding Hood being chased through the woods by a man disguised as a wolf who, on catching her, threw off his disguise and started ravishing her. It was in fact a blue movie and it was taken off the screen during the next 24 hours, but only after quite a few families had sat through it too embarrassed to move from their seats. Indeed letters were written to newspapers! The owners of the cinema maintained it was an honest mistake.)

In those days Kampala boasted four very well run cinemas showing both Western and Indian films. Sometimes Willi and Carruthers would enjoy watching an Indian film, as they combined beautiful scenery, singing, dancing, murder, intrigue, blackmail and lust all in one film. Good value for money! (Perhaps if Amin had watched these films he might not have had such a jaundiced view of the Asian community in Uganda. Or maybe he had and learnt from them.)

Their departure for their Mombasa holiday was imminent. It should be said that at that time in the early 1960s eyebrows were raised when a black and white couple went about together; it was just not done. Such feelings existed on both sides of the racial divide. For instance, Carruthers' parents and Wilfrieda's parents were not at all happy with the situation and both had opined that marriage was not to be countenanced.

On a recent occasion they had been invited to a farewell lunch for an expatriate who was returning to the UK. On arriving they were informed by the host that in fact the luncheon was for their expatriate friends and the one they should have attended was the next day for their African friends.

'But come anyway,' their host said.

The assembled male expatriates didn't seem put out by Wilfrieda's presence, and in fact many of the females were her customers. However, things started getting out of hand when Wilfrieda related to the increasing circle of white male admirers details of certain ladies' preferences in the lingerie department and even suggested a fashion show of underwear. At that stage Carruthers felt it was wise to leave. They didn't feel the need to go back the next day, especially as their host's wife had looked distressed as they left. White wives generally were deeply suspicious of black girls, who they were convinced were trying to steal their husbands – which, of course, sometimes happened. That was why Carruthers always stressed to anyone who cared to listen that Willi was his first wife.

Carruthers and Wilfrieda had decided it would be more romantic to travel to the coast by rail. The train left Kampala Railway Station in the late afternoon, crossing the Uganda/Kenya border during the night. Their private compartment converted into two bunk beds, one up one down. It was a long but interesting journey, with the train meandering through hills and forests and at one stage over a bridge crossing the Nile where the river emerged from Lake Victoria on its long journey to Egypt.

It took nearly 24 hours to reach Nairobi. While the

journey through Uganda and into Kenya was mostly downhill into the bottom of the great Rift Valley at Nakuru, the train had to climb out of the Rift Valley and up on to the vast plain where Nairobi was situated. That was what took the time. The views were breathtaking and the tedium of sitting on not too comfortable leather bench-type seats was worth the inconvenience. Lakes, mountains and plains, shimmering in the heat, fell away before them. This was the great Uganda Railway which the British colonial government had built to reach Uganda and which had led to the creation of Nairobi.

At Nairobi extra coaches were added to accommodate the Nairobi passengers. The platform was busy, mainly with expatriates saying farewell to friends or relatives leaving the country by sea via Mombasa, either for good or to go on leave. In fact one of Nairobi's social events was to see off the passenger train to Mombasa as there was a good bar and restaurant at the station. Carruthers saw that some Nairobi acquaintances of his were gathered together further down the platform, seeing off someone. He decided to keep his distance and not provoke any racial asides by introducing Willi to them. Coward, he thought, but he didn't want anything to spoil his holiday.

Two nights on the train and two days later, they were in the humid heat of Mombasa. Another two hours journey by taxi and ferry from the coral island of Mombasa to the mainland and they were at their chosen hotel on the south coast.

Of course eyebrows were raised again by many of the guests at the hotel, who were exclusively white except for his beautiful Willi. She looked gorgeous in her beach shorts and even more gorgeous in her swimsuit. He felt very proud to be with such an attractive person.

They spent ten days at the hotel. It was the first time

Wilfrieda had seen the sea and, apart from exploring each other, they explored the coral reef, the old town on the island of Mombasa and the exciting souvenir shops. All too soon their holiday was over and the return by train to Kampala didn't seem so exciting.

Only one thing had marred, as it turned out later, an otherwise most successful holiday. One of the other guests at the hotel was a secretary with the same company Carruthers worked for, but based in Nairobi. He knew her by sight but couldn't remember for whom she worked in the company, and didn't find out during the holiday as they didn't really socialise.

As fate would have it, their fellow guest turned out to be the secretary to the Chairman and she was quick enough to get on the phone to her boss and say, 'Guess who is here staying in the same hotel – Mr and Mrs Carruthers!'

In turn the Chairman was on the phone to Carruthers' MD in Kampala, and in turn the MD was questioning Carruthers on his return to Kampala! It was bad enough to be seen with a black girl, but to say she was one's wife, well!

(Returning to Mombasa many years later on leave from Nigeria, they were to find their old hotel transformed into an air-conditioned palace. No more quaint cottages on the beach with natural cooling from sea breezes. Everything had changed. Jumbo jets brought tourists straight from Europe to Mombasa airport. Even notices on the hotel boards were in German. To make matters worse, a security guard accused Willi of being a prostitute as she and Carruthers entered their bedroom after dinner one night. The guard was roundly abused by both of them but they laughed about it later.)

So some of the glitter was taken off the 'honeymoon' and both Carruthers and Wilfrieda were furious with people interfering in their lives. They decided there and then that they would get married and would tell everyone, including both sets of parents, after the event rather than before.

Their plans were, however, delayed by surgical operations, which they both had to undergo at Mulago hospital in Kampala. First Carruthers had to have a hernia operation. Then Wilfrieda had to have a cyst removed from one of her ovaries. If it was not removed, the doctor said, it would grow as big as a football. Willi was horrified. Carruthers wondered if these conditions had arisen because of too much sex. He wouldn't be surprised! But he didn't mention that to his partner lest she decide to take remedial action. (Much later in life Carruthers would have another hernia operation, that time a double hernia! What one had to pay for lust!)

At the first opportunity and after recuperation from their operations, they took time off and went to Nairobi, where they applied for a special marriage licence and were legally man and wife within a week. 'Sod 'em' was their comment on the rest of the world. Thus the first black Mrs Carruthers entered into the history books. The fact that Mrs Carruthers was a Catholic and her husband a Protestant meant a double mixed marriage. (The wedding ceremony had been in the Registrar's office and would later, much, much later, after the children were born, be blessed in a religious ceremony in Kampala after many years spent in enforced exile.)

Apart from being together nightly, life continued as before for Carruthers and his beautiful Willi. The MD, the Chairman and both sets of parents had been presented with a fait accompli. The MD tried to bluster and said that the company secretary of the mine they had visited, one of the company's major clients, was upset and could take his business away as he didn't approve. On hearing this, Carruthers felt a bit sick at this prospect and even guilty. He was angry at what he felt was an unfair world.

It so happened that the mine secretary came into the office the very next week and Carruthers, always one to take the bull by the horns, told him that he knew he didn't approve of his marriage and it was too bad because the deed had been done. Carruthers thought the secretary was going to hit him, and physically recoiled. It turned out that the MD had no knowledge of the secretary's feelings and was merely trying to frighten Carruthers. In fact the secretary was very supportive and invited the newlyweds to spend a weekend at the mine, where he was sure his MD and his large wife would be happy to see them both. He then threatened to report Carruthers' MD to the Chairman in Nairobi.

As it turned out, Carruthers did nearly cause the company to lose the mine account but for a different reason. Conscious of the fact from his last visit that the mine's MD's wife needed a new bra and the thought that it would be a nice present from Willi on her first visit, Carruthers hastily wrote a note and popped it into the unsealed envelope the Chairman had asked Carruthers to pass on. Addressed to the managing director's wife and ostentatiously inscribed *From the Chairman*, it was a letter of thanks for the recent hospitality given to the Chairman on their last visit.

The brief note Carruthers wrote said: 'Dear Flora, what is your bra size? Let me know. Thank you for a lovely evening.' Very unfortunately, Carruthers in his haste, forgot to append his name.

Sitting on the edge of her sagging bed at the mine, Flora opened the envelope, which had been thrust into her hand by her husband as he headed to the shower after a hard day's work. She was a bit puzzled by receiving two notes in the same envelope from the Chairman and was holding the note about the bra and murmuring quite audibly, 'Naughty, naughty', when her dripping wet husband grabbed it from her hand and scrutinised it. He immediately thought of that photograph of the girl with large breasts with the Chairman, and putting two and three together assumed that the Chairman's lust for heavy-breasted women even extended to seducing client's wives. He was outraged and started to froth at the mouth.

The next morning around noon Carruthers in his Kampala office received a phone call from the Chairman in Nairobi.

'What the hell is going on?' he said. 'I've just had a furious managing director from the mine on the telephone to me who shouted, "It's 42B, you bastard, and I'll make sure you never, never get your filthy hands on them, you bloody pervert", and then slammed down the phone!'

Carruthers felt a distinct sinking feeling in his stomach and weakly told the Chairman he would find out and let him know. His ambitions about being a chairman were fast slipping away. Head in hands, Carruthers ruminated. He knew it must have something to do with the note he had written. He decided the only way to save matters and find out what had happened was to get up to the mine soonest. He was on the phone to the secretary immediately, saying that he and Wilfrieda would love to take up the invitation for a visit that coming weekend. The secretary said they would be happy to see them, but his MD had said that he should not bring 'that bloody Chairman'.

Well, Carruthers thought, at least I have learnt the size of Flora's bra. He had Willi choose a couple of the best bras from the leftover stock from her shop, one black, one red, while he bought the most expensive brandy he could find and some cigars to take as a present for the MD. He phoned the Chairman to say he and Willi had been invited to spend the weekend at the mine and he would find out the problem. We will save the day, Carruthers said, stressing the 'we'.

The look on the mine MD's face when his wife Flora showed him the present of two bras was a sight to behold.

He went bright red and spluttered, 'Who, who are these from? Not your bloody Chairman, Carruthers?'

It confirmed to Carruthers what had happened and, after explaining, they all fell about laughing and got stuck into the brandy bottle.

'I don't know why you married that bloody young fool,' the MD fondly told Wilfrieda, to which she replied mischievously that it was the underwear in her shop which was the real attraction, not her. He liked to try them on sometimes, she remarked wickedly. The MD looked at Carruthers in a new light.

On returning to Kampala, Carruthers phoned the Chairman and told him that it was his fault in the first place for showing the MD the photographs, because the MD had hallucinated one night after a heavy drinking session, convinced that the Chairman had phoned up in his absence to inquire about the size of his wife's tits. The MD sent his apologies, Carruthers added. The Chairman, who had forgotten about showing the photographs, mumbled his thanks to Carruthers for sorting the matter out. The Chairman privately thought that being stuck up at that mine was having an effect on the MD's sanity. Anyway, no harm had been done to their business contact. In fact, Carruthers thought he had sorted out that incident in a chairmanly fashion!

Chapter 7

Frivolities

Carruthers and Willi sat in a spacious hall, part of the large Lugogo indoor stadium in Kampala. They were attending a Round Table function hosted by Carruthers' MD, the current President, who was moving around greeting people and looking very important. His wife and mistress were both present. Willi thought this very sad as both vied for his attention, one blatantly, the other surreptitiously. The function was a jazz concert given by the Dutch Swing College Band, which was on a charity tour of East Africa.

Being a traditional jazz aficionado, Carruthers thoroughly enjoyed the music and kept time to the beat of *St Louis Blues* and other exciting pieces. He had a couple of their records and was impressed that such a well-known band would come all the way to Kampala to play to what was actually a pretty sparse crowd as far as they were concerned.

Lugogo stadium was where President Obote had been shot in an assassination attempt, the bullet going through his mouth and missing all vital organs. That had been a very near miss (the bullet, in fact, had been slightly deflected before hitting the President) and who knows what the political outcome would have been if the plot had succeeded. (Probably no different; Amin would have stepped in anyway.)

The band was now playing *Love for Sale* and Carruthers sat back contentedly, his loved one by his side but certainly not for sale. He was reminded of his youth in Edinburgh when he used to sit in the back room of a pub listening to Sandy Brown and his traditional jazz band. Sandy Brown, an architect and clarinettist, had moved to work in London, played once or twice with Humph (Humphrey Lyttelton), and then died. What a sad loss. Carruthers knew he had made the correct decision in not moving to London and instead going to East Africa. He at least was still alive, just.

After the concert, Willi and Carruthers went to a Chinese restaurant for a bite to eat. He showed off to Willi by demonstrating his mastery of chopsticks, although he did find it quite difficult. Willi disdained using them and concentrated on eating with her fork. She was quite correct, thought Carruthers. If you didn't look like a Chinese, why pretend to eat like one? The world was full of people trying to pretend to be what they obviously were not. No wonder people got ulcers.

On that note, Carruthers' MD breezed into the restaurant, the band in tow. To impress the diners already present, he drummed his fingers on the table, hoping he would be thought a member of the band, and looked round smugly. Of course as the band weren't carrying their instruments they were indistinguishable from the rest of the diners. He then started banging on the table with a couple of spoons. He certainly wasn't amused when he spotted Carruthers and Willi quietly killing themselves laughing in the corner. He gave a weak wave and a sheepish grin. His wife looked in a foul mood and raised her eyes to the ceiling. There was no sign of his mistress.

This was the second Round Table function to which Carruthers and Willi had been invited. The previous one had been a charity showing of the film *The African Queen*, where the boat bearing the same name and the actual one used in the film – part of which had been shot in Uganda – was on display in the foyer of the cinema. Both these events had raised sizeable amounts of money for the polio clinic in Kampala.

(Carruthers himself became involved quite heavily with the Round Table some years later, after his Managing Director had left the country. That was how Carruthers and family acquired a donkey. In the UK it was quite common for Round Tables to organise Donkey Derbies, and it was decided to do the same in Kampala.

The only donkeys available near to Kampala were roaming free on hills surrounding a sugar estate 20 miles away. They had been used in the past to pull wagons full of sugar cane from the fields to the factory but had long been supplanted by motorised transport. The donkeys therefore were not the docile type and had been used to their freedom for some time now. Catching them was a nightmare. Getting ten of them onto a lorry even more so. However, the team of Round Tablers succeeded and returned jubilant to Kampala after toiling all day, strongly smelling of donkeys.

After the Donkey Derby, which proved a great social and monetary success, especially as a result of the tote they had set up, they had decided to auction the donkeys. To Willi's dismay, Carruthers bought one of the donkeys, which he put in a spare plot of land adjoining their house. It was supposed to be for the children but it proved too wild to ride on a regular basis. However, it was fed and well looked after for some years before being sold to a neighbour after the Carruthers' forced exile. The donkey had also been something of an embarrassment, especially for lady guests sitting on the Carruthers' verandah, when the donkey displayed its male virility. Sometimes he was sure he heard the words 'if only' softly whispered by the same ladies.)

Carruthers and Willi had now settled into the daily routine of married life. Both sets of parents had accepted the inevitable and in fact Carruthers was now on very good terms with Willi's parents. Carruthers and his father-in-law shared a common hobby: drinking Scotch whisky. Perhaps one day his own parents would visit them in Uganda, Carruthers hoped.

Being married to a local girl with good connections, Carruthers had decided that his future life would be in Uganda. He was still ambitious about being Chairman but would, for the time being, strive to obtain that post in Uganda rather than in London. Can't be in two places at once, he thought. There were many opportunities apart from insurance. He had decided they should have their own house, and set about finding an architect who would draw up plans and obtain the necessary approvals for building at reasonable cost. Through his good connections in the insurance world he would easily obtain a mortgage.

They were also involved in another building at the Kabaka's Lake, on the shore of which Willi, with the help of Carruthers, was building a small house to rent out. The lake had been made a hundred years ago by one of the Kabakas, just below his palace grounds. The house was nearly finished and Carruthers, with the help of the person employed to guard the premises, was putting in some finishing touches.

While painting, Carruthers had foolishly taken off his wedding ring and left it on a shelf adjoining the kitchen sink. On returning to wash his hands he noticed to his consternation that it was no longer there. There was only himself and the guard, so it was obvious who had taken it. He searched carefully to ensure it hadn't dropped on the floor. He thought it would be pointless openly accusing the guard as it was an expensive ring and he might just take off and not come back. Instead, he called the guard and informed him that he had dropped his ring somewhere and couldn't find it. He would have to get the police to come if it didn't turn up, as a police report would be necessary to make an insurance claim. He then went back to his painting. On his return to the kitchen about 20 minutes later, he found the ring in its original position. Tact, thought Carruthers, was a powerful weapon.

(Years later, this house would be destroyed by army shells as war raged round the city. But it had provided a haven for some days to a university student who had miraculously escaped from the boot of a car where he had been thrown by Amin's secret agents. He had eventually been smuggled out to Kenya.)

In the meantime, waiting to move into their newly constructed house, they were living in a small rented bungalow in one of the city's suburbs where strawberries grew in the garden.

The Ugandan wife of a British journalist who wrote for the UK *Telegraph* newspaper owned the bungalow. He had recently been deported for writing an article which had upset the Government, and his wife had left to join him in New Zealand. When they moved into the bungalow Carruthers, to his surprise and consternation, found a loaded revolver lying in one of the bedroom cupboards. Nothing else remained from the previous occupants except the revolver. This made him feel a bit nervous, and he and Willi drove out to the shores of nearby Lake Victoria one evening and threw it into the depths of the lake. One could never be too careful; it could have been a set-up, for all they knew.

Another discovery they made was a family of field mice under a wardrobe. For some nights Carruthers had thought Willi was squeaking in her sleep, until further investigation proved otherwise. He didn't kill them but swept them up and deposited them in the far corner of the garden.

Another British journalist, who was retired but still acted as a stringer, had also shared the bungalow with the previous occupants, but with the Carruthers' arrival had moved out at his own insistence into the servant's quarters, which had been partially converted to accommodate him. He had at one time been the editor of the local English newspaper in Kampala, the *Uganda Argus*, during the colonial times. His original career had been in the British Army but that had come to a halt when he caught his commanding officer in bed with his wife and thereupon shot him dead. He served time in prison for manslaughter, came out to the colonies, and ended up in the servant's quarters next to Carruthers' rented bungalow. He had some very interesting stories to tell, and he and Carruthers built up quite a close friendship although he was very much older.

The Carruthers' female house servant inhabited the other part of the servant's quarters, but Carruthers' frequent visits to the quarters were genuine in his desire to share a noggin or two with his journalist friend and not to visit the house girl.

The house servant in fact did not have a favourable impression of Carruthers, whom she could hear through the wall often telling her journalist neighbour the latest dirty jokes he had picked up at the club. Being an ex-convict, the journalist couldn't of course get into the club as he couldn't get past the righteous membership committee.

There was an unfortunate incident involving the house

servant when Carruthers, going for a bath one evening, stripped off in his bedroom and backed completely naked down the corridor to the bathroom. Sighing with relief that no one had seen him, he slid into the bathroom, quickly locking the door. He heard a gasp behind him, and turning round found the house servant cowering in the corner where she had been washing some of Wilfrieda's clothes. Hastily opening the door, Carruthers laughed as she fled down the corridor. Wilfrieda was never quite sure if this was a genuine foolish mistake on Carruthers' part or an attempt to seduce the maid. What would have been the result, for instance, if the maid, instead of cowering, had advanced provocatively and touched him? Carruthers himself was not quite sure. Life was so full of surprises.

Carruthers and Willi drove the short distance into town at the start of what was looking like a very busy day. They passed a restaurant and bar which bore a prominently displayed sign saying, 'Open 24 hours'. Outside, staff were unlocking the doors for the start of the day's business. He dropped Willi off at the Land Office, where she was going to sort out a title deed for the piece of land given to her by her mother, and then drove to his office.

He passed a widely grinning technical director as he entered his office. This was obviously an omen for what was about to befall poor Carruthers later in his office that day. An older expatriate colleague, the technical director, who was very staid in his ways until recently, had suddenly decided to catch up on life. It was probably the male menopause. His wife, who suffered terribly from asthma, to which the Uganda climate was not conducive, had recently returned to live in England. Let loose for the first time in his life, Carruthers' colleague had developed a taste for ballroom dancing – more particularly with a visiting large female inspector at one of the international banks. He had started buying new clothing and having his hair permed. If it hadn't been for the female dancing partner, Carruthers would have had grave doubts as to where his colleague's sexual inclinations now lay.

It was therefore with shock and disbelief that Carruthers witnessed his colleague march into his office, close the door and drop his trousers to reveal a pair of Y-fronts, which he had only purchased the day before. The poor man who had never owned such items of clothing and was anxious to show off his trendy underwear, stood there beaming, his trousers round his ankles.

Carruthers was aghast, afraid that someone might come in and immediately gain the wrong impression. He urged his colleague, after giving him appropriate words of congratulations, to pull up his trousers quickly or all would be lost. This was done, and his colleague went out of the room, leaving Carruthers quite shaken. If it had been a female who had done that, Carruthers would have coped admirably. But a man! Ugh!

As Carruthers thought about what had happened, he remembered that his colleague had a habit of putting his foot in it. Not so long ago they had taken a recently arrived Indian expatriate who was the new boss of one of their clients' local operations out to lunch. Carruthers' colleague, who had very black hair and a deep tan, was very well read and prided himself on having a bit of knowledge about everything. Over lunch, although he had never visited India, he regaled the newly arrived Indian expatriate with details about Bombay and its environs. Intrigued, the Indian asked quite seriously, 'Are you coming from Bombay?'

Carruthers' colleague got very angry with this and shouted that of course not, he was a true London cockney born within the sound of the Bow Bells. Carruthers laughed out loud, the Indian looked puzzled and Mr Know-All, muttering to himself, got stuck into his food. He didn't say another word. Serves you right, thought Carruthers.

He remembered the last time his colleague had got carried away. He was trying to convince the Indian manager of a large sugar estate to take out medical insurance for his staff. His colleague went into such great detail of various medical conditions that the manager, who kept taking snuff and blowing his nose into a quickly dampening handkerchief, got very excited and, although he well knew who the technical director was, started calling him 'doctor'. This time his colleague didn't object to such a title and the conversation and the sniffing and blowing continued. Carruthers sat back amused.

His office colleague had also recently arranged a couple of fancy dress parties, to which Carruthers and Willi were invited. The men were asked to appear in drag, which Carruthers refused to do. He would much rather take women's clothes off than put them on, for goodness sake. His colleague did of course appear in drag and had gone so far as to shave his legs and wear nylon stockings. Willi was quite shocked by all this and told Carruthers to keep his distance, especially as another two guests were in drag. Either that or they were manly-looking women. However, Carruthers couldn't resist pinching his colleague's bottom, and in return was thrown a male kiss, whereupon Willi urged Carruthers to leave immediately.

The next day his colleague insisted he had been followed home by a strange car, which had only stopped chasing him when he took off his wig.

On another occasion the same colleague arrived in

the office one morning with a large plaster across his nose. He had been visiting a friend who had a large Alsatian dog. He assured his friend that he got on well with dogs, but the Alsatian took a chunk out of his nose when he mistakenly encouraged the dog to share the chair on which he was relaxing.

Chapter 8

Events at the Club

Frivolities aside, Carruthers spent a lot of time and energy in his job and also in his position as honorary treasurer at the Uganda Club. The latter was not a sinecure, especially as the majority of members who regularly attended were MPs and Ministers in Government. Some of them didn't take kindly to a white man pursuing them for their outstanding bills and membership dues. But although at times he was abused and even threatened, he had the full support of the committee, the Chairman of which was a senior minister. The Chairman on one occasion even offered to provide an armed soldier to accompany Carruthers to collect dues from recalcitrant members, but this was politely refused.

Carruthers' very close friend, the Clerk to the National Assembly, was the honorary secretary to the club. They were about the same age and shared the same interests: women, booze and politics. Carruthers thus became a regular visitor to the Strangers' Gallery in Parliament, as his friend alerted him to attend, often in the evening, to witness history taking place. MPs would glance up at the gallery to see who was there, and some would recognise him. The Speaker and Clerk both wore white wigs. The Speaker in his Indian accent frequently had to shout, 'Order, Order', as members became overexcited.

Carruthers would witness the accusation made by an

MP that the head of the army, one Idi Amin, had been involved in gold shipments from the Congo into Uganda, money from the sale of which – it was alleged – ended up in his personal bank account. (This was the beginning of the crisis which would lead to the coup by Idi Amin, an act of self-preservation.)

It was exciting to witness such events, although he felt slightly nervous as a white stranger. However, he felt he belonged in Uganda and was treated as a Ugandan by many Ugandans, and he felt very proud of that.

Instead of dealing decisively with such events building up, Obote hid behind legislation that he pushed through, allowing a state of emergency to exist and renewed such state of emergency on a regular basis. Criticism was answered by threats or imprisonment.

Even the President, the King of Buganda, was aware of the threats against his life by Government. A close friend of Willi's father, a senior Cabinet Minister, at great personal risk alerted him to a plot to arrest the Kabaka. The Kabaka was scheduled to make a visit outside Kampala, and troops had been positioned at a certain point on the route to stop the official convoy. The Kabaka was duly informed, and a relation was put in his place while he remained hidden in his palace. True enough, the convoy was stopped by the army, who were furious at not finding their quarry.

Being 'on the inside' also had its advantages. On one occasion Carruthers was asked to sit in the Speaker of Parliament's official car along with the Speaker and his friend the Clerk to the National Assembly. They were on their way to the crematorium as the Mayor of Kampala had died. A prominent Asian lawyer, he had served with Carruthers on the committee of the Uganda Club and Carruthers had enjoyed his company. The

Government of Obote had appointed him Mayor not so long ago and crowds lined the streets as he had been popular. In traditional Hindu fashion the body was placed openly on the pyre and burnt. It was an emotional sight.

Cremation was not usual in Uganda. Indigenous Ugandans normally interred their dead in family burial grounds, often many miles away from the city and towns. European families wishing to cremate loved ones would either have to send the body to Europe or follow the Indian custom and watch their loved one burn before their eyes.

It was also the custom in Uganda for the body to be put on display at the home of the nearest relative for the whole night prior to the burial. Relatives and friends would congregate at the house to offer condolences and sympathise with each other. Those who were seriously religiously inclined (mainly the women) would sing hymns and pray all night, while others would share the odd bottle or two round a burning wooden fire in the grounds of the house.

The funeral over, Carruthers and party headed for the club, where quite a bit of drinking ensued and tributes were paid to their former colleague. (African, Asian and European members got on very well with each other in those days. It would be Amin who would cause great animosities between the races and tribes.)

The secretary and treasurer occasionally carried out stocktaking of the club bar, in addition to weekly stocktaking by the club manager. Money was being lost in the bar and it took quite a while, and a considerable amount of time spent at the bar, to find out how the head barman was cheating, for it could only be him. It was in fact simple and obvious, which was the reason it took so long to detect. One doesn't look for the obvious unless you have been trained to do so. Quite simply, the barman, on being asked for a second drink, retrieved the chit he had given the member for the first drink and wrote on it the details and price of the next order, conveniently omitting to place it on top of the carbon paper so that it would not appear on the copy of the first chit. The money for these repeat orders went into the barman's pocket. He was sacked immediately.

Carruthers and his secretary friend carried out the subsequent stocktaking on a Sunday morning, which was a blessing in disguise as it gave them a whole day to partly recover from their morning's activities. This had involved imbibing quite a few glasses of liqueurs. Six or seven or more dusty bottles were found at the back of one of the bar shelves, some with names they had never heard of before. As there were no more than a couple of glasses in each bottle, they decided to write them off and taste and drink the contents between them.

Some hours later, members arriving in the club bar for a mid-day Sunday drink found the secretary and treasurer giggling away uncontrollably and quite incapable of serious conversation. Some joined in the merriment and more drinks were ordered, so that by mid-afternoon there was no pain being felt by anyone. Eventually they had some food in the club restaurant, which sobered them up a bit. The next morning they both had monumental hangovers and Carruthers was quite glad that his Willi was not around to see it. She had gone to visit a sister in Nairobi. But soon the club would have a new secretary.

* * *

They stood on the tarmac at Entebbe airport, Carruthers, his friend the ex-Clerk of the National Assembly and former club secretary, and another close acquaintance of both of them. The ex-Clerk had been appointed Ambassador to France and was waiting to board the Air France aircraft in front of them. Unfortunately there was a mechanical failure and it was delayed by about five hours, so the new Ambassador and his two friends imbibed heavily in the VIP lounge. He was also coached by his friends on how to greet French officials on his arrival in Paris, which was quite hilarious as none of them spoke adequate French. They lost all track of time and the Government car which had brought them to the airport had long since returned to Kampala.

Carruthers and his partner in crime didn't leave the airport until the sun was rising above Lake Victoria and long after their friend and the aircraft had gone. They had had to wait for an early morning taxi as their cars had been left outside the Kampala hotel where they had all met before departing for the airport, which was 20 miles away. Their wives, of course, were distraught with worry and thought firstly they were with other women and secondly that there might have been an accident. Such was their husbands' reputations that it took some weeks to convince them that their first suspicion was not correct.

The pressures of being honary treasurer at the club without his friend the secretary eventually persuaded Carruthers he had to leave his post. This was prompted by an incident involving the then club manager, who it was thought had been fiddling the books. Because it was really a government club, a senior CID officer was called in to investigate. Nothing, however, could be proved but nevertheless it was decided to terminate the manager's service. Carruthers was not altogether happy with the committee's decision and felt it was more a matter of tribalism than dishonesty. The manager was from the majority tribe, the king of whom was also the then President of the country and an enemy of Obote. Carruthers insisted that as no proof had been found, the manager should be paid his full entitlements, which had been withheld during his suspension and the subsequent investigations. There was a threat of legal action, he said, although he knew that was not true.

The ex-manager had been given a job by his king as a sub chief quite a few miles outside of Kampala, and Carruthers was given the task of finding him to hand over a cheque from the club. A police escort was provided and they set off. About an hour and a half later, driving along murram roads, they managed to find the local headquarters where the ex-manager now worked and lived. As Carruthers approached the office building, the ex-manager emerged looking very apprehensive. After they had greeted each other, Carruthers explained the reason for his visit, which was met with visible relief and eventually great happiness. On seeing Carruthers with the police escort, the sub chief had thought that Carruthers had come to arrest him and was rightly suspicious.

Carruthers felt he had done a good deed but at the same time didn't like to think that people should fear him through his position as treasurer of the club. Although his announcement at the next committee meeting of his intention to retire was at first met with refusal by the Chairman, Carruthers was adamant. A compromise was eventually reached, however, and Carruthers now found himself appointed Vice-Chairman, a position that he felt he could hardly refuse. It always surprised him that he, a white expatriate, was so trusted.

Nevertheless, people knew where his loyalties lay: in Uganda, which he now considered his home. Secretly, he felt quite pleased as his advancement to becoming a Chairman was getting nearer although his actual ambition, he reminded himself, was to be Chairman of a quoted commercial company and not of a social club!

His fond lingering memory of the good old peaceful days at the club during 1964 and 1965 was once when he was sitting in the club library reading a newspaper and Prime Minister Obote and two of his senior Ministers came in to listen to the BBC news on a portable radio. Carruthers out of courtesy got up to leave but was waved back by the Prime Minister, and the three of them went off to a corner of the library, leaving Carruthers to his reading.

Tribalism played a big part in Uganda politics; these three politicians were not Baganda and all came from the north of the country. Carruthers reminded himself that many of the politicians on the Opposition benches had been persuaded or bribed to join the Government side. Some of them had felt threatened by the aspirations of the Baganda as a tribe with their King as President – a clever ploy by Obote, who knew this would lead to chaos, and the Kabaka had ignored the advice of certain of his advisors not to accept the Presidency. Religion had also played a big part in all of this. The King's Protestant advisors told him not to listen to his Catholic advisors, and vice versa. A letter written to the United Nations by the Baganda unrealistically appealing for assistance and stating Buganda's desire to secede didn't help matters, more especially as copies of such letters went publicly on sale in Kampala. Obote considered this an act of rebellion. But the United Nations, manned by highly paid and mainly ineffective bureaucrats, were toothless bulldogs and weren't interested in some distant (from New York) African state. The Organisation of African Unity showed no concern either.

As the Prime Minister got too close to his army generals and his security people, he started to believe too much of what some of his selfish colleagues told him and became isolated from genuine friends. The Government's security apparatus grew as people spied on each other and were paid to do so. A prominent intellectual magazine, *Transition*, was closed down and its Ghanaian proprietor deported; the Government wouldn't countenance criticism of any kind. Paul Theroux, who was to become a famous author, but was at that time attached to Makerere University, wrote an article for the magazine entitled 'Tarzan is an Expatriate', which upset some whites in Uganda.

Obote would soon alienate the largest tribe in Uganda, the Baganda, to which his wife belonged. That had been a political marriage.

On 24th May 1966 Idi Amin with his soldiers was then ordered to depose and arrest the President of Uganda, the Grenadier Guards King of Buganda the Kabaka. By God's grace the Kabaka, King Freddy, was able to escape from his besieged palace, while hundreds of his followers were mowed down. After a long trek cross-country, he eluded his pursuers and was eventually able to reach England, where an arrogant British Government largely ignored his presence. Tyrants make better political allies than deposed kings for politicians.

Obote didn't then realise that as Amin had kicked out the Kabaka, he would do the very same to him. Prime Minister Edward Heath even persuaded Queen Elizabeth to host an official dinner for Amin and his wife.

As Carruthers and Willi sadly looked at the smoke rising from the Kabaka's ruined palace and wondered what was coming next, Willi reminded Carruthers that she had anticipated trouble but he had not cared to listen. What in fact followed was an abolition of all the kingdoms and a suspension of the constitution. Obote had mounted a coup against his own Government.

When all this was happening, Carruthers' duties still took him to the Uganda Club. On the day after the King was deposed and his whereabouts were not yet known, Carruthers and an older expatriate colleague from his office visited the club in the late morning to have a drink and pick up any gossip. The club was deserted, except for the Minister of Defence sitting alone in the lounge puffing on a cigarette. Carruthers' colleague naively asked the Minister if he would call in the British Army, little realising that the Minister was the one who had given the attack orders to Amin. The Minister replied vehemently that as far as he was concerned the Baganda should suffer, as they had never had to fight for Independence. Carruthers shifted uneasily in his chair.

However, his colleague's remark about the British Army was in fact not so naïve, as a couple of years earlier the same Minister had been briefly detained by his own rebellious soldiers and it was he who had had to call in British soldiers from Kenya to quell the riots. Still, the danger signs of army involvement in politics went unheeded.

A curfew had been imposed, during which nightclubs could not of course operate, but at the weekends they opened on Saturday and Sunday afternoons and were always packed. The benefit was that in daylight you could see whom you were taking in or taking out!

During this time Carruthers, Willi and her girl cousin would meet with a lawyer in a bar overlooking the main street in Kampala. Army jeeps kept whizzing by, manned by surly and fully armed soldiers. Willi's cousin's mother, the Kabaka's sister, had just been imprisoned by Obote as he didn't want her to be used as a rallying point by the agitated Baganda. Her house, which Carruthers and Willi visited regularly and where Willi had spent much of her childhood, was a meeting point for Baganda traditionalists, the supporters of their king.

Tension in Uganda was therefore high. At one stroke Prime Minister Obote had dissolved the kingdoms and made himself an un-elected President, and thus alienated all those in Uganda who loved their kings – more people than he ever suspected. Such alienation extended to some of his Ministers and advisors and forced the Government to rule by the gun. Ministers were arrested and prisons became full of political prisoners, the army to all intents and purposes became the police and eventually Idi Amin would step onto the political stage and give two fingers to Obote and his cohorts. After all, they had asked for it. Their arrogance had blinded them to the dangers of too much security and those who controlled it.

Carruthers could no longer sit in the library of the Uganda Club and share space with the former Prime Minister, now President. Before the new President came into the club, plain-clothes security men would now rush in and move everyone out of the library. Carruthers continued his duties as Vice-Chairman of the club but didn't feel entirely comfortable. He didn't like being eyed up and down all the time by security operatives. Although some of his Cabinet Minister friends remained close to him and not aloof, they in fact were as nervous as he was.

He was able to shake the President's hand – and commiserate with him after an assassin narrowly missed killing him on 19th October 1969 – when the President attended a dance at the club. At such dances, which were held regularly, the looming presence of the Army

Commander Idi Amin, huge and always smartly dressed, often in a beautifully cut grey suit, was seen and felt by all. Amin, while happy on the dance floor, was not so happy trying to make social conversation, which was mainly in Swahili. On shaking Amin's hand in the bar one evening, Carruthers felt he didn't want to linger in his presence too long and retreated quickly. His Swahili was not good enough, anyway.

Wilfrieda Carruthers refused to attend these dances. As it turned out, she was correct. Even then, before the coup, it was not wise for an attractive female to be 'spotted' by Idi Amin or his henchmen. Thus Carruthers went alone to any functions at the club.

On one Saturday night dance at the club Carruthers asked a very attractive lady to dance as she was standing by herself. Despite Carruthers' persuasive charms, she refused, saying her husband was about and he wouldn't like to see her dancing with anyone else. Rebuffed, Carruthers retreated to the bar, where he stood and chatted to some friends. Then someone shouting at him from behind shattered his peace. On turning he saw the ugliest man he had ever seen in his life, who demanded to know why he had been talking to his wife. Talk about beauty and the beast, Carruthers thought. The tirade went on and on and Carruthers began to feel a bit scared, as this person was important and involved in security. Luckily, one of the people Carruthers had been talking to was a good friend and a Cabinet Minister, and he eventually intervened, told the ugliest man in Uganda who Carruthers was and and that he should shut up. At an appropriate moment Carruthers hurriedly left the club, making sure his tormentor didn't spot him. Or had he, Carruthers, been the tormentor? Well, Carruthers thought, it serves him right for not staying at home with his beautiful Willi.

The next day, Carruthers told Willi he would go and get a carry-out curry for lunch and promised not to dally with any cronies in the restaurant bar. He was standing ordering his curry at the carry-out counter when he glanced into the bar to his right, and to his horror saw his ugly antagonist from the previous night. Their eyes met, and the fear Carruthers had felt then returned to him and his heart started thumping. Carruthers didn't move, but the ugliest man did, towards him, and indeed came right up to him and said hullo. Carruthers remained impassive. Then, to Carruthers' great surprise and everlasting relief, the man referred to the previous night's incident and said he would like to apologise as he had clearly been out of order. He offered to buy Carruthers a drink, which was refused politely, and Carruthers left immediately his order was complete. Carruthers was certainly relieved and he respected the man for having the guts to apologise. However, he remained disturbed by the whole incident.

(Years later, Carruthers was to meet the same man, who was in exile in Nairobi, at the home of Wilfrieda's sister, who was also living there as her former husband – a former Cabinet Minister and also a good friend of Carruthers' – had been murdered by Idi Amin and his henchmen. Carruthers was by this time also in exile and didn't refer to the previous incident. In any case, the ugly man didn't seem to remember him, for which he was glad. He made sure, however, of helping him to nearly finish a bottle of whisky to further destroy his memory. After the overthrow of Amin the ugly security man returned to Uganda and ended up being killed in Southern Sudan, where he had gone on some undercover Government or personal mission. At that time that area was very dangerous – and in fact still is.)

There was tension at the club and members knew

something was going wrong. Certain Cabinet Ministers were becoming openly critical of the President and said in the bar that he was becoming a law unto himself and to hell with democracy.

One of the President's vocal supporters in government employment was a middle-aged Englishman working with the Ministry of Information, whose chief asset was that he had a pilot's licence and was able to fly various persons on undisclosed missions, including, reportedly, the army commander, Idi Amin.

He would meet him occasionally at the club bar, where they would have a few drinks together, but they didn't discuss political events. He had few white friends. Some said he was a British spy, although Carruthers suspected that many also said that about him. Carruthers felt he was keeping dangerous company and this time did resign from the club. He had had enough and it just wasn't safe. Willi was delighted.

Despite the political uncertainties, Carruthers and Willi concentrated on getting plans ready for the bungalow they intended to build some six miles from Kampala on the shores of Lake Victoria. It took a bit longer than anticipated but eventually they were able to move in. It was so peaceful sitting on their verandah and surveying the lake spread out below, and this was to be a favourite place to entertain their friends and relations on a Saturday or Sunday afternoon. By this time Mr and Mrs Carruthers were the proud parents of two boys and a girl, one of the boys still a baby.

Chapter 9

The Coup and the Parrot

The nearest Carruthers got to being a British spy was when he rang up a contact in the British High Commission – shortly before Idi Amin overthrew Obote in January 1972 when the latter was in Singapore – to advise him that a coup was imminent. No surprise was expressed and Carruthers suspected the British already knew.

He had received that information from a highly placed Uganda CID officer who was a friend. Somewhat sinisterly, he had come into Carruthers' office one morning and said he was not on a social but an official visit. Carruthers was immediately nervous. His friend wanted to know what the British High Commission was advising British citizens residing in Uganda, because he had heard of meetings being held between the High Commission and British residents. Carruthers replied that as far as he knew these were regular meetings held to brief British residents on the current security situation in the country. Carruthers' CID friend then revealed that Obote had sent a message from Singapore that every effort should be made to trace the reason why rumours were going around at home and overseas about a coup.

However, it was too late: two days later, on 26th January, there was a coup. (Unfortunately, the CID officer, who was an efficient and dedicated public servant, was later to be murdered by Amin and his henchmen. This was because of his earlier involvement in the investigation into the murder of a Brigadier and his wife where suspicion had fallen on Amin.)

The coup was a relatively peaceful affair, as far as Kampala residents would remember. The BBC was widely listened to and the news that Uganda radio had stopped its regular programmes and was playing martial music led everyone to tune into this music and wait for the announcement that would surely come.

Most people stayed at home to await developments. Carruthers had a tape at the ready. Then some army sergeant came on the radio and announced the various faults of Government that had forced the army to take action. Idi Amin would speak later in his halting English.

One of Carruthers' neighbours was the editor of the local English newspaper the Uganda Argus and also the BBC Africa correspondent in Kampala. He walked over to his neighbour's house after the announcement, tape in pocket. Another couple of expatriate neighbours had already congregated there, and the correspondent assured everyone that he had copied down everything from the radio broadcast. But he had been a bit unprepared and various jottings were written on pieces of paper, newspapers, book flaps etc, all scattered round the room. As the correspondent went round gathering these up, Carruthers smugly thought of the tape in his pocket. But he wasn't going to reveal its presence just yet as he found it quite amusing to see the correspondent trying to piece all his notes together. After the correspondent had read his notes to all those assembled, Carruthers then handed the tape to the correspondent. There was a stony silence and Carruthers thought it best to leave there and then. What a laugh, Carruthers thought as he walked back up the road to his nice bungalow and family.

When Idi Amin was sworn in as President, it was the brother of Carruthers' close business friend who as Chief Registrar officiated. The photograph of him, white wig perched on top of his head, and Idi Amin in his army uniform, would be seen around the world not only then but for years afterwards. But he had his leg pulled unmercifully as Amin went from a supposedly docile dictator to a sadistic killer. 'It's all your fault,' he would be told chidingly by friends and acquaintances. However, he took all this in good part and would recount how he had to coach Amin on how to pronounce certain words.

It was time for another visit to the mine, and this time his colleague with the shaven legs would accompany Carruthers. Willi was not impressed when she heard this, and Carruthers noticed that she took an unusual interest in the clothes he was taking with him. He caught her going though his suitcase, in fact.

Because of the coup and army activity, it wasn't considered safe to travel by road, so they hired a single-engine Piper Aztec to take them to the grass airstrip near the mine, where the mine secretary had his driver and car awaiting them. As they circled the airstrip on their approach, their pilot, an Irishman who had been around for some years, announced they couldn't land right away as the airstrip was covered by elephants. Sure enough, the small black dots they had seen from a distance soon turned into elephants as they came lower and lower.

'We'll have to buzz them,' the pilot announced, 'so brace yourselves.' Down they went over the airstrip, back and forward, while the elephants, ears flapping, lumbered away. It was quite a sight and one Carruthers would never experience again. Amin's soldiers started shooting the elephants for their ivory and it would take nearly 30 years for the herds to return in anything like such numbers.

They had no time for golf on this visit, and anyway his colleague didn't play. The driver dropped off the pilot at the hotel, and Carruthers and colleague left their bags and then proceeded straight to the mine offices, where meetings lasted through lunchtime (sandwiches were served) and most of the afternoon. Because of the coup, contingency plans had to be made and every possibility, good and bad, considered.

Again, because of the coup, most expatriate wives had left the country and the buxom Flora, the wife of the mine MD, was not present to entertain them. However, at dinner a passable meal was served by the mine MD's cook, with brandy and cigars providing a fitting conclusion to the repast. They laughed again about the Chairman and his photographs and the bras. Carruthers' colleague, who had not heard the full story before, was highly amused and showed particular interest in the part about the bras. Indeed, a sheen of sweat could be seen on his upper lip as he asked the MD to repeat the story.

'Look, mate,' said the MD, 'the next time you are up, I am sure Flora will be happy to show them to you – assuming, of course, she is not wearing them.'

Carruthers' colleague nodded enthusiastically and the MD raised his eyes to the ceiling and said to Carruthers, 'Next time, bring someone normal.'

Back at the hotel, they stopped for a nightcap.

'Let's go to the bra,' his colleague remarked tipsily.

They were surprised to see their pilot propping up the bar, where it turned out he had been most of the evening. Evidently dinner had consisted of goat meat and rice that had been served cold, so he had retreated to the bar for sustenance. Standards had fallen since the coup. He was so happy to see them he ordered another round.

'I hope you will be fit to fly us out of here, Paddy,' said Carruthers. 'We aim to get away around eleven a.m. tomorrow, after we tidy up at the mine.'

'No problem,' said Paddy. 'A piece of cake! Have another one.'

Eventually they made it to their bedrooms. There was no point in trying to adjust the early morning tea callboard this time because there was nobody else staying in the hotel and there was probably no tea.

About three in the morning Carruthers was sure he felt the bed moving but put it down to an excess of brandy. However, in the morning the staff were talking about quite a sizeable earth tremor which had hit the area – they were quite common in these parts. Paddy swore he had heard Carruthers' colleague shouting, 'Mummy, Mummy' in the middle of the night and he had replied drunkenly, 'I'm here, me darlin'.' But nothing more was heard and Paddy went back to sleep.

'You had a lucky escape, old boy,' Carruthers said.

Soon after 11 a.m. they were in the air. They didn't see any elephants this time, but they had an extra passenger, a priest whom Paddy knew. An hour into the flight back to Entebbe everything suddenly went silent. The engine, the only engine, had stopped. The priest crossed himself, and Carruthers and his colleague glanced anxiously at Paddy, who himself was anxiously examining the control panel. Suddenly he relaxed and pushed a switch and the engine spluttered into life. He'd forgotten, he said, that the fuel gauge wasn't working properly and although showing half full, should have showed empty; he had now switched over to the reserve fuel tank. They arrived back at Entebbe without any further incident.

(A few years later Paddy was to commit suicide by flying his plane into the waters of Lake Victoria. It was assumed he had killed himself because of some pressure or threat from Amin and his cohorts. The truth was, however, that his pilot's licence had been withdrawn because of medical reasons. That was the only life he knew and it was soon to be finished, unfortunately.)

Meanwhile, people who had welcomed the coup, which was the majority of the major tribe, the Baganda, were having second thoughts and were beginning to realise that the genial giant, Idi Amin, was not so genial. Although he had released all political prisoners and brought back the King's body from London, where he had died in exile on 21st November 1969, for a proper traditional burial, his rambling utterances were causing concern.

Like many others present, Carruthers felt embarrassed listening to Amin address the business community at the International Conference Centre in Kampala. He could hardly speak English, the official language of the country, and the feeling after the meeting was of extreme pessimism.

People were also starting to die in mysterious circumstances. The first incident involved a well-known rich young Uganda businessman who was not involved in politics and was found dead in his burnt-out car in Kampala. Similarly, a priest who was the editor of a local vernacular newspaper died in the same circumstances.

Rumours of retaliation and invasion by Obote and his

colleagues, who had fled to Tanzania, abounded. Both sides hurled insults at each other. There was a lot of tension in the air. People didn't smile much any more.

Obote's former Minister of Information, who had been in Kampala at the time of the coup and was married to Wilfrieda's sister, kept a low profile, abandoning his Mercedes and driving around in a Volkswagen Beetle. They sat on Carruthers' verandah one Sunday afternoon discussing the situation, and Carruthers' advice to him was to get out of the country as soon as he could; Idi Amin just could not be trusted.

(Carruthers never saw his friend again after that Sunday. He went to Tanzania and joined an ill-planned Obote invasion of Uganda, which took place on 17th September 1972. After he was captured, he was paraded before diplomats at a function held in Kampala's top hotel and attended by Amin. Hands tied behind his back, he was barefoot, naked to the waist and without his glasses. No diplomat had the guts to lift a hand to help him, such was the fear Amin instilled in people. Soon afterwards he was killed, and the manner of his death, like many others, does not bear thinking about.)

Another visitor to Carruthers' verandah, who came with his wife, was the Governor of the Bank of Uganda. He was a good friend of Carruthers and his wife was related to Wilfrieda. But he made the mistake of making some public statement which was contrary to Amin's view, and was picked up, put in the boot of some henchman's car and never seen again.

And so it went on, almost unbelievable but unfortunately true. While Obote had imprisoned political foes, Amin killed them without thought. (Sadly, when Obote came back the second time after the overthrow of Amin, his army would also follow that line of action. But the Carruthers would have left the country by then, only making occasional visits but never together because of the danger.)

Carruthers and his colleague arrived back in the office in Kampala from the mine to find that their MD was leaving the company and the country. His wife, on learning that his secretary was pregnant by him, had taken herself and their two children off to South Africa to live with her parents. The MD was going to follow them, and his secretary was going to follow her MD and the father of her child – she had no previous children. What a mess! So Carruthers now found himself in charge of the company – instant promotion! Although he wasn't appointed Chairman, Carruthers felt that it would only be a matter off time before he was. The present situation was fortuitous but he knew he deserved it!

Carruthers and the MD went for a farewell drink to the well-known bar of a large hotel, known as The Imperial in colonial days but changed to The Grand after Independence. Idi Amin, guest of honour at a dinner at The Grand, had, in his typical style, suddenly announced at the beginning of the dinner that he was changing the name back to The Imperial. The hotel manager, Willi's cousin, suddenly remembered that all the old Imperial crockery bearing that name was still under wraps in the store and quickly had his staff uncover and wash it. As a result, the main course was served on the old Imperial crockery, which the manager pointed out to Idi Amin, who smiled broadly and nodded his head in approval. There was a certain amount of self-preservation in the manager's action because Idi Amin could as easily have ordered the manager's arrest for using Grand Hotel crockery when he had already changed the name, albeit only half an hour before! (Willi's cousin, however, still didn't escape being victimised and was later to be imprisoned for some weeks on some spurious pretext. One of his jobs in prison was to load the dead bodies of victims of torture onto trucks.)

So the MD and Carruthers sadly sat down to their drinks in the Copper Bar of the Imperial Hotel. It was May 1969, and the place was packed. People gathered together to discuss and piece together what was happening. It was early days and many couldn't really comprehend a situation where people were suddenly being arrested just because they were important or well-off. Eventually, as the truth sank in, people would keep away from such bars. (This was one of the places the Governor of the Bank of Uganda used to patronise.)

The MD was devastated by what had happened to him. He said he couldn't stop himself having an affair with his secretary and was well aware he had brought his family misfortune upon himself. He would sort it out, he said, probably living and working in South Africa. Anyway, it wasn't a good time to be in Uganda, so it all could be a blessing in disguise.

Carruthers pointed out that he had married Willi and built his own house, and would have to stick it out in Uganda. He couldn't just turn a blind eye to his investment in the country and run away. He would have to give it a go. Perhaps things would improve, but he was apprehensive. Carruthers was actually sad that the MD was going and he was sure he would feel a bit isolated now.

On leaving the bar, Carruthers was delighted to greet an old friend, the Town Treasurer of Jinja Town Council, who had been imprisoned by Amin on some false charge. It was surprising to see him alive and out of prison and they greeted each other warmly. (However, a few months later he was again picked up and imprisoned, probably because he wouldn't give in to threats, and was never seen again.)

After the departure of the MD from the country, his Chairman asked Carruthers to visit him in Nairobi to discuss future plans as far as Uganda was concerned. Carruthers wondered if that would encompass the position of Chairman. He decided that he himself would bring that matter up. Carruthers hadn't been to Nairobi since his marriage and was quite happy to have such a break. He was frightened for the safety of Willi and the children and arranged for them to stay with her parents while he was away.

The early morning flight from Entebbe to Nairobi was uneventful except for the delay before take-off. Apparently, someone had put a parrot in a cage on board and the bird had escaped and was wandering around the cabin. The captain asked over the public address system for the person who owned the parrot to identify himself or herself.

'The next announcement you will hear,' Carruthers said to the person beside him, 'will be "This is your parrot speaking, squawk, squawk!"'

The lady sitting next to him thought this was terribly funny and almost choked. Carruthers noticed her bra was black. She had been to Kampala to attend a meeting of the East African Orchid Society. Such was the confusion over the parrot, which was eventually caught, that one of the stewardesses started serving drinks before take-off, which of course Carruthers and his new acquaintance took immediate advantage of. It turned out that the lady knew the Chairman and, from what she said, had spent some precious moments with him. Carruthers mused about birthmarks and wondered.

Carruthers was booked into the Muthaiga Club as a visitor by the Chairman, who was a long-standing member. This was the private members' club in Nairobi set up by the original Kenya settlers and was something special. Carruthers felt privileged to stay there, firstly because of its history and ambiance and secondly because the staff were so polite and friendly. Run by a very efficient voluntary committee, it was a place where the older local white members could show off their knowledge of Swahili by addressing the staff in the vernacular. The staff could speak perfect English but politely humoured the members. Interestingly, however, the white members conversed only in English with the black Kenya members. Their kitchen Swahili didn't extend to business Swahili.

Members were apt to say strange things like, 'I was having a pee in the Muthaiga Club the other day with old so-and-so, as one does, and we were discussing so-and-so...' The club was something very special and reciprocated with similar clubs all over the world.

It still boasted a men's bar, where before lunch he bumped into some old chums from his Kenya days. He made discreet inquiries as to what had happened to his ex-girlfriend. Evidently she had been persuaded to go back to the UK because it wasn't seen as proper to be co-habiting with a black person, particularly one of the same sex. His chums, not knowing the real background, complimented him on getting out of that liaison. They weren't particularly put out by his marrying a black girl because they had for some reason more respect for the Ugandan girls than those of Kenya.

Carruthers was only staying one night in Nairobi, so he spent much of the afternoon holding discussions in the office. It was agreed that despite the uncertainties in Uganda the office would remain open, but that at the slightest hint of any threat to expatriate staff they would be pulled out, and they were to be in possession of an open airline ticket to Nairobi for themselves and families.

The position of chairman was raised by Carruthers. The Nairobi Chairman's opinion was that appointing Carruthers chairman could have an adverse affect on Carruthers and his family's security by putting him in the limelight. It would be more appropriate in the unusual circumstances to maintain a black Ugandan chairman for the time being. Carruthers could see the sense in that but nevertheless felt disappointment.

That evening the Chairman hosted a dinner at the club and brought along some guests, one of whom turned out to be Carruthers' flight companion of that morning. He was seated next to her, with her husband, a distinguished-looking lawyer and close friend of the Chairman, on the opposite side of the table. There were eight of them altogether, and as the Chairman's wife was one of the party the Chairman was on his best behaviour.

On the other side of Carruthers was the Chairman's wife. She was a haughty old bird and Carruthers could well understand why the Chairman let his hair down, as well as his trousers, when he went on safari.

'We should never have given Uganda Independence,' she intoned. 'See what they've done with it. Jumped up Generals, Colonels who were floor sweepers, a very bad lot. It's going the same way here. I don't know why we stay.'

The Chairman shifted uncomfortably in his chair. Carruthers made some inquiries about her stable of horses in order to change the subject and then turned his attention to his other dinner partner.

By now quite a lot of wine had been downed and

Carruthers felt slightly reckless. He inquired in low tones how long she had known the Chairman and she whispered that about ten years before they had a very serious affair at a time when the Chairman's wife was spending too much time with her horses, and her own husband too much time with his legal briefs rather than his cotton briefs. However, they had stopped the affair after she and her husband viewed a video he had picked up in Soho, which had suddenly opened a new chapter in their sex life. She said she would lend it to him and bring it with her on her next visit to Kampala, and asked if he owned a pair of handcuffs.

Things had also got a bit awkward, she said, when the Chairman insisted on setting up a camera with a timing device on it.

'Just at a crucial moment in our lovemaking,' she said, 'this bloody flash would go off.'

It resulted in making her very nervous, with a resultant loss in her libido.

'I hope he destroyed the photographs,' she said, 'because they are not the sort to leave lying about.' She giggled.

Carruthers now put his foot in it. 'You don't by any chance,' he whispered tipsily, 'have a large birthmark on your left buttock?'

His neighbour slowly turned to face him, hand to mouth, and her face was deathly white. 'Oh my God, oh my God,' she moaned, and passed out.

There was consternation at the table. Everyone stood up. The Chairman looked accusingly at Carruthers, while the lawyer husband set about reviving his wife. She soon recovered and insisted on being taken straight home, and the dinner party broke up.

'What did you say to her, what did you say to her?' the Chairman questioned Carruthers, who replied, thinking rapidly, that he had been telling his partner about some of the atrocities being committed in Uganda. The Chairman gave a grunt and departed with his wife. Carruthers went straight to bed, wondering what the repercussions of the evening's disclosures would be. Interesting, very interesting, he thought. Who would have thought?

Presumably her mother at the tea estate didn't realise her daughter had been living in Nairobi for some years. Carruthers decided that he would have to get them to meet each other. That could compensate for the embarrassment he had caused her, even although instigated by the Chairman and his photographs.

The next morning Carruthers was awakened by the telephone ringing at 6.30 a.m. It was his flight and dinner companion, telling him, then pleading with him, to retrieve the photographs from the Chairman. She would do anything, she said; even supply her own handcuffs. Carruthers said he would do his best and would have to work out a plan of action. She should phone him in a week's time in Kampala. Why, Carruthers thought, why do I get involved in people's lives like this? Was it fate or lust?

The flight from Nairobi to Entebbe left on time. He was seated next to a friend, a partner in a firm of chartered accountants in Kampala. Prior to checking-in at the airport, he had asked Carruthers how his weight was, to which he had replied that although he had been putting it on a bit, he thought he now had it under control.

'No, no,' the accountant had said irritably. 'I mean your luggage.'

Carruthers, who had only had one small bag, then agreed to put some of his friend's luggage with his for weighing-in purposes. Why were accountants so mean and irritable, he thought?

Carruthers' first call after landing at Entebbe airport was to his in-laws' house, where he collected Wilfrieda and the three children. Of course he had bought various gifts for them, mainly confectionery for the kids, bottles of perfume for Willi and his mother-in-law and a bottle of whisky for his father-in-law. It didn't take much prompting for the bottle of whisky to be opened there and then, so that by the time they returned to their house on the lake Carruthers didn't have a care in the world. He was very happy to be back in his home, he thought as he drifted off to sleep in his armchair.

He was awakened by the sound of a helicopter. It grew louder and louder and then came into view and slowly landed at the plot in front of their house, where the expatriate government photographer lived. It was an army helicopter and some armed soldiers jumped out and took positions along the fence. Keeping away from the verandah but looking through the windows, the family saw their neighbour being lifted from the helicopter and carried to his bungalow. Soon after, the helicopter took off. Carruthers, seeing the soldiers had gone and always curious but cautious, went over his fence and into his neighbour's bungalow. There he found him sitting in his armchair, with one leg in plaster resting on a stool and one of his arms heavily bandaged. He said he had been on an official assignment following Idi Amin on an upcountry visit to one of his battalions. At a certain stage on their journey on a murram road the car in which he was travelling was crashed into by an army personnel carrier from behind, and the car overturned. He was taken to a nearby hospital for treatment, then Amin directed that he be flown back to Kampala.

The neighbour had his suspicions as to whether it was an accident or a plan, which had in fact succeeded, to get him out of the way. The barracks to which they were travelling was where two American journalists had been arrested, imprisoned and then murdered. The fewer expatriates, particularly photographers, that visited the scene the better. Amin had always denied that the Americans' disappearance had anything to do with the army, and in his usual fashion had appointed a committee of inquiry to investigate. But he had underestimated the tenacity of the British-born judge he appointed to head the inquiry, as it was discovered that the journalists had been killed inside the barracks and their Volkswagen car pushed over a nearby cliff. The report was so damning against the army that the judge completed his report and posted it from Nairobi, resigning at the same time from the Uganda judiciary. He was correct; Amin and his henchmen didn't care who they killed and there was a good chance he would have been next.

In time Amin would personally arrange for the death and murder of both the Chief Justice and the Archbishop of Uganda, both heinous acts. No one was safe. A sense of fear pervaded the whole community; the army, the civilian secret police and the State Research Bureau behaved as they liked, with impunity. People were spied upon and local Ugandans feared to be seen talking publicly to expatriate friends. In fact Amin banned meetings of more than three people, as well as banning mini skirts and wigs. He also announced that Uganda girls married to expatriates were to be considered as spies. Naturally this made Carruthers and Wilfrieda very nervous – indeed, so nervous that it was decided to send Wilfrieda and the children to stay with her sister in Nairobi for some months.

Alone in the house, Carruthers felt quite lonely and miserable and worried constantly about the future; he couldn't go to the local nightclubs any more as it was downright dangerous with the soldiers picking up girls at random. Those girls who refused were simply murdered.

His future now lay in the balance. He hadn't amassed any wealth and still hadn't attained the position of chairman. He had thrown his lot in with his wonderful Wilfrieda and Uganda, certain at the time that he was going to get involved in Uganda business and make money on top of his regular salary. Idi Amin had destroyed his dreams, as he had done to so many others of all races, and he would have to deal with the current situation as best he could, but he was very apprehensive.

He tried to concentrate on his golf. In fact the Golf Club became one of the few places where people could meet in safety, especially as some influential Ugandans, including army officers, were members.

Carruthers also concentrated on his office work, which increasingly became more difficult as the internal security position worsened and international companies required more advice. Some just closed shop. Many such companies had recently been partly nationalised by Obote's Government before the coup, in a socialist strategy called 'The move to the left', an action which was doomed to failure and did not have the full support of members of the Cabinet.

Around that time, July 1969, Carruthers had been quite amazed one evening in the bar of the Uganda Club to hear one of Obote's then senior Ministers loudly denouncing the move. This Minister was close to Amin and his remarks were a portent of things to come.

The other club to which Carruthers belonged, the mainly expatriate one with the men's bar, was where the expatriate tribal societies held their functions. So it was that the St George's Society's annual function, an all male affair, to celebrate St George, was to be held the following Saturday. Carruthers had been invited and asked to bring guests, so he decided to invite his Ugandan business friend and his colleague from the office as his guests. It was also rumoured that Idi Amin was to be chief guest. It was a formal occasion, black tie.

True enough, on the night Idi Amin was there, resplendent in army mess kit. He made a speech in his halting English, telling the assembled all-male dinner audience that the Queen of England was his very good friend. He asked to meet all those who had served in the British Army during the Second World War in a room adjoining the dining room after the main course had been served. (The organisers had, incidentally, made a mistake in serving him pork, which as a Muslim he was not allowed to eat. So he refused it and ate the vegetables only. That caused a bit of consternation.)

In the anteroom Carruthers' office colleague and others who had fought in the Second World War met the General. He wanted to shake their hands as he himself had fought for the British in Burma, he said. That, of course, was a complete lie but many believed it at the time. Likewise he would tell people he had been to Sandhurst, which was quite true, but only on a short visit. He was not a Sandhurst-trained officer.

Soon after that, Amin left the function, much to everyone's relief; heavy drinking followed. Carruthers' friend decided to tell everyone at his table a dirty joke but promptly fell asleep just before he was due to deliver the punchline. The German Ambassador stood up and sang *Lili Marlene*. Carruthers' office colleague was outraged, stood on a chair and, giving two 'V' signs, the rude ones, to the Ambassador, got everyone to follow him in a rendering of *It's a long way to Tipperary*. Carruthers felt a bit embarrassed at this, especially as the cheerleader was his guest, but nobody seemed bothered. Things settled down drunkenly and soon it was time to leave.

On the verandah of the club sat several ladies, wives of the dinner guests awaiting their husbands. Some of them were there because of love and affection, others, the majority, because they didn't trust their husbands to hurry home.

Carruthers had promised to give his colleague a lift home, although he was in no fit state to give anyone a lift, far less himself. However, he was spurred on by the action of his colleague, who had incurred the wrath of a senior member of the British community. He had espied the handsome wife of the be-medalled senior British citizen standing on the verandah beside her husband, who was wearing a white dinner jacket that provided a splendid backdrop to the colourful row of medals pinned to its breast. This very respectable-looking couple was suddenly set upon by Carruthers' colleague, who drunkenly leapt at them, smothering the wife with kisses and jangling her husband's medals up and down with his fingers, causing the husband's Bloody Mary to spill over his jacket. The husband went as red as the Bloody Mary and chased the colleague along the verandah, shaking his fist, medals jangling, jacket dripping and shouting, 'How dare you, how dare you, come back here.' The club secretary joined in the chase, which Carruthers feared was for some ulterior purpose. He quickened his pace.

Carruthers managed to get his colleague into his car before the irate husband caught up with them, praying that everyone would be too drunk to remember the incident by the next day. In that he was mistaken.

That the next day was Sunday was a blessing as Carruthers felt decidedly dizzy all day. By the Monday the dizziness had partly subsided, but when walking he felt that he was constantly on a slope walking sideways. He suddenly remembered that on arriving home in the early hours of Sunday morning he had walked into the edge of an open door and hit his head quite sharply, although there was only a very slight cut on his forehead.

Fearing to go to the only British doctor, who would have been at Saturday night's dinner, as he did not want to be reminded of any embarrassing incidents, Carruthers consulted a Uganda doctor friend. Lying on a bed in his surgery, he noticed on top of a cupboard a human skull and some bones staring down on him. He jokingly asked his doctor friend if that was his last patient but the doctor only smiled nervously. (Later, this particular doctor would try and get close to Amin by building a statue of the General and presenting it to him. He would end up fleeing to Nairobi, only to be wooed back to Kampala with promises of money – and never seen alive again. Foolishly, he had agreed to meet someone on the Uganda side of the Kenya border and had crossed the border by foot. He never returned to the friend who had given him a lift and was waiting for him in his car.)

Carruthers was diagnosed by his doctor friend as having a dislodged nerve in his head and after a few days, with the help of some drugs, he was back to normal. He took Monday off.

On the Tuesday an envelope marked *Strictly Personal* was placed on his desk. It was from the senior British citizen and enclosed a dry cleaner's bill and a request that he have a word with his colleague telling him to behave himself and that he, Carruthers, should think carefully in future as to who he invited to functions as his guest, because in such circumstances it was he who was ultimately responsible. Carruthers accepted this rebuke and penned a reply saying so. He felt humble.

As for his colleague, he told Carruthers that he reckoned the senior citizen's wife fancied him, and although there was a disparity in their ages he intended to pursue her. Carruthers was convinced that in his office he was surrounded by raving lunatics driven by lust. He told his colleague that he had better be very, very careful.

And as for the club secretary, he had decided to keep his lustful desires to himself, after one of the club members who had witnessed the amusing chase from the verandah said to him, 'You had that chap Carruthers by the seat of the pants. Pity he got away!' The secretary's wife had thought the whole incident most unbecoming and berated her husband for getting involved, little realising that he did in fact have an ulterior motive!

Chapter 10

Changed Days

Wilfrieda's relationship with her father was now back to normal and he had accepted the marriage. He had in fact become a good friend of John; the whisky bottle was the mediator.

The tragic events that had befallen their beloved country drew Willi and her parents closer together again. They were very fearful of the future, and Willi's mother urged her to consider leaving the country with her husband and children and go to the UK. Willi knew, however, that John would not do that voluntarily. He was just completing their new house and he was not sure that he could get a job back in the UK, although Willi was certain that he could. She knew he just didn't want to admit defeat.

Despite all the troubles, John continued to take an optimistic view of life and this sometimes angered Willi. He seemed to think that going to parties, boozing with his friends etc would take their minds off the events unfolding in the country. She knew and felt the underlying fear of her tribespeople, which John would never know, despite what he said. One day he would realise.

During all the commotion she had been upset when one of John's colleagues organised a fancy dress party which John insisted they attend. Men dressed up as women! What next? Couldn't people be serious? She decided to keep a close eye on her husband, although he himself had not dressed up as a woman.

She knew, however, that John loved and cared for her and she smiled when she thought of their holiday in Mombasa and their visit to the mine, especially the latter, where she had made such good friends.

Also their children were a great source of comfort and delight. Events seemed to have happened so fast that she could hardly comprehend that they had three children as part of their family. She grimaced when she remembered the ovarian cyst she had to have removed. She was certain that the lump that was there was a child and she had been shocked when told the actual facts. Thank God it was not cancerous.

While her immediate family were at present safe, she worried about her other relations, especially her aunty the Kabaka's sister, who had been imprisoned by Obote and later released by Amin. She wasn't in good health as a result of her imprisonment and was very doubtful as to Amin's supposed good intentions to members of the former royal family.

Everyone in her family had been happy when Obote was overthrown but now Amin was proving just as untrustworthy – and more dangerously so. She was conscious of the lascivious stares of army officers when she ventured into town, which frightened her but, she kept her feelings to herself. She had heard stories of married women being picked up by the military, and when their husbands made efforts to find out what happened they were threatened or simply disappeared. But she knew John wouldn't believe her if she communicated her fears to him. She felt he was rather naïve at times.

One of her sisters, a nurse living in Nairobi with her Swedish husband, was soon leaving Kenya and going to live and work in Sweden. In a way she envied them. They would be further away from family but at least they would be living in a country where safety and peace of life was guaranteed. When they married in Nairobi, her sister and brother-in-law had been matron and best man respectively, even although they had only married in a Registrar's office. She fervently hoped they would one day get married in a church because her religion was very important to her. She didn't want to do that now – but later, in hopefully happier times.

Life was becoming a bit boring for her because many of her friends had left the country and this also had an effect on the children's friends. It was not safe to move about too much, especially with a white person, since Amin had said that people married to whites were spies. Spies for whom, she wondered? How ridiculous. The man was going mad, if he was not mad already.

John's Managing Director had left the country, leaving him in charge of the company, and she didn't see him as much as before as he was always home late. She hoped he wasn't seeing girlfriends, which was always a danger with so many beautiful women about, but there was nothing she could do about it.

Because of the spy accusation nonsense, John had decided that it would be safer if she and the children moved to Nairobi to stay with one of her sisters who had a couple of spare bedrooms in her flat. She didn't really want to go but there was no doubt that she would feel much safer, and her parents were urging her to go.

Settling into Nairobi life wasn't too difficult. She had the car they had driven from Kampala to Nairobi. They managed to get their kids into a good primary school and they adapted quickly to their new environment.

The downside was that she wasn't with her husband,

although he did manage to visit a couple of times a month. He stayed alone at their Kampala house and Willi made sure that her father drove out to visit him most weekends, just to ensure he was well and that there were no girlfriends hanging about the house! So far there were no adverse reports on that front. She herself had been out a few times with her sister and some Swedish men, friends of her Swedish brother-in-law. She told John that she couldn't be expected to remain cooped up in a flat all the time. She knew John was jealous, but what could either of them do? It was very difficult.

She was actually quite glad that she didn't have to entertain John's Chairman any more when he visited Kampala. She wasn't quite sure what those two got up to, but whenever they were together they had late nights, hangovers and John had a guilty look about him. She just didn't want to think about it.

Nairobi was full of Ugandan exiles and she was always hearing the latest rumours and gossip. There was no doubt that the Asians were being targeted by Amin and his army, a popular move with many Ugandans, but Willi had now lost some close Asian friends who had decided to leave. The army also took their wrath out on the Baganda people. Willi was frightened for her parents and other relations, but then they had seen troubles before.

She remembered during the 1950s, when her father was a Minister in the Kabaka's Government and there was an uprising against the Government. She, along with other Ministers' children, had had to be hurriedly collected from boarding school by armed guards and transported to the safety of relatives' homes. They had all survived that.

In that respect Uganda was unique. There was always

some conflict going on. Was it just tribalism, Willi wondered or was it that life in Uganda was just too pleasant, perhaps boring, and the men took out their frustration on each other? The climate was perfect, there was regular rainfall for the crops, nobody starved, and the women were beautiful and in their own subtle way controlled the men.

Since the British had handed over their role in 1962 as protectors – or was it really rulers of Uganda? – there were no foreigners for the men to take out their frustration on except themselves. Looking back, Willi wished the British had stayed. Surprisingly, when she had conversations with John on that very subject, he did not agree and argued that the Uganda society should develop itself free of outside influences, whatever the hardships.

All very well for him, Willi thought. If he really wanted to he could just disappear back to the UK, leaving her and the children behind. She had heard of that happening before, with the white husband breaking off all future contact. How cruel! She was sure John wouldn't do that but in the present situation she couldn't stop her mind dwelling on such unsavoury situations.

In a way, she thought, John personified the Uganda male in the period just before and after Independence in 1962. Life, the good life, was a triviality. John was enjoying this good life, or had been until recently, while around him a brutal African regime was emerging. Would he ever wake up, Willi wondered? Perhaps some more babies would concentrate his mind on his responsibilities to his family. She must work on that!

At least the British and American Governments were now taking a hard line with Amin, she thought, whereas the usual political troublemakers – the French and the Russians – were helping him. Traitors!

Chapter 11

Mother Meets Daughter

As Wilfrieda wasn't around, Carruthers felt it was a good time to go on safari again. He would visit the tea estates in the west of the country and also his friends at the mine. The night before he was due to leave he received a phone call from Nairobi from the lady in the Chairman's photograph and his erstwhile Muthaiga Club dinner companion. She was arriving in Kampala the next day and just had to see him. She would bring her own handcuffs, along with the video she had told him about. She laughed wickedly. Carruthers rearranged his travel plans.

Carruthers tenderly stroked the purple birthmark and asked if it hurt. Oh, I wish it did, she moaned. They were lying on the bed in her hotel bedroom in Kampala. They hadn't managed to watch the video as there was no TV in the room, but as far as Carruthers was concerned, it didn't make any difference. They had fallen into each other's arms almost as soon as he had arrived at her room a couple of hours before. Everything was perfect, except for the disconcerting habit she had every couple of minutes of glancing over her shoulder, or his shoulder, depending on their position. It was the effect of the Chairman's flash. At first Carruthers had followed her glances, thinking someone was there, until he remembered the cause.

He knew he was being unfaithful to Willi but excused himself on the grounds that it was a state of emergency. He wanted to get the woman into a receptive state so that he could reveal details about her mother. She was certainly being receptive, of that there was no doubt, he thought.

As they lay getting their breath back, Carruthers asked her about her parents. Her father had been a doctor in Mombasa, while her mother, she said, had run off with some tea planter who had been visiting Mombasa regularly to attend the tea auctions. She didn't know anything about him. She hadn't seen her mother for over ten years and assumed that she couldn't trace them after her father had gone to live in South Africa. She herself had married her lawyer husband when she was only 18, so she had not accompanied her father. As she had never come across or heard of her mother in Kenya, she assumed she had left East Africa. She had forgotten, or not been aware, that there were tea estates in Uganda as well as Kenya.

Carruthers gently asked her if she was still interested in tracing her mother because he thought he could help her. At first she didn't take him seriously and it was only after another session, with the handcuffs on this time, that he was able to convince her. She could hardly believe it but got very concerned and confused when he told her the circumstances of her mother's discovery. In fact, she was so distraught she insisted that he stayed the night. He unlocked the handcuffs.

It was a strange situation. Although deeply ashamed that her mother had seen them, she realised that if it hadn't been for the photographs her mother's whereabouts would never have been discovered. Carruthers advised that if she really wanted to re-establish contact with her mother she would have to brazen it out and put the blame on the Chairman for seducing her and at the same time photographing her; she could say it was against her consent. She needed, and was given, a lot of comfort that night. Carruthers was in charge.

The next day they were on their way to the west of Uganda. She had phoned her husband to say that the Orchid Society AGM had not taken place because of a lack of a quorum and that she had heard out of the blue the whereabouts of her mother and was going to find her. Her companion and guide was her dinner partner from the Muthaiga Club. The husband felt concerned when he heard that, but didn't say anything.

Carruthers thought it best that the news of her daughter should be broken gently to the mother, so he arranged to stay with the daughter at the Mountains of the Moon Hotel in Fort Portal, about 20 miles from the tea estate where her mother lived. He would go first and visit the mother, then bring her to meet her daughter in Fort Portal. Carruthers thought it diplomatic to stay in separate rooms. There was an adjoining door, however, which opened without difficulty.

Carruthers was off early the next morning to the tea estate, leaving his partner in a highly nervous state. He had comforted her in the only way he knew – and it wasn't with a cup of tea.

At first Carruthers was given a very frosty reception by the mother, who well remembered his last visit. He apologised for the incident, stressing it was his Chairman who had the photographs. Anyway, she would be pleased to know, he said, that by a strange coincidence he had met her daughter at a dinner at the Muthaiga Club. They had been talking about people he knew on Ugandan tea estates and the description he gave of her had convinced her daughter it was her mother. The mother seemed to swallow this fabricated story and excitedly got into his car for the drive to Fort Portal.

When they arrived at the hotel, Carruthers took the mother to her daughter's room. The door opened slowly when he knocked. Mother and daughter stood facing each other.

'Mother, is that you, is that really you?'

'You slut, you slut,' the mother shouted, and slapped her face. Then burst into tears.

Both women fell into each other's arms and sobbed uncontrollably. Carruthers left them alone and headed for the bar. Another good deed, he thought as he downed his first beer of the day.

Later, in the bar the two ladies told Carruthers that it was essential to retrieve the photographs – and the negatives – from the Chairman. They wanted to destroy them themselves. As far as Carruthers was concerned, the only way to get the photographs was to get the Chairman away from Nairobi on safari, as he would probably carry the photographs with him.

Carruthers decided to solicit the help of the mine MD, who he was sure would love to get his revenge for the Chairman's lustful thoughts about his wife. As he was within a couple of hours' drive of the mine, Carruthers planned to drive there immediately and promised the ladies he would return the next day and hopefully reveal a plan.

The drive to the mine took longer than expected. A single-lane bridge over a river tumbling down from the mountains had two lorries crashed head-on into each other, and they were right in the middle of it. Both drivers had refused to give way, thus causing inconvenience and delays to hundreds of travellers. Carruthers sat on a hillside overlooking the bridge, sipping a cool beer from a local bar and watching breakdown trucks tow the lorries apart. All this took a couple of hours, and he also had to go through some army road blocks, so he only reached the mine just before dusk. He went straight to the MD's house.

Over dinner they discussed the best way to get the Chairman to leave Nairobi. As it turned out, there was indeed a good and genuine reason. The Canadian mine owners didn't trust the Amin regime and hoped to persuade the Government to buy them out, and the Chairman's knowledge of political risk insurance would be crucial to any deal. The MD said he would phone the Chairman in Nairobi the next day with an offer to fly him from Nairobi to Kasese. He would spend the night at the nearby hotel, probably in a couple of days' time, and be told that Carruthers was already at the mine.

The next day, Carruthers drove back to Fort Portal and then to the tea estate where the daughter was now staying with her mother. It was agreed that they would all stay at the hotel near the mine the same night the Chairman was there. They would thus be on the spot, hopefully to take possession of the photographs.

The following morning they drove back to the mine and booked into the hotel as the Chairman was due the next day. The MD had asked him to bring the photographs and the negatives as he wished to make some copies. He hinted jocularly that his wife, who was back at the mine, could be interested in doing some modelling for him. The Chairman was sold.

Carruthers was at the airstrip the next morning to meet the Chairman, who came off the aircraft beaming, with a camera slung round his neck. He reckoned Carruthers had done a good job getting the client to use his specialist advice. They drove straight to the mine where everyone behaved professionally and discussed the particular issues on which the Chairman's advice was needed.

Invitations were made for dinner and the MD nudged the Chairman and reminded him to bring you-know-what. Meanwhile, mother and daughter remained incognito at the hotel. Dinner was, as before, a jolly affair with plenty to drink. The photographs and also the negatives were handed over to the MD with great laughs and sly looks. Even Flora agreed to have photographs of her bare breasts taken as long as her face didn't appear, and in a funny way her husband felt quite proud. He asked the Chairman to make sure he sent him some copies. Then Carruthers insisted on some photographs with Flora wearing the bras which Wilfrieda had given to her some little while ago.

Carruthers had a lifelong interest in breasts, starting from his days in Nairobi where one of the nightclubs featured Tessi the Tassel Tosser. Tessi, a European lady, had tassels fixed to her nipples, and to the accompaniment of music swung the tassels round, first clockwise then anti-clockwise. Carruthers was intrigued at such an erotic spectacle. Since then, however, he had been spectacularly unsuccessful in persuading various ladies, including Willi, to repeat Tessi's performance and was sometimes accused of being sexually deviant. Anyway, it was more interesting and amusing than trying to train seals to balance balls on their noses, he mused. Life was a circus.

Before driving back to the hotel after dinner, the MD had slipped Carruthers the Chairman's photographs and negatives. When the Chairman insisted on a nightcap at the hotel bar on their return, Carruthers first quickly went to the ladies' bedroom and passed over the photographs and negatives. There was certainly a look of relief on both faces.

The Chairman was in a very happy mood and they had a few nightcaps before retiring. On the way to his bedroom Carruthers could smell the burning photographs as he passed the ladies' room.

While the Chairman was at the mine for dinner, the ladies had managed to gain access to his room and gone through all his belongings. As they suspected, they found one of the photographs that he had not taken with him.

'Oh, how could you let that devil treat you like that?' mother moaned to daughter. 'Destroy it immediately! But I think we should teach him a lesson,' she mused.

Seeing a bottle of after-shave in the bathroom, luckily the non-spray type, she emptied the contents down the loo and peed into the bottle. It was the same colour and he probably wouldn't notice until the heat of the day had an effect after he had put it on his ample cheeks. She also gave the toilet a good clean with his toothbrush. Finally she took the drawing pins from the notice behind the door and placed them under the sheet where she estimated his buttocks would rest. This brought back memories of her school days and she left the room humming happily and clutching the Chairman's pyjamas, which she thought could be a useful tool of embarrassment sometime in the future.

'How was the night?' the waiter asked Carruthers at breakfast.

'Excellent,' replied Carruthers.

He left the breakfast table before the Chairman appeared but was there to drive him down to the airstrip to catch his flight to Nairobi. There was a distinct odour of kidneys emanating from the Chairman but Carruthers couldn't remember seeing them on the breakfast menu that morning. How did he get them, he wondered? He had also noticed how the Chairman had hobbled to the car with one hand rubbing his right buttock, but Carruthers thought he had better not inquire as to the reason for this. Now he remembered that shortly after turning in last night there had been a loud cry of anguish from the Chairman's room, followed by a series of oaths. This had been followed, he was sure, by girlish laughter. Perhaps the Chairman had been having an orgy. He wouldn't put it past him.

Carruthers drove back to the hotel from the airstrip to pick up the ladies, now the Chairman was airborne. Halfway back to the hotel he had the distinct feeling that he was being watched. Turning his head to glance behind him he nearly leapt out the open car window, for perched on his right shoulder was the largest locust he had ever seen in his life. It was fastened onto his shoulder and wasn't budging. Of course it wasn't dangerous but it did look like something from outer space when viewed at such close quarters. He slowed down the car and parked at the side of the road, and gingerly got out. The locust hadn't moved. He shrugged his shoulders a couple of times and it was off. Some poor farmers were going to lose their crops if there were many swarms of locusts that size in the vicinity, he thought.

The MD had asked Carruthers to bring the two ladies to meet his wife and stay for lunch, so he dropped them off at the house and after making introductions went to the mine offices. The secretary had to attend a meeting with some of the mine engineers at the entrance to the main shaft halfway up one of the mountains, and he asked Carruthers to accompany him.

The mine was designed so that the copper deposits could be reached by shafts going deep into the sides of the mountains, up or down from the main shaft. Carruthers had walked, crawled and climbed up and down ladders inside the mine on a couple of previous occasions and it was hard work. He didn't envy those who worked inside the mine, although as far as he was aware there had been no serious accidents. Some of the mineshafts went through the mountain as far as the Congo border.

To reach the main shaft, mine workers used a ski lift that had been specially imported and installed. Up they went, halfway to the top of the mountain not for a skiing holiday, unfortunately, but for some very hard and dangerous work. When they first installed the lift, the mine secretary said, it wouldn't work properly because the grease used for the cables kept melting in the tropical heat and they had to import a special type of heat-resistant grease.

The meeting over, Carruthers and the secretary returned to the base of the mountain and went on to the MD's house for lunch. The ladies had obviously been swapping stories about the Chairman, with the daughter providing an insider's view, so to speak. They had also attacked a bottle of Gordon's gin quite successfully and lunch therefore was quite a hilarious affair, and seemed to pass quickly. Breasts were not on the menu.

After lunch and promising to keep in touch, the ladies piled into the car and Carruthers drove at a fast pace, reaching Fort Portal just before a violent thunderstorm. Rather than brave the murram road and slide all over the place on their way to the tea estate, they stopped to refuel at the Gluepot Bar, a well-known meeting point for tea planters visiting town. All the expatriate gossip was exchanged there – who was sleeping with who, what had happened on the way home from their last visit, etc, etc.

Eventually they made it to the tea estate and Carruthers was offered a bed for the night. All had been forgiven and the customary bottle of Glenmorangie was produced.

Carruthers was able to give account of all the happenings to his tea planter host, who was highly amused. Having known the Chairman when they were both young, he wasn't in the least surprised he had grown into a dirty old man. He hinted that the Chairman had been sent off to the colonies from England after being involved with a much older woman, his aunt or something.

Fond farewells were said the following morning. Mother and daughter parted reluctantly and promised to keep in touch. The mother asked Carruthers for the Chairman's address and said she must know when the Chairman was next travelling out of Nairobi. Something to do with pyjamas, she said.

Carruthers and the daughter decided to spend the last night in Fort Portal at the Mountains of the Moon Hotel. This was a long, straggling, single-floored establishment built in the 1930s. Black-painted wooden beams contrasted picturesquely with the white-painted walls and red corrugated-iron roof sheets. It had been a favourite watering hole for local elites and tourists alike. Afternoon tea on the verandah overlooking the large and well-kept gardens was very relaxing, and later on in the evening the bar off the verandah became a popular spot, with a log fire providing a convenient backdrop and some badly needed heat for chilly nights at certain times of the year.

A favourite tourist excursion from the hotel was to drive through the Rwenzori Mountains over a long and winding murram road and down into the plains bordering the Congo. There hot springs bubbled away merrily and in the nearby forest a tribe of pygmies would emerge to be photographed and to sell various small carvings or skins. They themselves wore skins but as the years went on they would be persuaded to wear western clothes.

The drive back to Kampala was uneventful. The rain had stopped, the sun shone and the road, although murram, was reasonably smooth with little dust because of the rain. The countryside was lush green and it was as if one was driving through a botanical garden. Butterflies were everywhere. Carruthers dropped off his partner at her hotel and promised to pick her up later for a farewell dinner. They both made phone calls to their respective spouses in Nairobi. Just as well they didn't know each other, Carruthers thought.

The lawyer husband was delighted to hear from his wife and to know she had met and mended fences with her mother. But she didn't inform him of her visit to the mine with her mother, just in case he mentioned this fact to the Chairman, who was his friend. She merely said that Carruthers had dropped her off at her mother's place on his way to meet his Chairman at the mine and picked her up on the way back, all very innocent.

Her husband told her that in fact he had bumped into the Chairman at the club at lunchtime and they had a couple of drinks together, but he had not said anything to the Chairman about his wife going to Fort Portal with Carruthers. The Chairman said it had been a strange visit. Apart from getting some sort of gum disease, from the business point of view everything went well but he had found pins in his bed, which had actually drawn blood from his right buttock. A stupid prank by one of the hotel staff, he thought. Also the pilot who had flown him back and who was Australian had been very rude to him and suggested that the next time he flew with him he should wear incontinence pads. The Chairman said there had been a distinct smell of urine in the plane but it was certainly nothing to do with him. The pilot even had the temerity to refer to him as 'mate'. He also had a pair of pyjamas stolen, although, he leered, he didn't often wear such things on safari.

Carruthers' phone call to Mrs Carruthers was more worrying. His beautiful wife and her sister, with whom she was staying, had been going to a nightclub at weekends with a couple of Swedish guys. She said she had the kids to look after all day, she was away from home and was bored, and Carruthers couldn't expect her to sit in her sister's flat day in, day out. Carruthers was madly jealous. He didn't trust Swedes, whom he considered promiscuous – free love and suicide was what he knew about Sweden. It was not healthy to be apart and he would have to seriously consider his family's return soon. But of course he himself was not entirely blameless, he admitted to himself.

Later that evening Carruthers and his Nairobi friend sat at the bar of the only expatriate-owned continental restaurant in Kampala. They were studying the menu before going to their reserved table, and the head waiter, a white homosexual who liked black boys, hovered nearby to take their order. Carruthers told his partner the story of his friend the mine secretary who, not knowing the head waiter's predilections, had taken him at his word some time ago when he had offered to bring his 'girls' to the mine one weekend. The secretary had fixed a date and spread the word to senior management. They would meet the girls at the senior manager's club and there was great excitement, especially from the South African Boers, famed for their randiness and whose wives and girlfriends were all down South. Imagine the mine secretary's consternation and extreme embarrassment, Carruthers said, when the head waiter accompanied by six young black boys turned up. It took the secretary a while to live that one down, especially when he was referred to as a 'bloody poofter'and other unsavoury remarks were made to him.

'And what would madam like this evening?' lisped the head waiter, giving Carruthers a knowing look.

Orders made, the head waiter scurried off to the kitchen and they both sat surveying the restaurant. It was quite early and still quiet. A small tubby Indian gentleman wearing glasses and sitting alone at a nearby table had a large bottle of champagne open in an ice bucket on a stand beside his table. He got up to make a phone call, probably checking on the whereabouts of his expected dinner partner. As he returned to his table he walked straight into the wine stand, nearly knocking it and the open champagne bottle over. The stand rocked back and forth – it was almost the same height as the Indian – and the champagne started frothing at the neck of the bottle. The man trying to stop the wine frothing out with one hand and with the other trying to stop the stand from falling over was one of the funniest sights Carruthers and his partner had ever seen. Back and forth rocked the man and his stand; he was clutching it as if in some macabre dance. He eventually had it under control, and sat down and mopped his brow while the two onlookers at the bar nearby nearly wet themselves laughing. His expected partner never did join him.

Dinner over, another night of passion lay ahead and it was a bleary-eyed wife who returned to her husband in Nairobi the next day and a very tired Carruthers to his Kampala office.

An excuse was needed to explain the non-return of the photographs, so one of Carruthers' first telephone calls was to his Chairman in Nairobi to tell him that there had been a fire at the mine secretary's office, nothing serious, but his photographs and negatives had been among the things burnt. The secretary was very apologetic but hoped that the photographs the Chairman had taken on his visit would make up for the loss. The Chairman wasn't too happy, especially as he couldn't find the spare photograph he had left in his case, but he promised to send copies of the photographs of the mine MD's wife's breasts to Carruthers under confidential cover once they had been developed and printed. These were eagerly awaited.

Chapter 12

The Aftermaths

Idi Amin was now becoming more and more schizophrenic. He was going to bomb South Africa and, although he said the Queen was his friend, he was going to take action against the imperialist British. He also awarded himself the Victoria Cross. He warned the Israelis to be careful and said Hitler was correct in his treatment of the Jews. This was after Israel refused to supply him with armaments. And he wasn't happy with the Asian community. Some of its leaders attempted to bribe him to keep quiet but that only added to his anger. Carruthers was present at the President's Lodge at a reception for Asian community leaders when this happened. Amin said he would put them in concentration camps but they would be well looked after. He fell out with Kenya and Tanzania, too.

Two books appeared from the Uganda Government Printer, one named *Contributions* and the other *The Shaping of Modern Uganda*, both supposedly written by Al-Hajji Field Marshal Dr Idi Amin Dada, VC, DSO, MC. The former contained pictures and speeches he made while at an Organisation of African Unity meeting in Addis Ababa, while the latter contained genuine copies of early maps showing parts of Kenya within the present borders of Uganda. To add to his various titles he was now an author of books.

Idi Amin's announcement that he was expelling the Asian community was met with shock and disbelief. They were the traders, the village moneylenders and the backbone of the economy. Apart from the humanitarian angle, it would spell disaster to the economy. But all appeals failed.

To many Ugandans, however, it was a popular move at the time. As with the Jews of Europe, people were jealous and suspicious of communities who kept to themselves and were moneylenders. Out they went, therefore. Many could claim British citizenship and went to the UK. Others went to Canada, some to the USA, France, etc. Very few went to India. For many Indians it was in fact a blessing in disguise. They were a hard-working community with close family ties and they helped each other financially, and some were to make fortunes in their chosen country of exile.

But the hardships of leaving the country of their birth were great for the Asians. Many had their passports torn up by immigration officers and thus became stateless. Many lost their jewellery, which was taken from them as they left the country. Some deposited valuables with officials of western embassies, some of which to this day have never been returned: stolen by a diplomat, not Idi Amin.

After the Asian community was deported and before Amin started handing out their properties to his friends, printed notices started to be affixed to many of these properties, stating that they belonged to the banks and anyone tampering with them was acting illegally. However, these notices were soon removed, probably because on second thoughts the banks did not want to draw attention to themselves. But many people were amazed that so many properties had been mortgaged to banks. Of course the Asian businessmen, always shrewd and cunning, had probably suspected the worst when Amin took power and had cleverly made contingency plans well ahead of his decision to expel them. The businessmen had seen the warning signs while the politicians had not.

The Indian community meekly accepted their fate and left the country without any real protest. Like the Jews of Nazi Germany, most of them had not believed it was really going to happen. However, the Asian community never actually physically fought by taking up arms then or later to protect their interests. They were the manipulators rather than the warriors in East Africa.

(Years later, they would be able to reclaim the properties they had left behind after Idi Amin had been deposed, as the British-trained Uganda Civil Service kept detailed records of all properties that had been taken over. Somebody in Idi Amin's Government was far-sighted enough to realise that future financial assistance from the likes of the World Bank and the IMF would be dependent on the state returning what it had stolen.)

After the Asians had gone, although a few stayed at great risk to themselves and survived, Idi Amin handed many of their properties out to his cronies. Hotels, shops, etc were now managed and owned by soldiers and their families. The state nationalised factories and put soldiers in key positions. Naturally, most became run-down from lack of management experience and the economy began to collapse. Coffee sales on the international market kept the economy alive and provided money to buy weapons, torture equipment and whisky, much of it provided by Britain from Stanstead Airport. Game in the national parks moved across the border into the Congo, and soldiers gunned down the elephants for their ivory. Both animals and humans were to suffer terribly under that brutal regime.

Of course, not all the soldiers were wicked and brutal. There were a handful of career officers who abhorred what was happening, but they themselves had to tread carefully, as a lot of old scores were being settled within the army. Too bad if you were from the wrong tribe; you were dead. It was only years later that people would say, 'Oh, so and so in Amin's army was okay, he was a good guy.' The bad guys were the gatekeepers, tractor drivers who were suddenly brought into the army and made officers overnight because they were from the same tribe as Amin. There were also killers from Southern Sudan who joined the army to kill for purely personal gain.

It was a frightening scenario and the terrified citizens of Uganda did not take Idi Amin's many utterances, seen as amusing in the Western world, lightly. He was a sinister, evil man, not a stand-up comic as parodied by some foolish English comedian who came to visit him. Indeed, he really was the village tyrant as depicted by the author Denis Hills in his book *The White Pumpkin*, who was imprisoned for saying so. The British Foreign Secretary, Callaghan, bravely came out to secure his release in June 1974.

The Israelis in Uganda were the first people to be kicked out, however. They had a large construction company operating in Uganda and they also had army advisors stationed in the Ministry of Defence Headquarters in Kampala, but they were soon gone. Carruthers had seen them in that building soon after the coup when he had visited there with his new Uganda Chairman, a lawyer and the expatriate managing director of one of his clients, whose car had been damaged by a car belonging to Idi Amin's Minister of Defence. The Minister didn't see why he should offer any recompense, and Carruthers had brought the lawyer and client to meet and discuss this with the Minister. Carruthers felt distinctly uneasy as they walked through the Ministry building and hoped it would be as easy to get out as it had been to get in. He was therefore quite relieved to see the presence of the Israeli Army advisors. When they met the Minister, after introductions were made, the Minister asked them to leave except for the lawyer. Carruthers and his client sat in an anteroom. Half an hour later the lawyer emerged and muttered, 'Let's get out of here.'

Later, over a drink he said that the Minister, while agreeing to meet the repair costs of the client's car, had given him a very hard time and indeed threatened him. Carruthers was full of respect for the lawyer's courage and told him so. Soon afterwards, however, the lawyer felt it wise to leave Uganda and go into exile in Kenya, which was probably a very wise thing to do. Carruthers felt a bit guilty at having dragged him into the affair, but they would meet over the years in Nairobi and reminisce about the incident. The Minister in question was later to be murdered by Amin and his henchmen.

A new Uganda Chairman now had to be appointed. It was still out of the question for Carruthers to take over that role, the Nairobi Chairman decreed. Carruthers made the argument, as events had proved, that it was just as dangerous for a black Uganda Chairman as for himself and he was prepared to give it a go. The answer was still 'no'. Frustrated, Carruthers soldiered on.

Soon after the expulsion of the Asians, Idi Amin announced that he was going to take action against the British. I wonder what that will be, mused Carruthers as he sat with a colleague in the restaurant of the International Hotel watching a Uganda businessman on his own table getting very drunk and shouting, 'I'm a tycoon, I'm a tycoon.'

The businessman had recently been given a departed Asian's factory and warehouses. It was in one of these warehouses that Idi Amin, on a fact-finding tour accompanied by one of his soldiers called Lieutenant No Parking, found a supply marked *India rubber tyres* and wondered aloud why, if he had expelled the Asians, there should be Indian tyres coming into the country.

The action against the British was to be announced on television the next evening by Idi Amin. Opinions varied amongst the British community as to what would happen. Everyone agreed that their club, the Kampala Club, or the Top Club, as it was known, would almost certainly be taken over, so the dwindling numbers of white members agreed to show solidarity and try and drink the place dry the following evening. One of the members who had been staying at the club was a client from Nairobi and he thought it would be safer to move out, and Carruthers agreed to put him up for the night. They would watch Amin on television from home.

There was a feeling of apprehension and a certain amount of sadness at the club that evening, particularly among the staff, who would undoubtedly all be sacked. It wasn't as busy as it should have been, as some members felt it safer to stay at home. Carruthers and his friend did their duty as far as they were able but were still in a reasonably fit state to drive home after shaking hands with staff and members alike. One member didn't want Amin and his henchmen to benefit from the well-kept snooker table and took all the snooker balls home.

Amin was due to come on TV at 9 p.m. By 11 p.m. he still hadn't appeared. It was obvious that there was serious discussion about what action to take. One of Amin's Ministers, a lawyer with very left-wing views, was the one behind many of Amin's political decisions in the early days of the regime. (Typically, he was anti-British, but when he himself eventually had to flee from Amin he sought haven in Britain, the country he had vilified.) Around midnight Amin appeared in his army uniform, somewhat hesitantly, as if someone had pushed him from the wings onto centre stage. Probably the lawyer, Carruthers thought. Amin announced he was taking over British-owned companies, company properties, etc, including the Kampala Club, which was to become a prison officers' mess.

The company Carruthers worked for was now Kenya-owned, so he was okay and wouldn't have to leave the country as many other British expatriates had to do. However, without the club to go to and with many friends having to leave, the place was going to become very boring. He had been worried about his property but it turned out that it was only British company-owned property that would be taken over, not personal property.

In a way Amin's speech was a bit of an anti-climax as everything he announced had been anticipated. And it could have been worse. Carruthers' chum who stayed the night was fast asleep and would have to be informed about it the next morning.

In the morning they pondered over events, sitting on the verandah and sipping a mixture of whisky and milk. It was a Saturday, so there was no need to go to the office now Saturdays were holidays.

However, on the Sunday Carruthers did go to the office and removed some personal files and other confidential files which could have been compromising if they had got into the wrong hands, such as some of Amin's uneducated henchmen. He walked past the army guard on the office building and luckily wasn't stopped. On getting home he burnt the files in the garden. One couldn't be too careful; these were dangerous times. He even went through all the drawers in his house and burnt certain items, including the Obote shirts he used to wear for events at the Uganda Club. Willi had hated those events, and the shirts.

Included in the items which Carruthers burnt was a set of photographic slides which he had taken from the centrefold pages of a collection of *Playboy* magazines he had once owned. In his bachelor days he used to show the slides on a projector to some of his friends, pretending that they were of past girlfriends who had posed for him. Amazingly enough, he was often enviously believed, which certainly did his ego a lot of good. Amin's Muslim regime would not view these kindly, Carruthers thought as he threw them into the fire. Anything which could be used as an excuse to harass, blackmail or deport him had to be destroyed, he had decided. Better safe than sorry. But life certainly was going to be very boring indeed.

Although Amin was a Muslim, Uganda did not become a Muslim state. However, he did try to impose some Muslim beliefs and customs on the country, and even persuaded the King of Saudi Arabia to visit, which he did in 1973. The Christian community was large in Uganda and Amin was constantly at odds with their leaders, accusing them of trying to undermine him. (Amin was not a credit to his faith and after he was overthrown some Muslims would, sadly, be killed in reprisal.) Certain government institutions were forced to employ Muslims. Because of the number of Christians employed by the Central Bank (the Bank of Uganda), it was accused of being a seminary for Christians, and soon had its first Muslim Governor.

The Commissioner of Insurance, who had been trained by Carruthers when he at one time worked in his office, obtained that position because he was a Muslim. Some time later at an international Insurance conference in Lagos, the same Commissioner told delegates that everything was peaceful in Uganda. Carruthers objected and then told the Commissioner in the Luganda language that he was lying. If looks could kill, Carruthers would be dead.

Carruthers' British planter friends were particularly badly treated at the tea estates in the west of the country. They were abused and beaten by Amin's soldiers and forced to leave their homes and the tea estates that they owned, and Uganda as well. And so started the decline of the tea industry in Uganda. In fact the decline of the whole Uganda economy started and would continue for the next nine years.

So it was that Carruthers' tea planter friend and his wife arrived in Kampala en route for Nairobi where they were going to stay with the wife's daughter before going to Australia, where they would spend their time in exile. At some future date, hopefully, they would return to Uganda. They weren't really in a mood to be entertained and it was wiser for them to maintain a low profile, so Carruthers just had a few drinks with them in their hotel room. As they reminisced, the wife said with some glee that despite all their problems she had not forgotten to bring the Chairman's pyjamas with her, and as she was going to Nairobi she would ensure they were returned to him with interest.

Carruthers heard what happened when he visited Nairobi a few weeks later. The mother had wrapped up the pyjamas in a parcel addressed personally to the Chairman at his office and marked *Very Urgent*. This had been delivered purposely when the Chairman was out of Nairobi for a couple of days, and an anonymous caller asked the Chairman's secretary for the parcel to be sent to his house as it was urgent.

The mother had put a note in the parcel, addressed to the Chairman on a piece of stationery from the Kampala hotel she and her husband had been staying in. It said:

> Hi, sexy. You said you would be back soon but long time no see. Did you know you left your PJs under the pillow? I don't know why you brought them anyway. Most of the guests at the hotel now are soldiers or drunkards and I may not be around on your next visit, and I may even come to Nairobi. I am dying to see those photographs you took, you naughty boy. I miss you so much. Love from your secret lover, F.
>
> PS: You know what F stands for, don't you? So many times! Keep it up! F.

The parcel was duly delivered to the Chairman's house and was found lying on the hall table by his wife on her return from the stables. As it was marked urgent, she thought she had better open it, which she did inquisitively. She recognised the black Christian Dior pyjamas. Then the note fell to the floor. 'Oh my God!' she said to herself as she read it. She had always suspected that her husband had the odd fling when he was away on safari, but this was someone intruding into her home and she was not amused. She was worried about her social standing and didn't want stories spreading around. She certainly had no wish to be known as one of the 'Are you married or do you live in Kenya?' set. What if this F came to Nairobi? And what about the photographs mentioned in the note? The bastard!

But she could deal with her husband. If it came to the crunch, he wasn't going to jeopardise their marriage any further. She was rich from an inheritance and her husband's lifestyle needed a lot of that money to supplement his income. Photographs – camera, of course! It was upstairs in his bedroom. Perhaps the photographs were in the camera case. A frenzied search revealed nothing except an unfinished film in his camera. Could this be it, she wondered? She wound it back and unloaded it.

She couldn't have it developed in Nairobi. If it was pornographic it could get into the wrong hands. Of course she could destroy it but she was interested in seeing who this F was. It would also be good ammunition to use against her husband if things ever got nasty. All this had emanated from Kampala, so she would have to rope in Carruthers for assistance. She had got to know Wilfrieda and the children and had helped them out in their temporary exile in Nairobi, and Carruthers was well aware of that. She also knew he had an uneasy relationship with his Chairman. In fact, she decided to ask Wilfrieda to request Carruthers' help, and that is how Carruthers came to hear what had happened. Of course he couldn't let on that he already knew the background. How intriguing, he thought.

During his next visit to Nairobi he and Wilfrieda had agreed that she and the kids would return to Kampala soon. That, after all, was where Carruthers' job was, and their home and also her family. They couldn't live apart for ever. They planned to reunite in about a month's time when Carruthers would drive to Nairobi to collect them.

Back in Kampala, Carruthers had the film developed privately and as he suspected the photographs were those that had been taken at the mine. He had extra copies made for the mine secretary and his MD. They only showed breasts, covered and uncovered, so there would be no problem showing them to the Chairman's wife. No one would be compromised. He had also been asked to find out who F was at the hotel. Of course he knew there was no such person, so he made up the story that F was the customer services manager, who had recently been murdered by a jealous colonel in the army, which in fact wasn't far from the truth. Such incidents were common.

The Chairman's wife was actually disappointed with the photographs, which Carruthers brought from Kampala personally. They were quite tame, she thought, and no faces shown. Wilfrieda didn't say anything but she recognised the bras and to whom they belonged. She would make her own investigations and judgement later.

The Chairman returned home a day after Carruthers had hurried from Kampala with the photographs, to be confronted by his wife. He had never seen her in such a furious mood and the tongue-lashing he got was frightening. She even threatened to divorce, which was even more frightening. He recognised the photographs and his pyjamas but he couldn't understand the letter, and could only assume he had got really drunk at the hotel one night. Could the F be Flora? He was confused and could only ask for forgiveness and promise to behave himself in future. How could this have happened, he wondered, and indeed suspected that Carruthers might know something about it all. He was so embarrassed he didn't even tell his chums at the club.

The Chairman's wife had, however, confided in the wife of her husband's close friend the lawyer – who, of course, was the daughter of the sender of the parcel. When her mother received details from her daughter some weeks later in Sydney, she found grim satisfaction in the plight of her daughter's abuser. After a few tinnies she and her husband laughed and laughed.

Back in Kampala, Carruthers sat on the verandah of his house nursing a newly opened bottle of J & B whisky. As it was a Sunday, he hadn't ventured out. Willi and kids were still in Nairobi and it was all very boring. However, another month and they would be back. That morning he had thought his house was being attacked by the army when a platoon passing his gate made a hell of a noise. He had been lying in the bath and leapt out to peer out of the window. However, it turned out they were only on a training run.

    A car hooted at the gate and Willi's father drove in. He must have smelt the whisky, Carruthers thought. It was nice of him to check up on me, Carruthers decided, and by the end of his visit the bottle of J & B was finished. But thank goodness there were no birds about.

    Willi's father was one of the few Africans to have tasted whisky before the Second World War. A close friend of the father of the deposed Kabaka of Buganda, he had been asked by the Kabaka to try it and since then had become a firm aficionado. The Kabaka had had a Scottish tutor in his youth who had introduced him to the taste. That was one benefit of colonialism to the locals, Carruthers thought.

    The next day was a Monday and Carruthers sat in the doctor's surgery after his boring weekend. He picked up a ladies' magazine with the words on the cover 'Eight steps to healthy breasts'. His mind started to wander. He had seen many healthy breasts in his time... The reason for his visit to the doctor was that around this time Carruthers had developed a severe sore throat and he hoped this would be his final check-up. Over the past year or two these sore throats had bothered him every three or four months but they soon cleared up with a dose of antibiotics. He had no tonsils to absorb germs, these having been removed around the age of three at Edinburgh Royal Infirmary. He could still remember sitting in a brown rubber smock and hat along with other children waiting to be gassed. While recuperating in hospital from the operation, he had gone missing one night and been found in the cot of a female patient of similar age. His early urge for female company would continue into later life.

Anyway, a new young expatriate doctor had arrived in Kampala and refused to give Carruthers antibiotics, reasoning, quite correctly as it turned out, that the body's natural immune system should be allowed to attack the infection and destroy it for ever. With the lack of tonsils, Carruthers was told it could be a painful and uncomfortable process. Indeed, his throat throbbed with pain and swelled up. It got so bad one night that he panicked and phoned the doctor at home, worried that his throat would close completely. But he was told to ride it out that night, which he did, and to his great relief the swelling had gone down a bit by morning. In a day or two it had gone completely and would never return. (The same doctor would remain in Kampala throughout all the various dictatorships and in Carruthers' eyes and many others would always be considered a one hundred per cent professional, dispensing not only excellent medical advice but good common sense.)

Cured of his sore throat, Carruthers drove to Nairobi from Kampala to collect his family and return again by road to Kampala. It was January 1973. He didn't feel completely happy because of the security situation in Uganda and Amin's rambling threats. However, there was no job at present available to him outside Uganda, and he didn't particularly wish to return to work in the UK.

The Chairman, who was a bit unsure of Carruthers' family going back to Kampala, had not mentioned anything to Carruthers about his embarrassing face-down with his wife, so over lunch in Nairobi's New Stanley Hotel, Carruthers prompted a reply by asking how the photographs had turned out and could he have some copies for his client at the mine. The Chairman replied that something must have been wrong with the film because on developing it there was nothing to be seen.

'We'll need to arrange another sitting,' Carruthers replied mischievously.

'Mmm,' was all the Chairman would say.

He confided over the lunch that he had received a letter from someone with the initial F from the Kampala hotel, along with his pyjamas, which had puzzled him because he didn't know who this person was and he was sure that he had left his pyjamas at the hotel near the mine on his last visit. In fact, when he thought about it he had not stayed in Kampala as he had flown from Nairobi to the mine and back. Carruthers reminded the Chairman that there had been a very attractive receptionist at the mine hotel and perhaps she had been transferred to Kampala, taking the pyjamas with her as remembrance of a night of passion with the Chairman. The Chairman stared into space.

'Well, I still can't remember,' he said, 'and I hope to God she doesn't pitch up in Nairobi.' Unless, of course, he could keep it discreet, he mused.

Chapter 13

The Army

On the journey back to Kampala the Carruthers family had an extra passenger in their car, the elder sister of an expatriate friend. She had flown into Nairobi from the UK and Carruthers had arranged to meet her and transport her to her brother's house in Kampala. Airfares were much cheaper through Nairobi than direct to Entebbe, and the British High Commission had told her it was reasonably safe to travel by road – if that advice really meant anything.

Prior to their departure from Nairobi on a much earlier occasion, Carruthers had heard on the early morning BBC Africa Service that there had been an attempt on President Obote's life in Kampala. Someone had taken a shot at him. Wondering whether it was safe to travel, he had phoned the British High Commission in Nairobi, to discover to his amazement that nobody seemed to know anything about the incident. So much for giving advice to British citizens, Carruthers thought. However, he had decided to set off and hope for the best, and apart from a lot of army roadblocks there had been no problems then.

Two events, one amusing and one not so amusing, happened on the way back to Kampala. Again there were a series of army roadblocks outside Kampala, and at one a soldier speaking in Swahili wanted to know who everyone was in the car. Carruthers' friend's sister was sitting in the front of the car, while Willi and the kids were in the back. Without even waiting for an explanation, the soldier said that he understood who everyone was – there was the *bwana* and his white wife in the front seat and the *ayah* (nanny) with the kids in the back. To the soldier it was an obvious explanation, and Carruthers flashed Willi a warning look not to disagree. Willi bristled with indignation but kept mum, and Carruthers smiled to himself as his imagined wife was old enough to be his mother.

On the outskirts of the city one of the children suddenly started babbling incoherently and tossing and turning. She clearly had a high fever, so instead of going straight to the friend's house, they drove speedily to a mission hospital, where cerebral malaria was diagnosed and a couple of injections given. What was frightening was the suddenness with which the attack had manifested itself, as there had been no apparent symptoms before they set off. They were lucky it had not happened earlier into their journey. The sister was subsequently delivered late but safe to her brother's house.

Carruthers was always very cautious when questioned by Amin's soldiers, or any soldiers for that matter, as they could turn nasty very quickly. Before the family had left to go to Nairobi they had had an encounter with the army which had shaken all of them. They had been to visit Willi's parents one afternoon and were pulling out onto the main Entebbe–Kampala road about a mile from Kampala when an open army Land Rover full of armed soldiers and going in the opposite direction passed them. The soldiers shouted and waved at them and slowed to turn their Landrover round. Willi was in the front of the car, while the kids, including the baby, were in the back. Carruthers knew the soldiers' waves were not friendly greetings and put his foot down on the accelerator, hoping to lose his pursuers, but they also came faster, weaving in and out of the traffic as they followed them. Carruthers realised he wouldn't outpace them but was determined not to stop on the outskirts of Kampala, where anything could happen to them. In the centre of the city it wouldn't be so easy to hijack a whole family in front of witnesses, although that hadn't deterred the hijacking of individuals by soldiers.

The kids were shouting 'Daddy, Daddy, they are coming after us!'

Willi was shouting 'Stop, stop', and crossing herself.

Carruthers drove on grimly, saying nothing and dangerously overtaking other cars until he reached the city centre and screeched to a halt in front of the fire station. Luckily, no shots had been fired. The army Land Rover parked menacingly behind them about 20 yards away. Nobody got out. Carruthers told Willi to hold the baby in her arms and asked everyone to lock the car doors after he himself got out. He had decided to take the bull by the horns and marched up to the army Land Rover, where he was relieved to see a young army officer sitting beside the driver. He looked human.

'What's the problem?' Carruthers said. 'I am driving with my family, who you can see sitting in the car.'

'You were driving dangerously,' was the answer.

'Well, I don't think I was,' said Carruthers, 'but if you say so, then I apologise.'

There was a long silence. The officer eventually got out of his Land Rover and accompanied Carruthers to look in the car. Willi stared straight ahead, sweating.

'Just be careful,' he said after staring angrily into the car for what seemed a very long time. Then he walked away and drove off with his sullen-looking soldiers.

Passers-by had stopped to look but quickly hurried on. Carruthers never knew the real reason why they had been chased, though a white man and black woman together were always objects of suspicion in Amin's Uganda, and more particularly so if the woman was attractive. That was a very close call, he thought, and if the kids hadn't been with them he hated to think what would have happened. They waited until the army Land Rover was out of sight before driving slowly home. They were all shaken.

For the first few weeks after their return from Nairobi and living together as a family again, they tried to be optimistic, hoping that politically things would get better. However, there was still the same constant feeling of tension in the air as before, brought about by Amin's complete unpredictability. Also many friends and acquaintances had left the country and social life became non-existent.

Their young son, however, made them laugh one Saturday afternoon when they were at the swimming pool of the hotel managed by Willi's cousin. He told them he had been talking to a white Negro at the swimming pool! Most of the American programmes on TV were comedies featuring black Americans and that was the only description he could come up with. They thought that very perceptive of him and also very amusing.

In a vague way Carruthers had contacts within the Amin regime. There was Amin's British advisor whom he knew, and one lunchtime a Princess of one of the

Ugandan royal families who still used their titles despite having had their kingdoms abolished by Obote invited Carruthers out to lunch. (Tall, slim and beautiful, she would one day when in exile feature on the front page of *Vogue* magazine.) Amin had appointed her as his roving ambassador and Carruthers secretly hoped she would do a bit of roving in his direction. However, it was not to be and it was strictly business. She wanted life assurance, which Carruthers was able to arrange.

(Their platonic friendship was to continue for many years but Willi was never convinced that it was indeed platonic. A barrister by profession, then a diplomat, a model and a film star, the Princess was far too sophisticated for a thug like Amin and she would fall foul of his moody jealousies, eventually being forced to flee the country. After Carruthers himself had fled the country, the next time he would meet his beautiful and elegant female friend was in Yaounde, Cameroun, when she was still Amin's roving ambassador. Coincidentally, they were both checking out at the same time from Yaounde's only five-star hotel, situated on top of a hill overlooking the city. If only he had known she was staying there! She was conversing with the receptionist in French and was amazed to find Carruthers standing next to her. No doubt Amin's spies would report back on this encounter. It was about this time that *Private Eye* magazine coined the phrase 'Ugandan affairs' after Amin falsely accused her of an incident in a Paris airport. She successfully sued every publication that carried that story.)

Sadly, one day he heard of the death of their old friend, the newspaper editor who had been cashiered from the British Army. He had been attacked in his small room beside the house they used to live in. He was an old man and his heart gave out from the shock. In a previous attack he had lost an eye and had to wear an eye patch. He often used to say that one day he could be mistaken for the Israeli General Moshi Dayan, who was well known for his eye patch. He had donated his body to the university medical school and this was announced at the funeral ceremony. Despite his age he had continued his connection with the press and used to regularly contribute a Uganda column in a Nairobi Sunday newspaper, sometimes making oblique references to his friends the Carruthers. Whether his death was a result of political thuggery or plain robbery no one ever knew.

When Carruthers resumed his golf, it was much quieter with so many people gone. However, new faces appeared who had never played golf before and it was encouraging to see Ugandans taking up the game in larger numbers. The golf course was situated right in the centre of Kampala and was very well kept. Over the years many threats were made about taking over the course for development purposes, but they never materialised – mainly because important Ugandans who played golf managed to step in and block any take-over plans. However, there would always be a constant threat from greedy property developers.

He smiled when he remembered one of his company's European secretaries who had got herself in trouble a while ago at the golf club when she forced her husband to leave a committee meeting to go home for dinner. This had outraged the all-white committee and she was forced to go before the next meeting and apologise and buy drinks all round. This she had accepted in good grace, and she enjoyed repeating the story.

One day at the Golf Club Carruthers found his German friend, the one he used to take to lunch at the Top Club, very much the worse for wear. He staggered across to Carruthers at the bar counter.

'Who are the Nazis now?' he shouted, giving Carruthers a Hitler salute. 'It is Amin. He will put you in a camp, my friend.' And he laughed hysterically.

Carruthers managed eventually to quieten him down and quickly joined him in being the worse for wear. It was sad really. The German had been told to leave because he had been working in a very senior position for an Israeli construction company that had been forced to cease operations. Anyway, he was lucky to be leaving alive, especially with his Israeli connections.

Another German whom Carruthers knew had suddenly had his contract with a government corporation terminated and was leaving the country. He had actually approached Carruthers about nine months before and asked if he could arrange some insurance cover to pay the costs of a broken contract and also repatriation costs, if ever the occasion arose. Carruthers had surprisingly managed to obtain cover with Lloyd's of London but the German had unwisely never taken up the offer.

It was definitely a time to keep one's head low. Another of Carruthers' friends, an expatriate working with Government, had bravely but again unwisely agreed to help the wife of one of his Ugandan colleagues who had disappeared to discover his whereabouts. He had actually been seeking out the Minister of Defence, whom he knew, when he went to a large government-owned hotel where the army had offices, some of which were used for torture. Barging into one of the office rooms, he suddenly found himself facing Idi Amin and nervously blurted out the purpose of his mission. Amin was not amused and angrily told some underling to get the white man out of his sight. The next day the expatriate was picked up at his office by security personnel and taken straight to Entebbe airport, where he was put on a flight to England. He had no time to inform his wife or friends or even to collect any clothing. The wife came to Carruthers' office the following day, seeking news of her husband, who hadn't returned home. At that time Carruthers was none the wiser and simply told her hopefully he would turn up – dead or alive he didn't know, but he didn't say that. Again this was a person who was lucky to get out alive.

Amin, being a Muslim, suddenly decreed that bars would only be open from 5 o'clock onwards. This was a blow to the hair-of-the-dog brigade who desperately needed the hair by lunchtime at the latest. Then someone told Carruthers of a bar near the Ministry of Defence which was open 24 hours a day despite the ban, so he and a colleague decided to find it – and true enough, it was open all hours. However, army personnel, many of whom were staggering about, were its main customers and Carruthers felt decidedly nervous being in such a place, especially as they were white and therefore very obvious. But he and his colleague didn't want to draw more attention to themselves by immediately walking out, which was their initial inclination, so they stayed and had a couple of drinks before leaving. Luckily, the soldiers ignored them, probably thinking they were Russians, who had replaced the Israelis in providing military assistance and advice. But if someone had questioned them they would have been in dire trouble. They didn't go back.

Another dangerous place was a military prison which Carruthers used to pass on his way to the office from home. It was a notorious torture and killing ground and he eventually thought it would be prudent to vary his route as the sight of a lone white man, sometimes accompanied by Willi, regularly passing by could be too much a temptation to bloodthirsty soldiers on duty at the main gate.

It was on his change of route that one day Carruthers spotted his English acquaintance from the Uganda Club now nicknamed Major Bob. Driving in the opposite direction, he had with him the widow and children of the first prominent and rich Ugandan to have been killed by Amin's soldiers, whose charred body had been found in his burnt-out car. By being friendly to that family he was certainly carrying out a good but dangerous deed.

Carruthers had been surprised. Major Bob was a supporter of Amin (and would play a prominent behind-the-scenes role in Amin's Government right up to the time of his overthrow). He had become a Uganda citizen and married a Uganda civil servant whom Amin made a Minister in his Government. Carruthers and Willi had been invited to the wedding reception at the Uganda Club, where the army band played and wine flowed freely. Carruthers was the only other white man there.

He really was a political chameleon. Carruthers had first encountered him in 1964 in the company of the Kabaka's sister, known as the official sister who accompanied the King on all official duties. This was during Obote's regime when relationships between Obote and the King, who would become President, were strained. Carruthers was with Willi at the Lake Victoria Hotel, Entebbe, one Sunday when he saw them, accompanied by others, coming out of the hotel. The King's sister was Willi's aunt and Willi knelt down to greet her. There was obviously quite a close relationship between Aunty and the moustached man because Willi's cousins referred to him not as Major but as Uncle Bob.

Uncle Bob became very close to Obote and would accompany him on upcountry visits and then personally introduce films of such visits on TV, referring to Obote as 'this great man'. Then Obote got kicked out and Uncle Bob was suddenly a close aide to Idi Amin. One had to admire his acumen and survival instincts, nonetheless.

(Uncle Bob would eventually flee from Uganda across Lake Victoria in his boat following the ousting of Amin in 1979. He was then arrested by the Kenya Police at the lakeside port of Kisumu and returned to Uganda, where he languished in prison for a couple of years before being deported to the UK, where the British (his masters?) restored his British citizenship.)

Uncle Bob was living dangerously but he was a survivor. He was also known to help British expatriates who got into trouble, but in many people's eyes he was guilty by association. He was even imprisoned by Amin for a short time because of a large radio that he owned and was suspected of using to communicate with the British! Carruthers was always convinced that was a set-up. Carruthers also suspected that Amin could never get rid of Major Bob because he knew too much about Amin's past activities.

Yet another of Carruthers' Uganda friends had escaped just in time from Amin's henchmen. He was the managing director and a shareholder in Kampala's only large department store, originally started by an Englishman. Although the MD was a black Ugandan, he was considered a prime target by the regime because of the wealth he had supposedly accumulated. One day Carruthers' friend received a phone call from a friend suggesting they meet urgently. She was a civil servant and had seen a secret list of prominent people who were to be arrested, and Carruthers' friend's name was on it.

Being a man of action, his friend made immediate plans to leave the country. He took his shareholding in the store in the form of new furniture, which he sold, and then arranged for his house, which was in a sought-after area, to be rented out to an embassy. He then went into exile in Kenya. Soon after he left, Amin's henchmen arrived at his now rented house and demanded to see him, but as it was a diplomatic residence they couldn't even get in. However, there is no doubt that he would have been murdered had he remained.

Chapter 14

Visits, to and from

All the expatriates at the mine were now moving out of Uganda, and when the MD passed through Kampala on his way to Nairobi Carruthers was given the negatives and the copies of the photographs of his wife taken by the Chairman. Carruthers had by now explained to Willi the circumstances in which the photographs had been taken, and over dinner at their house one evening he and the MD tried to persuade Willi to pose too, but she firmly refused. She secretly wondered if her husband was becoming a pervert.

The MD was pleased with the way the photographs had turned out. Carruthers' idea of getting him to rub his wife's nipples with a block of ice had certainly ensured that they were erect. Carruthers also remembered noticing out of the corner of his eye that the Chairman had picked up the discarded block of ice and started sucking it, slowly and delicately with a decided gleam in his eyes. Meanwhile the MD's wife had shivered in anticipation. Willi said the only decent thing about the photographs was her bras, and in fact they would make a good advert. She thought she might write to the suppliers.

Carruthers knew that the MD would be meeting up with the Chairman in Nairobi and stressed that the Chairman had only seen the photographs when his wife had produced them with a letter from a girl she thought was from Kampala. He explained the background and the MD was highly amused. He thought he might have some fun with the Chairman in Nairobi over these revelations. Carruthers fervently hoped this would not all rebound on him and once again felt that sinking feeling in his stomach.

Despite all these trivial and humorous incidents, mostly occasioned by Carruthers' warped sense of humour, he did work hard. Work hard and play hard was how he got by. Working hard, and he did work bloody hard, was his excuse for letting his hair down. He was a good insurance broker and his penchant for lateral thinking made the business a success even in these difficult times. He would make a worthy Chairman one day, he knew. He mustn't give up on his ambition.

About that time Carruthers had to visit the staff of one of his clients in Dar es Salaam, Tanzania, and was to meet up with their UK director, who would also be making a visit. Willi was not happy to be left alone in these troubled times and again she moved in with her parents.

Carruthers certainly felt the humidity of the coast the minute he stepped off the flight from Entebbe at Dar es Salaam airport. He and the director were booked into a newly built hotel on the coast a few miles outside the city, where they both met up.

The meetings with staff at the client's office took place in the afternoon and Carruthers and the director were back in their hotel by early evening. They decided they would have a swim and then meet later for drinks and dinner. There was also a nightclub at another hotel up the coast, which they decided they would visit after dinner.

The bedrooms of the hotel were romantically designed and all faced the Indian Ocean and the beach. Waves breaking over the coral reef some way offshore could be viewed while lying in the bath, which was situated at the end of and above the bedroom, separated by screens which could be pulled back. Carruthers' imagination went into overtime as he imagined himself leaping from the bath onto a naked body of a woman lying on the bed below. He didn't usually like baths, preferring showers, but this was something else. He started to fill the tub humming to himself.

Carruthers had actually drifted off to sleep in the bath and wakened as the sun was going down and the water growing tepid. He didn't have time to visit the open-air swimming pool before joining the director for drinks at the hotel bar. The visiting director, who had been very white on his arrival from the UK, was now, after a visit to the swimming pool, pink like a lobster and slightly uncomfortable. However, a few drinks soon sorted that out and he seemed anxious to see the nightclub. Carruthers assured him that it would not really get going until around 10 p.m., so they could enjoy their dinner, have a bottle or two of wine and then grab a taxi.

Dinner was excellent and they almost had the dining room to themselves. A bottle of white wine followed by a bottle of red had gone down well, which inured them to the bumpy ride in the taxi. The driver, whose name was Jim, so he said, insisted on singing them songs of Elvis Presley, which the two of them hilariously joined in.

The night club was in the open air under a huge thatch roof and adjacent to the hotel and the beach. A live band was playing Congolese music and the place was busy. There was no shortage of girls to dance with, and by one o'clock and after much dancing they were comfortably seated with drinks at their table, accompanied by two girls they considered the best of the bunch. The director seemed to have fallen in love with his girl and was all over her, but Carruthers was a bit more circumspect.

His attention was suddenly drawn to a table in a far corner where a white couple were having a violent argument. To his consternation and surprise he recognised his ex-girlfriend, or he thought he did. He had thought she was no longer in East Africa. She looked quite attractive, he thought, especially in her anger. Her poor companion was obviously not winning the argument and was in fact sinking lower in his chair and waving her away feebly. Carruthers shifted his chair so his back was to their table, although in the darkness of the nightclub it was unlikely she would spot him.

Meanwhile, his companion the director wanted to extend his knowledge of his partner's nether parts and they decided to leave and head back to their own hotel, accompanied by the two girls. This time they sang Beatles songs in the taxi, thus making a noisy arrival at their hotel.

The loud rendering of *It's a Hard Day's Night* alerted the couple, or rather one of them, alighting from the taxi in front of them. His ex-girlfriend stood mouth agape as she stared at him, her partner, completely drunk, hanging onto her arm.

'What are you doing here? Oh, my darling,' she shouted, and rushed to embrace him, leaving her partner to collapse on the hotel steps.

Carruthers mumbled that he was on a company visit from Kampala and had been seeing the sights. His dancing partner clutched him protectively.

'I must see you,' she hissed. 'That's my husband,' she

said indicating the forlorn-looking figure on the steps, 'and he's always getting drunk. I'll come to your room later. He won't know what's going on.'

Giving her his room number, Carruthers hastily followed the director and his chick, who had disappeared up the steps. He had to tell his own chick that she could not accompany him and she looked downcast. However, the director declared that he would make it a threesome, to which his partner angrily reacted by pushing her rival away and saying she wasn't going to share her darling honey with anyone. In order to avoid a scene, Carruthers gave his now rejected partner enough money for a taxi and a bonus for the great disappointment she had suffered. Maybe he would see her tomorrow, he said. She stomped off angrily.

Away along the hotel corridor a door slammed and a girl shrieked. That director was certainly enjoying his visit, Carruthers thought. Behind another door a certain lady carefully put her husband to bed, knowing he would sleep very heavily. Should she take her whip with her, she wondered? Carruthers used to be into that, she remembered, and it was that which had led to her dalliance with members of her own sex. She decided she had better leave it for the moment.

Carruthers checked the mini bar in his bedroom, then turned on the bath. A full moon shone down on the sea. Leaving the door unlocked, Carruthers slid into the bath, into which he had poured some foam gel. His ex-girlfriend soon came through the door and then, disrobing, slid into the bath beside him. She had brought a bottle of champagne with her. They were soon telling each other the story of their lives since their parting. She had in fact returned to the UK, where she had met and married a man who worked on a sisal estate in Tanzania. They had met in a sex shop in Soho while he was on leave. Unfortunately, he had become an alcoholic as a result of the initial stress he had suffered from her nightly whippings. She had tried to make him act positively but he just became a cringer and a whinger, she said. Her big toe with a nail that needed trimming explored Carruthers' anus. He winced. She smiled.

The bottle of champagne almost finished, Carruthers suggested they move to the bed down below. His fantasy of leaping onto a naked woman from the bath was not to be fulfilled, however, as his ex-girlfriend demanded to do the leaping and insisted he crouch down on all fours on the bed and she would jump upon him as she would a horse. Carruthers positioned himself, glancing over his shoulder nervously. Unfortunately the slipperiness of the foam bath on their bodies and the momentum of her body when she landed on Carruthers' back ensured that she slid off at great speed. Her cry of 'tallyho' turned into an abrupt gargle of pain as she hit the wall opposite with her face and then passed out.

Carruthers gingerly slid off the bed. He thought his back must be broken. He crawled over to his ex-girlfriend, who was now moaning. He wasn't sure if the moans were of pleasure or pain, but he decided that he had to get her back to her bedroom before something else happened. He still couldn't stand up straight, so in a bent position he managed to get her bathrobe on and found the key to her room in one of the pockets. Gripping her under her wet arms, he pulled her, with great difficulty, along the corridor to her room, from which came a sound of loud snoring. After bumping her down the few steps to the bedroom, he left her on the floor near the bed. As he released her arms, her eyes opened and she smiled up at him. He recoiled, convinced that the blood-splattered teeth were those of one of Dracula's female servants. Half crawling up the steps, he left the room, shutting the door behind him. As he did he was sure he heard the crack of a whip and the sound of snoring stopped. A night servant coming round the corner wondered what the naked white man loping along the corridor was up to. Carruthers muttered 'Good night' as he passed him. Glancing up, he noticed a look of pity on the servant's face.

Far too early, the telephone in his bedroom awakened Carruthers. He could hardly move. Had he had a bad dream or had it all really happened? He had a painful bottom, a painful back and a hangover. All of it was true, he now remembered. The call was from the director, who was in a terrible state and babbling incoherently. Carruthers suggested he come to his room, as he couldn't go to his because of his hurt back. The director arrived shortly, bringing with him his companion of the night. Both looked dishevelled. They were in love, he said. He was a bachelor, and he was going to return with her to the UK, where they would marry. She probably had a boyfriend and six kids, Carruthers thought, although she wasn't a bad looker. Carruthers asked the girl to wait outside while he talked to her partner but she refused to go and looked on suspiciously

'You mustn't rush into things, old man,' Carruthers said. 'This is your first visit to Africa and I am sure you would have many more similar experiences if you were to stay longer, or when you return, in fact. You have no idea who she is. Give it time, and write to each other. Just give her enough money and she'll be happy.'

The director's partner now brightened up and nodded.

'You're a heartless bastard,' the director sobbed helping himself to a beer from the mini bar. 'Anyway, I suppose I'll take your advice as you must know what you are talking about.' He sighed and stared at the floor.

He left to say fond farewells to his chick and departed on the plane that night for the UK.

(Carruthers never saw his director friend after that night and had no occasion ever to meet him on business. He did hear from someone, however, that he had subsequently been arrested on the banks of the River Thames near Reading, dressed in a long raincoat and exposing himself to women. Perhaps he had given him the wrong advice, after all, poor sod.)

Carruthers spent most of the day in his bedroom resting and taking hot baths and by early evening he was nearly back to normal, with just the odd twinge in his back. His director friend had left for the airport and there had been no sign of his ex-girlfriend. He was due to fly back to Entebbe the next day, and he managed to phone Willi to assure her that he was okay and was behaving himself. She knew he couldn't be; all men were the same.

That evening Carruthers decided to try and trace one of Uganda's exiles. Having been kicked out of the country by Amin during the coup, Obote and some of his Cabinet Ministers had been given refuge in Tanzania by President Nyerere, a well-known socialist. The person Carruthers sought was Obote's Minister of Foreign Affairs, an old drinking buddy in Kampala. After making some discreet inquiries from various acquaintances in Dar es Salaam and assuring people he was not an Amin spy, he managed to trace his friend to the bar of the Civil Service Club. They were both happy to see each other, although initially the politician was understandably cautious. Life was very boring, he told Carruthers, and money was short. It wasn't easy but one day they would all be back. He had been a very good foreign minister and had many international friends with whom he was keeping in contact. Quite a few drinks later they parted (and would not meet again for some years).

Back in Kampala Carruthers recounted the story of the director to Willi.

'Poor man,' Willi said, 'he must have been lonely. I suppose you were keeping him company? I hope you weren't taking any photographs?'

Carruthers reminded her it was only people like the Chairman who did that, and he merely looked at them. But he wondered if the Chairman and the mine MD had met up in Nairobi.

Within the next few days the company's UK Chairman and his wife would be visiting the Kampala office. He was flying in from Nairobi but would not be accompanied by the Nairobi Chairman, thank goodness. His wife had barred him from Kampala visits until further notice.

The visiting UK Chairman was an ex-Navy Commodore and was on his second wife, a much younger woman. They got off the flight at Entebbe and were met by Carruthers and a couple of colleagues, one black, one white. The wife, who seemed fairly tipsy, asked in a loud voice if the former spoke English. Probably better than you, madam, thought Carruthers as he shouted, 'Of course he does. It's the national language!'

He could also have mentioned that his black colleague, a university graduate, was well known for stripping woman with his eyes, which he had just done to her but in her tipsy state she hadn't noticed. Carruthers often found this quite embarrassing as his colleague slowly looked women up and down from head to toe, and when appropriate, leered. Some responded, many didn't.

That evening they had a cocktail party for the Chairman and his wife on the top floor of a city hotel. Only business associates and the wheelchair-bound expatriate Chief Justice had been invited. It was too dangerous to invite Government Ministers tainted by Amin and his brutal regime. Better not to draw too much attention to the company, its directors and employees.

Dinner after the party had been arranged in the same hotel. It was not a success. The Chairman's wife talked a load of rubbish, probably because she was drunk, and the Chairman himself seemed to have other things on his mind, such as getting his pliable younger wife into bed as soon as he could. The meat was undercooked and Willi felt quite sick. It was around the time of the first heart transplant operation being carried out in South Africa and Willi had visions of that as she poked at the lump of bloody meat. Carruthers was on his best behaviour and had kept quite sober, which was why he could sense that the dinner function was a bit strained. To crown it all, a junior expatriate colleague near retirement age decided, after imbibing many whiskies, to imitate a striptease artiste in front of the whole table. It was actually quite funny and well done, but it had to be stopped by his wife, who hustled him away before he could remove his trousers. His upper garments had all gone. The Chairman was not amused and cautioned Carruthers to 'keep that little man well out of my way!' A stiff 'goodnight' was said, and Chairman and wife retired. Phew, thought Carruthers, thank goodness they are only staying one night.

With a visiting chairman you had to either keep him completely away from other staff or get him to mingle, in which event you ran the risk of outspoken remarks and actions. Carruthers remembered the story of a visiting chairman who had asked his MD to introduce him to members of his staff. Many of the staff, while delighted to meet the chairman, wondered who the other man was!

Carruthers lay in bed that night hoping that the next day's activities would be free of any untoward incidents. He must make sure that the Chairman didn't bump into his elder colleague who, although a hard worker, loved letting his hair down and couldn't care less whom he offended. The incident at the Kampala Club came to mind. His colleague also had some interesting stories to tell. On one occasion when he was a civil servant in Tanganyika and visiting certain outstations, he had spent the night at the house of one of the officials looking after the local postal system. In the morning the official's wife had brought him a cup of tea, and on leaning down to place it on the bedside table, a breast had plopped out of her dressing gown. Never one to lose an opportunity, the visitor had quickly ascertained that her husband had left the house to open up the office. His tea was cold by the time his hostess had left his bed.

Another incident in the same country had involved him giving violin lessons to the young wife of an expatriate teacher, but it wasn't long before other strings than those of the violin were being pulled. He had been forced to give up the lessons after his pupil and lover had decided to move in with him without his knowledge – and without the knowledge of her husband – and had been found hiding under his bed quite naked. Luckily he had managed to get her out and back to her own house before her husband became overly suspicious.

Another time, before one of his binges, he had parked his car for safety outside the Kampala police headquarters and subsequently forgotten where it was. The next day, on coming out of the police station after reporting the loss of his car, he noticed with some embarrassment that there it was parked on the opposite side of the road. Such was his muddled but enjoyable life.

On yet another occasion Carruthers had witnessed an embarrassing incident when both of them were invited to a curry lunch at the house of an Indian merchant, a friend of his colleague. There were just the three of them. After the curry, lots of beer and whisky were consumed. Then Carruthers had been astonished when their host offered the services of his wife to them and said she was waiting in the bedroom next door. Unfortunately, she had not been young and attractive, and they had laughed off the offer.

The next day was quite uneventful. Willi arranged a wives' luncheon at which the Chairman's wife was the guest of honour, and the Chairman had a business lunch with important clients. Again Carruthers was on his best behaviour and in fact some of his clients wondered if he was under the weather, as he never seemed to refill his glass.

The Chairman and his wife were on the night flight to London and Carruthers made sure they were at the airport early. They were flying first class, of course and were able to sit in the first-class lounge. Carruthers made the excuse that because of Amin's tight security they couldn't accompany them to the lounge, although to be honest he never tried. He and his colleagues rushed back to Kampala, where they celebrated the departure with more than a few drinks.

Another former UK Chairman of the company was to visit in a couple of weeks. He was the current Chairman of Lloyd's of London and was visiting Kampala with the Nairobi Chairman, who had been temporarily let off the leash by his wife. The object of the visit was to meet the Secretary to the Treasury on the matter of insurance coverage through Lloyd's. As it turned out, it was a mission impossible because the day before his arrival Amin had appointed a new Secretary to the

Treasury, a civil servant completely untrained for that particular post, who happened to be from the same tribe as Amin. He didn't know what the Chairman was talking about but was brave enough to admit it. Carruthers respected him for that, but he wasn't to last long in that post because he kept on telling the truth.

The only positive achievement of the ex-Chairman's visit was that he had brought with him, at Carruthers' telexed request, a supply of pork sausages, which had been unavailable in Uganda for some time. Carruthers thought that would make a good newspaper headline – 'Lloyd's Chairman brings sausages to Uganda'.

The Nairobi Chairman had decided to spend a couple of nights in Kampala after putting the Lloyd's Chairman on a flight he was taking back to London. Carruthers knew that his own Chairman wanted to investigate who had written that letter sent to him with his pyjamas. Carruthers wondered if he should set him up again, and a bizarre idea came into his mind.

He went to see his queer head waiter acquaintance, first to book a table for lunch with his Chairman and second to discuss his plan for entertaining the Chairman the following night. A couple of clients came to lunch, which was a relaxed affair. A dwindling band of Carruthers' business acquaintances were also in the restaurant, which would soon close as its clientele, mainly expatriates, left the country, forced out by the circumstances of the time.

The Chairman spent the evening with the Carruthers at their bungalow overlooking the lake, and they sat on the verandah with their drinks and told the Chairman of their fears. Being a black and white couple, they were easily, too easily, identifiable and were quite frankly hesitant about going out together to public places where army men and informers abounded. The Chairman said the situation was, in his opinion, not going to get better and they should not hesitate to leave if they felt they had to, but should try to give him some warning of their intentions.

Most of the next day was spent discussing contingency plans if they decided to close the office. Carruthers explained to the Chairman that he would have to look after himself that evening as he had the annual general meeting of the Golf Club to attend. This would undoubtedly be a long-drawn-out affair, especially as one of the committee had been accused by members of fraud and complicity in bringing in private stocks of alcohol to be sold at the bar with no profit to the club.

The stage was now set for Carruthers' plan for that evening. He had arranged for one of the head waiter's 'girls' to dress up, wig and all, and visit the Chairman in his hotel. He/she would first phone the Chairman in his room and suggest a meeting in his bedroom, revealing herself as the mysterious F who wrote the letter. The disguise was so perfect that when Carruthers, who was lurking in the hotel lobby, saw her, accompanied by her minder, he fancied her/him himself.

She/he now phoned the Chairman from the lobby.

'Hullo, you naughty boy,' said the lispy voice. 'This is F and I hope you didn't bring those stupid pyjamas with you because you certainly won't be needing them tonight, big boy. Can I come up, I mean to your room?' Giggle, giggle.

The Chairman, surprised and shocked, his hand shaking, took a deep breath and said he would be waiting for her. 'Knock three times and ask for Joe,' he hummed as he sprinkled some after-shave on his face and you know where. He quickly downed a whisky. He would, he thought, have to pretend he remembered her if she wasn't recognisable; he didn't want her to feel insulted as it might cool her ardour.

When he/she came into the room, he was full of smiles for her/him and gave him/her a tight embrace, fondling the surprisingly tight buttocks. She really was a beauty, he thought, and he was going to enjoy himself – of that he was sure.

She demanded drinks first, then sat down and lit a cigarette. She said she had lost her job at the hotel since she last met him and hoped he would perhaps be able to give her an advance as she had no money, and he might remember that last time they met he had even suggested helping her to start a guest house, where, incidentally it would be so convenient for them to meet in future.

Good heavens, thought the Chairman, I certainly can't remember that – although in fact he couldn't remember anything of that previous meeting. What the hell, he thought. He would give F what cash he had in the room. Better to get it over with now, he thought, and handed F 300 dollars and about half that in local currency. F was delighted.

They were working their way through the mini bar quite well, the Chairman's hand resting on F's knee. Suddenly the Chairman said, 'Let's get on with it. I want you now, you are the most beautiful black girl I have ever seen.' He stood up to undress, visibly excited. F said she would visit the bathroom first. When F came out of the bathroom she switched the lights off and the Chairman, lying naked on the bed, drunkenly shouted out, 'Me Tarzan, you Jane, you black bitch.'

The next thing the Chairman knew was he being forcibly turned onto his stomach by a pair of very strong arms. What happened to him next was something he had not experienced since boarding school in England.

He prayed it would be over soon. He couldn't move. It was he who was Jane now. Somebody must have broken into the room, he thought, and F had fled.

'You're cool man, real cool,' said the male voice above him.

The Chairman certainly didn't feel cool at all.

Fifteen minutes later, a black youth went out of the Chairman's room, leaving a shaken Chairman behind. He only comprehended what had really happened to him when he found a wig lying on the floor behind the bathroom door. Surely this hadn't happened to him on his last visit, he thought? He must have been set up, and he had also given all his money away. Head in hands he pondered his fate, vowing to himself that he would start behaving himself from then on. The sooner he got home the better. He was safer with his wife, even if she smelt of horses.

The Chairman left early the next morning, saying nothing about what had happened to him. He had to borrow some money from Carruthers.

Carruthers noticed he was walking in a funny way. Must be age, he thought. But when he heard from the head waiter what had happened, he actually felt a bit sorry for the Chairman. He hadn't really wanted it to end that way, but nevertheless the Chairman had asked for it.

The Chairman had said on his way to the airport that he was getting fed up with travelling and Carruthers should visit Nairobi instead. In fact Carruthers, Willi and family would soon be visiting Nairobi on a more permanent basis, as the terror forced them to flee their beautiful country,

Despite the uncertainty, the expatriate community, what

was left of it, tried to continue life as normal. Carruthers, Willi and children were comfortably seated one evening in the National Theatre in Kampala, watching the annual pantomime performed by the Kampala Amateur Dramatic Society, known as Kads and mainly composed of expatriate thespians. Such pantomimes were usually of quite a high standard and very popular. The theatre was packed. Carruthers felt a nudge on his right side – but his family were seated on his left, so at first he ignored it. However, as the nudging persisted he turned to face the perpetrator. To his shock and dismay, there was his ex-girlfriend leering at him. He ignored her. My God, he thought, what is happening? First Nairobi, then Dar es Salaam and now Kampala. Was she following him to cause chaos in his life in retaliation for his having spurned her? Under cover of the dim light her hand closed tightly on his testicles. He ignored her and no introductions were made. When the pantomime ended they went their separate ways, Carruthers hoping it was all a bad dream. But it wasn't.

The next day she phoned him in the office. She and her husband were spending Christmas in Kampala with some friends and there was nothing sinister in her being there. She suggested they meet, which Carruthers resisted. It would be highly dangerous to meet her on his home territory.

'Maybe we will meet in Dar,' she then said. 'I keep track of your movements, you know.'

Carruthers gulped and murmured goodbye. But her assumption that they would meet in Dar was to prove correct.

Chapter 15

Fleeing Uganda

Amin announced in one of his many raving statements that some Ugandan spies had been caught and they were going to be publicly executed by firing squad. No proper trial had been held. They were young men who had probably been overheard criticising Amin, although one did have links with a rebel movement. This was horrific to Ugandans and brought home to them the real brutality of the regime and the way Amin wanted to rule – by terror and fear.

The night before the executions were to take place, Carruthers and Willi attended a family gathering to celebrate the forthcoming marriage of Willi's cousin. It was held at the home of the cousin's mother, the Princess who had been imprisoned by Obote but now freed, and was a fine function, family only, with plenty of food and drinks. Not as jolly, however, as it would have been in former times. There was always that underlying tension.

Carruthers and Willi left for home around midnight, just the two of them, after they had dropped off Willi's brother at his home. They were never quite sure when the car full of armed soldiers started following them. They had passed through the edge of the city and were heading home on the main road going towards the lake when Willi remarked that a car had been behind them for a while and implored Carruthers to drive faster. He did but it didn't make much difference. There weren't many houses around that stretch of the road. There was the police barracks and that was about it.

Carruthers' immediate thought was that they were in a no-win situation. They wouldn't be able to outrun the following vehicle as the road eventually came to a dead end at the lakeside. Furthermore, it could anger the followers and also suggest they were running from something. He also didn't want them to follow them to their house and discover where they lived. Nor did he want to crash at speed.

He told Willi to be prepared to get out the car quickly and run into the bush at her side of the road if and when they were forced to stop. They kept a steady speed – and the inevitable did happen and quite soon.

The car behind overtook them and screeched to a halt at an angle in front of them. Willi took off. Carruthers got out more slowly. A gun was stuck up his nose; his night driving glasses were thrown onto the road and his driving licence and identity papers removed from his pocket. He didn't know what had happened to Willi. No one spoke. Time seemed to stand still.

Suddenly the lights of a car appeared in the distance behind them, and just as suddenly the soldiers took off, piling into their own car and also Carruthers' car. He was left standing in the middle of the road. There was no sign of Willi.

Carruthers dashed to the side of the road and hid in the bushes. He didn't want to stop the car whose lights had disturbed their ambushers in case it was another army car. It was a dark night and he was scared. To his great relief, after the other car had passed he suddenly heard Willi calling his name from out of the darkness from the other side of the road. He ran over to her and eventually was able to hold her hand, but he still couldn't see her. He couldn't understand why she wanted him to give her his shirt until she told him she was completely naked. One of the soldiers had caught her near the side of the road and tried to drag her to their car. She had fiercely resisted and lost all her clothes in the process. It had obviously been quite a struggle. If they had succeeded in taking her, Carruthers knew without a doubt that he would never have seen his wife again.

They were now at the side of the road. Again the lights of a car appeared in the distance. Carruthers was worried that as their attackers had taken off so quickly, they might return to the scene of the crime. They ducked down out of sight as the car passed.

As they were near the police barracks, they decided to proceed there, all the time keeping to the bush and ducking out of sight as cars passed; luckily there weren't many. They reached the police barracks without further incident.

The police force, which had become completely demoralised under army rule, had lost much of their authority. But they were not considered a threat to people's safety and the Carruthers felt relieved to have reached there.

The officer in charge asked Willi if she realised that President Amin had banned the wearing of mini skirts. Carruthers' shirt only just covered her bottom! They quickly explained the circumstances of their dress and the police officers, genuinely concerned and sympathetic, offered a police car with two officers to drive them home.

The drive home took 15 minutes and in its own way was equally frightening because the policemen were very nervous and thought the ambushers would be waiting somewhere along the road. They kept glancing over their shoulders and peering at the sides of the road. Fortunately that was not the case and they arrived home safely, but very much shaken and in shock.

Carruthers and Willi swallowed a couple of large brandies immediately. While Willi narrated the details of their ordeal to their nanny, both of them in tears, Carruthers telephoned a colleague in his office to alert him to the situation.

The next day, Saturday, was the day of the public executions, and army roadblocks appeared around the edges of the city. There were also reports that the army was conducting a house-to-house search on the main road leading to the Carruthers' house. Were they looking for them, Carruthers wondered? Willi took the children and hid in the far corner of the garden. Carruthers nervously paced around the house. However, by late afternoon the army had given up their search, much to Carruthers' and Willi's relief.

Friends and relatives either called personally or telephoned to offer commiserations, and on the Sunday an official from the British High Commission came to see them. News had travelled fast. A neighbour gave Carruthers a lift into his office on the Monday morning. Apparently someone had seen his stolen car being driven in town by an army major, but although a full report of the incident had been given to the police, they weren't going to risk their lives by recovering a car from an army officer serving in a brutal military regime. Who could blame them?

During the morning a Ugandan gentleman Carruthers had never seen before came into his office and told him that a certain colonel in the army would be happy to offer him any help if he so required it. This made Carruthers decidedly nervous. He knew of the colonel, from the same tribe as Amin, but didn't know him personally. The less he was involved with the army, the better, Carruthers thought. Why was this person telling him this, he wondered? Perhaps the colonel had been one of the attackers. But that puzzle would never be solved.

Willi was also highly nervous. She was convinced that she was a target and was thoroughly miserable and scared all the time. Carruthers was also worried about his past connections with the previous regime through the Uganda Club. They discussed the situation over lunch one day, and Carruthers asked Willi the question which he had been dreading to ask.

'Do you want to get out of here? Do you want to leave?'

She nodded her head in the affirmative. She could hardly speak. Things had to be pretty bad, thought Carruthers, when you wanted to quit your own country, leaving your parents behind, because of fear. But he had to act to protect his wife and children, and himself, for that matter. It was a terribly sad moment.

Carruthers was still concerned about the man who had been nosing around his office, so he decided not to tell anyone he was leaving until the last moment. He personally purchased air tickets to Nairobi and phoned the Chairman to say they would be arriving that evening and could he send a car to the airport to meet them. Initially they would stay with Willi's married sister in Nairobi.

They decided to pack what they could in suitcases but without burdening themselves, as they didn't want to give the impression they were fleeing the country. Carruthers would return on visits and bring out their remaining possessions in suitcases as necessary. The TV, record player, etc would be transferred to Willi's parents' house and her father would keep his eye on their house. He had a car and could easily make visits to the property.

The 20-mile journey to the airport was nerve-racking. Willi kept looking out of the back window and was convinced a car was following them. This, however, was not the case, but it showed the state of mind she was in. The children were equally nervous. Relieved, they arrived at Entebbe airport without incident, checked in for their flight and proceeded to the customs area, where they had to clear their baggage before proceeding to the departure lounge.

It was bedlam in the customs hall. Departing Asians had their luggage piled up in front of them, and Carruthers and family found themselves at the back of a very long queue. And the longer they stood in that queue, the more exposed they were to scrutiny from roving security men. In fact an armed soldier approached them and said in Swahili to Willi, 'You are not going!'

The Carruthers ignored him. Luckily a customs officer who knew Carruthers by sight suddenly waved them to the front of the queue, quickly chalking their luggage and allowing them to enter the departure lounge.

Inside the lounge they huddled down in their seats, not wanting to make themselves conspicuous. It was relatively quiet; the Asians must have been departing through another way to another aircraft. Eventually they boarded their Kenya Airways flight and were soon airborne. All they felt was great relief – and a terrible sadness. Their plans for their future together in Uganda were gone; their lovely bungalow, recently built, was now standing empty. They had left relations and friends behind without properly saying farewell to them. What was their future now? However, their safety was paramount and with that foremost in their minds it had been a relatively easy decision to decide to get out.

The current Governor of the Bank of Uganda was on the same flight. Although he knew Carruthers, he studiously ignored him. Bastard, Carruthers thought; but perhaps he considered it dangerous to acknowledge them, as there were so many spies about.

A car and driver was waiting at Nairobi airport to take them to Willi's sister's home. It was now around 10 p.m. The house was in darkness and Willi got out of the car to rouse her sister and her husband. She seemed to be away an awfully long time. Eventually Willi was back at the car in tears and on her own. There was no room at the inn. Her own sister and brother-in-law had refused to give them a bed because they were frightened that if Carruthers and Willi were indeed on a hit list, then if word got out that they were staying with them, they too would become a target. Such was the fear of Amin's regime, which even extended outside the country.

Their immediate reaction was of shock, consternation, embarrassment and sadness. For this to happen at the end of a harrowing journey was almost unbelievable.

Carruthers decided that they would book into a hotel and sort things out the next day. With three young kids, their journey had not been an easy one and they were all exhausted, hungry and thirsty. So they secured a couple of rooms, ordered food and drinks and then tried to get some sleep.

But Willi did not sleep all night: she cried all night. Carruthers didn't realise the human body could hold so many tears. She was inconsolable. The effect of having to leave her own country and her parents and then being rejected by her own sister was too much to bear. It seemed to her the end of the world.

However, things brightened up a bit the next day. Friends who had previously lived in Uganda offered to put them up temporarily when they heard the news of their flight, and a week or two later they all moved into a large flat which was occupied by another of Willi's sisters. Their school-age children were put in a Nairobi school.

After settling into their new surroundings, Carruthers and Willi went to visit their lawyer friend who had felt it necessary to flee the country after his meeting with Amin's Minister of Defence, which Carruthers had set up. He was ensconced behind the largest bottle of whisky Carruthers had ever seen. It was so big it had a special pump attached to it, as it was too heavy to lift and pour. The duty-free allowance going into Kenya was one bottle of spirits but didn't specify any maximum volume. Carruthers' friend had taken good advantage of the regulation.

His friend had another visitor whose face appeared familiar. It turned out he was one of Amin's Ministers, who had fled the country in the past couple of days, quite rightly fearing for his life. As far as people in Uganda were concerned, he had just 'disappeared', and he was slightly embarrassed about being recognised. He said it was quite impossible to work for Amin as he was so unpredictable, dangerously so, like a snake poising to strike.

Carruthers made weekly visits to Kampala from Nairobi. He didn't, strangely enough, feel threatened any more, although he maintained a low profile. The fact that his family was safe had calmed his nerves. He even spent some nights at his bungalow, and each time he visited he removed their personal possessions bit by bit.

On one of his visits to Kampala, Carruthers had stayed in a hotel in town as at that particular time he felt it was safer than staying in his house on his own.

Ugandan friends would visit him in his room, where they would have a beer together as it wasn't safe for them to be spotted by Amin's spies conversing with a white man in the street or in a public bar. People were really very scared. There was no law as such and prominent people continued to be abducted by soldiers, put in the boot of a car and never seen again.

It wasn't safe for Carruthers and Willi to visit Kampala together after they had fled. Once Willi went to visit her parents in Kampala and travelled by road from Nairobi by public transport. At the Uganda border she was nearly abducted by soldiers again when they found her British passport in her luggage. She must be a British spy, they said, and the money she was taking to her parents had to be used to bribe the soldiers to let her go on her way. She was very shaken by that incident. The Carruthers had wrongly assumed that a British passport would give added protection, but to illiterate soldiers such a passport meant only suspicion. She would have been better without it.

The staff in Carruthers' former Kampala office were now all Ugandan – they couldn't run away – as the Asians and Europeans had gone. They continued their jobs in very difficult circumstances. Often on their way home from the office they would be stopped by soldiers and robbed at army roadblocks. Rumours abounded and at the sound of any heavy gunfire, the office would suddenly be deserted as employees fled to their homes on the outskirts of the city. The staff was very much like a large family and tended to look after each other, which was very important in these trying times. Carruthers often wondered if the overseas shareholders of foreign-owned companies were ever really aware of the trials and tribulations suffered by staff in looking after the shareholders' interest.

The Chairman and his colleagues were very kind to Carruthers but the prospect of regular employment in the Nairobi office was slim. However, apart from Kampala, Carruthers was sent on business visits to Dar es Salaam, Lusaka and Addis Ababa.

As the prospect of employment in the Company's Nairobi office were so slim, Carruthers now realised that a Chairmanship in the East African company was not going to materialise. That was it. He didn't even have any savings, having invested everything in their houses in Uganda. He was assured by the Nairobi Chairman that a position would be found for him in one of the company's branches outside of East Africa. But not as Chairman, Carruthers realised.

Chapter 16

The End of an Era

When she had gone back to Kampala, Willi had been so happy to see her parents again, and they were equally pleased to see their daughter and grandchildren. But they were obviously depressed and worried about the current political situation and were not sure that it had been a good idea for them to return.

Willi was not quite sure either. She would have been happier remaining in Nairobi, but Carruthers had been insistent that they return to their own house in Kampala and said they must give it a try. He couldn't believe that things would not get better and thought that Amin wouldn't last. As far as her marriage was concerned, Willi was happy they were back living together but she was fearful for their safety.

Their journey back to Kampala had been a bit of a nightmare, she thought. That stupid white woman pretending to be Carruthers' wife and sitting in front with him in the car; and the rush to the hospital in Kampala with their delirious daughter, all the time the white woman bemoaning the fact that she was going to be late to see her brother.

Another white woman she had met after her return had also been a pain, a drunken pain. She was the wife of John's UK Chairman, who was on a visit. She acted as if she was the Queen of England, and Willi had been glad to see the back of her. Also her husband, her second husband by the way, who had been aloof and stand-offish. He had been particularly disdainful when Willi refused to eat a very bloody steak. Didn't he know that Africans generally did not eat raw meat? It hadn't helped, of course, that she had been heavily pregnant at the time.

Now Amin was kicking out the Asians and threatening to do the same to the British. She was British by marriage, and this frightened her. How were they going to cope, she wondered, if they were suddenly rounded up by soldiers? She had been terrified by the threatening soldiers who had chased after them in Kampala, and she actually thought John was going to cause an accident in his attempt to get his family safely into the centre of the city – which he had done, to be fair.

Yet Carruthers seemed to dismiss such incidents and continue on his merry way, going on safaris and dining with princesses. She noted that she hadn't been invited to dine with them. It was business, John said, and she sincerely hoped it wasn't funny business.

Then there was the puzzling incident of the Chairman's photographs and naked breasts. Although Carruthers put all the blame on the Chairman, she was sure he was closely involved, particularly as some of the photographs displayed her bras, which she had given to the mine MD's wife. And did he really think she was going to expose her breasts for a photograph? He shouldn't have even asked, stupid man.

She was worried that John might be losing interest in her. He kept staring at other women, and she had noticed that the lady sitting next to him at the pantomime seemed to know him, although John had denied this later. She would need to keep a close watch on him, if that was possible, she had decided.

But all these incidents seemed like trivialities now that they had been forced to leave Uganda more or less at the point of a gun and were back in Kenya again, though this time it seemed for good.

She had so looked forward to going to the party at her aunt's house and also attending the wedding of her cousin, almost a brother, to one of her old schoolmates the next day. The party had indeed been good fun and they had left in good spirits to return to the children, who had been left at home with their nanny, a very capable and trusted servant.

John was reasonably sober as they drove home around midnight through deserted streets. Because everything was so quiet Willi was able to spot the car that was obviously following them. It had picked them up, she thought, somewhere near the centre of town. She knew it had to be Amin's soldiers or spies. It couldn't be anyone else. Her heart pounding, she quickly communicated her fears to John and urged him to drive faster. He did so, but not dangerously, and still the car behind kept pace. A long straight stretch of road lay ahead and John remarked that if anything was going to happen, it would happen there. They were in a no-win situation, he said, as they would never outrun their pursuers and if they tried to, they would only anger their followers. Willi prepared to leap out of the car and run into the bush immediately if their car was stopped, which of course it was.

She was soon caught by an armed soldier as she fled into the bush. It was very dark and all she was conscious of was this man dragging her back towards the road. She was so shocked she couldn't even scream. However, she then started to fight like a wildcat and put up such a resistance that her clothes were torn off by the soldier, gun in one hand and the other hand tugging at her clothes. All of a sudden the soldier was no longer there. He had left her and run back to the car. Doors slammed, engines revved, tyres screeched and then there was silence. The lights of another car coming down the road illuminated where they had been stopped, but there was nothing there. No sign of John. She crouched trembling in the bush, completely naked.

Eventually she found her voice and shouted John's name. To her great relief he replied from the other side of the road and was soon by her side and giving her his shirt to cover herself.

They were both shaken and frightened. John was insistent they did not show themselves for some while, frightened that their attackers would come back. Willi was relieved as never before to see policemen when they eventually reached the police barracks, and they were so sympathetic when they learnt of their plight. It was even slightly amusing when she had to explain that she was not wearing a mini skirt but John's shirt.

John had forced her to drink two glasses of brandy when she got home by courtesy of the police. She had never drunk brandy before and she fell into a deep sleep, thoroughly exhausted. John, she knew, had not slept at all that night.

The next day was equally terrifying for Willi. It was reported that armed soldiers had begun a search of houses around where they had been attacked, and they were proceeding in the direction of their own house. Whether this was connected with last night's events was not known. Willi took the children to a far corner of the garden, where they sat on mats under a palm tree with their books and toys. Everything had to appear normal, John said, and if the soldiers came they should show no fear. Luckily this didn't happen, but nobody could smile that day or the days after.

Willi still couldn't believe that she was no longer safe in her own country. But she had feared something like that was going to happen, which somehow made it all the more dreadful. Thank God they hadn't been killed. They could so easily have been.

To add to the confusion in the country, some people, so-called 'guerrillas', were being publicly executed the day after they had been attacked. A reign of terror had been unleashed on the citizens of Uganda, and Willi was determined to get her family as far away as possible.

Willi knew John had now realised that it had been a mistake to bring them back from Nairobi and she could see remorse in his face. When he asked her if she wanted to leave the country and she nodded her head, frightened she would break down and cry and be unable to speak, he immediately agreed and started making plans for their departure. Once John made up his mind to do something, he did it.

The drive to Entebbe airport after saying goodbye to her parents was frightening. Willi was sure they were being followed but John kept assuring her it was not so, although he kept glancing behind, too.

Once they reached the airport, she thought they would never get past the queues of departing Asians, and when a security guard told her in Swahili, 'You are not going – *Wewe hapana kwenda*', her heart sank. John told her to ignore him.

Once they were on the plane Willi was able to relax a little, but she felt terribly sad. Carruthers was also miserable and kept glancing at her. They didn't know what the future held for them or where they would end up. At least they were together, she thought, as she looked lovingly at her children.

But another nightmare awaited Willi. Although news had been sent to Willi's sister that they were arriving to stay in their guest wing and no negative reply had been received, her sister and brother-in-law refused to let them in their house. They said that the Carruthers must be on Amin's hit list and that if they put them up, the Uganda Government would accuse them of complicity. Willi was shattered and broke down in front of her sister. What had she done, she wondered, to be turned away by her own family? Was there no end to this cruelty? First her father had thrown her out of the parental home because she wanted to marry a white man, and now her own sister was denying her.

Willi returned in tears to her family waiting in the car outside. Carruthers couldn't believe it. Then he got very angry and said they didn't need relations' help and they would look after themselves. They went to a hotel, got food and drinks organised for the kids, and then went to bed, completely drained. But Willi couldn't sleep. She still couldn't believe what had happened. What would John think of her, not being trusted by her own family? She cried all night, clutching her rosary.

The light of day cheered up Willi a bit, and with John assuring her everything was going to work out, she felt a bit more positive.

When friends came to their assistance, life soon became more meaningful. There were also prospects of a job for John in Nigeria with the same company, and Willi felt that would be a good move – although John wasn't so sure. Her feeling was that she didn't want to live in a country close to Uganda, as she would always feel unsafe. And to hell with relations!

Chapter 17

White Mischief

Carruthers was on another business visit to Tanzania, and he remembered his last sojourn in Dar es Salaam as he rode in the taxi from the airport to the city. That had been rather a hectic visit, which he was sure, would not be repeated, especially as he would be staying in the company branch manager's flat who was returning from a visit to the UK the next day. The flat was in a large block overlooking the ocean. Thank goodness there was air-conditioning, thought Carruthers, as he slipped into his host's dressing gown after taking a cold shower in the empty flat.

He was bending down cutting his toenails with his back to the door when he heard the door click open and a female voice he knew well say in a surprised tone, 'Binky, you rotter, you didn't tell me you'd be back today. I thought you said tomorrow.'

It was his ex-girlfriend, who assumed he was Binky, the branch manager, with whom she must be having an affair.

Carruthers froze *in situ*, so to speak. His ex-girlfriend let out a shriek of shock as, throwing her arms around him, she realised it wasn't her Binky.

'Oh it's you! My God!' she screamed as she saw his face. 'Binky never mentioned you were coming to visit him. Let's celebrate – champagne, champagne.'

She was on a visit from upcountry to do some shopping, leaving her husband behind on his sisal estate. She had first met her Binky at the yacht club, then one thing had led to another, she said, and she had heard all about Carruthers' escapades from him.

Carruthers mischievously asked how her teeth were, as she may remember, he said, that last time they met in Dar she had injured herself trying to mount him! She laughed, and he could see they were perfect. Almost too perfect, he thought.

Evidently when Carruthers had left her lying on the floor beside the hotel bed on which her husband was snoring, she found she could hardly move. Because of his snoring, her husband couldn't hear her pleas for help, so she had managed to whip him awake, using the whip which was lying beside the bed. On wakening, her husband had peered over the side of the bed and thought he was seeing a bloodstained ghost leering up at him. He had panicked and, jumping from the bed, fled into the hotel corridor, where he bumped into a hotel servant and gabbled his story. They both went back into the bedroom, where the husband was then able to recognise his wife and, with the help of the servant, lift her onto the bed.

The servant wondered if she had been attacked and whether he should call the police – he remembered the naked man loping along the corridor. But she assured him that she had passed out crawling back to bed. Her husband, whether he believed that or not, had decided to let sleeping dogs lie.

'What a life, there's always something happening,' his ex-girlfriend said as she slid her hand under Binky's dressing gown. 'You seem to have grown a bit since we were together,' she remarked. 'Let me show you the way to heaven.'

She removed her three top front teeth and moistened her lips.

'You wee hussy,' groaned Carruthers.

After that experience, Carruthers felt the need of a good hot curry and some cold beers, which they soon found at a nearby Indian restaurant. Prawn masala with chapattis and no rice was an excellent pick-me-up.

Binky seemed quite amused when, early the next morning and straight from the airport, he found them together in his double bed.

'I suspected you two might bump into each other. Is she still a good lay, Carruthers?' he leered. 'All I can say is that you trained her very well, the little whore.'

'Oh, Binky, you say the nicest things,' she said as she kicked him playfully in the crotch.

Carruthers thought he had better get out of there before he got caught in a threesome, so he leapt out of bed and headed for the shower. After dressing, he shouted, 'Enjoy yourselves! See you in the office, Binky old boy,' and went downstairs to catch a taxi. He had stressed the 'old boy' as Binky must have been at least ten or more years older than him.

Binky reappeared a couple of hours later and they managed to finish the business that Carruthers had come to do.

'You're a dark horse,' he said to Carruthers over lunch. 'How did you get into whips and all that?'

Carruthers assured him that the use of whips and all that had been taken to extremes by his ex-girlfriend and it wasn't his usual *modus operandi*. In fact, he considered it dangerous. Binky scratched his back thoughtfully.

From Dar es Salaam Carruthers flew on to Lusaka in Zambia. He was just in time to join the party to celebrate the arrival of the local branch manager's new son. More champagne. Luckily he was staying in the branch manager's house and wouldn't get into trouble. In fact, only two incidents happened, both involving urine.

During the party – which was all male, the wife still being in hospital – one of the guests, growing tired of standing in the queue for the toilet, relieved himself into the large metal drum containing iced beers, much to the amusement and cheers of all present. People still kept drinking the floating beers and said it added to the flavour – a bit like putting salt on the back of one's hand before downing a tequila, Carruthers thought.

The second incident happened after the party was over and sometime in the middle of the night. Carruthers had consumed quite a number of beers and had to get out of bed to relieve himself. Being in a strange house, Carruthers had difficulty finding the light switches and the bathroom. He eventually gave up and staggered back to the bedroom. All he could do was open the window and stand on the inside windowsill while he relieved himself. It was totally dark so he couldn't see outside, and conversely nobody from outside could see him. The only outcome of that incident was the remark made by his host the next morning that he thought there had been a shower of rain during the early morning. A smelly shower, Carruthers thought.

Back in Nairobi, Carruthers prepared his company reports at home – Willi's sister's flat. It wasn't safe to do this in the office as the immigration authorities had a habit of making physical checks that expatriates had work permits, and Carruthers and family were really in transit while the company tried to find him a job in one of the countries in Africa where they had offices.

The company was thinking of opening an office in Addis Ababa, and that was where Carruthers was sent on his next business visit. Addis was high – 8,000 feet – and it took a bit of acclimatising. One got out of breath quickly, especially if you had a beautiful Ethiopian girl above or below you. Carruthers was proudly shown round the red light district by an Ethiopian business contact who was dressed in a beautiful overcoat with an astrakhan collar – it was cold there at nights. Many of the bars or clubs were private houses where drinks and girls would suddenly appear whenever a client entered.

Carruthers visited the local gold market and bought Willi a pair of gold earrings and a gold necklace. The quality of the Ethiopian gold and design were excellent. He also bought himself some electrical goods at a huge duty-free shop in a converted hangar at the airport. The shop was named King Solomon's and it was packed full of everything imaginable, including motor vehicles. Of course, the city was full of diplomats, being the headquarters of the Organisation of African Unity. That was probably why there was such a thriving red light district, Carruthers thought.

It was ironical that the magnificent building specially built to house the headquarters of the OAU was situated in the capital city of a country ruled by an Emperor, when many of the leaders of the member countries were outright socialists, if not communists, bitterly opposed to monarchies.

The company had a member of staff, a young expatriate, working in Addis seconded to a local company. Carruthers was pleased that his colleague had been so well accepted by the executives of the local company and also by the local girls, who were quite beautiful. Visiting his colleague's small flat one late afternoon on his way back to his hotel, he was offered tea or beer and chose the latter. His colleague, while very cheerful, also seemed a little uneasy, especially when Carruthers decided on a second beer. Carruthers was aware, as he sat sipping his beer, of sounds of movement from within the wardrobe of the bed-sitter. He looked questioningly as his young colleague opened the wardrobe door to reveal a gorgeous scantily-clad Ethiopian girl, who nimbly stepped out, flashed him a grin and headed for the bathroom.

'You lucky blighter,' Carruthers gasped, downing the remainder of his beer in one go. Does she have a sister, he wondered aloud? The reply was affirmative, but nothing could be arranged in the short time left of Carruthers' visit. (He later found out that the girl was a university student who often visited a relation in the block, and his colleague had gained her confidence on these visits, leading to a love affair.)

Carruthers was meeting some business colleagues that evening for dinner at The Cottage Restaurant, a local hostelry where one could get draught Amstel beer. Quite a bit of it was consumed, and the effect of the beer and the altitude convinced Carruthers that he should have an early night, which he duly did. Halfway through the night, he woke up feeling sick, combined with imminent diarrhoea, and rushed for the bathroom. He had no control over either end of his body, so he decided to sit in the bath and let it all come out. It proved very practical, but what a mess. Carruthers felt quite shattered and was glad he was alone. He did, of course, clean up the mess, which was a gruesome task.

He awakened to the sound of cracking whips. Oh God, not again, he thought, but he was quite safe. His hotel bedroom overlooked the Emperor's stables where his horses were being exercised, so he was able to survey this equine scene as he worked his way through the continental breakfast that had been delivered to his room. Not a bad job being an Emperor, Carruthers thought. He remembered that the Emperor's son, the Crown Prince, regularly used to visit Kampala, where he could be seen dining in the Grand Hotel. An expatriate friend of Carruthers told him that he had once been sitting at the side of the road outside the capital having a picnic when the Emperor passed in his Rolls Royce, stopped and had a chat to him. The Emperor was evidently a very approachable man, and he had even hosted Idi Amin amongst other heads of state when they visited Ethiopia for a conference. (Perhaps he was *too* approachable, because he was eventually overthrown and murdered by a gang of army thugs masquerading as communists who, like Amin, went begging to the Russians for assistance and unfortunately received it.)

Carruthers left that morning with a promise from his colleague that suitable arrangements would be made for his next visit. The Ethiopian Airlines flight, one of the best if not *the* best airline in Africa, arrived on time in Nairobi, where Carruthers was told of a possible transfer to one of his company's offices in West Africa.

The prospect of returning to work in Uganda in the near future was out of the question because of political events. In fact the company had withdrawn all its expatriates from Uganda, and Carruthers had been given the task of persuading and eventually ordering the last of them to leave. The place was just not safe. (To their credit, the local staff, under the directorship of their Ugandan managing director, were to keep the office running as a going concern during all the years of turmoil that were to follow.)

Carruthers was now asked by his Nairobi Chairman to visit the Chairman of their West African operation in Lagos – who was based in London – to discuss a position which, all things being equal, would be offered to him. Carruthers wondered if his new Chairman, assuming he accepted the job, would be such a handful as the one he had come to know so well in East Africa. He seemed to spend most of his working time meeting with Chairmen of the various companies in his Group, he thought, and yet he, the one that deserved to be a Chairman, had never attained that position. Perhaps there was more to being a Chairman than he thought.

His East African Chairman had decided to retire and go to live on the Kenya coast at Malindi. He intended to spend his time deep-sea fishing, and his wife would still be able to visit Nairobi to keep an eye on her stable. He told Carruthers he had had his fill of Uganda – in more ways than one, Carruthers thought – and didn't intend ever to return there. There was already a successor in the Nairobi office, a long-time expatriate business partner of the Chairman.

Carruthers and Willi discussed the future. He knew little about Nigeria except that it was very hot and noisy with a huge population, a very big difference to the temperate climate and wide-open spaces of East Africa where he had been so happy. To his surprise, Willi was keen to go. She had been so upset about what had happened to her in Uganda that she would be happy to be far away, although still in Africa, and see a new country.

At Heathrow airport, Carruthers was met by the West African Chairman's driver and Jaguar car and was whisked off to Northampton, where the Chairman was presiding over a company conference and where Carruthers would spend a couple of nights. He already knew some of the people participating in the conference so he didn't feel out of place.

The type of job and terms of service were all explained to Carruthers and he was happy enough to accept, especially as the salary was much more attractive than he had been receiving in East Africa (although he would find out that the living conditions and quality of life were not nearly so attractive). In the colonial days it was common for senior civil servants to be transferred from East to West Africa as they neared retirement so that they would get a pension based on a higher final salary.

He flew back to Nairobi from London via Lagos as he had been given the opportunity by the Chairman to look at the place, and if he wasn't happy he could withdraw his acceptance of the job offer. The expatriate MD of the West African company, who was on his way back to Lagos from his biannual leave in the UK, accompanied him.

Browsing though the glossy airline magazine on their way over the Alps en route to Lagos, Carruthers was astonished to see a photograph he recognised, with details and pictures of a photographic exhibition which was being held in Amsterdam. The photograph was entitled *Before and After*, and showed two shots mounted within one frame. The top photograph showed a bra-covered pair of breasts, while the lower photograph showed the naked breasts only. These were undoubtedly the photographs of the mine MD's wife. The caption said the exhibitor wished to remain anonymous, but the press had shown such interest that there was a search to find out the owner and bearer of such luscious breasts. His new MD didn't believe him when he pointed to the magazine and remarked that he knew whose breasts they were. All he said, rather crudely, Carruthers thought, was 'I wouldn't mind getting my kissing gear round those.'

Carruthers gathered a few copies of the airline magazine to take with him to Nairobi. He was sure Willi and the Chairman would be amazed. And he idly wondered if he could sell his information to the press.

Lagos was hot, sticky and very humid. His glasses, which he sometimes wore, steamed up the minute he set foot outside the aircraft. He spent a couple of days meeting people and being convinced by the MD what a wonderful posting it was. It was a much bigger and more opportunistic business environment than Carruthers had been used to and he thought he would relish the challenge. He therefore didn't change his mind on the job offer he had tentatively accepted. Initially he would understudy the Managing Director of the Nigerian company and take over in about a year's time when the MD returned to London. Still no promise of a Chairmanship.

Back in Nairobi, he apprised Willi of his visit and said that apart from the heat he was sure they would all settle into their new environment quite well. Schools were available for their kids, although their secondary education would probably have to be in UK boarding schools. However, the company would help with school fees. They would leave for Lagos in a couple of weeks' time.

Willi was highly amused at the photograph in the airline magazine. She thought, as she had before, that it could be worthwhile approaching the bra makers and if they were interested in using it as an advert, she could negotiate the purchase of the photograph, after obtaining permission of the lady in question. All for a fee, of course, and she might also negotiate a good commission from the mine MD's wife. Of course the *Before* and *After* photographs would have to be reversed for a bra advert. It would be up to Carruthers to make contact with the MD, who had the negatives, as he had his contact address.

The Chairman was astonished to see the photograph in the magazine, which Carruthers showed to him, especially as he had thought that it was only his wife who had the photographs. Could his wife be the exhibitor, the Chairman wondered aloud? Carruthers said he was as puzzled as he was. The Chairman had told the mine MD when he passed through Nairobi on his last visit that the photographs hadn't turned out, and the MD had feigned great annoyance. He must have taken a new set, the Chairman mentioned enviously. He asked Carruthers if he could keep the magazine, to which Carruthers readily agreed.

In the end the idea of using these particular photographs for a bra advert didn't work out. As the bra manufacturers pointed out, the photographs should show benefits of their bras to sagging breasts and not the pert, ice-induced ones shown in the magazine. However, they were grateful for Willi's continued interest and her suggestions and sent her a handsome cheque, with which both Willi and Carruthers were delighted.

Carruthers was now hot on the scent of more money, and he made contact with the *News of the World* in London, asking if they would pay for information on the breast photographs that were making so much publicity. Two days later, a *News of the World* photographer and a reporter arrived in Nairobi.

Carruthers hadn't wanted things to go so far, and thought the newspaper would eventually be satisfied with the contact address of the mine MD. However, the newspaper sensed a good scandalous story, especially as the source came from East Africa and more particularly Nairobi, the former headquarters of 'white mischief'.

When the newspaper people contacted Carruthers and discussed terms with him for information, he was adamant that all he could provide was the name of the owner of the photographs. He proved he was a reliable source by producing copies of the photographs which he had kept when he had the film developed.

However, as fate would have it, and as often happens in the newspaper world, a remark overheard by the reporter led him down another route and on the trail of the Chairman.

The reporter had been taken by a Nairobi newspaper friend to the Muthaiga Club for lunch and, being typical journalists, they decided to make it a liquid lunch. In the men's bar there was the usual convivial lunchtime crowd, amongst who was the Chairman. Someone in his group had mentioned the photograph in the airline magazine and asked whether anyone had seen it, and the Chairman, full of pink gin, bellowed out, 'Seen it? Who the hell do you think took it? Me!'

There was great laughter all round, but his cronies didn't believe him. However, the reporter decided to follow the matter up with Carruthers.

He told Carruthers that the Chairman, who was a friend of his colleague, had told him that he had taken the photograph. Now, said the reporter, he was giving Carruthers the first opportunity, for a substantial sum of money, to reveal all. If not, he would make a similar offer to the Chairman and Carruthers would be sidelined.

The temptation was too great. Carruthers did reveal all, giving the reporter the name and address of the mine MD, the Nairobi address of the Chairman and details of where the photographs were taken. He reckoned that as he was leaving East Africa soon and the Chairman had already retired and would move to Malindi, there was no great harm being done. However, he insisted that his own name should not appear and advised the reporter not to talk to the Chairman as he had friends in high places who could make it awkward for him.

The following day, the Chairman noticed a photographer taking pictures through the gate of his house when he happened to be with his wife in their garden. His house was next to the Muthaiga Club, and as tourists often hung around taking photographs of the club where the white settlers had partied in the old colonial days, he thought nothing of it. He merely muttered under his breath, 'Oh, fuck off!' and gave two fingers, all duly recorded on film.

The issue of the *News of the World* the following Sunday bore the headline WHITE MISCHIEF AT MOUNTAINS OF THE MOON. Photographs of the mountains, the Muthaiga Club, the Chairman's Nairobi house and of the Chairman and his wife all appeared alongside the bra photographs. The article gave details of the Chairman, saying he had actually taken the photographs, and promised that in their next Sunday issue they would reveal whose breasts they were, with details from the lady in question of the circumstances in which the photographs were taken. Money had already been promised to the former mine MD and his wife by the newspaper and their cooperation was assured.

As the British Sunday newspapers didn't reach Nairobi until the Monday, it wasn't until the late afternoon that the Chairman was phoned by a friend, saying, 'I see you've made the front page of the *News of the World*, old boy.'

The Chairman putting on dark glasses and pulling a

hat over his eyes, rushed in his car to the nearest bookshop where he knew he could buy the newspaper which was one he didn't usually read. He was deeply shocked. His wife, who had been at the stables and picked up the story from so-called sympathetic friends, was almost suicidal. Already the local journalists were phoning and some gathering at the gate of their house.

Typically, it was the lady of the house who after a few stiff brandies refused to panic any further and decreed they must leave that very night for their house at the coast. Even if it was dangerous driving at night, it was essential to get away. She couldn't bear to face anyone, she said, and her husband silently agreed.

Only a few close friends knew where they were by the time the next edition of the newspaper came out. The headline this time was OWNER OF BOOBS REVEALS ALL. A photograph of the mine MD's wife in a swimming costume appeared, along with one of the MD and his wife smiling together fully clothed; he was wearing a miner's hat. The article was not really detrimental to the Chairman and mentioned that in far-flung outposts of the former Empire people had to make their own amusements, which sometimes included wild parties.

However, the article ended by mysteriously saying that further revelations might be made in future editions after further ongoing investigations by their reporter. 'Is this the tip of an iceberg?' said the article, referring not to the breasts but to the further investigations.

The Chairman had made no contact with Carruthers, assuming that it was the mine MD who had spilled the beans. He hoped the further investigations didn't involve those pornographic photographs which the MD had salivated over and which he said had been burnt in a fire. The Chairman was in a very nervous state and his local grocery was doing a good trade in Gordon's gin.

His wife refused to speak to him and seemed to be weeping most of the time.

What Carruthers and the Chairman didn't know was that the wife of the Chairman's lawyer friend and Carruthers' one-time mistress had, on reading the newspaper articles, approached the *News of the World* with the titillating news that she had a photograph which the newspaper might like to see. It showed the Chairman and some unknown lady in a compromising situation. She was sure she wouldn't be recognised because she had managed to find a clever photographer who had made a negative out of the photograph and airbrushed out the tell-tale birthmark on her left buttock.

'Got you, you bastard,' she said to herself.

So it was that in the next edition of the Sunday newspaper, the third in a row, headed MORE WHITE MISCHIEF AND CHAIRMAN'S NAUGHTY ANTICS, the latest photograph was shown. Carruthers realised that the lawyer's wife, being typically sentimental, had not destroyed all the photographs of her and the Chairman.

The Muthaiga Club was now querying the Chairman's continued membership, and the Government wondered why this deviant expatriate should be allowed to live in their country. The Chairman's wife was asked to move her horses elsewhere. It was thought she was the lady in the latest published photograph because a horsewhip was lying beside the handcuffs on the floor.

Nothing more was ever heard of the Chairman and his wife, although it was rumoured that she had gone to live with some distant relations in Albania. On his part, the Chairman loaded his fishing boat with some provisions and personal possessions and as many bottles of gin as he could safely carry and headed out into the Indian Ocean, where he was said to be living alone on some solitary island.

As for Carruthers and family, they were already on their way to Lagos, when the third edition of the newspaper appeared. It was the ideal time for them to be leaving, especially as neither their names nor any suggestion of their existence had appeared in any of the articles. They were off to start afresh, and Carruthers hoped he would keep out of trouble in his new posting. That, however, would prove to be an impossible task.

The whole family's excitement at going to a new country was, of course, tinged with sadness at leaving their home behind, and their relatives, who would continue to suffer in Uganda under two brutal regimes.

On the money front things were a bit rosier. The money from the newspaper swelled the Carruthers' almost depleted UK bank account and the money he would earn in Nigeria would swell it even more. In a way that would make up for his disappointment at not being a Chairman, which, nevertheless, was still his goal.

Chapter 18

Going West

In May 1973 Nigeria was certainly a different kettle of fish from Uganda and East Africa in general. It was extremely hot and humid, a complete contrast to the temperate inland climate of Uganda, and initially Carruthers and family thought they would never get used to the humidity. Sweat poured from them whenever they moved or sat outside the air-conditioned houses, offices and cars. Generally houses were big but gardens small, and anyway it was too hot and humid to enjoy big gardens.

They really missed East Africa and were quite homesick. However, as time went on they became used to the climate and began to enjoy the hustle and bustle of Lagos life. There were so many people and so much was happening in the streets of Lagos, with hawkers selling everything from plastic combs to the latest films and videos. Smuggling was rife and street markets sold all the latest electronic goods from radios to refrigerators. During the day, Lagos streets were all crowded and noisy, and pickpockets abounded.

Smuggled booze was cheap and could be bought from Nigerian smugglers who visited offices and homes, bottles hidden in special pockets sewn inside their flowing robes. Up to 20 bottles of spirits could be accommodated, a travelling Aladdin's cave of booze on display.

As Lagos was on the coast, the main weekend leisure activity was going to the beach. Luckily, the company owned a motorboat that would take the family some miles through the Lagos creeks to beaches bordering the Atlantic Ocean. A beach hut had been constructed from local materials, palm fronds and the like, to provide shade from the scorching sun, and they got into the routine of going to the beach most weekends, leaving from the local boat club, where they had become members. Carruthers in fact became secretary of the club for some years.

It was certainly much easier negotiating the Lagos creeks by boat than negotiating the traffic on dry land. Driving in Lagos was a nightmare. This was caused by the sheer volume of traffic attempting to get onto Lagos Island, the business centre of Nigeria as well as the seat of government, where only two bridges provided access. (Later, more bridges would be built.) Such was the traffic problem that Government decreed that only vehicles with an even first digit on the number plate could enter Lagos Island on certain days, and those with an odd first digit on other days.

This solved the traffic problem for a couple of weeks only. Wealthy Nigerians and companies met the challenge by buying extra cars so that they owned one even-numbered and one odd-numbered car. Where wives worked and had their own transport, the result was that households had four cars parked in their driveways. Car sales rocketed. Nobody bothered to think that the whole exercise could have been controlled through the licence numbering authority. That would have been too easy, and corruption being rife, there had probably been some collusion between the government ministry involved and the representatives of the car industry.

Traffic policemen, clothed in their dark yellow uniforms

and nicknamed the 'yellow peril', certainly benefited by soliciting bribes from car owners who either forgot abut the new regulation or just got the days mixed up. It was all good but frustrating fun.

The expatriate community where the Carruthers lived in Lagos was quite sizeable, which suited them just fine. Soon they made some good friends and started enjoying the very good social life in Lagos, which centred on the Boat Club, private parties and Lebanese owned restaurants and nightclubs. The Lebanese were the wheeler-dealers of the expatriate business community and socially they integrated well with all other communities. (Years later, they would lose some of their influence to Indians moving in to purchase and set up businesses, who sadly would not be inclined to mix socially to the same extent as the Lebanese.)

Willi enjoyed living in their particular area in Lagos. It was completely cosmopolitan, unlike certain parts dominated by Brits. They had good Scandinavian, Brazilian, English and French friends. Willi zoomed about in her new Austin Mini (bought according to today's prices for a ridiculously low sum). Soon after she got it, however, she had the misfortune to sideswipe a Nigerian man who was languidly crossing the road in front of her. He wasn't knocked down, but he pursued her into the driveway of a nearby house where she was going to visit a Swedish friend. Nigerians took maximum advantage of such incidents, especially if a foreigner was involved, but Willi's Swedish friend took charge of the situation. The man claimed he was a footballer and that his future prospects had been affected. In actual fact, it was only his elbow that had been hit, and he had probably instigated the incident. He was taken to the doctor, who pronounced no serious damage, and Willi gave him some cash in compensation. For weeks afterwards he kept turning up demanding money, until Carruthers paid him a final sum and got him to sign a disclaimer. Getting authorities such as police involved in such incidents was not recommended as the money demanded would be even higher.

Carruthers found the business environment challenging and stimulating. The Nigerian businessman was tough and was capable of all sorts of tricks in order to compete and retain or gain business. Early on, Carruthers was arrested by the CID and taken to their headquarters. Sitting in an air-conditioned office with piped music playing, he was informed by the CID officer that a Lagos businessman had complained that he was working in the country illegally and stealing his business. Fortunately, Carruthers' papers were all in order, and he heard nothing further on the matter. If that had been Uganda under Idi Amin, Carruthers thought, he would simply have been bumped off or deported.

Willi and the kids eventually settled in well. Despite the Lagos traffic, having her own car gave her the opportunity to get out and about, especially when Carruthers had to travel upcountry, which would become a regular feature of his business life.

From age ten the children would go to England to attend boarding schools. In the meantime, however, they attended local British-run schools supported by the British business community. Carruthers at one stage became the chairman of the newly formed parent/teachers association. He was Chairman! Not, however, a company Chairman and so he mentally discarded that title.

Willi had been pregnant when they arrived in Lagos, and gave birth painlessly to a daughter. Typically, Carruthers was not around when the waters broke, being stuck in a traffic jam, and Willi had to beg a lift from an expatriate neighbour to get to the hospital.

Traffic jams were always a problem and the next and final time Willi was pregnant, her doctor recommended she be admitted a day or two prior to the birth and he would induce the baby. This was duly done, and another hassle-free delivery of another girl took place. The total was now three girls and two boys, and Willi and Carruthers decided to call a halt.

The birth of Willi's last child coincided with a visit to Lagos of the Chairman of the Nigerian company from London. As we have seen, Carruthers' relationship with chairmen was ambivalent. On the one hand he had to give them the respect they deserved as his superiors, but on the other hand their behaviour at times didn't warrant such respect, especially when they came without their wives.

The visiting Chairman was used to staying at the company bungalow occupied by the Carruthers. He had been responsible for buying the property some years ago and was very proud of his acquisition. (Carruthers would eventually install a swimming pool in the garden to enhance its value and provide amusement for the kids and exercise for himself. Willi had taken up tennis, while he had found it too hot for golf and he never had time anyway.)

Carruthers set off for the airport to meet the Chairman, who, coincidentally, knew Carruthers' former East African Chairman and had once spent a week with him at his house in Malindi. He had been meant to visit Uganda after that Malindi visit on his way back to England, and Carruthers had gone to Entebbe to meet him, but he had never got off the aeroplane. Evidently both chairmen had spent the week in Malindi accompanied by a couple of East African Airways hostesses, and the visiting Chairman was so exhausted he had slept through the stopover at Entebbe and gone straight on to London, no doubt well ministered to by one of the hostesses.

It was therefore with some trepidation that Carruthers waited outside the doors of the immigration and customs hall. There were windows to each side of the doors, and he was able to spot his Chairman, whom he had met briefly on a couple of occasions in England, passing into the customs hall and lowering himself into a chair. His luggage was collected for him by a baggage handler and placed beside him. Carruthers was thankful that everything was happening quite quickly as Lagos airport was famed for its hold-ups.

Half an hour later, a now anxious Carruthers saw his Chairman get up and walk about slowly then resume his seat. It occurred to him that the Chairman had probably imbibed heavily on the flight and wasn't sure of his whereabouts, and this in fact was what had happened – as he later found out. While he was waiting, a client and friend of the Chairman, who was also meeting someone, chatted away to Carruthers.

An hour later the Chairman suddenly rose and headed towards the exit. Carruthers braced himself. To his astonishment the Chairman walked straight past him, marched up to the client, extended his hand and said, 'How very nice of you to come and meet me.'

Smilingly, the client turned him around and pointed him in Carruthers' direction. It was all very embarrassing. On the journey home the Chairman remarked that he had met a friend on the flight who worked in Lagos and that they had both had one too many. He had waited for his friend in the customs hall, but he hadn't shown up.

Carruthers learnt later that the Chairman's friend's entry permit was out of date and the immigration official had demanded some payment to let him through. The friend had refused and drunkenly walked back to the aircraft, where he seated himself and refused to move. Eventually two armed soldiers had come on board, forcibly removed him, frog-marched him through the customs hall and unceremoniously thrown him officially into Nigeria without going through immigration. By then, Carruthers and his Chairman were on the way home.

Willi, of course, was still in hospital when they arrived at the Lagos bungalow, and the Chairman was anxious to renew his acquaintance with the steward who had worked at the bungalow for many years, but there was no sign of him either.

'Where's James, where's James?' complained the Chairman.

To which Carruthers rather guiltily replied, 'I sacked him. He stole some of our things.' That in fact was true, although sad, but something that had to be done. This often happened when there was a change of guard.

The Chairman was distraught and Carruthers had the feeling he didn't believe him. After a few nightcaps they both retired for the night.

In the morning the Chairman had sobered up and it was business as usual. A board meeting had to be prepared for the next day, and there was a luncheon with clients etc. Lunch was at a Chinese restaurant, of which there were many in Lagos and indeed all over Nigeria. These were mainly Nigerian-owned, often in partnership with the Chinese who came in to conduct other business, such as textiles, casinos and money-laundering. As the Chinese chefs could not come into the country as chefs under the immigration laws, they were often brought in in the guise of engineers for the textile factories.

On his return to the office Carruthers learnt that Willi had given birth to a baby girl, and the Chairman decreed that after visiting Willi in hospital they would celebrate the birth in style with a champagne dinner.
Willi sitting up in bed, baby at breast, looked radiant. The Chairman's eyes, Carruthers thought, rested longer on the bared breast than on the baby, and his moustache quivered in anticipation as if expecting his turn at the fountain of milk. Carruthers' thoughts wandered as he remembered how Willi used to have, and perhaps still did, a baby-feeding bra where a patch of the bra when pulled away revealed an erect nipple. Such possibilities, Carruthers thought... Then he wondered how the mine MD's wife was coping after all that publicity.

After leaving Willi at the hospital, Carruthers and the Chairman returned to the bungalow for a shower and change of clothes and a couple of drinks. They decided to visit a local club and then go on to a popular Lebanese restaurant. The club was a members' only club and was really a colonial legacy, although membership had always been open to whites and blacks alike. Before being admitted, one had to be interviewed by the Chairman of the club and his committee, but it was really a waste of time as all types of rogues and vagabonds seemed to be members. Carruthers' Chairman referred to it as the workingmen's club. They had gone there instead of the more upmarket Boat Club, where they would never have left because too many friends would have insisted on buying drinks. Under the Boat Club's chit system, with payment at the end of the month, it was all too easy to buy a round of drinks for everyone at the bar, which of course was regularly reciprocated, and before long one could be legless. Luckily, breathalysers were unknown in Nigeria.

Carruthers had already booked a table for two at the

Lebanese restaurant in the centre of town. It was as usual very busy and very friendly. The Chairman bought a bottle of champagne. Eventually they were the last diners left, apart from a group of about 20 Lebanese celebrating some event. The Lebanese loved a good party, and also their Scotch whisky. Carruthers and his Chairman were asked to join the group when they heard of the new baby, and one thing led to another. Through an alcoholic haze Carruthers saw his Chairman dancing on top of the bar with a very beautiful Lebanese girl, the coloured lights hanging above the bar swinging wildly as the two dancers banged into them. The girl's boyfriend or husband, who was becoming exceedingly jealous, was being restrained by his companions. It was a really wild evening and Carruthers sought to attract his Chairman's attention and get him to come down from the bar. But the girl kept him and the lights swinging to the music. Eventually they tired and climbed down, and Carruthers quickly hustled his Chairman out of the restaurant, promising the owner to return and pay the bill the next day. There was real danger of a fight, and as they left there was a slanging match going on between the girl and her partner.

The following day was the board meeting and they were on their best behaviour. The board was composed of Nigerian chiefs, professors, *alhajis* (Muslim gentlemen who have been to Mecca) and the heir to the throne of Benin. The meeting was very formal and uneventful, and it was agreed that those who were available would all meet for lunch at a Chinese restaurant. Uneventful though the Board meeting was, there was one embarrassing moment when Carruthers' thoughts turned away from the meeting and to Willi and her breastfeeding. The meeting had suddenly gone silent and all his fellow directors were looking at him. He had no other course but to apologise and ask the Chairman to repeat his question which he had missed. His stumbled reply was met with some amusement.

The Chairman was proud of the fact that he had secured the most prestigious private room in the restaurant. When one of the Nigerian directors commented upon this, the Chairman explained he had bribed the manager of the restaurant quite heavily. After a pregnant pause the director said that he found that quite interesting, especially as he had recently been appointed by the Government as Chairman of an anti-corruption committee. He wasn't joking. The Chairman didn't comment and busied himself with his chopsticks. That reminded Carruthers of a colleague who had given money to a tout at the airport in an effort to obtain his boarding pass quickly. Then the 'tout' had announced that in fact he was an undercover policeman checking on touts and their activities at the airport. But the money was not returned.

One of the company's local directors was an Emir from a kingdom in the north of Nigeria. The Chairman had ensured that a cross-section of local dignitaries representing different ethnic groups were on the board of the company, and this had proved to be a very useful contribution to the company's activities, especially during political instability and army coups. Carruthers first met the Emir when he had newly arrived from East Africa and was sitting in his office on a Saturday morning with the door open. He noticed a Nigerian gentleman with robes and cap at the reception area, and thinking he was a smuggler or something he beckoned the Emir in a somewhat imperious manner to join him in his office. To his shock, the Emir introduced himself and said he had come to collect his director's fees before returning to the North. Carruthers made appropriate apologies for not recognising him, but the Emir was very gracious and kind and they soon struck up a rapport.

Another director was the heir to the ancient throne of Benin and currently a highly placed civil servant. (He would remain a director even when he assumed the title after his father died, and Carruthers would make visits to his Palace in Benin, where in the reception room pride of place on one of the walls was given to a picture of his father playing snooker.) During the day, as a civil servant, he wore a smart business suit probably bought in Savile Row instead of the long robes of rich material and beautifully embroidered that were the traditional dress in most of Nigeria, particularly in the north of the country. If one was used to seeing someone regularly wearing robes and cap, it was often difficult to recognise the same person in a suit. Conversely, the same difficulty arose when someone donned robes and cap instead of his usual business suit.

One of the expatriate wives of a colleague of Carruthers' had spent a lot of time at a company Christmas party dancing with a Nigerian gentleman dressed in flowing robes who looked so distinguished she didn't like to refuse his invitations. It was only after a few of these dances that she realised the gentleman with whom she had been dancing was the night guard from her house. They all had a good laugh about that, and the husband was warned to check up what night guard duties the chap was actually doing.

Another of Carruthers' colleagues had gone to visit a prominent Nigerian director from the North who was staying at a Lagos hotel, to interest him in some shares the company was selling. He hadn't met him before. Sitting in the hotel room, the colleague took the businessman dressed in his flowing robes through the company prospectus, extolling the future prospects of the company. After some 20 minutes, no response was forthcoming from the Nigerian businessman. It turned out that he was a common trader who spoke no English but shared the same name as the director. Fuming, Carruthers' colleague, feeling an utter idiot, left the room to seek out the proper businessman.

In the evening the Chairman and Carruthers had been invited by close friends who lived a few houses down the road from the bungalow. He was the general manager of an international brewery, so there was plenty of beer flowing. It was a very relaxed evening and there were many friends and clients present. Willi was still in hospital, so unfortunately she wasn't there to keep her eye on her husband and his Chairman.

At one stage in the evening some of the men organised a weight-guessing competition where everyone had to accurately guess their own weight. A set of scales was used to check the accuracy. Carruthers didn't take part but was made well aware of his Chairman's participation by the sound of shouting from the corner of the room where the scales were. To try and prove that he had guessed his own weight correctly, the Chairman had taken off his shoes, socks and his trousers. The problem was that he wore no underwear and his manliness was exposed to everyone, including the ladies, who looked on in shock. Their hostess left the room in anger. Again Carruthers had to get his Chairman away from the scene of the crime quickly and they both staggered up the road to the bungalow.

In the morning the Chairman couldn't remember the events of the previous evening and was severely embarrassed when told. Their hostess had phoned to say that she would never speak to the Chairman again. However, Carruthers was sure she would eventually relent and he persuaded the Chairman to buy her a bottle of champagne and a large bunch of flowers. These gifts were presented to her that afternoon before the Chairman left for the airport, and she accepted them and said he was forgiven – but that he should always make sure he wore underwear! He could be in an accident or whatever. (Many years later, the now retired Chairman would walk into a London hospital near to his Dolphin Square flat, complaining of a severe headache. He was kept in overnight for observations. By morning he was dead. He had become a good friend of Carruthers and all his family since their Nigeria days and he was sadly missed.)

Not too long after their arrival in Lagos, there was a military coup in Nigeria, one of several which Carruthers and Willi would experience. Carruthers felt quite depressed when the announcement came over the radio in May 1975, after a few hours of the obligatory martial music common to most African countries after such coups. Having had to flee one country after a military coup, it seemed the same thing could happen again. Coincidentally, the military leader, General Gowon, was attending an OAU conference in Kampala presided over by Idi Amin when he was overthrown. (General Gowon ended up in England at Warwick University studying politics.)

Just a few weeks before the coup, Willi and Carruthers had met Gowon's Foreign Minister, at the latter's residence in Lagos, and pleaded with him to bring pressure on his own President to halt the excesses of the Amin regime. The Foreign Minister was an old friend of the Chairman – both were Gray's Inn barristers – and he had accompanied General Gowon to Kampala.

On his return he was no longer Foreign Minister. The Chairman asked him to join the board, and he readily accepted.

Another dignitary they met, and indeed renewed acquaintance with, was Prince Buchartz of Prussia, a relation of the British Royal Family who bore a striking resemblance to Prince Charles. He worked professionally for a large German reinsurance company and travelled the world on their behalf. He was a lovely gentleman, tall and very polite, and was famed for his capacity in taking Scottish whisky at any time of the day or night. Offering him a coffee in one's office would be met with stiff resistance.

Willi and Carruthers had met him previously on his visits to Kampala, and when they met again in Lagos he told them the story of when he had returned to Addis Ababa on his first visit since the overthrow of Emperor Haile Selassie. He had been a guest of the Emperor on previous visits. His favourite restaurant, to his surprise, was still open and the same head waiter was in attendance. The head waiter was so happy to see the Prince that he rushed up to him and threw his arms around his neck. The Prince had been quite taken aback and remarked to Willi and Carruthers in a serious tone that the waiter certainly wouldn't have dared to take such liberties with him in the days of the Emperor. Previously he would have bowed and moved backwards, but waiters could now greet princes as equals under the new Marxist regime.

The military coup in Nigeria had been peaceful and the army posed no real threat to civilians. Businesses had closed for one day only. Luckily it did not affect their day-to-day activities and business continued as usual.

About 18 months later, however, there was a nastier

coup and fellow officers assassinated the military leader of Nigeria. Factions of the army were initially fighting each other and there was panic amongst the civilians in Lagos. The business populace started to flee their offices and return to their homes during the day of the coup. One of the Carruthers' sons was at day school on the other side of the island of Lagos from their bungalow. As it was quite close to the army barracks, Carruthers decided to go and collect his son immediately with the car and driver. As they came off the bridge onto the island, they met panic-stricken drivers streaming out of the city. Some were on the wrong side of the road. Carruthers' car was one of the few going into the city. The driver did a good job weaving in and out of the traffic until they reached the school, where they were able to collect Carruthers' son John. He was one of the few children left as most of his schoolmates lived near to the school. They headed back to home, but this time progress was painfully slow as they were heading out of the city along with hundreds of other cars. Some army checkpoints manned by nervous soldiers had been set up and that slowed their progress even further. Eventually they reached home, many hours later but safe and exhausted. Willi was relieved to see them, not knowing where they were as she herself had only learnt of the coup later. Fortunately, once again the civilian population did not suffer too much; it was an army affair. A curfew was imposed but after a few days business was back to normal. Some army officers would be executed for their part in the coup, but a TV news programme showed army members of the new Cabinet dancing with each other in the army mess.

So life went on in Lagos. The Carruthers had a love-hate relationship with Nigeria. Life could be very frustrating but also rewarding. Carruthers' job took him all over Nigeria, where different cultures provided a fascinating insight of life outside the southern city of Lagos. He enjoyed the North, where the pace was more leisurely and people seemed to have more time to devote to their culture, mostly Moslem. The East of the country was also interesting, where its Catholic influence reminded him of Uganda, but the Yoruba of the South seemed to spend their time shouting at each other and everyone else.

Travelling upcountry to other parts of Nigeria was mainly achieved by flying on the local network of Nigerian Airways, which in those days was not very efficient. One was never sure if flights would be on time or even arrive to take passengers back to Lagos from upcountry destinations. They tried their best but it was always a nerve-racking experience waiting in the departure lounges and trying to guess which flight was going to leave and when.

When announcements of flights leaving were made, there was always a mad rush to reach the steps of the aircraft. This was because there were no seat allocations and it was quite common for more boarding passes than seats to have been issued. The sight of planeloads of passengers, young and old, mothers with babies on their backs, businessmen with their briefcases, traders with heavy bags, some in their flowing traditional robes and dresses, rushing across the tarmac was a sight to be seen. It was the survival of the fittest. Ladies and children were only first if they were fast enough to reach the steps first.

At upcountry airports travellers eager to get back to their homes would often swarm out to meet an aircraft even before it had stopped taxiing. Carruthers was all part of this, and it even had its humorous side. Once, he was at an upcountry airport waiting for a flight to

Lagos when an announcement was made that all passengers should form a queue on the tarmac to await the incoming aircraft. The usual rush started but an orderly queue was eventually formed. An elderly expatriate gentleman clutching a bag in each hand emerged from the terminal building and made his was across the tarmac towards the queue. Suddenly his trousers dropped to his ankles and the bemused traveller, still clutching his bags, stood there not moving, a foolish smile on his face. He seemed at a loss what to do. Carruthers did a double take to ensure it was not his Chairman. It was some of the Nigerian ladies in the queue who went to his aid. These were not mini-skirted young ladies but matrons who rushed to him and encircled him as if on a rugby field. The circle eventually broke and a sheepish-looking gentleman emerged, trousers back where they should have been. Everyone applauded and had a good laugh.

On another occasion, far in the North at Sokoto, the passengers, Carruthers amongst them, sat in the aircraft, which had been on the tarmac for about an hour, unable to take off due to some engine problem. The airport mechanic had tried but failed to rectify the problem. It was the last flight on a Friday and passengers were anxious to get to their destinations. A discussion ensued amongst the passengers and one, an employee of the airline, said he could sort it out and went to talk to the pilot. The pilot doubted his claim and pointed out that it was against all regulations for him to allow the passenger to tamper with one of the engines. A shouting match developed, with many passengers insisting that the pilot give his permission, which eventually he did – under much pressure. The passenger then announced that all he needed was a stepladder and a screwdriver, much to the disbelief of many passengers.

This was provided, and in about 15 minutes, to everyone's amazement, the engine started. Carruthers almost got off the aircraft when the pilot announced he was proceeding to the next destination en route to Lagos. Luckily they made it to Kaduna, but there the pilot discontinued the flight, probably quite wisely, and Carruthers had an unplanned overnight stay. The next morning another flight took him back to Lagos.

Airport lounges provided a great deal of human interest. They were full of passengers from as early as 5.30 a.m., with various hawkers and tradesmen moving around discreetly selling gold watches, rings and necklaces, while others provided manicure and pedicure services. These traders had bribed officials to allow them into the departure lounge. Carruthers once saw his former night-watchman, whom he had recently sacked, moving around selling watches and wondered if he had paid him too well, or if the man had stolen something he had not yet noticed.

The event leading up to the sacking of that particular night watchman had been a rather frightening experience for Carruthers. It was a well-known fact that most night-watchmen spent much of the night sleeping, and when Carruthers sometimes woke up in the middle of the night and couldn't get back to sleep he would prowl round the garden, usually carrying a panga to give him courage, to check up on the night-watchman. On this particular occasion he had found the night-watchman lying fast asleep on his back, covered up to his shoulders by a blanket. A security light above him outlined his head and shoulders. It was 3 o'clock in the morning. Carruthers crept up to him and, crouching down, slowly placed the panga across the night-watchman's throat, increasing the pressure to awaken him. The night-watchman's eyes opened in terror. He placed both his hands on the blade and slowly started to rise, Carruthers with him, both of them still gripping the panga. There was complete silence and Carruthers suddenly realised that the night-watchman had no idea who he was. He was in a trance-like and very dangerous state and perhaps thought he had seen a ghost. Carruthers felt fear; anything could happen. They stood facing each other, staring and gripping the panga. Then, to break the night-watchman's trance, Carruthers gave an almighty shout that fully awakened him and loosened his grip on the panga, which Carruthers then quickly hid behind his back while he shouted abuse at him for sleeping. His heart pounding, Carruthers hurried back indoors, vowing never to do such a stupid thing again. Willi could easily have found a husband with his throat cut lying in the garden in the morning.

Once, in the international airport departure lounge on their way to UK, Willi and Carruthers saw an expatriate couple come in and sit talking for some minutes. The wife pecked her husband on the cheek, wishing him a good flight, and watched as he entered the first-class lounge, where he turned at the door and blew her a kiss. She then hurried off. About ten minutes later the same man appeared at the door of the lounge, his gaze searching among the passengers. He beckoned with his head and another lady detached herself from the other passengers and disappeared with him, his arm about her, into the first-class lounge. Carruthers was amused, Willi shocked. Such were people's infidelities.

Another couple had once asked Carruthers and Willi if they were interested in wife-swapping. It was at a party and the wife kept coming up to Carruthers and saying that her husband wanted to ask him and Willi something. Again Carruthers was amused and Willi shocked. Carruthers certainly wasn't interested, especially as the other lady was quite ugly. The answer, of course, had been 'no'.

Chapter 19

Meetings and Visits

Carruthers and Willi were in the departure lounge of the airport to catch a flight on their way to the UK, but were actually going to the Bahamas to attend a conference of all the worldwide offices of the company. As now the country head of the Nigerian company, but not the Chairman, Carruthers was moving up in the company hierarchy. To keep cost to a minimum everyone had been requested to fly economy, from the Chairman down. They spent a night in London and caught a flight to the Bahamas from Heathrow the following day. Others from the group were on the same flight, and contrary to instructions, one was in first class; Carruthers espied him through the separating curtain. It was his friend the MD from Uganda of all people, who quite correctly took the view that as things were so difficult in Uganda he may as well enjoy the perks of first-class travel.

The conference took place at the Lyford Key Club, scene of a James Bond film, which faced the ocean. The surroundings were immaculate and exquisite, but not really the sort of place to concentrate on a business conference. Their first activity, while members of the group congregated and checked in, was a round of golf. All the equipment had to be hired, so one of the group decided to put his hiring charges on the bill of a senior director who had not yet arrived. Everyone else followed his lead, hoping the director would take it all in good part and put it down as a company expense. Unfortunately, the director, while checking in that evening, was handed the equipment-hiring bill and was furious. He was that type of person. He found out who had instigated the matter and within the next six months that person was out of a job.

Anyway, the conference went on. A separate programme was arranged for the ladies and Willi enjoyed herself immensely. Nothing material emanated from the conference. Carruthers didn't hear of any scandals or involve himself in any, although he became part of a fishing group which incurred the wrath of the conference Chairman.

They were split up into syndicates one afternoon, with instructions to debate a certain matter and report back to the conference on their deliberations the next morning. The syndicate to which Carruthers belonged decided to hire a boat and go deep-sea fishing accompanied by a generous supply of cold beer. Any deliberations would be done offshore. It was great fun and they even got involved in the rescue of a boat that had broken down and was drifting. They alerted the coastguard, who had staged a rescue operation. This was duly reported in the local press the next day and mention was made of the name of the company whose employees had rented the boat. The Chairman, as luck would have it, read the local paper the next morning and asked the Chairman of the syndicate if he was taking the conference seriously. He was hurriedly assured that appropriate deliberations had been carried out on board and they had in fact paid for the trip themselves. Nothing more was said.

Willi and the Uganda director were the only black

members of the group. Those who were not aware of Carruthers and Willi's relationship wrongly assumed that she was the wife of the Uganda director, especially as she was also Ugandan. Strange looks were often directed at Carruthers and Willi as they went around together and went to bed together.

After the conference Carruthers and Willi flew to New York, where they were going to spend a few days with a couple they had known in Uganda. The man, who was with the UN, showed them round the headquarters building. Altogether they had an exciting time and Willi spent a fortune on clothes. When Carruthers went to book their return flight home they were offered Concorde seats by British Airways at no extra cost and this was gladly accepted. What a coup, Carruthers told Willi. No one will believe we travelled Concorde. Willi, who didn't like flying, was a bit apprehensive. However, as it turned out it was the smoothest and fastest flight they had ever experienced and they had no jet lag. What a way to travel! The taxi driver taking them to the special Concorde check-in at the airport had obviously expected a big tip but with Carruthers' aversion to tipping he had merely tipped him a paltry $5. They left him shouting abuse at them and Willi was extremely embarrassed, more especially as he was black. On one occasion in London Carruthers had refused to pay anything to a mini-cab driver who had got lost; another embarrassing incident.

They were now back in Lagos, where Willi's younger sister had been looking after their youngest daughter. The sister had also fled Uganda and Nigeria Immigration had magnanimously agreed she could stay as a dependant of Willi, although at 25 years of age she was a mature adult. However, she paid her way and opened up a nursery school, which proved very popular.

The senior director who had bitterly resented being charged for the hire of golf equipment in the Bahamas had now become the Group Chairman and announced he was making a grand tour of Africa, accompanied by his wife, starting off in Nigeria.

He had arranged the dates of his visit to coincide with public holidays celebrating the anniversary of Nigeria's independence, thus causing maximum inconvenience to his staff. Carruthers managed to obtain VIP tickets for the military parade on one of the holidays and a cocktail party afterwards to meet the President. To further complicate matters, the Chairman had decided to arrive not at the capital Lagos, but at the northern city of Kano, where he would spend a night.

Such was the reputation of the Chairman that Carruthers decided to keep out of his way as much as possible. The local Nigerian Chairman was quite happy to play a prominent role as host, and flew to Kano to welcome him. Carruthers stayed in Lagos, pleading pressure of work. However, he and Willi accompanied the Chairman and his wife to the military parade in a huge open-air stadium in the centre of Lagos. The parade ground was a former cricket square which had been concreted over, and there were massive concrete stands surrounding it. Huge concrete statues of rearing horses were on either side of the entrance to the stadium. It was an impressive sight.

Willi had prepared salmon sandwiches to go with the champagne they carried in a picnic basket, and it was all demolished as brunch as the Chairman and his wife, Willi and Carruthers sat watching the march past and a fly-past by the Nigerian Air Force. All went smoothly but Carruthers winced when the Chairman tapped the shoulder of a senior Air Force officer sitting in front of him to ask what type of aircraft were flying past. Senior Nigerian officers don't like being tapped on the shoulder by white men.

In the late afternoon they attended the cocktail party held in the grounds of the Presidential residence and actually managed to shake hands with President Shagari. The Chairman and his wife were suitable impressed. The President, in fact, on emerging from his residence, clothed in flowing robes and accompanied by his retinue, had walked straight up to them. Probably had his eye on Willi, Carruthers thought. (A few months later he was ousted in a coup.)

That evening the company hosted a dinner in a Chinese restaurant for friends in the insurance industry. Carruthers noticed some Nigerians smirking as the visiting Chairman fulsomely referred to being in their 'great' country. The next day the Chairman flew off to visit offices in East Africa and everyone breathed a sigh of relief.

(When Carruthers was working in England after leaving Nigeria, he came across a file in his office containing a report by the Chairman of his visit to Nigeria. In it he said, 'Carruthers seems to be slowing down and his medical condition should be checked upon from time to time'. Carruthers' decision to keep in the background during the Chairman's visit had obviously been noticed. But then Carruthers survived while the Chairman did not. He lost his job soon after his visit to Africa.)

To add to the reputation of overseas visitors to the Carruthers' household, a London broker attempted to climb into the bed of Willi's sister, whose shrieks brought Carruthers and Willi running to her bedroom. The culprit, however, fled to his own room and denied the accusation, suggesting she must have been dreaming. He wasn't invited back.

But one visitor who didn't give any trouble was a future Vice President of Uganda, who spent a night at the Carruthers' house. He and Carruthers had been attending an international insurance conference in Cameroon, but he had missed his connecting flight. The Carruthers were more than happy to look after him. One of those involved in trying to topple Idi Amin, he was closely allied to Yoweri Museveni (who seized power in 1986). At that time he was living in Uganda but would soon go into exile. Carruthers used to pass letters to various contacts of the future Vice President when he visited Nairobi from time to time.

Another Ugandan friend of Carruthers also in exile in Lagos was the former Chairman of the Uganda Electricity Board, who had fled the country in fear of his life. He would sit and write poetry on occasions when they went to their beach hut on Sundays. He too would become closely allied to Museveni. A former supporter of Obote, he had eventually seen the light. (Sadly, he would die of a heart attack soon after returning to live in Uganda after Museveni had taken power.)

One Sunday morning after a late-night party at their house in Lagos, the Carruthers were awakened by what they thought sounded like singing coming from the lounge area. On going through there from their bedroom Carruthers found a senior Nigerian colleague and director dancing by himself on the bare wooden floor. The houseboy, who had been clearing up from the night before, had allowed him into the house. Carruthers had last seen his colleague in hospital when he had visited him there a few days before. In fact, his admission to hospital had been prompted by Carruthers. The colleague had been off work for some days, and Carruthers had entered his house to find him seated in a chair and hardly able to speak. He was suffering from malaria and was treating himself with some tablets he had in the house. There was a strange musty smell – Carruthers likened it to the smell of death especially as his colleague looked a bit like a corpse – and persuaded his colleague to go to a hospital immediately. There was no sign of his colleague's wife.

His wife had eventually appeared and had been making regular visits to the hospital to visit her sick husband. On the evening of the Carruthers' party his wife went to the hospital and was sitting in a chair beside his bed. After a while, realising that she had been unusually quiet for some time, the husband saw she had fallen asleep. Leaning from his sickbed, he shook her shoulder and to his great shock suddenly realised that she wasn't asleep, she was dead! Apparently she had suffered a sudden and swift heart attack. So while the wife was wheeled off to the mortuary, the husband discharged himself to make funeral arrangements – but not for himself, as Carruthers had at one time envisaged.

His morning dance at the Carruthers' bungalow was the dance of death, and as he moved slowly round the floor he chanted, 'She's gone, she's gone.'

After what seemed a long time, Carruthers managed to get him to sit down and recount his story. They both had an early morning beer as he had now fully recovered from his bout of malaria.

* * *

Another chairman to visit Nigeria from London had arrived the day before an army coup and was holed up in his hotel, which was a bit distant from the Carruthers' residence. In fact he was the same chairman who had visited Kampala soon after the Idi Amin coup. He wasn't too amused when Carruthers refused to visit him on the day of the coup on the grounds that it was too dangerous. The Chairman was a former naval commodore and could well look after himself, Carruthers reasoned. He was the type of Englishman who would probably call his coup visit a lot of fun. Carruthers, however, did do him a favour by getting him on the first flight out of Lagos after the coup, a Pan Am flight to Nairobi. In doing so he also did himself a favour as he considered visiting chairmen an extreme pain.

But one visiting chairman whom Carruthers actually liked was a fellow Scot and ex-banker. He and his wife had once taken Carruthers and Willi to the ballet in London, which both found incredibly boring. On going out of Sadler's Wells after the performance, the Chairman was accosted by someone who turned out to be an ex-colleague in India. The ex-colleague, much to their host's embarrassment and in front of everyone, expressed absolute amazement that the Chairman had achieved such a high position in a public company. Carruthers thought there must be a story there, but he never did find out.

It was during one such visit to London that Willi and Carruthers attended the annual dinner of the Institute of Directors, where a Tory Government Minister embroiled in a spat with his former mistress was the guest of honour. His after-dinner speech was completely forgettable and Willi and Carruthers and two of their table companions, the London-based Nigerian Chairman and his wife, left soon afterwards to go to a nightclub.

Lots of champagne was drunk and they returned late to the over-warm bedroom of their Park Lane hotel, which had also been the venue of their dinner. Before he fell asleep Carruthers remembered that he had a medical check-up in Harley Street at 9.30 a.m. the next morning, or rather now the same morning.

They had a hell of a rush checking out and reaching Harley Street on time. Carruthers, with hangover, was certain the results of the check-up, an annual company requirement, would be disastrous. When the results of various tests including liver function were shown to him a week later, he was astonished to see everything was normal. Perhaps the examining doctor also had a hangover, Carruthers thought.

Prior to sitting down for the Institute of Directors' dinner there had been pre-dinner cocktails at a cash bar. Carruthers hated that name. He felt strongly that if one had paid for tickets for a function, that should be the end to spending. Anyway, standing at the bar to get drinks for Willi and their companions, he had overheard two directors at the bar discussing Willi, who stood out in the crowd because of her colour and beauty.

'I've never had a black job,' one said.

To which the other replied, 'Neither have I, and I wouldn't mind that one right now.'

Carruthers smiled inwardly. He could tell them a thing or two. In fact, Willi was feeling a bit distraught and downed her drink quickly. She had met someone wearing exactly the same dress and she felt somewhat cheated, considering the money she had spent on it.

A couple of days later the four of them were thrown out of the Charing Cross Hotel on the Strand when they refused to eat and pay for their ordered dinner, which took well over an hour to arrive. When they were asked to leave, Carruthers and the Chairman, angry at their treatment, started throwing about advertising fliers displayed in the elevator. Looking back, Carruthers was quite ashamed of the incident, although it was good fun at the time, and it took him some years to pick up his courage and enter the hotel again.

On one of his trips outside Lagos, Carruthers was seated in one of the Government-owned hotels in Benin City having lunch with his branch manager, when he noticed a familiar figure seated on the other side of the dining room. He mentally rubbed his eyes and told himself he must be dreaming. However, he was convinced, as the meal went on – and it was a boring meal (both food and company) – that the familiar figure must be the former MD of the mine in Uganda. Carruthers tried to attract his attention, to no avail. Eventually the meal finished and as his old friend was still seated, he rushed up to him at his table. The person sitting there was aloof but grudgingly admitted that he knew Carruthers. Carruthers felt rebuffed but nevertheless plunged on and reminded him who he was – after all, it was only five or six years since they had last met.

Carruthers found out later, when they were in the hotel bar by themselves, that his friend had felt a bit awkward as the Nigerian he was having lunch with knew nothing about his background. He had therefore been a bit cagey talking about himself in front of what he called 'the Nigerian Mafia'.

The former mine MD was now working for a company starting up business in Nigeria and because of his African experience had been appointed to run the company. (In fact, the job didn't last long as 'Africa experience' is no way equivalent to 'Nigeria experience'.)

The conversation led on to bras and the former MD's

wife. The MD was a bit miffed about what had happened and said that his wife had capitalised on the situation and put most of the money she had earned from the publicity into her personal bank account. He then, after many double whiskies, ranted on about Carruthers' former Chairman and said, indeed shouted, that it was all his bloody fault and that Carruthers had not helped matters by having his wife Willi give a present of bras to Flora, which bras had eventually been publicised worldwide – including her bare tits, for God's sake.

By this time the former MD was really uptight. Carruthers tentatively asked about Flora and where she was, to be told that she was arriving in a couple of days' time to visit her dear husband, who because of work commitments wouldn't be able to meet her at Lagos Airport. However, he had a good travel agent who had assured him that he would meet her and put her on a plane to Benin City.

Carruthers then stepped in. There was no way that Flora could be met by a stranger, he said. He and Willi would meet her, accommodate her for a night at their Lagos bungalow and put her on the plane the next day to her eagerly awaiting husband. Carruthers wasn't sure about the eager bit, but one had to be optimistic. The former MD looked doubtful but Carruthers persuaded him.

As it turned out, Willi and Carruthers couldn't physically meet Flora at the airport as they had an important function to attend. They sent their driver with a name-board and Flora was duly delivered to the bungalow, where Willi and Carruthers, just returned from their party, were there to welcome her.

Flora delighted in regaling them with stories of what had happened following the revelation of her name as the barer of the breasts. She had made money, she had been propositioned, and she had on occasions allowed male lips – and on the odd occasion female lips – to sample her youthful breasts. Her husband had been madly jealous and in a huff one day had applied for this job in Nigeria. She really wasn't sure why she was there but she wasn't the type of person to break up a long-standing marriage. 'Standing' was the operative word Carruthers thought!

The next morning a bleary-eyed Carruthers wandered through the corridor of their bungalow, for a cup of coffee. As he passed the guest bedroom, the door suddenly opened and there was Flora resplendent in a very sexy bra and not much else. She stepped forward and grasped his testicles through his purple flared trousers and croaked, 'You son of bitches!'

Carruthers didn't have time to correct her grammar. He coughed, blushed and fled, glancing over his shoulder and hoping Willi had not witnessed the attack, especially as he felt he could have taken things a stage further if Willi had not been around.

He groaned in frustration as he sipped his coffee. He had not felt that way about Flora while in Uganda, but she had improved her appearance considerably since then, what with all the publicity over her breasts.

'I've always wanted you,' she hissed as she sat down opposite him and poured herself a cup of coffee. Carruthers raised his eyebrows and smiled weakly.

Willi had still not appeared.

'Maybe we'll have a chance to meet later, once you have settled in to your new home upcountry and, after all,' Carruthers said, 'you will no doubt have to make shopping trips to Lagos.'

She looked at him thoughtfully and leered.

Willi, of course, was nobody's fool and had witnessed the encounter between Flora and Carruthers through the slightly ajar door to their bedroom. As she approached the breakfast table she remarked somewhat frostily that Flora had better be off soon or she would miss her flight. She suggested to Carruthers that they send the driver with Flora, to which Carruthers felt obliged to agree. After she had gone, Willi told Carruthers that 'that woman' would not be welcome in her house again as she considered her a whore. Carruthers decided not to argue and tamely went off to the office in his other car. Very difficult creatures these women, Carruthers said to himself.

For instance, he remembered that the wife of one of his friends had phoned Carruthers up and complained that he had led her husband astray as he had come home from lunch with Carruthers very much the worse for wear. The wife, a volatile and attractive Italian, had vowed that her husband would never have lunch with Carruthers again and she refused to speak to him for some weeks after.

Yet another wife stopped speaking to Carruthers after he called her a bitch. That was when she suggested that Willi had stolen one of the fillets of steak which she was storing in her deep freezer while the woman was away on leave. Willi, in fact, had been very careful to count the fillets and knew that the person concerned was jealous and just being bitchy. This very same wife had once said to Carruthers during a Hogmanay dance at a Lagos nightclub that she intended to have one more affair before she was 40, and looked meaningfully at him. However, he had not risen to the bait or the challenge and reported the matter to Willi, who was never sure whether Carruthers was being serious.

Carruthers smiled when he remembered another incident over meat stored in their freezer for other friends. This time it had been a turkey and had lain there for nearly a year. Carruthers and Willi had got fed up seeing it and decided to cook it and invite their friends to join them in eating it, without telling them beforehand. After the meal Willi was complimented by their guests for the excellent meal, to which she replied that it was really for her and Carruthers to thank them because that had been their own turkey. Luckily their friends took it all in good part and they had a good laugh. These were genuine friends.

During their time in Nigeria, Carruthers and Willi kept abreast of events in Uganda and wondered if they would ever be able to live there again. Willi's father kept in constant contact by letter and reported on the upkeep and renting of their lakeside bungalow. As the bungalow was some miles from Kampala city centre, it was difficult to find regular and suitable tenants because of the danger of hijacking and attacks by undisciplined army soldiers. One tenant had his car taken at gunpoint, and a neighbour had their baby thrown against a wall by soldier intruders. Fortunately it survived.

Another neighbour, a lawyer, was lucky not to have disappeared when Idi Amin appointed him as Secretary to a Commission of Inquiry into missing persons. Some of these missing persons had been lucky enough to escape the country, but many prominent persons had disappeared into the car boots of security agents and thereafter been tortured and murdered. Only oral evidence was to be accepted by the Commission, although evidence in the form of phone calls and letters to the Secretary was sent by some brave but anonymous souls. As no one physically turned up to accuse the Military Government of complicity in the disappearances, the report of the Commission was inconsequential. This was just as well for the Secretary and members of the Commission because if the report had pointed a finger at the military they would themselves have joined 'the disappeared'.

On one of their few visits together to Kampala after the overthrow of Amin, Willi and Carruthers managed to visit their bungalow. An Indian who was holding his own wedding reception there in a week's time was renting it and they were both invited, along with Willi's father and mother. It seemed strange sitting in their own garden being entertained by a stranger renting their house. Carruthers espied someone he used to know sitting at the other side of the garden but purposely ignored him. He had been one of Obote's spymasters and Carruthers didn't feel it was wise to acknowledge him, and perhaps have to admit that this was his house and that he was living outside Uganda. One couldn't be too careful, he thought.

Thinking about being careful, Carruthers remembered making a brief visit to Kampala by himself from Nairobi after a visit to the then apartheid South Africa. He had requested South African immigration officers not to stamp his passport, as he didn't want to get into trouble with immigration officers at Entebbe airport. As he was waiting in the airport lounge at Entebbe to return to Nairobi, he was sitting minding his own business when a Ugandan who was not a passenger but probably some security official came up to him and asked if he could provide a light for his cigarette. Although Carruthers didn't smoke he did have a book of matches in his pocket and passed them over. The man lit his cigarette, handed the matches back to Carruthers and wandered off; Carruthers idly looked at the book of matches in his hand and realised with a start that they bore the name and address of a prominent Johannesburg hotel.

He looked round guiltily but there was no sign of the smoker. Carruthers was glad when the flight to Nairobi took off on time. Luckily he hadn't told the man to keep the matches.

Airports in the days of apartheid, cold wars, currency restrictions, hijackings etc were, in Carruthers' opinion, hazardous and nerve-racking places to get through. Officialdom in any form could frustrate your progress and you couldn't do anything about it except sweat it out and try to be patient.

Carruthers had at various times hidden currency in the underpants he was wearing and carried unopened letters for various people hidden away in his luggage and fortunately never been found out. A lady security officer at Entebbe airport who for some reason had taken a shine to Willi and Carruthers used to wave them through without checking and also ask them to post her own letters outside the country.

Customs at Lagos International Airport was well known for being very difficult. Once approaching the customs with Willi after a flight from London and with too many suitcases as a result of Willi's excessive shopping, Carruthers knew he was going to be in trouble and with some trepidation struggled to put four heavy suitcases on the counter in front of the customs officer. The customs officer looked at him fiercely. On being asked what the suitcases contained Carruthers on a sudden inspiration pointed out that two of the suitcases belonged to him and his wife, nodding at Willi, and the other two belonged to his other two wives who were waiting to greet his arrival outside. The customs officer considered this so funny and outrageous that he laughed uproariously and waved Carruthers and Willi through without examining anything.

On only one occasion had Carruthers ever had to

bribe an official. This was an immigration officer, in order to allow a newly arrived colleague without the correct paperwork to enter the country. Generally he resisted such practices, although many people regularly gave backhanders.

Carruthers' visits to various upcountry towns and cities in Nigeria continued. It was a vast country with many different tribes and cultures, including visiting foreign tribes. For instance, he was amused to see a dozen Japanese businessmen wearing white smog masks at Sokoto airport to keep out the desert dust. In another part of the country locals were hanging out clothes on lines alongside the main road, but not as he first thought to dry them. They were clothes belonging to recently deceased persons and were to accompany their spirits. Even briefcases were displayed.

The ancient city of Kano in the North with its centuries-old market and dye pits was also fascinating. On Fridays certain roads would be blocked as the Muslim population knelt in the road to say their prayers. He once went on a business tour of the North with a colleague bearing the romantic name Ali Baba during the Muslim period of Ramadan and followed the fasting laws with him.

The war-ravaged areas in the east of the country, the so-called former Biafra, was a source for souvenirs of that sad episode – Biafran currency and stamps were for a while easily available.

He only had one more encounter with the former Uganda mine MD and his wife in Nigeria. Carruthers had been visiting an insurance company in the city where they lived. It was a state-owned company and one of the most prominent features of its annual report and accounts was on the progress and fortunes of the company's football team, which was one of the leading sides in Nigeria. The insurance section of the business made a loss sustaining the football team, and the boss of the company was better known for his football activities than his insurance ones.

That evening, the boss and his wife invited Carruthers out for dinner at a local restaurant situated in a nearby hotel. Both of them were in a boisterous mood when they picked up Carruthers from his hotel and it was evident that they had already been imbibing quite heavily. They drove erratically to the hotel and as they progressed round the car park area looking for a space, they approached a car sticking out a bit from the rest. It was obvious to Carruthers that if they continued on their present course they were going to crash into it. He was undecided as to what to do. After all, there were two of them in the front of the car with two sets of eyes, bleary eyes perhaps, but they could surely see the direction they were taking. Luckily, they were moving slowly so Carruthers decided to keep quiet and see what happened. They crashed straight into the side of the other car.

The wife mumbled, 'What was that?'

Carruthers shouted, 'What's happened, what's happened?' pretending astonishment.

The insurance boss staggered out to inspect the damage, which was mainly to the other car, managed to reverse and then parked his car as far away as possible from the damaged one. Nothing more was said on the matter. The dinner was a disaster as his hosts were too drunk to say anything about anything, and he persuaded them to allow him to go back to his hotel in a taxi!

The former mine MD and his wife insisted on taking him out to dinner the next evening at a Chinese restaurant, during which the ex-MD excitedly told him that he was returning to Uganda to reopen the mine as there had been a change of regime and because of his experience he was the only man for the job. Carruthers urged him to exercise caution, as he didn't consider the place safe. However, the MD was determined to return with or without the much photographed bra owner, Flora, who was not at all keen on this latest move. She had better things to do, she told her husband, giving Carruthers a painful kick under the table. A prawn almost went down the wrong way.

By this time they were getting quite tipsy and Carruthers suggested some Chinese tea to wash down the food and alcohol. Teapot and cups duly arrived and were placed on the moving centre part of the table, the 'lazy susan'. By this time Flora's left foot was nestling in Carruthers' groin area and she was leaning back smirking, her husband unaware of what was happening beneath the tablecloth. Flora's exploring toes suddenly found a sensitive part and as Carruthers jerked forward in pain, his hand, which had been resting idly on the lazy susan, inadvertently spun the centrepiece round at speed, causing the pot of china tea to come off it and land on Flora's lap. There was a scream of anguish. Flora's husband and Carruthers leapt to their feet and the crowd of diners in the packed restaurant stared in fascination. A female acquaintance of Flora's at a nearby table rushed over to give assistance and hurriedly escorted her to the ladies while shouting for one of the waitresses to bring ice. Whiskies were ordered and Flora's two male companions awaited her return anxiously.

'What were you doing?' her husband asked Carruthers accusingly.

Eventually she returned, seemingly none the worse for wear. Luckily, her skirt had absorbed most of the scalding tea, but her private parts still had to be treated with ice blocks until the heat had been taken out of that very sensitive area. Considering the state of excitement she had been in before the accident, Carruthers wondered if steam had arisen on application of the ice blocks. After a large whisky Flora declared that the experience was the opposite of an orgasm, a remark that caused great merriment. Carruthers tipsily remarked to Flora and husband that that was the second time ice blocks had featured on Flora's sexual organs, reminding them of the time her breasts had been iced and photographed in their presence at the mine – and look what that had led to. Flora's husband didn't seem to take that very kindly, but Flora smiled and looked thoughtful and absentmindedly massaged her breasts.

That was the end of their evening together and they departed promising to keep in contact and hopefully meet in Uganda sometime. Carruthers said they unfortunately wouldn't be able to see them in Lagos on their departure as he and Willi would be visiting Togo. He wasn't sure if that was the time they would be away but he knew he had to keep Willi and Flora apart. He wasn't even sure he would tell Willi about the incident at the Chinese restaurant, as she would be deeply suspicious.

Chapter 20

Comedy and Tragedy

The Carruthers' visit to Togo was in connection with the annual meeting of the West African District of Lions Clubs, a worldwide charitable organisation started in the USA. Carruthers was a Deputy Governor for Nigeria, and the mixture of charitable work and social activities with like-minded people, Nigerians and expatriates alike gave Carruthers and Willi something to do with their spare time.

They drove along the coast road to the Nigerian border and through the Republic of Benin and then into Togo, going through immigration and customs controls in each of the three countries. There were tight currency restrictions in force and Carruthers had secreted a sizeable wad of money in his suitcase. The President of the Lions Club in Benin couldn't attend the meeting as he had been imprisoned by the tin-pot dictator of that country, an ex-army sergeant.

While the delegates met in a large hotel in Lomé, the capital of Togo, the wives had a special programme organised for them, which included a visit to a well-known juju market where fetishes and charms were sold to cure and ward off various illnesses and spells. Dead bats, monkeys' hands and heads and goodness knows what else were on display.

Another popular place to visit on that trip was a

French-owned supermarket where all sorts of goodies such as apples and cheeses, unavailable in Nigeria, were on sale. Carruthers used his good supply of Nigerian currency and he and Willi spent a happy time in the supermarket.

The return journey to Lagos was not quite so happy as Nigerian customs officers, famous for their corruption, had mounted a series of at least six roadblocks on the road from the Nigerian border to Lagos. Some apples and cheese were lost to these thieves in uniform, as well as some cash, but overall Carruthers and Willi were in profit. It was no use getting angry at the roadblocks. Each one had to be treated as a challenge to see to what extent one could bluff one's way through. While the customs' officers always tried to look fierce, Carruthers always smiled and joked. Although neither he nor Willi smoked, they had bought packets of cheap cigarettes and doled them out to smooth the way through.

To celebrate their return to Lagos a couple of their Lion friends, a Frenchman and his Nigerian wife, had invited them to dinner at their home, along with some others. Halfway through the excellent meal the lights went out, which was a not uncommon event in Nigeria. Their host urged them to sit still as his generator would soon burst into life, which it duly did, and light was restored. But after about five minutes the lights went out again, and their host got up from the table and went outside to see what had happened. He was soon back, urging everyone to be patient as there hadn't been enough fuel in the generator and he had instructed his night guard to fill it up. Soon the lights were on again, but only for a matter of seconds. Once again an increasingly angry host disappeared and came back carrying paraffin lamps, his face bright red. He announced that his night guard had put paraffin instead of diesel into the generator and he was so angry and fed up about the whole situation that he was going to bed. There was a stunned silence as he departed, leaving his guests at the table. His wife shrugged her shoulders and advised everyone to eat, drink and be merry. Although their host never reappeared, which cast a slight pall over the evening, they made a dent in his nice French wine sitting in the near dark.

Willi was well known for her excellent dinners and Saturday or Sunday lunchtime curries, and Carruthers always ensured that their generator was filled up with fuel by himself and started by himself or, in his absence, Willi. So their guests were never disappointed with a failed generator. Much of their entertaining was centred around visitors from various businesses in Europe and was usually reasonably sober and non-controversial; although on one occasion, at a barbecue round the swimming pool, the managing director of a large brewery disappeared, leaving his open car and briefcase full of documents in the driveway and didn't turn up until late the next day to claim his possessions. Over a hair of the dog he tried to remember what had happened but couldn't. All he knew was that he woke up in the house of his brother, a navy commander, late the next morning and some miles distant from the Carruthers' residence.

During one dinner at home an expatriate friend of Carruthers accused a visiting London director of Carruthers' company of only holding onto his particular job because his wife was an heiress with excellent connections. In this he was actually quite correct, but it was an embarrassing moment. At some stage the visitor must have insulted Carruthers' friend, and they sat opposite each other at the dinner table trading insults.

An even more embarrassing moment happened in a

friend's house over dinner when a female friend, who was on her own as her husband was away, stated that she hated Jews. She had no idea, of course, that her hosts were from Israel! Everyone else metaphorically crawled under the table. She had to apologise profusely when Carruthers told her aloud that her hosts were Jewish.

In Carruthers' opinion Willi's hospitality sometimes went too far. Once he had carefully planned a Sunday barbecue lunch at their beach hut, which could only be reached by boat. He had worked out the transport details so that one set of guests would be whisked up to the beach at a certain time and the boat sent back to collect the other set of guests. Timings had been communicated to everyone.

Carruthers sat at the Boat Club bar having an early morning Star beer, once he had ensured the boat was in working order. He was awaiting the first set of guests, who were going to collect Willi on the way and bring her to the club. Carruthers had already loaded the boat with booze, food etc, and the motor was idling ready to take off the minute Willi and guests appeared. The second set of guests would arrive later, after the boat had been sent back to collect them. An hour and a half later Willi and guests appeared at the same time as the second set of guests. Carruthers was furious and wondered what the hell Willi had been up to. She replied that when the first set of guests arrived at the house they mentioned that they had been in such a rush they had not had breakfast. To Carruthers' astonishment, Willi said she had therefore prepared breakfast for them, thereby ruining Carruthers' well-made plans. He shouldn't really have been astonished: it was typical African hospitality. The guests had been the UN High Commissioner for Refugees and his wife, who was an old school mate of Willi's from Kampala. By the time both sets of guests had been ferried to the beach, back and forward, Carruthers had consumed quite a few beers at the club bar and the rest of the day passed by in a haze. No one else seemed to be worried, and Willi's attitude, with that terrible female logic, was, 'Why all the rush? Be happy.' One had to smile.

One of their friends, the Agence France Press correspondent for Nigeria, was their guest at the beach hut one Sunday and decided to go for a swim. The Atlantic Ocean off the west coast of Africa is notorious for its strong tides and a close watch has always to be kept on children and tides. Their friend, swimming in deep water some 30 yards distant from Carruthers, who was standing in the shallows, started waving feebly. He couldn't get back to shore because of a strong undercurrent. Carruthers' immediate inclination was to start wading out towards him, but Willi, who happened to be nearby holding their baby, immediately spotted the danger and took charge. Shouting earnestly to Carruthers to stay put, she rushed along the beach towards some local fishermen who were tending their fishing canoes and nets and shouted to them for help. One of them, young and strong, was in the water within seconds and swam out to the rapidly weakening newspaper correspondent. He managed to reach him before he disappeared under the water and brought him safely to shore, but the correspondent was in a complete state of exhaustion and it took him some hours to recover. It had been touch and go and everyone felt shocked. Swimming in the sea was never quite the same after that. The rescuer, of course, was duly rewarded with a sizeable amount of money.

The Boat Club was a favourite meeting point for Carruthers and his cronies: good restaurant, good bar, constant social functions, parties etc, and too easy to get stuck at the bar. Ringing the ship's bell hanging at the end of the bar signalled drinks all round at the expense of the bellringer. No cash passed over the bar; it was all chits. At Christmas time snow was made from white polythene for a kids' party and Father Christmas arrived in a boat, and at Hogmanay a Scottish piper playing his bagpipes would arrive by boat at midnight, resplendent in his kilt. Carruthers was Secretary to the Boat Club and also Vice Chieftain of the Scottish Caledonian Society. Willi regularly went to Mass at the church conveniently situated near to the Boat Club, where the local Irish priest had honorary membership and was known as Father Heineken.

News from Uganda continued to filter through. Willi's brother, a major in the Uganda army, was killed in action. Amin had been overthrown and the brother had joined up in the euphoria that followed. But his own colleagues probably killed him as he came from the wrong tribe.

Willi's father had been pulled out of a taxi near Kampala, made to sit at the roadside and been accused by drunken soldiers of being father to the rebel leader Museveni. Patiently he had explained his identity and eventually they let him go.

He had been through many crises before and was therefore able to deal with events calmly. He was from a warrior family, his mother having been a sister to Semei Kakungulu, 'emissary and loyal servant of His Majesty the King', as written on a plaque erected in 1901 in Eastern Uganda. The King referred to was King George V. Historians would visit her at her son's house to ask about her brother and life in those days.

Carruthers and Willi were very fond of their grandmother who died on 12th December 1979 at 103.

During the invasion of the city of Kampala during Amin's overthrow, Willi's parents and family, including the grandmother, had fled from their house to seek refuge in the Catholic Cathedral. The grandmother couldn't walk and there was no fuel for the car, so she was pushed the three or four miles in a wheelbarrow. They all survived, but Willi's small house near to the lake and the cathedral didn't. It was hit by shells and demolished. Luckily, no one was inside.

Sometimes soldiers forced their way into Willi's parents' house but a photograph on display of her brother in military uniform sometimes helped to convince the intruders to leave them in peace. Once, Willi's father fired the hunting gun he kept out of his bedroom window in the dark, scaring the soldiers away. (Years later, he would die a peaceful death in a peaceful Kampala.)

Willi's father came to visit them in Nigeria, his first visit to that country. He was of course well looked after and had a well-deserved rest after all the trials and tribulations suffered under two brutal Uganda regimes. He was a courageous man and it was he and men and women like him that brutal regimes could not destroy.

One of the great cultural events which Willi and Carruthers were able to experience in Nigeria was the Festival of African Arts and Culture held in Lagos and certain other parts of the country in 1977. All African countries sent teams of dancers, acrobats and actors, etc to attend the event. The opening parade in Lagos was breathtaking. Participants from all the different countries, dressed in traditional costumes, paraded before a crowd of 50,000. Drumbeats and the sound of flutes and horns reverberated round the stadium. Each new entrant to the stadium brought gasps of delight; some were on stilts, many in masks, each depicting their country's culture. To date it has never been repeated. Willi was pregnant at the time but managed to attend the opening ceremony and witness Uganda's entry in the stadium.

Later, Carruthers and his visiting Chairman went north to Kaduna to witness the Festac Durbar, a parade of emirs and sultans with their retainers, all mounted on richly adorned horses and camels and shielded from the sun by gaily coloured large umbrellas. It was a once in a lifetime experience.

On another of his visits Carruthers arranged for his Chairman to visit the former war-torn Biafra to seek out a Nigerian colleague he had not seen for ten years. He didn't even know if he was alive. A practising lawyer, the colleague had originally left Lagos to go to the new Biafra's aid. Indeed, they did manage to trace him and it was an emotional reunion. Carruthers' Chairman was very grateful for the trouble Carruthers had taken and it made their bone-jarring taxi journey from Enugu to Owerri over a pot-holed road worthwhile. They stayed a couple of nights just outside the town at a local hostelry known as La Perch, but the motif on the board hanging at the entrance was not of a fish jumping out of the water, as one would have imagined, but of two blackbirds perched on the branch of a tree. This was where, for the first time in his life, Carruthers actually witnessed someone rolling on the ground in laughter. It was one of the barmen at La Perch reacting to a joke told by the Chairman, the one about a black woman looking in a shop mirror at the cosmetics counter in a just independent Zimbabwe. She looked at herself and said, 'Mirror, mirror on the wall, who is the most beautiful of them all?' To which an outraged white shop assistant shouted, 'It's still Snow White, you black bitch, and don't you forget it!' Even Willi laughed at that one. Carruthers used to balance such racial jokes by telling jokes against whites, such as the definition of a black girl going with a white guy – somebody getting up to a bit of honky panky.

While Carruthers found his stay in Nigeria culturally interesting and the work challenging, it was also frustrating. As long as you were useful to them, the Nigerians put up with you and indeed could be very hospitable and sociable. They were, however, generally very much concerned with their own importance, and money was their god. Their arrogance was not only directed at foreigners but also at their own people who displeased them.

He remembered seeing a Nigerian male passenger waiting to board a plane being angered by an armed soldier who was making a cursory search of passengers queuing to board the aircraft – and showing his anger by opening his fly and peeing on the tarmac at the soldier's feet. On boarding the plane, the same passenger had refused to fasten his seat belt and the flight was delayed while a big argument ensued between him and the captain of the plane until he eventually agreed to conform.

An expatriate friend of Carruthers, who had been born in Nigeria and was going to join his parents and work in the UK after spending all of his life in Nigeria, had proudly announced this to the immigration officer who was giving him his final exit stamp in his passport. He was immediately rebuffed by the comment, 'Good riddance, don't come back.'

On the other hand, Nigerians often complained that they were racially abused in the UK, and while Carruthers was sure that this did happen on occasions, he was also sure some asked for it with their attitude to authority, white or black. No wonder there were so many coups in Nigeria.

Sometimes the house stewards could be difficult and the expatriate wives had a problem determining who was boss in the kitchen. The male Nigerian was a chauvinist at heart and the mistress/servant relationship was fraught. Servants also pretended not to understand their master. Once when Carruthers phoned home from the office the steward asked him if he wanted to speak to the donkey, mistaking the name Carruthers had badly pronounced! Carruthers was furious as he shouted into the telephone and then slammed it down. How could someone think he wanted to talk to a donkey? But he started to laugh as he thought about it.

It was about this time that Carruthers thought he would deflate the ego of an expatriate acquaintance who was himself becoming arrogant. He was also cheating on his wife, who happened to be a good friend of Willi's. This gentleman was a manager of a British-owned company and, because he was very handsome, also appeared in a well-known TV commercial surrounded by pretty girls sipping beer. He visibly preened himself in front of others, which of course didn't go down very well amongst some of his hard-drinking male friends like Carruthers. Using a couple of sheets of guest stationery which he had obtained from a prominent Lagos hotel, Carruthers composed a letter from an imagined Hollywood talent scout who supposedly was visiting Lagos and had seen his friend on the TV commercial. The letter said that his appearance fitted exactly what a Hollywood film producer was looking for to star in an African adventure based loosely on the Tarzan stories. The letter was sent by post from Lagos as the scout said he had only seen the commercial the evening before he was flying out, but in the short time available he had traced his name and address through the advertising agency. The letter asked for some photographs, if possible in a loincloth, that should be sent to the studio in Hollywood, whose name and address he gave.

The friend, of course, couldn't resist mentioning all this to his drinking partners and various rude suggestions were made as to how he should pose. He talked of having to resign from his job and going to the USA to become a star. His friends offered to take the photographs and help him choose the best prints of the various poses. (Carruthers had not divulged to anyone that he was the one behind this. Certain of his friends said that it must be some joke but the aspiring film star would not be persuaded otherwise.) The hilarity shown at the photo sessions should have warned him that all that glitters was not gold, especially when Carruthers suggested the odd nude shot after the loincloth kept slipping.

Undaunted, the friend sent off copies of the photographs to Hollywood and nothing more was heard. He had also sent some copies to his advertising agency, and one of his poses in a loincloth appeared in a local newspaper under the heading TARZAN IN LAGOS.

'You've been set up, mate,' opined his friends, and eventually he had to admit such a likelihood.

Soon afterwards he left the country on a posting – to Calcutta, not Hollywood. Carruthers never heard from him again but he did hear that he had separated from his wife. Her name was Jane.

* * *

The Carruthers came across all sorts of weird characters in Nigeria. Among the weirdest but most talented was the musician Fela Ransome Kuti, famous for his stand against military regimes, which he vilified in his songs and music. Carruthers was a fan, despite the fact that at Fela's club, called the Shrine, a picture of Idi Amin and the Uganda flag was prominently displayed, alongside those of Bokassa and Mandela, on a shrine; however, due homage was paid to them all by Fela at some stage during his performance. Scantily clad girls sang and danced, some in swinging baskets, beside the band on stage. It was heady stuff and the music was excellent. Fela during that time was beaten and imprisoned by the military authorities and his family house was burnt down but he refused to be cowed. He said that the law restricting Christians to one wife was colonial in outlook and he announced that he was marrying 27 wives, as was his right as an African. He then bought a bus and travelled around with them. When he died, his son Femi Kuti took over the band, but not the 27 wives, and the Shrine was renamed Kalakuta Republic and moved to the outskirts of Lagos. Despite the notoriety of these places, they were perfectly safe for expatriates to visit and huge bouncers were on call to prevent any racial or drunken behaviour.

   Another weird character, an expatriate friend of Carruthers, had the most beautiful blonde-haired Scottish wife. Maybe she was *too* beautiful, because he couldn't seem to handle the situation. She wasn't promiscuous or anything like that but men couldn't help ogling her, Carruthers included. The husband took to drugs at first occasionally but later more regularly. The wife's sister was very plain compared to her sister and was attached to the drug squad at Scotland Yard of all places. When she came out on a holiday visit, seeing her brother-in-law involved in drugs was a shock and, as she told Carruthers, she was in a bit of a quandary but felt she had to protect her sister. Not long after the sister's visit the marriage was over. Carruthers kept in touch with his friend, who remained in Lagos and somehow got involved with certain local political issues, which eventually resulted in his arrest and detention. While he was in prison a Nigerian female intelligence officer interrogated him, and such was their rapport that on his release they were married. Carruthers could hardly believe his ears when he heard this latest episode in his friend's life on bumping into him at a hotel in Lagos. And he had stopped his drug-taking. All's well that ends well, he thought.

Two other expatriate friends also had problems with marriages. One had been married twice in England to English girls, divorced them, and moved to Kenya and married a Ugandan, then moved to Zambia and married a Zambian and finally moved to Nigeria and married a Nigerian, all at great cost to his emotions and bank balance. Another long-married friend had returned to the UK from Nigeria and secured a job in London. Because his matrimonial home was far from London, he took lodgings in London during the week. After a few months he announced to his distraught wife and two children that he was going to marry his landlady, which he did. Two years later he died from lung cancer brought on by heavy smoking. Now if he had stayed with his first wife and family he might have given up the habit and still be alive.

One of Carruthers' Nigerian colleagues occupied a high position in an Adventist Church. Once when they were in a hotel bar together he said he would have a soft drink and then proceeded to order champagne! The Church attracted converts who sang, clapped and danced and spoke in tongues. They danced in the aisles in their long robes, clouds of incense obscuring them. It was said that if a Nigerian member of staff didn't join that church, his or her path to promotion would be blocked. Hallelujah! Carruthers attended one service, when his colleague was being installed in a senior position. He wore a bishop-type hat and carried a crook, which was an apt name, Carruthers thought. After two hours Carruthers made a discreet exit. He desperately needed a cold beer to wash away the taste of incense. If only it had been incest, he thought, he might have stayed longer. The family of that church certainly seemed to get on very well with each other, and goodness knows what these tongues were really saying or suggesting. Perhaps an orgy was on the cards.

Carruthers' attendance at churches was very irregular. Willi was the leader in that respect and regularly attended Mass. Carruthers' last visit to church before attending the church of shakers and frothers had been to a memorial service for the deceased wife of a prominent Nigerian, a friend of Carruthers. The Protestant Cathedral was packed and Carruthers seemed to be the only white face in the congregation. When it came to the time when the priest asks the congregation to shake hands in friendship and peace with each other, Carruthers was completely ignored, his extended hand unclasped. He felt ashamed and extremely angry at what he considered racial ignorance. It was about that time that he thought seriously of changing his religion and leaving Nigeria. He was sure that he would be more welcome elsewhere (and years later, he was).

A visit to the UK became necessary at very short notice as a tragedy had struck the Carruthers family. Their son John, aged 17 and at boarding school in England, had knocked his knee during a ski trip to Switzerland. On his return to England, John had been referred by the school doctor to a specialist in Reading, who had confirmed the doctor's diagnosis – cancer of the bone.

Carruthers and Willi managed to get a British Caledonian flight out of Lagos the very same day that John's guardian had phoned up to give them the news that John was in hospital. They travelled first class – the only available seats. A few large whiskies and a cigar calmed Carruthers' nerves. (Looking back, it now seems strange for cigars to have been offered on flights but no one seemed to object in those days.)

On landing at Gatwick they hired a car and went straight to their flat overlooking the Thames at Teddington. They had an appointment with the specialist that afternoon in Reading.

Both Willi and Carruthers were very nervous as they waited to be called in to the specialist's room. They felt devastated. And soon they learnt the seriousness of the situation. John's chances of survival were only 25 per cent. The cancer would soon spread quickly and the only remedy was, in the specialist's opinion, amputation and chemotherapy. He was happy for them to get a second opinion but time was not on their side.

It was worse than they had imagined. Clutching at straws, Carruthers decided to get a second opinion, and the next day took the x-rays to another specialist at London's top cancer hospital, the Royal Marsden. This specialist told Carruthers bluntly that cancer was a killer disease and his own wife was in fact dying from it. However, he thought that because of John's young age it would be worthwhile to try a course of radiation on the knee. He would start as soon as he received instructions. Carruthers rushed back to Reading full of hope, and once again they visited the consultant. But he was adamant that amputation was still the only course. Radiation might well reduce the tumour but the cancer could quickly manifest itself in the lungs. The consultant was very sympathetic but practical, and what persuaded Carruthers and Willi to allow the amputation to go ahead was the caring and pleading look in his eyes as he begged them to allow him to operate. He wanted to do it the next day.

John meanwhile was lying in bed at the Royal Berkshire Hospital in Reading. His father had told him of the possibility of amputation and he and Willi now went back and told him the operation would take place the next day. It was a life or death situation, he was told. The operation in itself was not necessarily serious but the consequences of not having it were. (Carruthers would, for the rest of his life, always remember his son saying he didn't want his leg amputated. Likewise a John Lennon song popular at that particular time would always bring tears to Carruthers' eyes whenever he heard it.) John bore the news with great fortitude. He didn't say much; what could he say? He knew that what his parents had told him must be true. He had always trusted their judgement in his life to date and would have to do it again this time, although he hated to do so. He could run away – but where to? – and he didn't want to die alone.

Willi and Carruthers didn't sleep much that night, and John can't have either. Both prayed almost nonstop. Phone calls were made to relations and friends. Tears flowed. However, they knew in their hearts that they had made the correct decision. The outlook was more positive than the alternative treatment, where there would always be doubt and fear.

In the morning Carruthers signed the consent form for the operation. There were no tears or recriminations from John. He continued to bear it all stoically and was wheeled off to the operating theatre around midday. Carruthers and Willi went to watch a film about the Bermuda Triangle to keep their minds off things but it didn't really help.

The operation was the easy part. There was also a whole long course of treatment by chemotherapy, coupled with the fitting of various false legs constantly being adjusted to fit the shrinking stump. John was angry at these legs, which was probably a good thing as his anger kept him fighting and he never gave up on the legs. It must have been painful. The chemotherapy treatment was administered initially at the Royal Berkshire Hospital then the Royal Marsden Hospital. The legs were fitted at Roehampton Hospital. The level of treatment was excellent.

John started to smoke. He put on weight and lost his hair and learned to vomit regularly. That was the effect of the chemotherapy. Carruthers and Willi bought him an automatic Mini car so he could drive to the hospitals for his treatment. He had to eat before the chemotherapy treatment and would call in at a cheap transport café for his breakfast. Being the son of a good Scot, he knew there was no point in wasting money on an expensive breakfast when he would vomit it up a few hours later.

Initially Willi remained in the UK while Carruthers returned to his job in Nigeria. She made no fuss and gave John all the loving care and attention he needed in those early days of treatment. Regular blood tests and x-rays of the lungs were made to check if the cancer was spreading and these would continue for the next five years.

(Almost 20 years after the amputation, no one on seeing John walking about would ever guess what had happened to him. Running his own business in London, he is able to benefit from free public transport because of his disability. He won the war, backed up by good supply lines provided by consultants, hospitals, parents, brother and sisters, relations, friends and above all God.

Interestingly and very sadly, a girl of the same age whom John knew and whose parents decided on the alternative treatment died within six months.

By a strange coincidence many years after, Carruthers suffering from a recurrent knee problem caused by an old rugby injury, was referred to the same consultant who had carried out his son's amputation. He was able to report to him that after ten years John was alive and well, and again offered him his grateful thanks.)

Chapter 21

Life in Nigeria

Life in Nigeria certainly opened Willi's eyes. It gave her an opportunity to see how the rest of Africa lived and she wasn't initially impressed. Despite all the troubles in Uganda, she considered the people more sophisticated than their Nigerian counterparts, who were very noisy and rude.

The climate in Lagos was so hot and humid she didn't know how she was going to exist in that country. She had been looking forward to going to Nigeria when she was in Nairobi but now she was not so sure.

The days in Nairobi before their departure had been quite hectic. Since John had got back from England and confirmed their move to West Africa it had been non-stop activity, and all this while she was in the early stages of a pregnancy.

She had been astonished to see the photographs of her bras in the airline magazine John brought from London. And soon after that the revelations of the Chairman and his goings-on appearing in the British Sunday newspapers!

John had spent hours reading and rereading the newspapers chortling to himself. He had managed to keep their names out of the newspapers, thank goodness, and had shown a certain amount of dexterity in doing that.

Willi had felt quite sorry for the Chairman and his wife, especially the latter, whom she had got to know quite well. She wondered if John regretted masterminding the whole incident because, whether he admitted it or not, it was he who had encouraged the presentation of bras and taking photographs etc.

He told her that he couldn't help letting his hair down from time to time because the pressures of working in Africa demanded this. As a white expatriate, there was the constant worry of being asked to leave a country because of political pressures or military action as had happened in Uganda. Carruthers, she knew, believed that if one didn't live one's life to the full there was no point in living; everything being equal, Willi to a certain extent agreed. At least her husband was upbeat and amusing and not downhearted and morose like some expatriates she had come across.

One thing she could never understand was why there were always chairmen of John's company visiting him. It was quite confusing and she was beginning to dread that name. In Uganda they had visits from the Nairobi Chairman and the London Chairman. In Nigeria, four chairmen, all from London, would visit at different times. John explained that it was to impress their colleagues at home when they announced they were going on an overseas tour. It was also an all-expenses paid unofficial holiday where they could relax. She was sure they didn't realise the effort that she and John had especially put in to ensure their stay was comfortable and their visit a success. It was understandable that with all these pressures John sometimes behaved irrationally after such visits. She knew that Carruthers aspired to be a Chairman and kept mentioning that he would do a much better job given the chance. She knew he wouldn't give up on his desire and would one day no doubt tell her 'I told you so'. Let us see, she thought.

Talking about visits, she was surprised to see the wearer of the bras, Flora, appear in Lagos, and John even arranged for her to stay with them. She had been deeply suspicious but put on a brave face when Flora first appeared at their Lagos bungalow. John didn't think that she had seen them as she watched through a crack in their bedroom door and saw John greet a half-naked Flora, throatily murmuring good morning and grasping her bra-covered breasts. But she had made sure that Flora didn't remain long as their guest.

Willi made some good friends in Lagos, particularly with some Swedish and French ladies, as well as a couple of Nigerian ladies who taught her how to cook certain Nigerian dishes.

The traditional Nigerian food was hot and spicy and very healthy. While she liked the food, John could not get on with it so she rarely cooked it at home. He preferred the Chinese food plentifully available in restaurants.

Willi found the Nigerian way of life completely different from East Africa. Everyone was always in a rush and constantly moving about. There were so many people and they were very noisy, shouting so they could hear each other above the hubbub. Traffic was horrendous and it took so long to get from one place to another that everybody was always late. Telephones didn't work properly, water was erratic and as for electricity, well, if you didn't have a generator you were finished.

Perhaps that was why Nigerians loved a good party. They would all dress up in their finery, especially the ladies. Willi knew that these ladies spent a fortune on colourful dress materials, and they made a breathtaking sight at their various functions. Often a live band was in attendance. Willi became an expert on Nigerian timing. If you were invited to a party at 8 p.m. then you knew that nothing would happen before 11 p.m.

If your house or garden wasn't big enough to host a large party, you simply held it in the street outside, which would be closed off by tables and chairs. Nobody objected, and in fact the neighbours welcomed it because they had to be invited.

As time went on, Willi decided that she wouldn't mind living in Nigeria if it was a bit cooler, not so noisy and she had plenty of money. The children seemed to relish Nigeria and were happy. As they grew older, however, they would go to boarding schools in England. John had a lot of trouble paying their fees because of foreign exchange restrictions, and she knew that was a constant worry to him and the reason for their eventual withdrawal from Nigeria. Yes, she could understand why he had to let his hair down at times.

News of her army major brother's death in Uganda came as a shock to Willi. She and her family had been fearful that would happen from the day he insisted that he was joining up. He left a widow and four children. Even from afar she was being affected by events on Uganda.

Willi, however, brightened up when she heard that her father was coming to visit them from Kampala. He needed a good rest – and also to get away from the turmoil that was rocking his country. His visit was a great success and John took him to visit the north of the country. All too soon the visit was over and the 70-year-old man returned home.

So, Willi didn't feel too cut off from Uganda, especially as they regularly visited Nairobi on holiday and sometimes she ventured across the border into Uganda while Carruthers looked after the kids in Kenya.

She had two babies delivered in Nigeria, which was quite an experience. Carruthers was stuck in a traffic jam when she delivered her first baby, but luckily an expatriate neighbour took her to the hospital. The staff thought he was the father which was a bit awkward! She agreed on the second occasion, on the advice of her Lebanese doctor, to enter the hospital and have the birth induced, which she did. The only hiccup was when John brought one of those bloody chairmen to visit her when she was feeding her baby.

Much of Willi's life then was concerned with the day-to-day activities of looking after and bringing up her children. This enabled her to meet up with other young and not so young mothers. There were lots of tea parties and also parties for the kids. It was, despite the heat and bustle, a good time for Willi even if it wasn't home.

Although they were safe from attacks by army soldiers as had happened in Uganda, they were still threatened by armed robbers, who were a constant threat at night. They broke into their bungalow one night, unknown to Willi and the rest of the family, who were fast asleep in the bedroom area, behind locked doors and gates. Only electronic goods were stolen which were easily replaceable.

Because John had a more senior position in Nigeria as head of the company, he was invited to conferences occasionally organised by his head office in London. Willi sometimes accompanied him, and she enjoyed being in the Bahamas and Scotland. It gave her the excuse to get some new clothes, which John had to buy her.

Their visits to the UK were much easier now that Carruthers had decided to buy a flat overlooking the river Thames in Teddington, Middlesex. Willi would occasionally stay there on her own when John had to get back to Nigeria to look after the company.

It was a blessing they had that flat when it was discovered that their son John had cancer of the left knee. Willi couldn't believe that amputation was necessary, but John and the specialist surgeon persuaded her that it was. It was a painful time for her and she decided to stay in the flat with John Junior after the operation so she could take him for treatment and the fitting of various false legs. She thought he was very brave and he appreciated her presence greatly.

Eventually she decided John was able to cope on his own, and she left him in the flat while she returned to Nigeria to the other John, who couldn't really cope on his own even with both legs.

Willi was happy to be back in the heat although it was stifling. She didn't really like the cold of England, although she liked the excellent shopping facilities. She was an ardent shopper and could spend hours window-shopping. She met another black lady, a magistrate, while she was shopping one day who told her that as there weren't many black ladies in that area they should get to know each other. This they did, and a long friendship between their respective families started.

John was now starting to get itchy feet in Nigeria. It was 1984 and he was becoming increasingly frustrated, he told Willi. He thought he should start looking for a job in the UK. That's okay by me, Willi thought. Let's wait and see what happens.

Chapter 22

Wind-down

On his various visits to London, Carruthers would always call in at his Head Office and would be wined and dined by the various Chairmen. It was obvious to him that it was a bit late in his business life to try and get his foot in the door of the hierarchy at Head Office, where the people at the top were well entrenched and unlikely to welcome an intruder from overseas. He actually didn't have enough time or money to start politicking for a top job in London and was beginning to feel a bit despondent. He had spent most of his business life in Africa and that is where his fate would be. But he certainly didn't want to spend much more time in Nigeria, where he was being frustrated by ambitious Nigerians in his company and by Nigerian business people who loved to frustrate the white man, especially the bankers who wouldn't remit his savings which were devaluing day by day as the Nigerian economy started to wobble.

On returning to Nigeria, Carruthers felt alone and miserable away from his wife and son. He drowned his sorrows more than he should have but eventually managed to get a grip of himself and threw himself into upcountry visits. The strain, however, took its toll and he suffered a haemorrhage in his right eye, partially blinding him. It was back to London and Moorfields

Eye Hospital this time. Luckily it was nothing serious and he was told it would clear up in a matter of weeks, which it did, to his great relief.

On one of his upcountry visits to Kano, where Carruthers had appointed a new expatriate branch manager, he had to sort out a serious problem concerning booze. The manager and his family didn't drink as they belonged to an evangelical church that didn't allow alcohol to pass the convert's lips. As he was staying at the branch manager's house, Carruthers' request for a cold beer to wash down the dust blown off the Sahara Desert could, therefore, not be fulfilled. This was swiftly remedied by Carruthers informing the manager that while he respected his views, one of his duties was to entertain clients, including his visiting MD and a certain amount of booze should therefore be kept in the house. It could all be put down to expenses, he said, and a gleam appeared in the manager's eyes. From then on quite a bit of entertaining was carried out at his house and he himself was even known to drink the odd glass of wine.

Carruthers hoped his colleague wouldn't go the same way as the Kano manager's former boss in Lagos. That particular manager, Carruthers had noticed, had a very awkward gait and although he appeared sober in public, it turned out that he was an alcoholic. He was in fact a sick man because of his alcoholism and had to be sent back to the UK, where his employers tried to assist him but unfortunately all to no avail. He was retired early on health grounds and died a year or two later. This was an all too common problem in West Africa.

Not learning from their mistake, the same UK employer sent out as a replacement a man in his late 50s with a heart condition. That was to be a death sentence, coping with the harsh climate and a business environment more suited to a younger man. He only lasted two years and died shortly after his return to England.

During his short stay in Nigeria this manager decided to launch a life insurance policy called The Crusader Life Policy. The motif on the sales brochure was a knight holding a lance on his horse. The intention was to sell it to a target group of Nigerians based in the north of the country. Carruthers was appalled and made his views known to the manager, who brushed them aside with a smile as if to say he knew better.

Carruthers pointed out that the majority of Nigerians living in the North were Muslims. First of all, their religion did not encourage them to insure (Allah will provide) and secondly and most importantly, didn't the manager know his history and that the Crusaders of centuries ago had ridden to attack Jerusalem to destroy the Muslims and their faith and restore Christianity? Of course the product didn't sell and the publicity had an adverse effect on the company's fortunes. A Nigerian was appointed to the soon vacant manager's position, but that should have happened much earlier.

The Nigerian manager's wife was a Yorkshire lass and the Carruthers became very friendly with their family. The manager was a friendly soul, not at all arrogant like many of his countrymen. It had to be said that many white women married to Nigerian men had problems coping with a different culture where the male was so dominant and often had a second wife or girlfriend tucked away. To assist each other, the white ladies formed the Niger Wives Club. Carruthers always felt that by doing this they were admitting defeat. Who knows, it probably still exists.

Carruthers and his visiting UK-based Chairman made a

visit to New York and Chicago. They flew direct from Lagos to New York on a Pan Am flight known as the 'grandmother run' because of its aging hostesses. It was ostensibly a business trip and they did do some business. However, Carruthers' main recollection of the visit was when they were thrown out of a New York nightclub after the Chairman attempted to greet the jazz band on stage by jumping on tables and leaping from one to the other to reach them. Bouncers caught him just short of the stage. Carruthers and the two girls at their table quickly left and helped to pick up the Chairman from the sidewalk.

Back in Lagos, the Nigerian branch of the Institute of Directors was formed, with Carruthers as the Vice Chairman. His appointment came about because he was a member of the London-based Institute and was one of the few expatriates to have shown interest in the formation of the Nigerian branch. The Director General came out from the UK for its opening and was given the royal tour, visiting local dignitaries etc.

It was about that time that certain buzz words appeared in business circles. Speakers at functions would talk about 'cash flow', 'level playing fields', 'moving the goal posts', 'transparency' etc. Charitable organisations lost their identities and became NGOs, even churches. It was all very boring and seat-squirming, in Carruthers' opinion.

The Chairman of the Directors' Institute was a prominent Nigerian businessman and a Chief. Any Nigerian of any standing had to keep up with the Joneses and would pay lots of money to be installed as a Chief in his or her local community and perhaps also have a street named after him or her. Often, however, a local community did give chieftaincies as a sign of respect and thanks to a son or daughter of the soil who had distinguished himself or herself or had contributed to the local community. Anyway, many Chiefs existed in Nigeria and sometimes foreigners, especially the British, mistakenly believed them to be minor royals, which of course the Chiefs were quick to capitalise on.

Carruthers became a sort of chief when he became Vice Chieftain of the Lagos Caledonian Society, a thriving organisation open only to those of direct Scottish descent. It was a sight to behold on St Andrew's Night, when the society members and their guests met for their annual ball at a local hotel. Many, including Carruthers, wore the kilt and there was always a piper or two and a Scottish band in attendance. Because the hotel couldn't be trusted to have the required stock of booze necessary, and to speed up service, most Scots brought their own cool boxes to the function. It was an amusing sight to see kilted Scots staggering in under the weight of heavily filled cool boxes and dumping them down to officially shake hands with the Chieftain and his lady, and then staggering off with their boxes to their table places. It was wise not to trust the hotel, because on one occasion Carruthers noticed a member of the staff wheeling blocks of ice in an open wheelbarrow to the bar through the mingled guests. No wonder stomach upsets were common.

On one occasion the Chieftain, having imbibed too much, slid off his chair under the table just after the opening grace and had to be carried out to his car to sleep it off. His wife was not amused.

Many Nigerians knew Scotland quite well and had enjoyed going to university there. They had formed their own Scottish Society and one day invited the office bearers of the Lagos Caledonian Society to a Saturday lunchtime function. This was held at the house of a retired Nigerian Major General. On everyone being seated and welcomed, the Major General announced that everyone should stand to sing the Scottish National Anthem. In those days there was no such thing as a Scottish Anthem, so Carruthers and team were puzzled, only to be highly amused when the Nigerian Scots burst into a rendition of *I belong to Glasgow, dear old Glasgow town*'! A good time was had by all, following that introduction.

About this time Willi and Carruthers made another holiday visit to East Africa to stay with Willi's sister, a nursing sister, and her Swedish husband. An attempted coup took place in Kenya on their day of departure and a curfew had been put in force from the early evening until dawn. The airline assured them they could still fly to Nairobi as the airport was still open, but on arrival they were not allowed to proceed to their relations' house because of the curfew. The army escorted them, along with the other passengers, to the local Intercontinental Hotel in Nairobi for the night, and they were collected by their relations in the morning.

The attempted coup was short-lived. Nevertheless, a lot of looting, mainly of Indian-owned shops in Nairobi, had taken place and the Indian community was highly nervous, as were many others.

Carruthers, Willi and their relations decided to get out of Nairobi and they managed to hire a cottage on the Mombasa coast, where they stayed for a week. The cottage was very old, not luxurious, but right on the beach and ideal for the kids, who were in the sea constantly.

Willi was nervous about the palm-fronded roof, which she said was sure to house snakes, and in this she proved to be correct. The first night they were there Carruthers was awakened by a rustling in the roof. It continued off and on for about half an hour. Everyone else was asleep. Suddenly there was a slapping sound as something fell onto the concrete floor. Carruthers had a torch handy and shone it round the vicinity of his bed. There was nothing to be seen. Gingerly he got out of bed and padded into the nearby open dining area. There on the floor was a long grey snake. It was motionless. Carruthers hissed to his brother-in-law to awaken him, keeping his torch shining on the snake. Luckily his brother-in-law wakened quickly, as did nearly everyone else. There was a panga on the verandah, which his brother-in-law crept out to get. Still the snake was motionless. The panga flashed down and the next moment there was a dead headless snake lying on the floor. It took a while for everyone to get back to sleep, especially as Willi insisted that there must be another one on the roof. However, the rest of the night passed peacefully, although it wasn't easy persuading the ladies to stay in the cottage for the rest of the week.

This brother-in-law was a good sport. Once, on a visit to the Carruthers' house in England he had offered to re-tile their kitchen floor. All the materials were bought and he worked halfway through the night to finish the job. In the meantime, being ever helpful, Carruthers and Willi had gone off to bed, leaving him with a good supply of canned beer in the fridge. At one stage the brother-in-law's back started giving him trouble so he went into the adjoining garage and lay down on his back, clutching a can of beer. The pain subsided and he thankfully raised his eyes to the roof. To his shock he saw a face staring down at him. Too tired to move, he just kept staring and slowly realised that he was staring at a reflection of himself. Carruthers had stored a broken mirror in the rafters of the garage some time before. Heart pounding, his brother-in-law gulped down his beer then fell asleep on the floor.

During that particular visit to Kenya Carruthers met up with an old friend who used to work for him in Kampala and was now working in Nairobi. At one time he had been among a group of expatriates arrested by Amin's soldiers in Kampala and accused of being British spies as they had been seen grouped together, obviously plotting something against the regime. In fact they were all members of the rugby club on the piss after a training session, and they were released later in the day after the intervention of the British High Commission. Soon after that, Amin had banned meetings of groups of more than three people, thus destroying what little social life was left to the population.

During lunch they reminisced about Kampala and Carruthers' friend said he had been very scared when Amin's soldiers had locked him up, because anything could have happened to them. Fortunately they were kept in a police station and not one of the notorious army detention centres. Some British journalists had been put in one of the centres, however, and they would write about their experiences after they were released and out of the country. One journalist had been arrested because when his baggage was searched on his way out of the country at Entebbe airport it was found to contain a Uganda telephone directory issued by the Post Office. He was accused of being a spy and of theft. Luckily, he got off with a fine and was deported.

Carruthers and his friend were in a comfortable steak restaurant in the centre of Nairobi. The steaks were of high quality and there was no pain felt as the meal was washed down by a couple of bottles of red wine. They were seated in a far corner of the large restaurant and so engrossed were they in their reminiscences, they had not noticed that all the staff had disappeared. They only became aware when a decision to have another bottle of wine was reached. The staff for some reason had not seen them in the corner when they were locking up and the restaurant was now closed until 5.30 p.m. It was now 2.45 p.m., and they were supposed to meet their wives in a quarter of an hour.

The outer doors were made of strong mahogany and were firmly locked, as was the bar, a metal grill with a padlock protecting it. On the shelf behind the bar, tantalisingly close but not near enough to reach, was a telephone. They wandered round the empty restaurant. There was no way out and, as the restaurant was some storeys up in a tall building, they couldn't attract the attention of passers-by.

Carruthers said there was no way he was going to sit and twiddle his thumbs for two and a half hours. They eyed the locked bar thirstily. The padlock to the bar grill was quite easy to force open and they were able to clamber over the counter. Unfortunately the telephone was not connected to an outside line so they couldn't raise any assistance. They could, however, operate the music system, which they did, and as there was a large and varied supply of drinks they did not die of thirst.

Just over two hours later the Asian proprietor of the restaurant unlocked the doors, to be greeted by booming music and two white men cheering and waving drunkenly from behind the bar. Their offer to give him a drink was surlily refused. Luckily Carruthers had meticulously written down what they were drinking, and after explaining the situation said they would happily pay for the drinks and the broken padlock but that they were also thinking of suing him for the trouble caused to them. He shook his head and told them to get out, which they did as speedily as they could, chuckling to themselves as they headed down the stairs to the street below.

When they eventually met up with their wives, because of their reputation they were not believed. They had no other explanation to give, so grudgingly the wives came round to accepting their version of the incident – but accused them of engineering the whole episode. You can't win, thought Carruthers. After that, Carruthers always chose corner tables in restaurants but there was no repeat of the experience.

On their way back to Lagos from Kenya, Willi and Carruthers had to spend a night in Addis Ababa before connecting with a flight to Nigeria the next morning. They were put up in an adequate hotel without frills. It certainly wasn't like the five-star Hilton in Addis, where Carruthers had stayed before on one of his business visits, so in the late afternoon they went to visit the Hilton. To their surprise and delight they bumped into an old friend, a former Major General in the Tanzanian Army whom President Nyerere had wanted to keep out of the way and appointed as Ambassador to Nigeria. He was now Ambassador to Ethiopia. They spent the evening at his house, where they met some other General on an undisclosed mission. Willi and Carruthers urged them to get rid of Amin (which of course the Tanzanians eventually did, after Amin made the mistake of invading Tanzania and underestimating the strength of the Tanzanian Army. They entered Uganda from the Tanzania border and marched all the way to Kampala, joined by Ugandans already fighting Amin.)

At Addis Ababa airport the next morning the renewal of old friendships continued as they bumped into

Carruthers' old drinking partner, the ex-Uganda Foreign Minister whom Carruthers had sought out in Dar es Salaam soon after Amin took over. He was in transit to Dar.

Apart from visiting Kenya, while they were based in Nigeria Carruthers and Willi also made holiday visits to Holland and Italy. Willi, being a strong Catholic, was thrilled at her visit to St Peter's Square and the Vatican, where she viewed the Sistine Chapel in hushed amazement. She didn't have the honour of seeing the Pope, but her sister, who was the Mother Superior in Uganda, was presented to him twice some years later, in Rome and Uganda, and her father was presented to him on three occasions. Popes made three visits to Uganda, once in the 60s and twice in the 90s. Security was no problem and Pope-mobiles were never used or indeed deemed necessary.

Carruthers would always remember Amsterdam for a haircut he got there. Espying a barber's shop, he suggested Willi take the kids to a café beside the canal while he got a badly needed haircut. On entering the shop he was immediately welcomed and placed in a chair in front of huge well-lit mirrors, and a couple of young chaps fussed round him asking what style he wished. Carruthers told them to just get on with it, and a glass of sherry was placed in his hand. A shampoo followed, then the cutting, styling and drying, and finally lacquering. Carruthers was shocked at the result. He looked as if he was wearing a lacquered wig and as well as feeling queer, was sure he actually looked queer. He paid his bill with a shaking hand and very self-consciously walked to the café, trying not to mince his steps, to meet Willi, convinced that everyone was looking at him. To her credit Willi said his hair looked nice, which it in fact was, too bloody nice. Carruthers insisted on going back to their hotel immediately, where he stuck his head under a hot shower and dried out his hair. He was now able to style it as it had been before and once again felt like a man. What an experience, an expensive experience as it had turned out. He could have bought a few bottles of sherry for what he paid for the haircut. Ever afterwards, Carruthers hated going to hairdressers especially lady hairdressers in England who asked inane questions during the haircut such as, 'Do you live locally?' 'Are you on your lunch break?' 'Are you working nearby?' 'Have you been on your holidays yet?' He used to make up answers as his mood took him. He once impressed one hairdresser so much after he convinced her he was a business tycoon that he felt obliged to give her a large tip. He soon learned to keep his mouth shut.

While Carruthers was in Nigeria, his father died in Edinburgh from a massive heart attack brought on by many years of smoking at least 20 cigarettes a day. He had nearly died two years before that with another heart attack, and Carruthers' mother had then been told he would never leave the hospital. That remark, made by one of the specialists, was like waving a red rag to a bull, and his mother had taken her husband out of hospital and nursed him at home for the next two years with great loving care.

In those days telegrams still existed, and that is how the news of his father's death was conveyed. It was quite common in Nigeria for bosses to have male secretaries rather than female ones; but Carruthers had attempted to break that mould in his office and had discreetly made arrangements for interviews. The secretary he employed was tall, slim and black and she was efficient. Unfortunately, she didn't stay long, all because of Carruthers' father's death. Carruthers was very busy at his desk when his secretary brought in the telegram. He asked her to open it and read it to him; he was sure it couldn't be that important. She was very reluctant to do so, perhaps some sixth sense telling her it contained bad news, but Carruthers insisted. As she read out the news Carruthers realised that he shouldn't have asked her to open the telegram, and as well as feeling sad for himself felt sorry for the girl. When he returned to Nigeria after attending the funeral his secretary had left and he never came across her again.

The news of the rescue of the Air France hostages at Entebbe by Israeli commandos right under Amin's nose was received with amazement and delight by Carruthers as he listened to the BBC African service. Amin had been closely involved with the terrorists who hijacked the aircraft and although he pretended otherwise (a group of Palestinian terrorists actually lived in Kampala), it was in fact no surprise to him that the aircraft was forced to land at Entebbe. Amin had assured the hostages he was going to help them and he would negotiate with the terrorists. However, he was part of the whole plot. The Israelis knew this, and they also had an intimate knowledge of Entebbe airport, having been military advisors to the previous regime. With the assistance of the Kenya Government, who provided a refuelling stop for the Israeli aircraft at Nairobi, they swept into Entebbe, shot up the Uganda Air Force MIG fighters on the ground, killed the hijackers and some Ugandan soldiers and took off with the released hostages, heading for Israel. One unfortunate hostage, an elderly lady who had been taken to the main hospital in Kampala a day or two before for treatment, was beaten to death on the orders of an irate Idi Amin. The commander of the Israeli commando team, a brother to a future Israeli Prime Minister, also lost his life. So did the traffic controller at Entebbe airport, whom Amin accused of being a collaborator. Amin was now realising that he didn't have many friends left internationally except for the Russians, and even they were distancing themselves.

Amin was a good sergeant major and that was that. Confined to that position within an army, he was useful. Having said that, there had been a history of atrocities in which he was involved when fighting the Mau Mau in Kenya in the late 1950s when he was in the colonial British East Africa army. Obote had been warned about that but had ignored it at his peril when appointing him as head of the Uganda army.

As the President of a country, Amin couldn't cope. However, because he had the physical stature, was boastful, didn't outwardly show any fear or embarrassment and above all was feared, he managed to remain in that position for seven long and troublesome years. He loved women and children, of which he had many. He was also shrewd and knew exactly how his minions and henchmen thought and operated.

On a visit to a popular restaurant and club in Kampala run by a friend of Carruthers, a black Zimbabwean, Amin and his team landed by helicopter at a nearby hotel. He told the restaurant manager that he had heard of its popularity and was there to test it. The manager arranged for drinks and snacks; Amin ordered coffee and his bodyguards ordered soft drinks. Amin looked at his men for a while and then told the manager he knew very well that they didn't all like soft drinks. Some of them liked spirits, others beer, and he should serve them that. They all laughed. When they had finished Amin asked for the bill. The nervous manager said it had been an honour to host the President and there would be no charge. Amin insisted on a bill and the manager prepared one, which was heavily discounted. On receiving it Amin shook his head and asked how he could make a profit charging those prices. He then asked for a correct bill, which he duly got and which he paid in cash, telling the manager that he knew his own staff too well and if he had not paid the bill, some of his staff would have appeared in the future demanding free food and drinks. So despite his bad reputation he could be caring when the pressures were off him.

People in Uganda were to find that after Amin had been overthrown life was not going to be any easier. The civilian President who took Amin's place was a respected academic and not a politician. Willi and Carruthers invited their close friends to their Lagos house for a celebratory lunch, and the new Uganda President's son and his wife were in attendance as he was then working in Lagos. Unfortunately, the new President became dictatorial and was replaced by a fellow tribesman, a Queen's Counsel. Both were from the major tribe, the Baganda, and had come out of exile. The second President didn't last long either. Rigged elections then allowed Obote back, a situation most of the population of Uganda had never envisaged. Fighting eventually erupted between the Government and a small but effective guerrilla force led by Yoweri Museveni. Many civilians were killed in the hostilities, more than under Amin, and it was not until seven years after the overthrow of Amin (1986) that order was restored and a popular government installed and the country could once again go forward.

During Obote's second coming, when Carruthers was

on a visit to Kampala from Lagos he went to a luncheon meeting at the Kampala Lions Club. There a prominent Buganda leader and ex-Mayor of Kampala urged him to tell people outside the country that many of his tribe were being targeted and murdered by Obote's soldiers, and Carruthers repeated this story many times after he left.

By the time a stable government was installed in Uganda, Carruthers and Willi were getting tired of Nigeria, especially as it was becoming increasingly difficult to remit money out of the country for savings and school fees . They decided to leave, and Carruthers asked his UK head office to find him a job. The Nigerian directors of the company couldn't understand why he wanted to leave. As far as they were concerned there was no better place than Nigeria.

Carruthers had no idea what sort of job he would be offered by his Head Office. He couldn't very well tell them that he wanted to be a Chairman! He was leaving Nigeria out of necessity and would have to accept what was given to him, like it or not. His UK-based savings had again dwindled and as the saying went, 'beggars cannot be choosers'.

Chapter 23

Working in England

Carruthers and Willi left Nigeria on 2nd January 1987. They couldn't go to Uganda to work as there was no job available there. They would spend five years living and working in England, the first time in his life that Carruthers had ever worked there.

His new job, as an insurance consultant subcontracted to British Airways, would take Carruthers on business visits to places of which he had only dreamed. From that point of view it was an exciting and interesting job, 75 per cent of his time being involved with the airline. Coming from overseas however he found it hard settling into the life of a UK office where some directors resented and were wary of his presence. Whereas he had been his own boss, he now had three or four bosses above him, most of whom were younger than him. One of his bosses considered Carruthers' overseas visits as nothing more than an exercise in being able to collect duty-free goods, which Carruthers considered a very petty view. He was, of course, even more suspicious when Carruthers happened to be in New Zealand during the first World Rugby Cup and managed to see the final. Another member of staff, a white South African who thought she would be murdered when Mandela was released and had fled to England, was quite shocked when Carruthers told her his wife was black. He watched her reactions in amusement and bought her a drink next time he saw her in a pub near the office.

The one good thing about being in England was that he and Willi were near their children and also his aging mother. So he put up with the frustrations of working as a minion instead of a boss, and they managed to continue their children's private education, including colleges and universities. All was well on that front. Willi tolerated Carruthers' frequent visits abroad and even got herself a job. She also had to get a British driving licence and took a few lessons to get used to the British roads and driving standards. It was a wise thing to do after driving in Nigeria, where it was a free-for-all situation.

On one occasion Carruthers remembered a Nigerian driver in Lagos suddenly overtaking him and slowing down in front of him to show his superiority over a white driver. Although Carruthers braked hard, he still touched the back of the car in front, which went into an uncontrollable spin crashing into a barrier at the roadside. Luckily the driver was unhurt but shocked. Other Nigerian drivers who had seen what happened roundly abused their fellow driver, and Carruthers drove off without a backward glance.

Before Willi took her driving test, Carruthers bought her a car. The salesman at the garage was amazed when Carruthers paid for the car and told him Willi would collect it the next day, after she had sat her driving test. How could Carruthers be sure she would pass the test, the salesman asked? I know my wife, Carruthers told him. Sure enough, she passed, and on collecting the car found a large bouquet of flowers from the salesman. That was how Willi and Carruthers lived their life together – by positive thinking and always looking ahead. They never celebrated anniversaries, just the kids' birthdays.

They knew they would return to Uganda sometime. That was why Carruthers insisted that they should never sell their bungalow overlooking the lake in Kampala, although he received a telephone call from a lawyer saying that a client of his in Kampala was interested in buying it. At that time Carruthers could have well used the cash, but he turned down the offer. As far as he was concerned, the sentimental value was higher than the monetary value, even although it had been 15 years since they had lived in it.

The company Carruthers worked for in England was now no longer part of the group and had no overseas operations. The demerger turned out to benefit the company bosses financially; although they would deny that, it became quite obvious. Lawyers, accountants and merchant banks also benefited. Staff were given share options – all except Carruthers, who was told that because he had worked overseas he wasn't eligible. He bought his own shares privately. But he didn't like being sidelined and was even more determined to get another job, preferably in Uganda. He thought that if he could raise the cash he could buy a substantial shareholding which may persuade his Board to take him more seriously. He had already had one altercation with his boss, a Director, and had blatantly used his shareholding to warn the Director to back off. Another Director had told Carruthers that he was being presumptuous in asking for a seat on the Board. So much for my ambition to be a Chairman, he thought.

Carruthers and Willi's social life in England was vastly different from what they had experienced overseas. They had been used to constant cocktail parties, dinners etc. That now changed and it was all very boring for Carruthers, although Willi seemed to like living in England and made a lot of friends. Of course Carruthers' social life was affected by the fact that he had no expense account as such. He had to prove to his company that anyone he took out for lunch or dinner in the UK would without fail put business the company's way, but he got so fed up with this scrutiny that he didn't even consider entertaining possible clients locally. It amused him, however, that the scrutineer, one of his director bosses, the one always going on about duty-free, never picked up on the entertainment expenses claimed by Carruthers on his overseas visits, which he milked rather ruthlessly. Everyone had their blind spot, Carruthers mused, as he walked away with his signed-off expense sheet after another overseas visit. Soon after Carruthers left the company, he was happy to hear that the scrutineer had been asked to retire early. Too many expenses and not enough profit was the reason given.

To add to the frustrations Carruthers experienced, the company installed a clocking in and out machine. Everyone had to clock in and out of the office whenever they left or entered, as if they were working in a factory. Big brother was certainly watching. It was a farcical situation because the staff were nearly all of professional calibre, not the types to cheat on their times of leaving and returning, more especially as they had people like the scrutineer lurking around.

Willi's father came to visit them in England. The highlights of his stay were visits to Windsor Castle, Salisbury Cathedral, having lunch with the Uganda High Commissioner at the Commonwealth Club on Northumberland Avenue in London, and watching the World Football Cup on television. He also visited Sweden to see Willi's three sisters, all married to

Swedes. Finally he spent a weekend with a Knight of the Realm, no less, a former colonial servant in Uganda who later became High Commissioner there. He had known Willi's father when they were both young and both working in Uganda for the colonial service – Willi's father was aged 86 at the time of his visit.

Willi and Carruthers had first met the Knight at a memorial service in London at St-Martin-In-the-Fields for an ex-Mayor of Kampala – the very one, in fact, who had asked Carruthers to tell people that his tribe were being killed off by Government forces.

After the service, the Knight had approached Willi and said he was sure he recognised her, and Carruthers, standing nearby, pricked up his ears. As it turned out she didn't know him, so she said; but the Knight had seen in Willi's face the likeness of her father. That was how Willi's father came to spend a weekend at the Knight's home in Godalming, Surrey. They in turn reciprocated, and the Knight and his Lady visited the Carruthers. That, however, was the end of the association. The zebra skin on their wall and the elephant's foot table seemed to have upset them.

Carruthers made regular visits to his mother in Edinburgh, and she also came to stay with them for a short while. She was, however, getting old quite quickly. His first visit to her after leaving Nigeria was by car, and he drove past the site of the Lockerbie disaster only a few days after a bomb blew up the aircraft over the town. It was a sad sight and proved that he hadn't left terrorism behind in Africa.

Carruthers nearly got into a racial brawl on a business visit to Berlin, which was still divided. It was the eve of a conference organised by a large insurance group, and people were sitting in the bar getting to know each other. They were talking at one stage about Uganda, and Carruthers mentioned that his wife was a black Ugandan. For some unknown reason this greatly irritated an English broker working in Germany, who started saying some very derogatory things about black people. Carruthers was forced to respond by suggesting that his new acquaintance must have become a Nazi during his stay in Germany. The Nazi then launched himself at Carruthers and had to be forcibly restrained and persuaded to leave. One of the group, a newly found friend who knew Uganda well, tried to get the antagonist to apologise the next day but he refused. It turned out that the lady who was with him in the bar and who was sharing a room with him was not his wife, and he had perhaps been trying to show off to his girlfriend. Who knows? It would remain a puzzle. The only other highlight of the visit was an organised trip into East Berlin, where they visited a museum containing some old Egyptian temple that had been reconstructed. Carruthers would rather have done that in Egypt where as far as he knew there were no Nazis.

One of the positive things Carruthers did in England was to give up pipe smoking. An old expatriate friend in Kenya who was a regular pipe smoker had died suddenly from lung cancer. After coming out of the Forces, when he had been in Ensa, he had set up what was to become a well-known puppet theatre in Edinburgh, and he had been involved in broadcasting in both Uganda and Kenya. He had a fantastic collection of puppets, some of which Carruthers and Willi had seen, and before his death he donated them to a museum in the North of England where they would be properly looked after. After his death a further tragedy befell the family when his 20-year-old son died of cerebral malaria while on an international flight.

It was actually Willi who insisted that Carruthers give up smoking, and he complied, as a dutiful husband should. Although he hadn't inhaled he felt a certain peace of mind. But he still retained his collection of pipes, including two Sherlock Holmes meerschaums. About ten years later he thought to take up the habit again but found he had lost the taste for it so didn't bother persevering. Naturally, Willi was delighted. She wasn't so delighted when he suggested selling off his pipe collection and investing in a collection of whips, starting off with a *jambok* from South Africa.

He had seriously thought of buying a *jambok* at one time to add to their collection of African artefacts but thought that perhaps that would be too controversial with its racial overtones. He wished, however, he had one when he first met that objectionable fellow in Berlin; he deserved a good whipping.

Their house in South-East England was already full of artefacts, including Nigerian bronzes, ivory heads, paintings, a small elephant tusk, a large zebra skin, a zebra skin table and an elephant foot table. Conservationists would cringe, Carruthers thought, but some had been given as presents, some had been bought legally in Kenya, and the elephant foot had actually been bought in a Scottish antique shop – it was Victorian. He also had a buffalo head in his Uganda house. Sometimes he would tell people he had shot them all, but really he had never shot an animal in his life.

Willi and Carruthers socialised to a certain extent with quite a large Uganda exile crowd living in London.

Carruthers renewed acquaintance with the late King of Buganda's brother in London and they used to have lengthy monthly luncheons at the Commonwealth Club, where Carruthers was a member. Of course these were non-claimable expenses.

The brother of the late Kabaka, who had been very close to him, kept getting himself involved in great love affairs. On one occasion he told Carruthers that during colonial times he had announced that he had become engaged to a white girl he had met in the UK and they were travelling together from England to Uganda so that he could introduce her to his brother and family. The Kabaka was amused and secretly felt nothing would come of it, but the Colonial Government took a more serious and pragmatic view and insisted that the whole affair must be nipped in the bud. A mixed-race marriage, especially where a member of a royal family was concerned and where relations between the Colonial Government and the Kabaka were already strained, could not be countenanced.

The Prince duly arrived at Entebbe airport with his fiancée and was met by the Governor's representative and an Inspector of Police. He was politely but firmly told that the lady was not allowed to enter Uganda, and she was put back on the same flight – much to the consternation of both. He stayed, she went; he never married her. (The xenophobia of British governments on such matters would be repeated many years later with Diana and Dodi.)

Two of Willi's cousins – a lawyer and daughter of the late Kabaka's sister, Willi's aunt and her brother, an accountant – were also in London. The heir to the throne of Buganda was living in London too, and they would also meet up from time to time. The main topic of conversation was when they would all be able to return to Uganda. They once attended a dinner hosted by a junior Government Minister at the Palace of Westminster to officially meet the heir to the Buganda throne. Most Ugandans and their friends knew him anyway; however, it was a nice touch after the disgraceful way his father had been treated by the then British Government. An Asian MP, Keith Vaz, was supposed to address the dinner but couldn't attend as he had flu. He sent his mother instead.

The problem of when they would return to Uganda was soon solved. Through his contacts with his former colleagues, Carruthers learnt that the MD of the office in Uganda was going to be retired early due to his political activities. These had been against the company's interests as it was involved in business with certain arms of the government, and if such opposition continued, it would be digging its own grave, so to speak.

Carruthers let it be known that he was available if they were looking for a successor. A couple of interviews followed – which were really just friendly conversations with old friends – and he was offered the job. Not, however, as Chairman but as Managing Director. He had kept all this a secret from Willi and broke the news to her over a lunch he arranged for the two of them, again not claimable as an expense!

Contrary to Carruthers' expectations, Willi was not greatly excited. She had found her niche in a quiet and safe society after many years of living in crisis-torn and unsafe African countries. She relished her peaceful existence and being near her children.

Eventually she accepted that as they would certainly go back one day it was better to do it when a job was available and with an expense account! So Carruthers took the job and plans were made to leave for Africa in a couple of months' time. But first he would have to attend a conference at Victoria Falls in Zimbabwe where all the African office representatives were meeting. That was a good start, Carruthers thought, and he had great pleasure in telling his office colleagues of his move.

Having thought disrespectfully of his office bosses for most of the time he spent in England he was surprised to be presented by the board of directors with a Stuart crystal set of a decanter and whisky glasses. Carruthers put it down to a collective guilty conscience. A whip-round from the staff enabled him to buy some golf equipment.

It was a coincidence that Carruthers had been offered the job in Uganda at that time because only four months previously Willi and Carruthers had visited Uganda together for a couple of weeks. They had stayed with Willi's elder sister and seen her parents, and Carruthers had renewed acquaintances at his old office little realising that he would be back sitting there in about six months' time as the boss.

Carruthers had a nasty accident on that visit. It was a Sunday morning and they were getting ready to go to church. Willi's sister had an ancient but workable Volvo which had belonged to her late husband, and was waiting for them. But when Carruthers headed downstairs, the next thing he knew was that he was tumbling head over heels down the stairs ending up in a sitting position against a wall. His head had hit the wall violently and although he was not unconscious, Carruthers knew he was badly hurt. He managed to stand up and call for help from Willi and her sister, blood pouring from the back of his head.

Instead of the Volvo taking them to church, they went instead straight to hospital, where Carruthers had 18 stitches put in the head wound. Strangely enough, he never even had a headache. He reckoned that at long last he had had some sense knocked into him. The lady surgeon at the Catholic missionary hospital had done a good job in sewing him up and the private doctors he subsequently saw both in Kampala and London declared that everything was in good order, and soon the stitches were out.

Carruthers never knew how the accident had happened. It could have been a blackout, but more likely his knee, always weak from that old rugby injury, had given way, as it did occasionally. Or possibly it was a combination of both.

The private doctor in Kampala whom Carruthers consulted before he and Willi returned to England was the same doctor who had so ably treated him for his sore throat many years before. After examining the sewn-up scars, he said to Carruthers that it would be nice to see him back in Uganda again. This was another prophetic statement, as it turned out.

The Victoria Falls conference was just like old times for Carruthers amongst his former colleagues, who were delighted to see him back on board. The Falls were a magnificent spectacle, and to his surprise at the railway station next to the large colonial-type hotel was a long line of railway wagons painted in Uganda Railway colours. Another omen. They also were on their way to Uganda after being manufactured in Zimbabwe.

On his return from Zimbabwe Carruthers prepared for his return to Uganda. Willi would not accompany him initially as she wanted to see their youngest daughters through their 'A' levels. She would join him in a year's time and he would stay with her sister and her daughter during that year. There was no way Willi would let Carruthers stay on his own, especially when she remembered that the lady of the bras had returned to Uganda to be at the mine with her husband. That had to be one of his first client visits, Carruthers thought.

Chapter 24

Homecoming

It had been 20 years since Carruthers and Willi had lived together in their house overlooking the lake in Kampala. When Willi eventually joined him they would be by themselves this time as the kids were grown up and either studying or working in the UK.

As the Sabena flight flew low over Lake Victoria in its approach to Entebbe airport, Carruthers felt quite emotional. He was returning home. It was 1992. After leaving East Africa in 1974 they had spent 13 years working and living in Lagos and then 5 years in England. That was the first and last time Carruthers would ever work in England. His job in England as a consultant to British Airways had taken him all over the world, visiting 15 different countries. There was certainly enough material there for a book, Carruthers thought, covering his experiences outside of East Africa. All those interesting cities – Lagos, Kano, Enugu, Hong Kong, Kuala Lumpur, Sydney, Chicago and Bangkok and many more. However, he was more than happy to be returning to Kampala although it was still war-ravaged.

During their absence from East Africa, Carruthers and Willi had never cut off contact with relations and friends in Kampala and he was looking forward to meeting up again with all these people on a regular basis, as well as eventually living in his own house. Bearing in mind their past experiences when Idi Amin was in power, their previous visits to Kampala had been carried out separately until very recently as they didn't want to draw attention to themselves, especially as the Entebbe airport complex and the city of Kampala had security operatives moving about and spying on everyone.

On one of these visits to Kampala Carruthers had seen an old friend, whom he hoped to see again now he was back, sitting with others on the verandah of the City Bar, a once well known bar and restaurant, which was sadly neglected and a shadow of its former self when it was Uganda-Asian owned. Approaching his friend from behind, Carruthers had placed his hand on his right shoulder. He immediately regretted doing this as his friend shot a few feet into the air, still in a sitting position. He had thought he was being arrested by one of the many security operatives, and Carruthers was very embarrassed. He bought beers for everyone but there was a strained atmosphere and he left as soon as he could, not wanting to get anyone into trouble. (Carruthers wouldn't in fact meet his friend again as he had since died from a heart attack.)

On that same occasion, he had gone to visit his friend, the former Clerk to the National Assembly and former Ambassador to France, who had re-emerged from keeping his head down and moved back into public life as Secretary to the Cabinet. His office was next to President Obote's in an office block adjoining Parliament. Obote was on his second term as President after dubious elections, a term of office which sadly was not to do him credit.

Anyway, Carruthers was interested in friendship and not politics, so he was determined to see his old friend again. Getting past a lorry full of armed and malevolent-looking soldiers at the gate to the offices was a bit nerve-racking, and he forced himself not to look back as he crossed the courtyard. Approaching him, a quizzical look on his face, was his friend, the once exiled Minister he had met up with in Dar es Salaam and at Addis Ababa airport. They greeted each other warmly and Carruthers explained where he was going, and was directed to the appropriate office. Everyone seemed tense, Carruthers thought, but his reunion with his old friend was very emotional and friendly.

That evening his friend and his wife took Carruthers out to dinner at the only Chinese restaurant, and in fact at that time one of the few restaurants open in central Kampala. It had been a very happy evening for them. His friend was in a powerful Government position – but that would only last a few years until the army toppled the regime. (However, his friend would survive and emerge again.)

The runway at Entebbe came into view and it seemed as if the wheels of the aircraft would touch the waters of the lake as they approached the tarmac. Everyone applauded as they landed, the excitement of being home replacing the apprehension felt as they had come into land. There were many returning exiles on that flight.

Everything was very peaceful as Carruthers and the other passengers walked across the apron to the airport building. The sun was shining and an early morning mist was slowly dispersing. There was only one other aircraft on the ground, a Uganda Airways cargo plane.

He was met at the airport by a delegation from his office, Two men and one woman, who had worked with him all those years ago in the early 1970s. They didn't seem to have changed much. Probably they dye their hair like me, Carruthers thought.

On taking up his job in England, Carruthers, noticing that most of the people in the office seemed younger than him, had decided to apply dye to his emerging grey hair and he had done this diligently ever since. He had been determined to survive in his new environment, and didn't want anyone to use the image of an aging returning expatriate as an excuse for getting rid of him or blocking his promotion prospects. It had, however, been an exercise in futility. Carruthers had found it quite easy to spot dyed hair in other men and presumed the same would apply to him. However, it wasn't vanity – it was brought on by necessity. (He gave up the habit not long after his return to Uganda and told everyone that his hair had suddenly gone grey due to pressures of work, but he didn't get much sympathy.)

He was delayed at the airport for some hours while his colleagues negotiated the release from customs of new computer equipment that he had brought with him. Carruthers was bringing modernisation to the Kampala office, which had never possessed such equipment. Eventually it was released and they proceeded to Kampala in a clapped-out old Toyota. (In a few years' time Kampala would be flooded with computer equipment, as it would with new and expensive four-wheel-drive vehicles.)

A welcoming party had been arranged for him at the office. No one believed that his appearance in the office some six months ago had been a coincidence; however, everyone was happy to see the return of the prodigal son.

Later that day he settled in at Willi's sister's house, which was built on a hill with a fine view of the city. He was now back working and living in this intriguing and exciting African city. Life could begin again! Hallelujah! He was 55 years old but still felt youthful.

What amazed Carruthers when he had settled into his office was that all the files and records he had left 20 years ago were still there, neatly filed in cabinets. It was as if time had stood still. The same clients were still clients, although many of the personalities had changed. It was fascinating going through old records and photographs of staff. The immigration department still retained his old file going back to 1963. So in effect it was quite an easy process to pick up the pieces again.

He spent the first few months of his return looking up as many old friends and acquaintances as he could find and also making new friends and business contacts.

In the city, buildings, roads and sidewalks were slowly being repaired. The population had been exhausted after many years of war and it had taken time for the Government to restore confidence. But confidence there was and most of the population had breathed a massive sigh of relief when they realised that the Government of President Yoweri Museveni, who with his loyal followers had spent six years fighting a bush war against the oppressive Obote Government, was there to protect them and not to oppress them – and to encourage them to develop themselves and families, and indeed the whole country. Museveni was their saviour, and Carruthers knew he would never have been able to come back if it had not been for that man.

He had only been in his office a couple of days when his old friend, the aging Vice President, phoned him to welcome him home. He went round to his office the next day to swap reminiscences. His friend extolled the virtues of the Movement System of Government, whereby everyone from village representatives upwards was able to contribute in thought and deed to the future well-being of their country. Party politics was out for the time being.

Most of Carruthers' old haunts had gone. The army now used the Uganda Club, and the nightclub known as the Top Life Club was razed to the ground, and the Suzannah, another then popular nightclub, famed for its under-floor coloured lighting, was now an Adventist church. Those good old days had indeed gone. The other members' club was a shade of its former self and Carruthers felt no desire to rejoin.

(Over the next few years many new bars and restaurants would be opened bearing strange names such as Half London, Kaos and Tender Loving Care. A sports bar, Just Kicking, bore the legend above the door 'No Hookers Allowed'.)

The British High Commission had also opened a bar attached to their offices for the use of British expatriates at a time when it was dangerous to be out visiting local places. That was very popular and was open three times a week during certain hours. Carruthers made many friends and business contacts there.

His name also attracted some comment from newcomers to the expatriate scene who thought Carruthers was a fictional name reserved for old colonialists and spy books. When he introduced himself to one such expatriate, the man burst out laughing and said he must be joking. Carruthers very nearly punched him on the nose. Of course the man was English and didn't know that Carruthers was a good old Scottish name and that there was a town called Carrutherstown in Dumfriesshire. There was a series of old Carruthers' jokes, most of which Carruthers had heard. One was about the dinner table guest slowly sliding his hand up the dress of the heavily built lady next to him and having a note thrust in front of his eyes which said, 'Should you decide to go any further, please do not show surprise, [signed] *Carruthers MI5*'. Another was the one about the captured colonial explorer sitting in a steaming cauldron over a fire in the jungle and a native writing a menu card saying, 'Does Carruthers have one "r" or two?' Then there was another one about a gorilla or something, and so it went on. It was all very boring.

Carruthers, as a Scot, was in fact to become Chieftain of the Caledonian Society of Uganda, which had been formed in 1907. Twice, as it turned out; the second time at short notice when the Chieftain elect, a married man, decided that getting lessons in Luganda from the attractive Muganda lady with whom he worked would also improve his promotion prospects. Unfortunately, he was to learn bedroom Luganda rather than business Luganda and was forced out of his job and the country.

The Vice Chieftain who took over the Chieftainship from Carruthers after his first stint was a South African, but his father was Scottish-born. The new Chieftain had never been to Scotland or owned a kilt – which he certainly needed for the St Andrew's Day Ball over which he was to preside, and arrangements were made for him to have one made in Edinburgh and sent out to Kampala. It arrived just in time and he was able to wear it with appropriate dignity. He looked the part as he was a big man with a beard. It was lucky that Carruthers and Willi arrived at the function early because the new Chieftain, resplendent in his new kilt, had it on the wrong way round with the pleats in front. There were roars of laughter all round. On meeting the Chieftain's Scottish father, Carruthers was amused to find father and son talking away to each other in Afrikaans. Anyway, he turned out to be a very good Chieftain and he did eventually go and visit Scotland, which he enjoyed immensely.

* * *

Carruthers had established early on that business at the mine had more or less ceased and that the former MD and his wife were no longer there. He made a visit to that part of the country, driving himself in his company vehicle – now a Land Rover. That was the type of vehicle most suited to many of the roads in and around Kampala, although their condition would improve slowly over the years.

On reaching the mine he was saddened to see how run-down it was. What had once been a bustling mining town was now an almost deserted marketplace. There was no meaningful activity. The adjacent hotel, where so much fun had taken place, was in a similar state and the golf course was overgrown. At least he had his memories. You can't revive the past, Carruthers reminded himself. Look forward.

He travelled on to Fort Portal past a closed fish factory and a run-down cement factory. The tarmac road was full of pot-holes, although most of the road from Kampala was in very good condition up to then, as it had been funded by EC money. The well-maintained tarmac road stopped near the entrance to Queen Elizabeth National Park, as the purpose of the donors was to assist Uganda in attracting tourists to the park, which it did, on and off.

Apart from the roads, the countryside had not changed. It was green and lush, with large plantations of cooking bananas. The villages he passed through were poor and the clothing of the inhabitants reflected that. However, that also would slowly change for the better.

At Fort Portal, Carruthers was delighted to find the Gluepot Bar, the old meeting place of the tea planters, still functioning. It also was run-down but the beer was cold and relatively cheap. He was told that some of the tea planters had returned, one of them being the old friend of his ex-Chairman in whose house they had stayed – the one whose wife's daughter had been found by Carruthers in strange circumstances! If he hung around for another hour, the lady bar owner told him, she was sure he would call in.

And call in he did, with another old friend who had stayed throughout all the years of turmoil, keeping his head down. The other friend hadn't been deported as he had all his property registered in his wife's name before Amin took over. The exiled tea planter friend and his wife had gone to Australia for some years, then Southern Sudan and eventually came back to Uganda. The wife was at present staying with her daughter and son-in-law in Nairobi. Carruthers had not been in contact with the daughter for 20 years and he wondered how she looked. Her stepfather opined that she had matured well. Like a good wine, perhaps, Carruthers thought, and very tasty too.

Many beers later, they went their own way – the tea planter back to his house and tea estate which he had managed to repossess, the other to his farm and Carruthers to the Mountains of the Moon Hotel. This was now very run-down except for the gardens, which were more easily maintained than man-made structures. Carruthers promised his friends to return in the not too distant future.

Chapter 25

New Experiences

Back in Kampala, Carruthers was determined to get his house back into shape. He had about a year to do so before Willi would return, and their love nest must be perfect so as to make it easier for her to settle back into Uganda life.

Tenants occupied their house, and Carruthers gave them three months' notice to quit. The time passed quickly and at the end of three months they were not ready to move out. While he was sympathetic, he was adamant that he had to get the building contractors in to start renovation, and if they wanted to put up with the noise and dust it was up to them. They finally moved out three weeks later as the kitchen began to disintegrate around them. Carruthers was building a completely new kitchen for Willi. An Irish carpenter was making smart built-in cupboards, and all the electrical equipment, such as cooker, refrigerator and washing machine, had been bought in the UK and was on its way to Kampala. The measurements had been communicated to the carpenter, and amazingly it all fitted in exactly when the equipment eventually reached Kampala.

An expatriate builder who ran his own small business in Kampala carried out the overall renovation. Roof tiles were replaced and more security gates installed;

the verandah was extended and sunshades for it ordered from South Africa; and plastering and painting were carried out. The original unused study was changed into a library and TV room with a bar. It was, as a friend described it, a lovely inglenook.

Willi would look after the garden when she came. Carruthers hated gardening but enjoyed looking at gardens. However, Willi had green fingers and was an expert, so Carruthers quite happily left it in her hands. When she returned the first thing she did was cut down a very large mango tree that obstructed the view of the lake. Sad, but it had to go, as that was the reason he built the house in that location – to view the lake. Eventually the place where the mango tree had been would be replaced by a kidney-shaped swimming pool, which added a touch of glamour to the surroundings.

The walls of the house inside and outside were painted bright white and the metal window frames gloss black. The clay roof tiles, locally made, were red. The reason for the white walls was that as well as lightening up the house, mosquitoes that managed to get in the house could easily be seen when they landed on the walls; mosquitoes are brown but after a few sucks of human blood become black. Most of their African artefacts were in the UK and they would bring some of them out later. Willi had told Carruthers of an African friend's house she had been in which was full of such artefacts, to which Carruthers had replied that in Willi he had an African human artefact, a work of art that was surely better.

A generator big enough to run the lights, TV and fridge for four or five hours was also purchased as the power supply was erratic because of the demand outstripping the supply.

So everything was set for Willi's return to Uganda.

She had a beautiful house awaiting her, all her relations and a loving husband. It would almost be like starting their married life again, Carruthers thought, and in a way it was.

Carruthers was not the only one renovating his house. Asians whose houses and buildings had been possessed by Idi Amin were returning to carry out their own renovations and rebuilding where necessary. Many Asian families had prospered during their years of exile, and most of the sons and daughters who were very young when their parents had to leave did not return. There were not many countries in the world where one could return after 20 years' exile and move into one's old residence. Despite rebel armies on the borders of Uganda, Museveni had created a sense of security in the major urban centres and Asians and the like who did decide to return had no real qualms. And there was free movement of capital in and out of the country. However, many, like Carruthers, had armed guards at their residences.

Over the succeeding years Kampala would regain much of its beauty and cleanliness while sadly its neighbouring capital Nairobi in Kenya would go the opposite way. Despite that there was more money in Kenya and, more importantly, a middle class with disposable income. This was yet to be created in Uganda and was one of the priorities of the Museveni era. Many well-off, middle-class young Ugandans resided and worked in North America and Europe but were hesitant to return to Uganda for fear of losing their residential status in their host countries. They did send money to Uganda, however, accounting in part for a boom in housing construction. Carruthers was certain that if a dual nationality system was introduced in Uganda it would go a long way to solving the middle-class problem and encourage these Ugandans to set up industries and, more importantly, in Carruthers' opinion, further develop and expand the agriculture sector.

Carruthers had restored the fortunes of the Uganda company of which he was MD. Staff were more confident of the future and he had promoted a long-term lady employee to a Manager – the first lady ever to aspire to that title in the company's 40-year history. The male diehards in the company were shocked and tried to discourage him from going ahead with the appointment but to no avail.

Carruthers had mentioned to his London bosses that the position of Chairman of the company in Uganda was vacant and why shouldn't he fill it? They felt it was early days in the company's resurrection and would prefer a black Ugandan. Carruthers approached a good friend and highly respected businessman who agreed to take on the job in a non-executive capacity. He said he would recommend Carruthers to take over his duties in a few years' time. Carruthers was elated. His ambition was going to be realised although at a much later age than he had originally envisaged.

Carruthers sat musing about all this as he sat on his verandah. It wasn't easy thinking about economic matters in such beautiful surroundings. Three different species of birds were quenching their thirst at the side of the swimming pool in the far corner of the garden. He could see a heron, an ibis and a hammerkop. Occasionally a turquoise-blue kingfisher with its red beak would dive into the water. Sometimes the odd snake and frog would appear at the swimming pool and be quickly caught by the birds. Willi hated snakes and was not too keen on entering the swimming pool after one had decided to join Carruthers in an early morning swim one day.

Opposite the verandah was a large palm tree, which provided an abundance of palm oil nuts that were much sought after by various types of birds – kites, vultures, fish eagles, crows, parrots, lovebirds, woodpeckers, hawks etc. The strangely called plantain eaters preferred the young buds from flowering trees. And once or twice a day the large white freight ferries could be seen steaming across the bay from Tanzania and Kenya into Port Bell to offload their cargoes. One therefore could never really be bored sitting on Carruthers' verandah.

On various occasions he had also been able to observe human birds, in the alluring shape of young naked Ugandan ladies carrying out their ablutions on the flat roof of the garage attached to an unfinished house a little distance below. Binoculars to eyes, Carruthers found this an exciting early evening pastime as he sipped his whisky and soda. Willi spoilt this innocent bit of fun one day when she asked to have a look, thinking Carruthers was gazing at birds of the feathered variety. She had been quite shocked at this invasion of someone's privacy, but as Carruthers pointed out, the ladies seemed to welcome such invasion from the way they cupped their breasts in their hands and looked meaningfully towards the verandah. He suggested to Willi that she should get down there and sell some bras, but Willi had long ceased that trade. Anyway, the ladies disappeared not long after that and Carruthers suspected that Willi had gone to have a word. The spoilsport.

On her return Willi had decided not to resume selling underwear. She felt that this could prove too much of a distraction for Carruthers at his age, and with so many attractive young girls thronging Kampala, many with short skirts, she felt she had to protect her man from wicked thoughts. In that she failed miserably. She therefore took up pickle and chutney making and sewing American-style quilts, at which she became very adept. She also took up golf, which she really enjoyed. There were no female waitresses to distract Carruthers at this golf club; he played the course but not the field.

Carruthers could, however, get his eyes full of beautiful young girls when he occasionally stopped at a bar on the road to his home. His excuse was that he was having a chat with his friend the owner, which in fact was more often than not true. Mainly from Rwanda, these girls were real eye-catchers and their business was men. From the way they were walking one could see they were sexually active. A journalist friend of their son's from the UK who spent a few days with the Carruthers remarked that she had never seen so many beautiful girls before. Her father, a good friend of Nelson Mandela, used to produce *Drum* magazine, which featured beautiful females, and he suggested he make a visit. However, he was too busy writing a biography of Mandela to be distracted.

On one occasion at this same bar Carruthers and his Swedish brother-in-law, who was on holiday, were sitting minding their own business when suddenly a girl leapt on top of their table and started dancing, skirt whirling and nothing underneath. They were quite enjoying this when there was a sound of breaking glass and a girl at a nearby table rushed over, brandishing a broken empty bottle. Chaos ensued, the dancer fell to the floor with her assailant on top of her and Carruthers and brother-in-law fled the scene rapidly. The girls didn't look so beautiful in these situations.

* * *

With the lifting of apartheid and Mandela in charge in South Africa, it was now more conducive to visit that country. Carruthers visited there first on a rugby tour from Nairobi to watch the 1995 World Rugby Cup, and Carruthers and Willi both went together to Cape Town a couple of years later.

Uganda had been used as one of the training bases for the ANC during the years of apartheid. There was even an ANC rugby team, with one white member, competing in Kampala. They looked the part in a very new rugby strip but their play did not match their appearance.

South African businessmen were looking north, and a noticeable number of them appeared in Uganda, involved mainly in telecommunications, soft drinks, the beer industry, power generation and food outlets such as cash and carry and supermarkets. Some of the businessmen were naïve and overestimated the contribution they individually would make to the business and social life in Uganda. Although white, they considered themselves Africans and most of them seemed to enjoy Uganda and its environment; but they tended to mix only among themselves. The South African High Commissioner in Kampala was seriously concerned about his compatriots being too insular.

Willi and Carruthers enjoyed their visit to South Africa. While Carruthers had no qualms in sailing in the Atlantic off Cape Town, Willi was definitely averse to that and instead went up to the top of Table Mountain in a cable car. They spent a couple of nights in Johannesburg, staying with friends in one of the suburbs that was taking the shape of a fortress as law and order seemed to be breaking down. Early one morning the daughter of the white couple they were staying with came into Willi and Carruthers' bedroom to say goodbye.

This was probably the first time she had seen a black and white couple in the same bed but she showed no reaction. However, he felt slightly uneasy and was puzzled by his own reaction. Was he just being naïve, he wondered?

The couple they were staying with were in fact Carruthers' former MD in Kampala and his former secretary, now wife. The visitor to the Carruthers' bedroom was their hosts' love child, who had been born in Kampala. During all the marital upset her mother had returned to Kampala, announcing to Carruthers as he sat in her former boss's office that as the baby had been made there, it would be born there.

(They would in turn visit Willi and Carruthers in Kampala, going to the hospital where their daughter was born and to their old house. To their astonishment, almost 30 years later, they found their old gardener still there. He rushed up to them, recognising them before they had recognised him.)

On his verandah, the early morning chill obliged Carruthers to wear a sweater. He was sipping the strong dark brown tea from the estates of Western Uganda, sweetened with a spoon of Uganda honey. He had just finished the last chapter of a book, *The Prince, The Showgirl and Me*, written by Colin Clark, with a message on the flyleaf wishing Carruthers and Willi all the best. Colin Clark, brother of Alan Clark, was a friend of their son in London. He had become acquainted with the ultimate sex symbol, Marilyn Monroe, on a film set, hence the reason for the book. Carruthers had known a few sex symbols in his time, he thought, and also some sexual deviants.

Only recently he had received through the post from

the UK a members' magazine for The Beaumont Society. It was addressed to an expatriate friend of his who had died suddenly two years ago and who had occasionally used Carruthers' post office box number for his mail. The magazine had taken two years to arrive because it had been sent by overland post. The early Victorian explorers had travelled on foot quicker than that, Carruthers thought. The friend, who had seemed happily married, turned out to have been a cross-dresser, as it became obvious that The Beaumont Society catered for such people. Carruthers was amazed as he went through the magazine reading about males dressing up as females, a fact sometimes known and accepted by their wives. His friend must have made a very ugly female, Carruthers thought, and no hint of his friend's predilection had ever crossed his mind. He decided not to pass on the magazine to the widow, as he didn't want to upset her; he presumed she was a woman. He kept the magazine out of Willi's way too, as he knew she would jump to the wrong conclusions. He could imagine her teasing him. 'Did you wear that blue dress of mine the other night, darling? I can't seem to find it. I do wish you would buy your own clothes.'

People sometimes had strange ideas about others. There was that stupid survey of left-handers which revealed, said researchers, that more left-handers than right-handers were gay. Certainly no one had approached Carruthers on seeing him writing with his left hand to ask if he wanted a bit of you-know-what.

It was all very confusing, he thought. He put the book aside and stretched his legs. Time for a swim soon. Only yesterday he had shaken his head in disbelief when, on a women's BBC programme, a husband who was looking after the kids at home while his wife worked was asked by the interviewer, 'Are you confused about your role in life?' The husband said sometimes he was, and Carruthers knew he had been brainwashed.

Carruthers had switched off the radio in disgust. Anyway, why had he bothered to listen to a women's programme, for goodness sake? Come to think of it, that blue dress of Willi's was rather exotic. He took off his sweater and headed for the swimming pool. He must cool himself down.

They had a guest staying with them, the former Attorney General of the Falkland Islands. He had worked in Uganda as a young man at the same time as Carruthers and had also left during Amin's time. They were planning to visit a game park over the weekend, and that evening he took his friend out to dinner, and then to a casino, but he himself didn't gamble.

The journey to the game park, the Queen Elizabeth, didn't take more than six hours and they were there well before dark. The original lodge buildings and adjoining chalets, situated on a peninsula overlooking Lake Edward, had all been renovated. From there they could view the game park below them as well as the mountains bordering the Congo in the distance. In that region the name of the park and the lakes Edward, George and Albert all reflected the colonial past of Uganda.

Since the days of Amin the number of animals in the park had slowly been increasing. The lakes were full of hippopotamus and Carruthers could see at the water's edge a herd of nearly a hundred elephants. Lions could also be seen and were said to enter the lodge area at night in search of the young warthogs that sought refuge there. Certainly a large hyena roamed about which Carruthers had encountered one night.

Willi and their guests, including their youngest daughter and two of her university friends from the UK, decided to go on a boat trip to view chimpanzees on a nearby island. Carruthers himself was not interested as he had gone on that trip twice before, so after dropping them off at the jetty he parked his Land Rover at an open camping area overlooking a channel which joined Lakes Edward and George.

He got out of the Land Rover and walked round, partially shutting all the windows, and returned to his driver's seat, alternately reading his book and looking at the scenery for about an hour. Turning his vehicle round to go back to the jetty to pick up his party, he was astonished to see a lioness lying down and looking at him from the grass only about 30 metres distant. If he had known of the presence of the lioness, he certainly wouldn't have got out of his Land Rover, and it illustrated how very careful one should be.

Carruthers was reminded of an incident two or three years previously when, driving out of the same game park, he had come across an expatriate wife and her baby sitting on a rug having a picnic on the grass overlooking the channel. It looked an idyllic scene but was fraught with danger. He was amazed and stopped to warn her of the implications of what she was doing. The woman's face went bright red. Her husband, sitting in their vehicle, said nothing. Perhaps he was hoping to get rid of them. That bonny baby would have made a very tasty morsel for a lioness or a hyena. In fact where they were sitting was near to a path taken by elephants going down to the water. The couple had quickly packed up and Carruthers had reported the matter to the ranger at the exit gate, who likewise was astonished.

Their visit to the park finished, they headed towards Fort Portal, where they spent the night at a small lodge built on top of a lake some 40 kilometres from the town. It was a magic spot, surrounded by forest containing monkeys, chimpanzees and exotic bird life. The owner was an old friend of Willi and Carruthers who unfortunately led a lonely life and drank too much of his own distilled liquor. (He died six months after their visit.)

They left the next morning, after a night of excellent food by candlelight, for Hoima and Masindi, going over very rough roads and round the end of Lake Albert to reach Murchison Falls National Park. They stayed there at another lodge, on the banks of the River Nile, where the views were magnificent. There were oil deposits in Lake Albert and various foreign companies had investigated the commercial validity of them. Companies came and went; it was an ongoing process. A couple of Americans had fleeced some local shareholders, including Carruthers, then left.

They took the obligatory boat trip to the foot of the Murchison Falls where the river burst through a 6-metre gorge, spilling 300 metres to the River Nile below. It was an awesome sight. Winston Churchill and Theodore Roosevelt visited there in the early 1900s, the former wearing a beekeeper's veil to keep off the tsetse flies. There were still tsetse flies there. They seemed to get everywhere – hair, clothes, luggage – and their bites stung.

On the boat trip, the banks of the river were lined with crocodiles and many species of birds. It was also possible on occasions to see lion and giraffe. Regrettably, the rhinos, which had been there in the 1960s no longer existed as poachers had destroyed them.

On arriving back in Kampala, Willi and Carruthers found that their younger son from London had arrived for a holiday. He wanted to see the gorillas in the forests in the South-West of Uganda bordering the Congo. The ex-Attorney General, however, had no time for that and was soon on his way back to England.

Their son spent a week in Kampala just resting. He was exhausted from 14-hour days, including travelling, working at a bank in London. He graciously paid for his father's visit to the tented camp at the base of the forest in exchange for transport costs, which Carruthers reckoned was a very good deal for his son. This time they took a driver with them.

It was a ten-hour drive often over some rough roads, but they were able to stop on the way for snacks and drinks. The driver joined them at their table, which wouldn't have happened if Willi had been present. She insisted on the separation of the classes, which was how she had been brought up. They went through heavily wooded mountainous roads, sometimes a bit slippery when heavy rain fell as they journeyed along. Where the wooded areas ended, cultivated terraced fields on the sides of the mountains illustrated the perseverance and hard work of the local population. Of course it was the women who cultivated the fields. The men drank and discussed politics.

After passing through fields of tea and a tea factory, they reached their luxury tented camp just outside the entrance to the forest game park. Normally they would have stayed at the tented camp at the base of the forest covered hills inside the park, but six months previously it had been burnt to the ground by rebels who crossed the three kilometres over the mountains from the Congo, abducting 12 tourists, 10 of whom they murdered. This had, naturally, a devastating effect on the tourist industry, and the tented camp where Carruthers and his son stayed only had one other couple staying there.

To assure the tourists of their safety, the Uganda

Army were there to guard them. A large gun mounted on a tank was placed near the park headquarters and army patrols were stationed up in the mountains on the border. Soldiers also accompanied the tourists on their trek to find and observe the gorillas, which could only be seen in their natural habitat in that particular area of Africa.

Early next morning they arose for breakfast. The other couple going on the gorilla trek were Germans. Carruthers and son beat them to the shared breakfast table, demolishing all the butter before they arrived. The Germans were a bit shocked to know the reason why their preferred choice of the other tented camp had not materialised; no one had bothered to inform them of the terrorist attack. But Carruthers assured them they would be quite safe.

Soon they were at the base camp. It would be a gruelling six-hour trek up the mountains into the forests and back to base, so Carruthers senior decided not to go. He didn't feel fit enough because of his bad knee, which wouldn't be a problem going but certainly would be on the way back downhill. He told the Germans he had seen enough gorillas in Tarzan films when he was young, so what was the point. They looked at him in astonishment.

While his son and the two Germans set off with their army escorts, guides and bearers, Carruthers went back to his tent to write his book and have a cold beer. He enjoyed the solitude, had some sandwiches for lunch and a nap, and was wide-awake when the trekkers returned.

They had observed a family of 14 gorillas, including young ones, for about an hour and a half. For them it had been a most rewarding experience and Carruthers' son was determined to return and repeat it. Their guides had stressed to them that no matter how close the gorillas came, they must on no account touch them for fear of giving them germs. These gorillas were better protected that the human inhabitants, Carruthers thought.

It was millennium time and Carruthers' son had to get back to London for 1st January lest anything went wrong with the bank's systems. In Kampala also, great deliberations had been going on for at least a year as to the preparedness of various utilities such as power, telephones etc. Industries had checked out their computer-run machines, boilers and the like. The Americans, taking a pessimistic view, advised all their citizens in Uganda to stock up with food and fuel for a three-month period. Nobody else seemed unduly worried, and that laid-back approach proved to be correct. After all, Uganda had enough resources for anyone to live off the land for at least three months without worrying about such things as electricity and cooking gas.

In fact the whole exercise showed how up to date Uganda was. Because of all the internal wars and the breakdown of infrastructures over the years, Uganda had to start rebuilding from scratch, and much of the machinery and many of the systems, newly installed, were state of the art. There were also digital TVs and cyber cafés, and everyone of any importance was online. Two mobile phone companies also provided their services to an increasing number of customers. Even rebel groups operating on Uganda's borders used the Internet and satellite telephones.

The two main rebel groups had no political agenda except wanting to seize power for themselves and line their own pockets. Funded by international terrorism, their groups were made up of kidnapped schoolchildren and unemployed youths recruited with promises of wealth, or groups of thugs who were not prepared to conform to the norms of civilised society. Arms were easily, too easily, sourced from formerly communist-run countries in Europe. Like the vast open bush lands and forests of Africa a century and a half ago where game would roam unchecked, so the aircraft bearing arms could today roam the skies above Africa also virtually unchecked. There was always someone wanting to cause trouble.

Carruthers had started reading another book, *The Mustard Seed*, the autobiography of President Yoweri Museveni of Uganda. It clearly illustrated the commitment, courage and resourcefulness of a freedom fighter turned politician, although Carruthers suspected that the former title would be his preferred one. Ruling in Africa was a constant battle and there was always someone militarily or politically prepared to unseat you because of self-interest and monetary gain.

Since Museveni had taken power in 1986 he had given amnesty to some of Idi Amin's old officers, and that still made Carruthers feel uneasy when he encountered them sitting in hotel restaurants. He hoped and presumed a close watch was kept on those guys. Once bitten, twice shy.

One of Museveni's close allies – and now one of his Ministers – had told Carruthers that when they started their movement to rid the country of dictatorship and killing during the early years of Idi Amin's rule, they were just young graduates with strong ideological views who were not prepared to sit back and take what was meted out to them. Thank God, Carruthers thought. He personally would hear no criticism of the author of that book.

Chapter 26

The Past Catches Up

Carruthers sat on a concrete bench at the 16th tee of the golf course in Kampala, driver in hand, waiting for his partner to tee off. On the ground in front of him lay a couple of used condoms. He imagined what the bench must have been used for the night before. He preferred a mattress himself. But the fact that there were condoms lying there was a sign that the populace had heeded advice given by Government and various agencies to practise safe sex in the fight against Aids. Uganda, once recognised as the country with the highest incidence of Aids in Africa if not the world, was now the only country in Africa where the rate of new cases of Aids was actually falling. This was due to commitment by the Government to publicise and educate people, particularly the youth. Uganda was in fact a showcase for other African countries, if only they would listen.

His partner drove off and Carruthers followed, hitting a blinder. His golf was certainly much better than in his early days in Kenya. Probably that was because his marital condition created a more peaceful ambiance than when he was a bachelor. His partner's golf was not so good. He was a former Uganda diplomat, now working in the restored Kingdom of Buganda's Government, who fantasised about nuns – maybe because he was a Protestant. When they reached the clubhouse they had a few beers together and surveyed the wives and girlfriends who had either finished playing golf or had come to meet their husbands or boyfriends. Many wore jeans, which Carruthers considered a retrograde step as it wasn't so easy now to give a leg glance, to use cricketing parlance. Cricket was another popular sport in Uganda.

The previous weekend the golf club had hosted the All Africa Ladies Golf Championship, which was a resounding success. The Zimbabwean team were happy to be away from their home country at that particular time with racial tensions so high. Something had obviously gone very far wrong in that country, and even the new Minister of Finance in Zimbabwe had told Carruthers and other delegates over a year ago in an after-dinner speech in Harare, before he was in Government, that all was not well. His personal advice to their company regarding an African central office had been to choose Kampala. He considered southern African countries to be in a political mess, who said that they still had to come to terms with life in the new millennium. That man was a pragmatist, Carruthers thought, and would be a valuable asset in the new Zimbabwean Government if he continued to speak what he felt was the truth. One didn't often find honest politicians.

One of Museveni's most popular moves was restoring the kingdoms, which had been abolished by Obote, for those who wanted them restored. The largest tribe, the Baganda, certainly wanted their King back, and the heir, who had been living in London and who occasionally took tea with the Queen Mother at Clarence House, returned to Uganda. He had previously returned to Uganda to show solidarity and meet Museveni when the latter was fighting in the bush. Both men were certainly pragmatists too.

Fully enthroned and now married, the Kabaka and his wife the Nabagareka physically illustrated all that was good about Buganda and the Baganda people: good breeding, courtesy, magnanimity, handsome looks. The Kabakaship was cultural rather than political, although there were those who would have it otherwise, and the Kabaka successfully strode the narrow line between the different factions of his followers.

The Kabaka's subjects, the Baganda, and some other tribes in Uganda, could be secretive and sometimes it took a while to get correct answers to questions. Carruthers, being a blunt Scotsman, wasn't used to that. He put the caution down to history as in the past great care had to be taken in the giving of information to invading tribes and, later, colonial servants. They were protecting their culture, and this trait had been passed down through the generations. It was understandable.

The Kabaka and his wife were two of the most important visitors to Carruthers and Willi's verandah. As they were unable to attend the wedding and reception of the Kabaka to his American-educated wife due to the death of Willi's father around the same time, the Kabaka had phoned to say he was bringing his betrothed to meet them. Willi, of course, had close connections to the royal family through her own family. Carruthers was just a commoner, although a Scottish commoner, but over the years he had become a close friend of the Kabaka before and after he succeeded to the title.

Willi had prepared a sumptuous meal for the royal luncheon. They had only invited three other guests, Willi's elder sister and two close friends, a Danish Knight, no less, and his beautiful Muganda wife. It was a relaxed and successful afternoon. The security guards accompanying the Kabaka outnumbered the guests, and they also were fed. It was a very, very nice day, always to be remembered, and a rare honour to host a King and Queen at their own request.

Carruthers and Willi also came across royalty when they were presented to Princess Anne at a British High Commission reception, who was on a visit to Kampala. Carruthers pushed the German chargé d'affaires out of the way so she could gain access to them. They found her charming. She asked where they had met, and then they got on to Scottish rugby. Carruthers held two debenture seats at Murrayfield Stadium in Edinburgh and the Princess was the patron of the Scottish Rugby Union.

Their friend the Danish Knight had remained in Uganda through the various regimes and been knighted by his King for looking after the interests of Denmark and its citizens during the troubled times. In fact on Carruthers' return to Uganda to settle again, his first welcome-back letter was from his Danish friend, who at the same time asked him to arrange insurance on one of the buildings he owned. He had prospered but also suffered, his lovely house being burnt down during one of the wars. No gain without pain, as the saying goes.

One of the saddest events that Carruthers was near to after his return to Uganda was the massacres that occurred in Rwanda just over the Uganda border. Carruthers wondered how there could be so much hatred between people living so closely together. It was supposedly tribalism but there had been so much intermarriage over the years between the Hutus and Tutsis that one wondered if that was the real reason. Carruthers put it down to ethnic jealousies rather than ethnic hatreds. Idi Amin's soldiers had killed because of jealousies of wealth and position, for instance. There had to be a buffer between the elites and the peasants, and that was why Museveni was so anxious to create a middle class. We ignore history at our peril, thought Carruthers.

At the time of the Rwanda crisis Carruthers thought he was going to get involved in a Paramount Studios film called *Congo*. And he was to a certain extent – he was asked to arrange local insurance cover. He met the producer and site manager, who came out from Hollywood to set up their base. Regrettably, reports of corpses floating downriver from Rwanda into Lake Victoria and Uganda waters created a feeling of unease not only in the Hollywood filmmakers, but also in many Ugandans. Very quickly the Hollywood film office was closed in Entebbe and they relocated to Costa Rica. Another career opportunity gone, was Carruthers' verdict. He in fact had often thought of making a film of the girls who abounded in Kampala, called *Girls in the Mist*. Sometimes western films about Uganda did not accurately depict the customs of the country. A Canadian film, for instance, showed Ugandans wearing Nigerian dress, while a Hollywood film made mention of West African customs instead of East African.

Many of Carruthers' old contacts were no longer around. Surprisingly, the ex-mine MD and his wife were dead, killed in an air crash. He wondered who had inherited the bra picture. His ex-Chairman, the one who had fled to an Indian Ocean island, had also died and his wife had evidently lost her memory, which was probably just as well. He knew the stepdaughter of his tea planter friend was in Nairobi but had no idea of the whereabouts of his ex-girlfriend of many years ago whom he had last seen in Dar es Salaam. Goodness, that was going back.

He had a friend in Dar and must make discreet inquiries, he thought.

In fact Willi and Carruthers had been invited by this friend to celebrate his wife's 60th birthday at the Muthaiga Club in Nairobi at a dinner dance and they were to stay overnight at the club. They flew down on a Friday afternoon and after battling through the Nairobi traffic arrived at the Club with just over an hour to spare before kick-off, including getting into evening dress, which Carruthers accomplished quickly.

Leaving Willi to have a bath and get dressed, Carruthers headed downstairs to the bar for a quick refreshment or, as some would say, a quick stiffener. Passing the club library on his way to the bar, he heard a loud hiss and on glancing to his left saw a mature, good-looking lady peering at him over the top of an opened book. Staring, he suddenly realised with a beating heart that this was the tea planter's stepdaughter, she of the birthmark. Her appearance certainly belied her age. Making sure they were not observed, they kissed and hugged nervously and then petted heavily, less nervously. The library seemed deserted. She had seen Willi and Carruthers passing the library on the way to their bedroom and had purposely hung about to see if they would come down.

'When can we meet?' she asked breathlessly.

Carruthers said it seemed impossible that weekend because after spending the night at the club they were spending two nights with friends in Nairobi whom she didn't know, and after that returning to Kampala. Perhaps that is where they would meet, or at Fort Portal when she went to see her mother. In a rush they exchanged phone numbers and Carruthers, having missed his stiffener at the bar but having got one anyway, rushed back to collect Willi, who wondered aloud what a dishevelled-looking Carruthers had been up to.

'Ran into some old friends,' said Carruthers.

Willi sighed.

They went down the stairs then crossed through the club to the ballroom. Friends of the birthday girl had come from all over the place – Nairobi, Kampala, Dar es Salaam, Mombasa and Dublin. Carruthers and Willi already knew quite a few of the crowd and a lot of gossiping took place before the dinner. To his surprise and shock he saw his old colleague Binky from Dar, and hanging onto his arm an attractive-looking lady who, the longer he stared at, he realised was his ex-girlfriend. Gosh, they didn't seem to have aged all that much. Binky waved at him happily while she pouted and licked her lips.

His ex had ditched her sisal man, preferring to stay in Dar es Salaam with a man who didn't complain when whipped, as she told Carruthers at the dinner table. She was seated next to him, and Binky next to Willi. Carruthers had introduced them to Willi as very old friends, which they were in fact, but Willi didn't know the background.

'Do not show surprise, Carruthers MI5,' said his ex as she grasped his crotch under the table. 'I'm getting tired of Binky, I think he's into black women.'

Carruthers laughed out loud and her grip tightened. He smiled weakly at Willi across the table. She seemed to be having some sort of trouble with Binky, whose hand she kept placing on the table and patting firmly.

Soon the band started playing and Carruthers quickly rose and asked Willi to dance.

'I think that guy wants to rape me,' Willi said. 'How well do you know them?'

'Well enough,' said Carruthers, looking nervously over his shoulder, 'and I think we should keep our distance.'

They were able to do this by joining their hosts at their table as the guests began to mingle. Binky and partner kept their distance, luckily. Of course they drank too much wine and tumbled into their separate beds in the wee hours of the morning. When they woke up, their memories failed them. Willi found a stained beer mat in her handbag on which were scrawled the words 'Binky likes to stroke black cats', with a telephone number on it and a whip drawn alongside, while Carruthers found a string of pearls in the side pocket of his dinner jacket.

'Oh, my God, whose are these?' he said to Willi. 'And how did they get there?'

Certainly his ex had not been wearing pearls. He suddenly remembered that their hostess, the birthday girl, had been wearing pearls and they must be hers. However, the circumstances in which they got into his pocket eluded him. He shook his head in amazement. They decided to put the pearls in an envelope without any message and slip the envelope under the nearby bedroom door of their hosts, who must still be fast asleep, and this they did. Nobody saw them.

Then they went down for breakfast as they were being picked up by their friends earlyish, and found a few people in the dining room nursing hangovers. There was no sign of Binky and partner, thank goodness, nor their hosts, but a Uganda Government Minister and his American wife stopped to greet them.

Breakfast over, Carruthers paid the bill while Willi went to pack. As he was going back to their bedroom he passed his host on the way downstairs. Carruthers' bright greeting and inquiry after his host's health was met with a grunt and that was that. Was it a hangover or had Carruthers upset him somehow? Then he remembered the pearls. They left the club soon after that with their friends. No one thereafter ever referred to the pearls, although they did get an email in Kampala from the birthday girl thanking them for her presents and for attending her party. They never saw or heard about Binky and partner again. It is presumed they are still together, whipping the hell out of each other.

The rest of the weekend passed quickly. Their Kenyan friends had recently put up a large house on the slopes of the Ngong Hills outside Nairobi where they had a small farm. Stunning views of Nairobi and the game park on the plains below, and of Mount Kenya and Mount Kilimanjaro to the north and south respectively, led Carruthers to believe that their friends, if they were so minded, could turn the place into a small hotel, especially as it was built right above the site where Denys Finch Hatton and Karen Blixen had spent many of their days together. He had been buried there after his light aircraft, piloted by himself, crashed on take off at Voi. An obelisk erected by his brother Lord Winchilsea and bearing a quotation from the *Ancient Mariner* marked his grave. Their brief life together and their love of Africa was immortalised by Karen Blixen in her book *Out of Africa*. Sadly, many of the trees on the Ngong Hills above the grave were being cut down for charcoal. That particular area was no longer part of the game park, and the salt lick which game once used was now part of their friends' front garden. Lions had once been seen there regularly, sometimes lying on the grave.

There was a shortage of water in and around Nairobi because of a drought. This didn't affect their hosts, who had a borehole. Power was, however, a problem as the drought had affected the levels on the dams used for generating electricity. Uganda with its more abundant supply was selling power to Kenya. Masaii herdsmen were bringing their cattle into Nairobi searching for grass, and the centre of the city seemed to have been taken over by street families and beggars, many of them thieves. This was no longer a garden city. All these problems had been caused by lack of planning, political greed, and the blinkered view of officials that it was somebody else's problem. Carruthers' view was that African men had failed their own society and they should stand aside and let their women take over, a simple remedy if the men could swallow their pride, which they wouldn't, of course. Maybe they should become cross-dressers.

Back in Uganda, Carruthers stood looking down from his Kampala office onto the main road. He had a good view of the rear of a Chinese restaurant fronting the main road. If the diners in the restaurant had the view Carruthers had of the blackened kitchen with no mains water, they would never have entered the place. The roof of the restaurant was covered in a medley of old junk, amongst which hung tablecloths and napkins drying in the sun. No one threw away junk in Africa, it was always stored nearby in case it was needed in the future. It never was.

The British company Carruthers worked for had now been bought worldwide by Americans, which meant hundreds of years of British tradition gone in one fell swoop, he thought. Everything and everybody had its price, he supposed. Unfortunately, he hadn't been a shareholder or in any position to get a golden handshake, so he had soldiered on but had reached the end of his contract. In fact the US owners had made a big difference to the well-being of the Uganda company and its staff. State-of-the-art technology had been introduced and no quibbles about the cost, something that the former

British-owned company would never have done. So Carruthers was quite relaxed about the situation. It was progress, after all.

Carruthers was asked to remain as non-executive Chairman. At long last he had reached his goal! It had been a long and fortuitous struggle. He had gained respect from his peers! He wondered if any other offers would come his way from outside the company. He remembered ruefully the nasty things he had written about other chairmen! The new Managing Director, a Welshman of all things, was much younger and had come from another company in Kampala, which the Americans had also bought worldwide around the same time. It was a relaxed situation as they got on well together, and had done so even when they were competitors.

Carruthers now had more time to devote to his verandah, his swimming pool and the golf course. Willi was slowly getting used to having him around more and in fact even felt guilty, she said, when she left him at home to pursue her own pursuits. This may have had something to do with the fact that once three young ladies turned up at the gate and asked Carruthers if they could use his swimming pool. Knowing Willi was about, he had to refuse, but he would have liked to have seen them in their bikinis. Willi was very suspicious and wondered how they knew they had a swimming pool, and the house-girl had told her that was not the first time they had appeared at the gate. Carruthers' recipe for a long and successful marriage was to keep one's wife guessing.

After quite a pleasant day writing his book, Carruthers now sat on his verandah. He wondered if the Kabaka, who reviewed books on Africa for the *Spectator*, would be asked to review his book! So many memories past and present. He was sipping a malt whisky from the Isle of Jura that reminded him of his mother's death at 93 in Edinburgh a few months ago. The undertaker had displayed the same bottle in his office, so that was Carruthers' personal memory to cherish. Only a brother in England remained in his own family.

He had wondered at times if they were all going to reach the year 2000. Willi's father hadn't. Her mother had, and Carruthers' also. Willi had had an accident on Christmas Day 1999 when she slipped carrying the turkey from the oven in their kitchen and badly scalded her right leg, her beautiful right leg. They had to call out the doctor on his mobile. It turned out he was just about to pass their house to treat an attempted suicide in a house nearby, so he came to them first. Fortunately, Willi's leg had healed quickly with the aid of sap squeezed from an aloe vera plant growing in their garden.

Carruthers himself had also had an accident recently falling through the ceiling of their house and gouged a hole in his leg almost through to the anklebone. The wound had taken two months to close, so no swimming or golf for him during that period. Friends asked him what the hell he was doing up in the roof at his age. To be quite frank he didn't know, but he had had time on his hands. He had actually hoped in his semi-retirement to have spent more time with a close friend and neighbour and a former chairman of the company, but unfortunately he didn't make the year 2000 either.

Another sip of the malt and Carruthers decided that so far he had had a good life. He had a loving family, and all four children were working in England. If they wanted to come to Uganda it was their decision; he wouldn't pressurise them. One of them had shown interest in leasing a plot of land on an island on Lake

Victoria only half an hour's boat ride from Entebbe. The island was being developed as a tourist resort by an English couple, Tim and Ali, who had fallen in love with the island and Uganda, and sold up everything they owned in England to develop their dream. They were also visitors to Carruthers' verandah.

A further sip and he thought of the five African Presidents he had shaken hands with over the years. Shagari and Buhari in Nigeria, both still alive; Obote and Amin (now dead) and Museveni in Uganda. The former was alive and in exile in Zambia and the latter was still running his beloved Uganda.

The workers on the roof of the house below his, the Governor of the Central Bank's residence, had left cleaning the Governor's tiles for another day. They spent all day admiring the view and cleaned a token amount of tiles only. He was getting fed up with their idleness and their constant glances invading his privacy.

The sun would be going down soon. Three crested cranes flew overhead on the way to their nests, honking in unison; the haunting gull-like call of the fish eagle sounded down near the lake, and later that night outside their bedroom window they would hear the nocturnal shriek of the African barn owl. Willi was also known to give the odd nocturnal shriek.

The ringing of his mobile phone interrupted Carruthers' reverie. To his surprise it was his tea planter friend phoning from his estate at Fort Portal. For some reason deciding to speak in code, he announced that the lady representative of the East African Orchid Society based in Nairobi would be arriving the next week and had suggested a meeting with Carruthers. Carruthers looked round guiltily but Willi was inside the house talking to her sister, the now former Mother Superior, who was spending the night.

After assuring his friend that contact would be made – in more ways than one, Carruthers thought – he tossed back the remainder of his Isle of Jura and headed for the swimming pool. The sun had just dipped below the horizon as a dripping Carruthers approached the verandah. To his consternation he saw that the former Mother Superior was leafing through the manuscript of his book. Had she read some of the naughty bits, he wondered? They certainly weren't meant for such saintly eyes but perhaps again he was being naïve. He gently prised the manuscript away from her, unconsciously crossed himself and headed for the shower. Tomorrow was another day.

Chapter 27

Back From Exile

Willi had enjoyed living in England and she had made many friends. Shopping was so easy compared to what she had experienced in Africa. But it could be expensive, and fresh fruit and vegetables were not as fresh as they would have been in Africa. Meat was particularly expensive, she found.

One of the drawbacks of living in England was that she had no servants to do the housework and tend the garden. While she loved gardening, she particularly hated it in the winter.

As long as she had the right clothes she could put up with the weather, though she really hated the rain. In Africa you had rainy seasons when you knew it was going to rain, and even then it would usually only rain for a few hours at a time on any one day. In England it could rain at any time during the whole year and indeed could keep raining all day. She noticed that the weather was a topic of daily conversation for most English people and that amused her.

She also felt that Carruthers, while enjoying the travelling part of his job and going to all parts of the world, was not really happy working in England. He was used to being the boss and complained bitterly about those he considered incompetent bosses. He was also angry at not being appointed a Director on the

Board, thus again frustrating his ambition to be a Chairman.

Their social life was also completely different and she missed the constant round of parties, many of them business-connected and mostly paid for as a business expense, which she had experienced in Nigeria. No such facility existed for them in England, so most nights were spent at home. In a way it was lucky, she thought, that there was no pub within easy walking distance of their house or she might never have seen John.

She had not been particularly excited when John told her about his new job – or rather, old job – back in Kampala. During the period 1987 to 1992 she had managed to settle down in England and the kids were happy at school. She felt comfortable and really had no worries.

This would all change when she went back to Uganda. Although she would be near her own family, she would have the problem of having to help solve problems, both social and monetary, for the extended family. She would much rather do that from a distance.

Of course she had to follow her husband, who now seemed more of a Ugandan than she was! John was very excited. To soften the blow she decided to let him go on his own for a year so he could prepare their bungalow for their occupation once again. She was sure it needed extensive renovation. Meanwhile she would look after the kids and slowly get reconciled to the idea of going home.

When she did return to Kampala to join John, she found a newly renovated bungalow with a large kitchen specially designed for her. She was delighted. John had obviously spent a lot of money arranging it all.

Slowly she settled back to life in Kampala. John bought her a new car, a four-wheel-drive Suzuki, and this enabled her to make regular visits to her parents on the outskirts of Kampala.

The daily terror she experienced when she and John had last lived in Kampala was thankfully no longer there. It was safe to walk the streets again, even with a white man! Previously people used to stare seeing a mixed-race couple, but now there were so many such couples that no real curiosity was aroused. They even commanded a certain amount of respect at having returned as old timers to their beloved Kampala.

John continued his lifestyle of living and working hard but also playing hard. She felt he was drinking too much whisky, but he said he had to support his own country's products. This also extended to imported haggis, which she quite liked. There were also many young and attractive Ugandan girls in Kampala whom John ogled quite openly. She had seen it all before and wondered if it was worth the bother trying to check up on him. She knew she had her own male admirers, as she was still a very attractive woman, and men were all the same, her friends reminded her.

She threw herself into charity work for the International Women's Organisation and started up a small cottage industry growing chickens and producing hot sauces and pickles. She also made quilts. She was a busy woman.

Of course, she did experience the down side of being a reasonably well-off member of an extended family. Many demands were made on her time and on her bank account. For instance, she decided to take over the educational responsibilities for her eight-year-old nephew, an orphan. It was the least she could do.

The death of her father devastated her. They had been on holiday in England and had to fly back to Uganda immediately. He was given a funeral befitting such an important person, with two Prime Ministers in attendance among other VIPs, his coffin draped in the Buganda flag and the Buganda royal anthem played. Archbishops and Cardinals were also in attendance, and he was interred right outside the cathedral situated on top of Rubaga Hill overlooking Kampala.

She had now fully settled back into life in Uganda. They sold their house in England and for a whole year didn't even visit the place. Instead they made visits to Zanzibar and South Africa, where travelling and accommodation costs were much cheaper than in England.

As well as having been appointed non-Executive Chairman of the insurance broking company, John had two years later been appointed Executive Chairman of an Insurance Corporation and had then had another appointment thrust upon him as Chairman of a bank! He was now working full time again and seemed to be enjoying it. He had also completed their son's house on the island fronting the beach. She hadn't been so sure about one of his recent visits to the island when he was the only male dinner guest among the 20-odd Miss Uganda contestants who were spending the night on the island for a photo shoot. He said they had been heavily chaperoned. By him, she wondered?

She now sat on the verandah of their bungalow with her sister, the former Mother Superior. John was having his daily exercise in the swimming pool, which he had actually installed for such exercise in his old age. John's nearly completed book lay on one of the verandah tables. She wondered if it would ever get published. John had assured her that many of the amorous escapades related in the book didn't really take place, but she wasn't so sure.

She rose to go and make a pot of tea for herself, and her sister who was now admiring Willi's orchids which were hanging in pots round the verandah. She remarked to her sister that the lady representative of the East African Orchid Society based in Nairobi would be arriving next week and she had invited her and other orchid lovers to morning coffee at the bungalow. Strangely, John had not seemed startled when she mentioned that to him and he had mumbled that he was going to keep out of the way. He could be very moody sometimes.

Tea made, she carried the tray of teapot, cups and saucers and cakes out to the verandah, passing John on his way in, dripping wet and clutching his book. They smiled lovingly at each other.

MRS CARRUTHERS IS BLACK